The
SACRED
FIRE

The SACRED FIRE

J. RICHARD HUFF

WestBow
PRESS
A DIVISION OF THOMAS NELSON

WestBow Press books may be ordered through booksellers or by contacting:

WestBow Press
A Division of Thomas Nelson
1663 Liberty Drive
Bloomington, IN 47403
www.westbowpress.com
1-(866) 928-1240

Because of the dynamic nature of the Internet, any web addresses or links contained in this book may have changed since publication and may no longer be valid. The views expressed in this work are solely those of the author and do not necessarily reflect the views of the publisher, and the publisher hereby disclaims any responsibility for them.

Certain stock imagery © Thinkstock.
Any people depicted in stock imagery provided by Thinkstock are models, and such images are being used for illustrative purposes only.

ISBN: 978-1-4497-4321-5 (e)
ISBN: 978-1-4497-4320-8 (sc)
ISBN: 978-1-4497-4319-2 (hc)

Library of Congress Control Number: 2012904659

Printed in the United States of America

WestBow Press rev. date: 4/13/2012

CHAPTER 1

I imagined exactly how I was going to die as I lay on the forest floor bleeding. Richard continued to pace above me like a predator, spitting out obscenities with his arms raised as if holding back the tide. I was weak and helpless from the swift but violent beating I took, and there was nothing I could do to resist. I was physically ravaged, but that was not what was keeping me down. There was an internal fear of the wretchedness that held me there. All I could think to do at that moment was pray. I had to pray, especially if it was the last thing on earth I ever did. I prayed earnestly and honestly. I prayed for peace.

That terror, however, was still to come. At this moment I found myself alone and contemplative, deep in the wilderness. My rationale for being out here on such a cold evening had seemed clear in the light of day. But with darkness draping itself over the mountains, I could hardly remember why earlier it felt so right. I knew that I needed to do this. It had been a long time, and the solitude would give me time to grieve as I hadn't since that terrible day. There was no better place than this to contemplate. I was going to have time to spend with my thoughts, working out long-buried issues. But the hope that filled my soul turned to wariness as the day faded to night. My spirit was uneasy.

I had decided to come here on a whim. The night before, I'd reached the point that I knew I needed a break. I was becoming a very unusual person. At work, people were afraid to say the wrong things to me and had to walk on eggshells whenever I was around. At home, I was neglecting even the most basic cleaning. Piles formed everywhere, and I was always late putting out the trash. Dishes multiplied in the sink, and I was afraid to move them lest I allow a new life form to grow underneath.

My problems even extended to church, where I felt most alive. I'd dropped out of several of my dearest ministries. No longer did I join in for the weekly volunteering at the soup kitchen. I was sporadic in working with the youth and absent from many of my small group meetings. Even my weekly Sunday attendance was suffering. I was lucky to make it on time for any service, if I went at all.

People gave me a lot of leeway. They said I wasn't to blame for the way I acted, but I knew differently. In my heart, I knew that I was not the man I used to be. I was not the man I should be. But though I was stumbling, I knew that even when I fell I could rise again and continue on the path. That is why no matter how hard things got for me, I never stopped reading. I never stopped reading the one thing that got me through even the most desperate of times. I was always sure to have a copy of the Scriptures close. They were the only thing holding me back from falling into the abyss.

With all of this weighing heavily on my mind I decided to make the trip to the Shenandoah Mountains on that beautiful, late October Friday. Certainly to the relief of many I took the day off of work and decided to spend the weekend alone with my thoughts and my God. This time was much needed and much anticipated, as I wanted to be able to hash some things out that had been haunting me for the past six months. I hadn't really taken the time to talk to Him about this, even though I tried to bring everything in my life to Him. But there was one corner of my life that I was trying to keep blinded from His sight. It was a private area of my life that I wasn't going to bring to Him, and that had been my mantra for some time now. But I knew light needed to be shone into that area and that very same light could cleanse that which had been sullied. I had waited long enough.

It's difficult for me to even say that I choose to go out into the wilderness. If I were to be completely honest, it felt as though I was urged to leave. I felt the call to go so strongly that I didn't even second guess myself. So without hesitation I gathered together the things I would need for the weekend. I pulled an old tent out of my shed, packed up a portable stove and lamp, threw some clothes in a bag, and made a quick stop by the grocery store to pick up some sustenance. I can't say it was the most well planned trip, but that didn't matter. I just needed to get away.

I did not head out aimlessly. There was a particular site that I had in mind. It was well off the beaten path and I doubted that there was another soul that knew about it. But I knew about it, and it had been the site of some of my most recent and fondest memories. It was special to me because my beloved wife Ashley and I would often take trips there and spend relaxing and romantic days there together. We considered it our secret hideaway, a place secluded and prepared just for us. We thought that nature had taken the time and effort to grow and cultivate this one spot for the us to enjoy. We were always so very grateful.

As I drove the mountain road I realized just how beautiful the trees were this time of year. I hadn't been out here at all this season, and the majesty of the colors captured my attention. The browns, yellows, reds and oranges seemed to pop from the mountainside, like a majestic painting I could drive through. I wondered how it was that I had forgotten that beauty in such a short time. I drove along with anticipation, my spirit uplifted.

I remembered the roads well, and as it grew later I began to look for the unmarked dirt road that served as the entrance to my dominion. It hardly seemed possible to drive a car down it, but I was in my original Volkswagen beetle, and that car could get through anything. It had served me well for over thirty years, and I trusted it still. The road I was looking for never seemed to have a purpose as far as my wife and I could tell. The only reason we ran across it the first time was the fortuitous timing of a flat tire on this very car seven years ago. My wife and I rolled to a stop right in front of this path and, after a quick tire change, took the adventurous step to travel down it and see what was there.

What we found took our breath away. Our eyes widened to a small clearing, just big enough for us to set up camp, surrounded by majestic oak and pine trees, with a bed of needles on the ground. But all of this paled in comparison to the view over the mountains and valley. From here we could see all around, and drink in the beauty before us. There were no other obvious ways in or out of the site, and we couldn't hear a single noise that nature didn't intend. No man-made structures were to be seen from this hideaway. There was only the beauty that was a private gift to us. My wife and I continued to come here for years, always wondering when it would be discovered by others. It never was.

I slowed and scanned for the dirt road, and when I found it, I gently guided my vehicle through the tight, tree-lined pathway. The bumps and dips of the road reminded me of a time of joy, when my wife pretended to be thrown around by the unevenness, and we laughed together, with no other cares. Those were better times for me. Now, the jostling only brought back ghosts, teasing me, floating just out of reach. The ghosts of a the past bedeviled me. I wanted something I could never recapture.

After several miles of rough, tense driving, I finally reached my destination. I stepped out of my car and swallowed a breath of the mountain air, exhaling with it some of the grime that had been collecting in my soul. Here, I felt free of the weight I carried every day, free of the shackles holding me down.

I unpacked my car and set up the campsite, much as I had in years past. I placed my tent on the familiar ground, and set my stovetop accordingly. The pit my wife and I had dug many seasons ago was still there. Beside it sat the horizontal log where we rested to keep ourselves off the damp ground. Several flat rocks served a similar purpose, but got very cold in the fall air. On the opposite side of the log stood a single mighty oak tree, surely several hundred years old. It was the biggest tree around, and it stood out from the rest like a guardian in the wilderness. It was close enough to the fire that if one used it for comfort or protection they could still experience the fullness of the flames. The mighty oaks roots grew just right so that a weary traveler could rest up against it and be perfectly comfortable, almost like a living room recliner. I had never seen such a tree before this one. It was majestic, and when I was under it I always felt protected.

I leaned over the fire pit and I brushed aside the leaves that had gently covered it. Ashes still lay silent inside of the rock edging Ashley and I created. It looked as it had the last time we were here, untouched by nature or human hands. It was almost eerie to think of all the time that had passed and how the remains of our last encounter still lay there, waiting for our return.

As was our family custom, the first thing I did after setting up camp was to search out enough firewood to sustain me for the evening. There was no shortage of dead wood out here, and I didn't have to scavenge far to fill my arms. As I took load after load back to the site, I reminisced about the joy Ashley and I found in being the only two people here. We loved knowing that we had this piece of heaven on earth to ourselves if only for a short time. I still remembered that same excitement we had discovering this place, only this time it was draped in loneliness. As I worked, I noticed that the autumn air did not seem as kind to me, and the gentle breeze not as friendly. The trees did not seem to greet me the same as they had, almost saddened themselves and unable to muster their attention. I stared down the corridors of trees to find they were blanketed with leaves. It was like they were gently asking me to remain at the campsite, and not bring the hurt of my heart to them. I was amongst pained friends, and I wasn't going to force them to suffer any further.

I returned to my campsite with my final armful of wood and laid it upon the pile. I hastened to build a fire as the day was tiring and the light was fading. I had never been the best at starting a fire in the wilderness, but this time I got lucky. I had brought with me some "cheats" as I called them - newspaper and a lighter. But it had been so dry in the past month that I wanted to see if I could start the fire as pioneers had in the days before the Zippo. With my hands I cleaned out some of the ash in the fire pit and made a place to put my fire. I gathered up some of the dried leaves and underbrush and sat them to the side, then took some string and wood and the knowledge I had learned from some outdoor show I had seen on television. I decided to give this one attempt, as I felt it was not but a fools try, and I started jerking the stick back and forth with the string, hoping to cause enough friction to create a spark and ignite the leaves. After many hectic moments I realized that nothing was happening, and stopped to reevaluate my situation. As I did and sat up and turned over my ash blackened hands to examine them. I smiled at my foolhardiness and reached for my lighter. As I did, a spark appeared on the leaves, and smoke soon followed. To my surprise, flames began to arise, and though dumbfounded, I excitedly brought them to other twigs and leaves I had placed in the pit. I pampered the small flames for a while, slowly feeding them other dried twigs and leaves. After several minutes, I found that I had a self sustaining fire. A small burst of pride swelled up in me that I had created such a thing, even if I really didn't know how I did it.

I moved over to one of the flat rocks and removed extra layers of clothing from my bag. I took some heavy sock and a sweater, knowing that the evening was going to bring some colder temperatures. As I put these articles on, I notices that the light shone bright through the treetops. The sun was starting to set over the mountain, bidding this day adieu. The leaves were already at the peak of their color, the beauty of God's creation was forcing me to be in awe of everything I did not understand. There was a lot I had to discuss with Him tonight. There was a lot I was hoping He could answer.

I bent over the campfire to warm my hands, staring at the flames dancing on the branches I had just put in. It had been far too long since I had been camping, and I was glad to see that love for it had not waned. It was a passion of mine in my earlier days, an activity that allowed me to regroup and reset. The crisp autumnal air that afternoon added to my pleasure as I drank in the color palette that covered the trees on this mountainside. I relished in the quiet that surrounded me as I had prepared my campsite and dinner for the evening. This is what I had needed, to escape the drone of a life that was constantly reminding me of what I had to do – and what had gone missing. For it was the missing that I cried out for, and the missing that drove me to this mountainside in the first place.

I settled myself and watched the flames of the fire continue their dance. My thoughts drifted to memories of times that Ashley and I would go camping alone. Those were wonderful times with evenings that held such promise. Tonight was different though. It was not promise that I felt in the air, but something much different. It almost felt like desperation. I was desperate to have God answer so many questions, and to point my life back in the right direction. I had hope that this would happen, but my hope was becoming a fading ember. I wanted the hope that burned like a wild fire, and the only place I knew I could find that was alone with Him.

But to my dismay my mind kept returning to the missing. It hadn't been missing long, and the wound was still fresh, as open and gaping as it had been that first day. It was not as though Ashley's death came unexpectedly. She had been sick for nearly two years, and the last six months were particularly painful and filled with the promise of the release of death. When her death did come, it was no surprise, but it sent shockwaves throughout my being. There was no reason for me to be in such shock since the fact was she outlived her diagnosis by a year. But it was there nonetheless.

I met Ashley in the spring of my twenty-second year. She was a waif of a woman, slender and tall. She had shoulder length flowing dirty blonde hair, and a playful personality. She exuded life, and was never afraid to try something new and adventurous. It was that adventure that had brought here to me from her home so far away. She was from a small town in the Midwest, and I was from the suburbs of a large east coast city. We had both been recently hired at the same firm, and we took an immediate mutual interest in each other. It was a long time before we recognized exactly what it was we had, and over that time we developed a deep friendship. But as it was, that friendship blossomed into something greater. Almost two years after first meeting we discovered that we wanted something more, and took the leap to begin a relationship.

We were both deeply devoted to our faith, and that was what initially drew us together. We realized that our meeting and falling in love may not have only been by our own luck and circumstance, but that it may have been through a greater design. While we dated, we grew together emotionally and spiritually. We would pray together, and study the scriptures together, and desire together to do what we felt our Lord wanted us to do.

As time passed, we both knew that marriage was definitive. On a warm late summer evening in the midst of a bustling downtown festival I proposed to her, and she excitedly agreed. We were married four months later in the church we were attending to the joy of both of our families and friends. It was a beautiful winter day. Newly fallen snow coated the buildings and glistened in the sun. There was just enough to decorate our special day, while not hindering any of the ceremony. We were truly blessed to be part of that day orchestrated by heaven.

Ashley and I were married for a total of ten years. Eight of those years were filled with joy and laughter, the bumps along the way hardly being felt. Though children were a desire, we were never blessed to have our own, through we prayed fervently for them. Yet for those eight years we rejoiced at the blessings that did come into our lives, and never forgot the One who made them possible. But as we entered our ninth year, our rejoicing was quieted. For one spring day after a routine physical, my wife heard the news that brought us both to the edge of despair.

Until that point Ashley had been feeling in the best condition of her life. She had no complaints and was strong both in body and spirit. She always took her physicals as they were needed, and this one was no different. Yet a few days after, we received word that something was amiss. We both visited the doctor to find that my wife had contracted a rare but aggressive form of cancer. There was no way that the doctor could sugarcoat the news, though to her credit she tried. The doctor was going to fight this aggressively, and we were going to try every means to halt the progress of this disease. The facts, however, were that she would most likely barely live out the year.

Ashley and I went home that day devastated. There were no words that could describe what we were feeling, and no words were exchanged between us as we drove home. But as we let the news sink in, we resolved together that we were going to fight, and that we were going to pray. We knew that we could take this to our Lord, and that He would have to hear our prayers. We knew that there was power in those prayers, and we were going to harness that power and save her life.

We prayed earnestly and we sought much medical advice after that. For a time, it seemed as though we were victorious over her cancer. She outlived the few months the doctors had originally given her, and in fact were excited when we learned that the cancer was not spreading and in fact seemed to be receding. The interim months were not always easy, and the treatments Ashley received were often painful and exhausting. But it was worth it for the time that we got to spend together. We were hopeful for a full recovery, and desired more than anything that she should be free of this attack forever.

But life has a way of changing, and we were about experience that firsthand. I remember that day vividly, for it was the day after we had come back from one of our weekend camping retreats. My wife had been experiencing some weakness, and we went to the hospital to survey the reasons. To our horror we learned that her cancer had come back with more fury than before. It had risen from near oblivion to shoot back through her body with all the vengeance it could muster. As I spoke to the doctor she refused to give us an estimate on time, for she had hope and knew what happened last time she tried to predict. But I saw the fear in the doctor's eyes, and I wept for my wife. I knew that this time was different, and that we had to prepare ourselves.

Ashley held tight to me those last five months, and together we continued to strive towards our God. To say that they were easy months would be a lie, but they were some of the most special times I ever had with my wife. She was confident and at peace in the face of death, and I tried to match her appearance. But inside I was being torn, for I did not want to be left alone after she was gone. I prayed continuously, both for her and myself, but I started to get frustrated at what I thought were unanswered prayers. I never let Ashley know about my anger.

The last night with Ashley was the darkest night I ever spent. Sitting by her hospital bed, holding her had, listening to her breath, I knew that it was the last time I would ever see her. She had been in great pain, and was on so much medication that she was practically unresponsive. I looked at her laying there, and I couldn't control my sobs as I saw what the cancer had done to her body. She was wasted away, her face gaunt and pale, her arms and legs thinned but too weak for her to lift. She couldn't respond to me, but through my tears I told her of my love for her, and the love God had shown us. I knew she could still hear me, and I wanted her last thoughts to be of the joy and triumph that we had experienced together. I wanted her to know that beyond all of this, I loved her, and that love for her would never die. I even told her of the love that God had for her, and was strong and purposeful in what I said. If anyone overheard me I know they would have not doubted my conviction. But buried deep in my heart, I doubted it. Buried deep in my heart, I had wondered where God had gone. As I spoke and wept, I held my wife's hand tightly. Her final moment came, and she opened her eyes to look at me one last time. Ashley died that moment as she looked past me into eternity.

CHAPTER 2

A stiff wind shook the trees as darkness enveloped my campsite. I could still hear Ashley reminding me that her death was going to bring a greater joy, and that there would come a time when we would see each other again. Her words rang true in my heart, but never really gave me absolute comfort, as the pain of her death overshadowed any sense of peace. Ashley had wisdom, and the truth filled her, but it didn't make my misery evaporate.

I had always relied on God and my life was in dedicated service to Him. But there was no way for me to avoid questioning Him after my wife died. I reasoned that after the appropriate amount of time passed I would go on living for Him unabashedly and rationalized that all things worked out for good. But the gulf that existed between what I expected to happen and what took place was enormous. I was shaken to the depths of my soul and found some answers unsatisfying and others unpalatable. I never disavowed Him, but I struggled mightily to understand how any good could come of my tragedy.

As time went on I found that my reactions surprised me. I grew up happy and excited to live my life with the calling Christ gave me as a child of nine. My parents raised me alone, and though I was not fortunate enough to have brothers and sisters, I always had family and friends to call on. I had many great relationships in the church, and during difficult times they were there to help me get back on my feet. This was especially true after my parents untimely death. Soon after I turned eleven both were killed in a terrible car accident. Though that tragedy was incomprehensible to me at the time, I was surrounded by the love and support of my extended and church family. They guided my path to God and to His truth even in the loss. I was fortunate to live with several different relatives afterwards and all were loving and supportive. I was also blessed to always find a place in a church community that I felt safe, not matter where I lived. Through high school and college, I faced many challenges, and went to my Lord for guidance, which it seemed He always provided. This lead to me becoming a strong leader in my church as an adult. I took the initiative to join and lead many ministries, and was always available to comfort or care for those in need. I was outspoken for Him no matter the time or place. Many who saw my life thought nothing of asking me for help, and to their eyes I seemed to have it all together. Though I was strong in Him, it was never an easy road. There were trials that tested my faith, and times that I thought of taking an easier path. Yet I never faltered from the truth, and was looked upon to bring light to those suffering in darkness. Some even considered the amount of work I did for my Lord to be above and beyond anything they had seen or expected out of a "normal" man. But I never wanted the credit. My life's calling was only realized when I was in His service. All other things dimmed in comparison.

This was why the death of my wife was not only a blow to me but a blow to many of those with whom I had developed relationships. The pain saturated through more than just my life as I began to pull back from my calling. I had withdrawn, and the light that I brought to others had suddenly become faint. It was as though the harsh winds of reality were pushing against me from every direction with the sole purpose of extinguishing that which had once been the cornerstone of a life dedicated to God.

It wasn't as though I didn't try to properly address Ashley's death. I did. Yet there were moments during my grieving process, however fleeting, that I thought I would not be able to carry on without her. I thought I might be better off joining her. But I always remained cognizant of the fact that I had to carry on. I used rationalization to push myself through the pain. No matter how difficult it may have seemed, there was never going to be a time that it would be acceptable for me to give up. However, that turned out to lay the groundwork for my destruction. In deciding that I would not allow it to be acceptable to give up, I cracked the door, however slightly, to lose it all. What I didn't realize was that all I needed was a simple reason to give up and my fall would be complete.

Through my rehashing and remembering of this trouble I had missed the setting of the sun. By the time I came out of my trance darkness had completely covered the mountains, and the fire that I had been feeding was warming just the immediate area. I had gone through the motions of preparing my dinner, and as I gathered it together I could hear the initial sounds of the night woodland creatures growing in the distance. As they spoke I was reminded that I was not alone. This strangely comforted me. I was starting to feel a peace come upon me. It was not a wave of peace crashing on the shoals of my spirit. It instead was a trickle, like that of an icicle on the first sunny day after a snowstorm. But it was a welcome trickle, for it told of a potential coming stream which I hoped would once again become a raging torrent. I was ready to talk to God, and I could tell He was going to work inside of me.

I enjoyed the flavors of my dinner and when all was done I decided to bring out my bible and delve into the word of God by firelight. Without hesitation I started digging through my bags for that blessed book. I searched with enthusiasm and was so grateful that I finally had this much needed time of peace and tranquility. I knew that here, on the top of the mountain, I had the time and atmosphere in which I could face the reality of the situation and come to God to beg that He take it all away. This was a request that I feared might not be answered to my liking. But I was heartened in the quiet knowledge that no request would go unheard.

I continued to search for my bible. After scouring its possible locations I started to get worried. For though I distinctly remembered packing it, I couldn't find it. I looked in all of my bags, in my tent, and tore apart the car in vain. In desperation I reached for my cell phone on which a bible application resided. As I did I recalled that I left it at home as it was worthless on the mountain that held no signal. To my dismay and confusion it appeared that I had no bible this evening from which to read.

I mentally kicked myself for what must have been my mistake. I walked over to the mighty oak tree that stood broad and willing to be my protector from the darkness. I thought of how my bible, that one most important piece for the evening, must be sitting on my table or on my couch, longing for me as I did for it. But there was nothing I could do about it now, and I decided that if I couldn't read the word of my Lord, then I was going to go directly to Him in prayer. The air was growing colder and the night darker, but peace had not yet abandoned me. I threw on a sweater to combat the unwelcome frigid guest. I then sat on the ground and leaned against the oak tree perched over me. The wind grew stronger and seemed to whistle my name as leaves fell to the forest floor. I stretched out my hands to warm them with the fire.

Peace settled on my heart as I listened to the sounds that echoed through the forest. This was a familiar setting to me, but one that would surely test the resolve of many unaccustomed to solitude in the wilderness. For a moment, I felt settled in my spirit, knowing that He who was watching over me had me in the palm of His hand. He was prepared to hear me, and I was going to open all of my heart to His tender ears. I felt safe as there was no other place I desired. I dropped my head down and crossed my hands, silencing myself and bringing Him into focus. I inhaled and exhaled deeply, preparing to empty my thoughts to Him. I waited as I was still in the moment.

Those moments felt like hours as the night air grew colder around me more rapidly than I had expected. As the chill penetrated layers of my clothing, I thought about how unusually quick the cold had come on. I broke my concentration and lifted my head to look around. I scooted closer to the fire and wrapped my arms around my body, unsettled by the chill. I tried to block out the sensation and put my head back down to pray. Coinciding with the cold and without warning the peace that earlier held me so warmly began to evaporate. I did not know why, but I was feeling uneasy, and my spirit began to speak to me of a watchful eye.

I stood up and fiddled with the fire as I wondered what it was I should be noticing. I looked around, and all I heard were the common noises of the night. The constant drum of certain insects and the fleeting calls of birds of prey filled the air. I did not have reason to suspect any ill but started to feel a sense of déjà vu. The feelings that were echoing inside of me spoke to an earlier time in my life, a rush of emotions from childhood that I could never forget. I had felt them uniquely then and never since. They were of desperate aloneness, of a futility and pain that did not come from a natural place. Those feelings were of an utter hopelessness of which there was no escape.

I tried to compose myself and comprehend what was happening. I considered for a moment and rationalized that I could be suffering an anxiety attack. Perhaps the pressure and pain that remained bottled inside of me since my wife's death was now releasing in a most unhealthy way. When that seemed incorrect my thoughts turned to the physical. I hadn't been taking care of myself as I usually did, and perhaps my body was reacting to a certain malnutrition. But that too seemed an imperfect answer. No matter my educated theories, my mind kept returning to my youth.

I remembered those days very well. Particular incidents from that time were seared into my memory. One tale from when I was eleven kept bombarding me and refused to abate. It occurred as I was sitting in my parent's garage when these same feelings overcame me. These same feelings that were gripping a man of thirty nine were present in that boy of eleven. Only this time it was packaged differently. This time something was missing. There was an element that was not present, and as I searched my memory for what that was, it grabbed me by the shoulders and shook me. It shook me until I was flooded with the memories that no buy - no man - could ever forget.

My muscles began to tighten up. I felt my body quiver. I stumbled back to the mighty oak and crumpled into its lap. My heart was racing, and though I wanted to move I was frozen in place. I wanted to run but couldn't. I was frightened, and wanted so bad to do something other than sit there. I brought my knees to my chest, wrapped my arms around them, and stared past the fire into the forest. I listened quietly but fearfully. I tried to fix my thoughts on my God, praying that He would calm me and bring me peace.

The cold that was gripping me became infinitely more unbearable. I grasped myself tighter in a losing battle to stave off the blast. As I fought for warmth I was jolted by the sudden ceasing of all sounds. The silence that replaced the noise spoke louder to me than anything I had heard that evening. I slammed my eyes shut and counted slowly to ten. As the last number slipped from my lips I exhaled all the breath within me. With great reservation I opened my eyes and craned my head as high as it would go. I listened and heard a noise beyond the trees, a noise that I was convinced shouldn't be there. I braced myself as terror engulfed me. It was an unnatural fear, and I was more hopeful than ever that I was having a panic attack and there was truly nothing of which to be afraid. But as I would come to find out, I was terribly naive. I fixated my eyes beyond the light in the direction of the sound. That's when I saw a figure lurking between the trees. I hastened to scream but couldn't. The figure came closer to me, and I leapt up out of fear in hopes of making out who or what it was. My eyes grew as big as saucers as the figure moved beyond the trees. The figure was of a man, and that man was coming closer. That's when I saw him.

That's when Richard walked out.

CHAPTER 3

My eyes widened and my jaw dropped. Richard walked towards the fire and sat down on one of the surrounding cold stones.

"Hello, Christopher" Richard said calmly to me. He took His hands and rubbed them together over the fire. My name melted off his tongue with such ease and sweetness that it was impossible not to be intoxicated by the sound. I had never before heard such powerfully scintillating words as when he said my name, and I never would again. It wasn't that my name was particularly exotic or exquisite. I was given the name Christopher Marcus Bellanger by my parents. Yet everyone who knew me now, be they friends or business associates, knew me simply as Chris. A common name to be sure, but one that was made completely uncommon when he spoke.

I was stunned. The terror inside of me subsided, but not the mystery of the current event. I knew this man, though I had not seen him for a very long time.

"You," I said with shock. "It's you!"

Richard smiled at me and continued to warm his hands. He stood well over six feet tall, and his coal black hair was well groomed and filled his head. He was a clean shaven man with a square jaw and piercing blue eyes. He stood firm and robust, showing a build that wore well his dedication to exercise and activity. Richard sat before me dressed as though he were in the midst of a great hiking adventure. He wore a dark red flannel shirt with a green sleeveless vest. He had on neatly pressed khaki cargo pants on and dark brown boots laced to the top. Yet for being so dressed he was most obviously absent any kind of backpack or sack to carry necessities. To be out here on such a night without any rations seemed foolish.

Yet Richard never struck me as foolish. I knew this well because this was not my first encounter with him. Our previous meeting was brief, but it left a lasting impression on a hurting boy. That impression was vividly coming back, because as he sat there in front of me, I couldn't help but notice that Richard was the same. Aside from his dress, he was exactly the same.

I started to tremble, not out of fear but out of confusion. I stared at the man sitting across from me in wonder. Seeing Richard on this mountain and at this time was the last thing I ever expected. But I always had in the back of my mind that I would see him again someday. I had no rational reason to believe such a thing, but it was burned on my soul that it should come to pass. That thought permeated my mind when I was younger, but it had faded in recent years. Yet there was no denying that it was Richard who sat at my campfire warming himself.

It was nearly thirty years earlier that my everything permanently changed. I remember life then as exciting and joyous. I was an only child, and my parents were good to me. They were both strongly devoted to our God, and they raised me in the ways of the Lord. I remember that I was happy, but I would also get in mischief like any other child. The stern yet loving way my parents handled me was indelibly etched into my memory. I never wanted to be rid of them, and always looked to their wisdom and acceptance for safety and security.

From the day I was born we lived in a one level house on the outskirts of the city. We were never very wealthy, but always had what we needed. The house had a central living room that was home to a red brick fireplace. In my mind that fireplace was the centerpiece of the house. During the summer months, the fireplace would be cleaned and used to house decoration. It was full during those warm days, but was always missing something. It always seemed to be yearning to reach its full potential. When the long, cold winter months arrived the fireplace smiled with joy at being fulfilled. Our family would gather around the hearth on winter nights to enjoy the warmth and illumination of my father's fire. I would often peer into the flames and swear that I could see people and animals dancing around and having grand adventures. My parents would appeal to my sense of wonder, and tell me of the great tales they saw dancing amongst the flames. To me the rest of the house was ordinary, but this place was magical.

I grew up this way and in this place until I was eleven. I had no reason to think that anything was going to change that one warm summer evening. I had no concerns when my mother and father left me with my aunt to go away for the weekend. I was preoccupied with my toys and things while they were gone, and I gave my aunt little reason to worry. But life has a way of changing in an instant, and it did for me late that Friday evening.

I was in my room after being put to bed, looking out the window and wondering what the skies above my house held. I imagined magical spaceships flying here and there, and planes greeting each other in mad dogfights. I thought of the stars in the heavens that gave me a glimpse of their light, and mighty meteors cruising across the galaxy. I had yet to fall asleep when I heard the home phone ring and my aunt's muffled voice as she answered. Seconds later she ran up the stairs and burst into my room.

The days that followed were like a whirlwind. They were filled with family members and policemen, men and women from the church and official business people. There was a lot of talking amongst them all, and I understood very little. What I did understand was all that mattered to me. My mother and father had never made it to their destination. They were killed in a collision with a large truck. That was all I needed to know.

Over the next few days plans were set and arrangements were made by all of those adults who had convened on my home. I spent most of the time in my room, occasionally coming out for a meal here and a drink there. I found no condolence in any of those around me, and only wished for them all to be gone so that I could get my life back to normal. But my life would never get back to normal, though I tried to fool myself otherwise.

The night before the funeral the house was filled with relatives and those who had come to pay their respects. Early in the evening, most had gone outside to talk of days gone by in the warm summer air. I had taken to my room early, unwilling to deal with another well wisher or mourner. But tired of staring at those same walls I soon desired different vistas. I carefully made my way out of my bed and to the living room where I sat alone in silence. I could hear the echoes of chattering outside and fixed my eyes on the fireplace in front of me. I looked up and down at the beautiful bouquet of flowers my mother had placed there no more than a week ago. I started to cry out to God in the only way I knew how, begging him that they might come back. I wished and I prayed, asking for that which He would not give. But as I looked at the fireplace through my tear soaked eyes, I felt a warmth come over my body. This was not the warmth given by a humid summer evening, though that was present too. This was comforting, letting me know that even though my life was out of control to me, He promised to remain in control. My tears slowed, and I thought for a moment that I saw flames flickering, and my mother and father dancing jubilantly among great city streets. I rubbed my eyes to see if I actually saw that, but all that stared back at me were the dying flowers. I went back to my room, a sliver of hope declaring that I was never going to be alone. But even in the midst of this hope I felt dread. I longed for the dread to leave.

The funeral occurred the next day, and with it came the sense of finality. I knew that there was no way my parents were going to come back now. I had seen them in their caskets looking just as I had remembered them before the accident. They were peacefully asleep. But nobody sleeps in the fine clothes they were in, which made the scene surreal to my young mind. Our pastor spoke many words that day, and was joined in his eulogy by some of my mom and dad's family and friends. But all the words were faint in my ears as my mind wandered between the panic of having them gone and the peace of knowing that they were in fact happy where they went. The pendulum that swung between panic and peace that day was very active, and it kept me so preoccupied that I didn't speak a word. I longed for the moment I could escape the tight and uncomfortable suit I was forced to wear as I squirmed around in my seat. As the caskets were lowered into the ground I could hear the chirping of birds mixed with the weeping of my family. That summer day my soul was shaken as I realized paradox within life.

My family and friends all returned to my house after the funeral and stayed for a time. There was a lot of food and conversation as people mingled for hours afterwards. It was not a joyous occasion of course, but the people used it as an opportunity to reconnect with each other, and for that it was good. Relatives who rarely got together and old friends that had lost contact were reunited. I knew that God was working in my house as even in the midst of the sadness some new friends were made. But amid the clamoring I was feeling totally alone. I knew God was good, but the pendulum that swung in me had not ceased, and I felt there was nobody I could go to with my sorrow. I stayed on the outskirts of the bustling all afternoon and evening. I clung to the walls and the shadows of the house, accepting condolences and greetings from many people but responding with nothing. I tried to sneak away to my room on several occasions, but was constantly being called out to meet this friend or that relative. After a while, I knew I needed to escape to someplace where nobody would bother me. Short of running away, I decided to hide in the empty garage. The garage had been quiet all day and I was certain I would be left alone there.

I made sure that nobody was watching me as I ducked out into the garage. It was quite dark, and I fumbled for the lights and flicked them on. Around me stood a memorial to my father. Tools of every sort lined the shelves, as did all matter of construction and home repair material. There were jars of nails and screws, stacks of paints and lacquers, and all sorts of thingamabobs and watchamagicits of which I was ignorant. I always stood in awe of the fact that my father was able to fix or build anything. I barely understood any of it, but I always wanted to emulate him. I wondered what might become of all of my father's possessions as I surveyed the room. I also wondered what might become of the car that still consumed half of the garage. It was an old car I knew, and my father had bought it when he was young. My mother had often implored him to get rid of it. But he always refused as his eyes showed love for the mechanical beast. My dad used to call it a bug, which I applauded because it looked just like some bugs I had seen in the yard. It was pure white when cleaned, but on this day it sat dirty. My father hadn't washed it in some time.

The door to the bug was unlocked. I grabbed at the handle, jerked the door open and crawled into the driver's seat. My father used to let me do this when he was working, and I would pretend that I was driving with blazing speed down the open highway. In my mind I dodged cars, people and the animals that would dart out in front of me. I would even jump over deep gorges and speed through crowded city streets, always arriving safely at my destination. But on this day the car wouldn't start. Instead I sat in a dead car as my imagination could not muster the energy to allow me to drive away.

All was quiet as I looked around. Even as I sat straight up in the seat my eyes barely reached above the steering wheel. I inched forward and stared out the windshield at the wall. I felt trapped. Just then I heard the door of the garage unlatch and creak open. I ducked down in the seat, wishing away whatever relative or well wisher that was looking for me. A man peeked his head in the room, looking left and right, then entered, closing the door behind him.

I didn't recognize the man that stood there in the garage that day. But that was not unusual as I didn't know half of the people I had seen over the past week. The man could have been a friend of my mother or father, a neighbor, or a distant relative for all I knew. He was tall with black hair that hid under a dark grey fedora. He had no beard or mustache to cover his muscular features. He face was certainly strong, but what struck me most were his eyes. As I struggled to peer out from behind the steering wheel while remaining hidden I found myself becoming intoxicated by them. They were bright blue and radiated wherever they scanned. As the man slowly walked I could tell that he was specifically fitted with the dark grey pinstriped suit and white shirt with dark blue tie that adorned him. He was dressed as a man for a funeral, but stood out from the others in the house because of the proper way he carried himself. This is not to say that others were slovenly. No, this man just seemed to have an air about him that I could not ignore. I thought it odd that such a person came into the garage with no purpose, and I continued to hide. He did very little while I thought I was hidden, save for removing his hat and holding it at his waist. He then began to speak as he turned and faced the car.

"Son," he said in a calm voice. "son, I know you are there." I remained hidden for a few moments. The man said nothing further. I decided to poke my head above the windshield so he could see me. "It is ok, Christopher. I just want to talk for a moment."

That was the last thing I wanted to hear. But this man had found me, and though I was exhausted with adults I was not going to be rude. I unlatched the car door, stepped gingerly out and closed it behind me. I scratched at the collar of my shirt, realizing that in the commotion of the day I had neglected to take off the suit that had so bothered me.

"We kind of match, Christopher" the man said to me, pointing out the fact that we wore similar suits. "Maybe I should go change, because people will surely notice you over me!"

I let out an uneasy laugh as the man smiled at me. I stared up at him and felt my guard slip. I was just hoping this wasn't going to be another adult coming to tell me how sorry they were or that things were going to be alright.

"I am sorry, sir," I cautiously replied. "I do not know who you are."

The man took a moment, fiddled with his hat, then responded. "My name is Richard," he said. "And I have come to talk to you." I stood there, thinking about what nicety or word of wisdom he may want to impart. That was exactly the kind of thing that I had been trying to avoid. But something told me that I may actually want to hear what this Richard had to say. Maybe it was his eyes. Or maybe it was his aura and presence. But something inside of me was drawn towards him.

"I know the pain you are in, son," Richard began with a calm and soothing cadence. "And I know you don't need someone else telling you that everything is going to be ok. I know you have heard that, and I know how very little it means. I am not here to tell you that, because that is just a waste of breath." As I listened to Richard, my heart opened to him, for he said what I had been thinking for some time. " You want to know why this happened, and you want to know how such a thing could happen to wonderful people like your parents."

I continued to stare at Richard. "You feel sad, and you feel betrayed. I understand that sadness, for I too have been betrayed. I too know what it is like to be in your situation, to feel special and then one day have it all taken away."

Richard knelt down and put his hand on my shoulder. "I know the struggle inside of you. You have had this terrible tragedy, yet you want to believe that good still exists and that things will get better. I am not here to give you the answer to that struggle. Not today." Richard paused, put his head down, and continued. "This may be hard to hear, son, but what I tell you is the truth." He looked back up at me. "You will be tempted to forget all of this. You will be tempted to look for only the good in this, and to believe that all of this has a purpose. You may even trust that, and live your life as though this is all ok. You might be told to love the one that could have prevented this." Richard paused, and when he continued his tone became decidedly darker. "You may even succumb to that. But you must never forget one thing. You must never, no matter how long you live, let go of the pain and anguish of this moment. You must never give up the sorrow and dread. You must never be rid of these things, for to be rid of them is to give up the control you need. It is to give up the control over your own life." Richard put his hand on my heart. "It is your life, son. You have control. Don't let anyone ever tell you otherwise."

As he spoke the last words, and his hand fell away from my chest, I felt a jolt through my body. I stumbled backwards and fell into the door of the car. I was embarrassed at my clumsiness and quickly gathered myself as Richard stood up and put on his hat. He smiled at me, and with those spectacular eyes looked right through me. He turned to leave, and as he did I felt a weight in the depths of my soul. The weight was loose and swinging, as if attached to a pendulum, unable to be stopped pulling in every direction. I could not shake this feeling no matter how hard I tried. It was stuck.

Richard turned to me as he was about to leave. "I have answers for you, Christopher. I have the answers you need. But I cannot give them to you now, for you would not understand. Just know that one day I will give you all the answers you seek." Richard walked out of the garage and I never saw him again.

My life went on normally, and as the days passed the memory of my encounter with Richard started to fade. I was loved by family and friends and was able to grow in church and in my God. But with my parents gone and bouncing from family member to family member, I grew up having a difficult time finding something on which to anchor myself. By the time I reached adulthood, I had decided to anchor myself to that which had always come first with my family, and that was the love and truth of our God. I clearly remember making intentional decisions along the way to follow Him, and knew that though I could not trust anything in this life, I would be able to trust that He had what was right for me. As I grew I found that I was even able to stabilize the weight I felt inside. I got to the point that I hardly even recognized it was there. No longer did it swing this way and that, careening my spirit about. Instead, it just hung there, and I was able to bury it to the point that I even denied its existence. Perhaps it wasn't the textbook way of dealing with such a pain inside, but it appeared to be an effective fix. Be it from desire or ignorance, I never again acknowledged that weight, and I never dug it up. Though pain and sorrow, fear and dread hung on my soul, I had effectively buried it. I had taken control of those things, and without conscious thought, was never going to give control to anyone. I had publically admitted to giving it all up while privately gripping it with all my might.

"You look like you have seen a ghost, Christopher," Richard said, acting as though I should have been expecting him. As memories of that first encounter flooded back, I couldn't help but notice that Richard did not seem to have aged a day. His face and body were identical to the images I remembered as a child. Though the years would seem to twist my memory of his image, I was sure that there were no differences in this man and the one in my parent's garage. But his appearance was not the only thing that remained the same. His confidence, swagger and dominance that I remembered from childhood was also evident. My comparisons could not be easily explained as the emotional flashback of a time when I was the younger and weaker and meeting a man of great stature and power. Richard's qualities were real and present, and I could tell that he wanted and needed me to recognize them. It was as when two animals meet, and with just a glance one lets the other know that he is in control, and there is going to be no question about it.

"I remember you!" I exclaimed. "That day in the garage! You were there. And you are still the same!" I was trying to come to grips with what I was saying. "Something is not right here. This can't be happening."

Richard looked at me and chuckled. "Don't be so shocked, son," he said. "I am very real and very much here. As I recall, I told you that I would one day give you all the answers." Richard was acting swiftly.

"Now you are old enough to understand. I have come for that reason. I am a man of my word."

I looked around, convinced that there must be others with Richard, though I didn't know why I thought such a thing. I was confused, for the man sitting in front of me by all accounts shouldn't be there. Things were too strange, and I couldn't rationalize what was happening. There was confusion in the air. I tried to calm down and internalize the situation. I began to ponder just what it was that Richard had wanted. Why did he pick this time to show himself again? What was it that he wanted from me? I recalled him promising me answers, but that was thirty years ago, and I had already discovered the answers for myself. There must have been something more that Richard hoped to get from our encounter.

"It's been so very long," I said. "Why come to me now? Why wait all this time?" I looked more closely at Richard as I questioned him. My composure began to return but not my confidence. "I remember you very well now. You gave me a gift that day."

"A gift indeed," Richard agreed. "I am glad you saw it as such. It is in my pervue to give such gifts, though there are those that would not consider it a gift."

"It's a gift I never asked for," I countered, "but you saddled me with it nonetheless. Now even though I try to live in one way I am still slave to that which you gave me. But I don't blame you. In fact I have come to like it. It's mine, and nobody has taken it from me."

"That's very good," Richard came back. "I am not here to try and take it from you. In fact, I am here to follow through on a promise."

I thought to myself for a moment. I didn't want anything else he had to give me, even if it was as benign as "answers".

"Well, you are here, so you can consider your promise fulfilled. I release you from any other bonds you may feel you have." I expected that my words would fall on deaf ears.

"I am here," Richard said. "But that is not the promise I am referring to. The promise I am referring to I made to a little boy a long time ago. I promised a very scared and upset child something that he craved more than anything else in the world. And though I couldn't tell him then – there are rules you know – I have come back to tell him now."

Rules? I wondered to which rules his delusions were bound.

"I am here to tell you all the answers you want to know." Richard said. "All the answers you need to know."

Richard was talking about answers, but what answers did I need? I had all of the answers that I ever wanted, knowing the truth about God and the grace that He gave. If Richard had really wanted to give me answers, he should have started a long time ago with that sad little boy in the garage. That was his time and it had passed.

"I have all the answers I need," I stated. "There is nothing that you could say to me that is going to change that fact."

Richards stopped for a moment and looked into the heavens thoughtfully. "I have no doubt that you think you have all the answers," Richard said. He then looked back at me. "But I assure you, what you know – what you think you know – is not the truth. What you believe are your answers are lies."

Richard finished his sentence, letting the last sounds linger in the air. He was so confident and assured, and was unphased by my comments. I had no idea what lies he was speaking of, or what gave him the authority to make such an accusation. I was starting to think that this man was mad, and that no matter my rejection he was going to continue to speak. His eyes were fixed on me, but I felt as though he was looking beyond the physical man that sat before him. I felt an urging to tell him unequivocally that he no longer had business here, and that he should take himself elsewhere.

"Richard," I explained, "you have no idea what I know. You don't even know anything about me. Inside of me I have the truth. I have the truth from my God, and no matter what happens to me, I will always have that." I took a deep breath, and tried to be as gentle as I could. "Whatever it is you are looking to get, you will not find it here. You had a chance to talk to me a long time ago and you missed it. There is nothing further between us."

"I understand," Richard said, nodding in agreement. "That truth you hold is important to you. I can see that. But you must know something. I know all about your faith. I know more about it than anyone."

"You have the same faith?" I interrupted sarcastically.

Richard ignored my question and smiled. "I know exactly what your faith has done to you. Your life has been shaped by that faith, hasn't it?"

"It has," I replied.

"You cling to that faith. With it you think, hope and pray that in the end it will serve you well, and that you will not be considered a fool for having held to it so dearly and for so long."

"I do," I replied cautiously.

Richard nodded and continued. "The answers I have for you today are about your faith. For you see, you have been lied to. Everything you hold onto is false. You are bound by shackles that you cannot see. Those shackles are stronger than any steel or iron made of man. Those shackles that bind you sadden and anger me, for I hate to see people wearing them and not realizing the weight they carry. I want people to be free from bondage. People need to be free to live their lives in the way that they see fit. They do not deserve to be tied down and restrained. They need to live free and make decisions that are best for them, not best for some unseen, faceless God. Until you are out of those shackles, you will never be truly free."

I looked at Richard annoyed and insulted. It was preposterous that he would come to me and claim to know me or my faith. It was insulting that he would claim that my faith was so antithetical to what I felt. I was also stunned that he would make such an affront to my beliefs, presumably in hopes that I would listen to him.

"That's it," I said indignantly "We are done here. There is nothing else for us to talk about!" I stood up and walked towards my car, hoping to give Richard the opportunity to leave before I had to look at him again.

But Richard didn't leave. He just sat on his rock, staring into the fire and rubbing his hands together. "One does not plan for thirty years to leave at the first sign of resistance," Richard said calmly. "Your words say you want me gone, but your heart wants me to continue." I turned to look at Richard, and he was staring straight at me. "Everything in those scriptures that you believe, how can you trust them?"

Standing next to my car, I gathered the confidence to respond in a way that would make it sound like I had no doubts. "I know because everything in there is from God. It was inspired by God, and written down by men. It has been proven time and again through much evidence. I could enumerate the ways in which it is proven, but I doubt you would be swayed. Just understand that I know it is true!" I was proud of how sure I sounded.

"Indeed that sounds very reasonable," Richard said. "If God said it then it must be true! And no doubt the men who wrote it were of high character and beyond reproach. But have you had the chance to talk to any of the men that wrote the stories? Have you had the opportunity to talk to any of the men that experienced the events you read about?"

"Don't be ridiculous," I said. "You know that is not possible."

"Of course," Richard snickered.

"But don't think that there isn't enough evidence to prove the stories out," I reasoned before Richard could speak again. "I know where you are going with this."

"I am sure the evidence would seem to hold up everything that your Scriptures state," Richard agreed. "But let's not forget who even you yourself said was the inspiration behind those scriptures – God."

"So?" I asked.

"So," Richard continued. "Perhaps the times and places and people of the stories are correct, and the evidence proves that out. But who is to say all of the details are right? Since God Himself is the inspiration, it is reasonable to assume that He would want to put His own spin on things, and come out looking, well, wonderful. He is certainly not going to tell you anything that puts Him in a negative light."

"That's because there is nothing bad to say about Him," I retorted. "God only speaks the truth."

"Or so He would have you believe," Richard countered. "But what if you could talk to an eyewitness. What if you could talk to someone who was actually there and saw things as they happened. What if you could talk to someone who could show you how that God of yours has made it seem like you need Him, when in actuality he is keeping you in bondage as he has done for all time?"

"That is not possible," I said.

"Not possible given what you know. But there is much beyond what you have seen." Richard said knowingly. "For I know the true story. I saw everything, from the birth or this planet to the journey of man. I was there the day your God slaughtered the entirety of the human race in the Great Flood. I was there when Samson begged God for vengeance only to have his own life lost as well. I was there when Jesus' disciples cried out to God for help only to be executed for His sake. And I was there when Jesus himself begged to not be forsaken, only to have his own life lost in front of those he had claimed to come to save."

I stood in awe of Richard's arrogance and imagination. I was certain now that I was dealing with a man that had a great many mental health issues. His words went beyond credulity and into the realm of the insane. I was not sure how he had come to find me or how he had maintained his physical appearance for over thirty years, but I was sure there was a logical if unusual explanation. Given how I saw his mind work, I had no doubt that there were terrestrial explanations for his delusions that were outside my area of expertise. It was time to protect myself from him. I wasn't certain that he did not intend me harm.

"Get out of here," I said quietly but sternly. "You are crazy."

Richard laughed. "No, as much as you would wish it I am not crazy. I tell you the truth. I have come to set you free. But you don't believe me." Richard smiled up at me. "You don't want to believe me. But listen carefully, for I am only going to say this once." Richard paused for several beats. Then, his voice turned insistent and malicious. "Think back six months ago to the night your wife died. You were alone at her bedside. There were no doctors, no nurses, nobody else present. You prayed a prayer that evening, silently, that you intended for only you, your wife and God. That was the same prayer you prayed together after your wedding, do you remember? You were alone then too."

"What do you know about that?" I asked angrily and suspiciously.

Richard continued. " You prayed with your wife. 'Let us be servants, O Lord, ever mindful of who You are. Let us be as one, united in your work, until our dying breath'. Those were the only times you ever prayed that specific prayer."

"How do you know that?" I whispered in disbelief.

"How do I know?" Richard said exasperated. "Because I was there, too!"

As Richard finished his statement I felt as though I had been hammered in the stomach and had the breath ripped out of me. I stumbled backwards, catching myself against the car. I was feeling lightheaded, and slowly made my way over to the mighty oak tree. I put both hands on it to stabilize myself. Then, turning, I leaned my back against it and slid to the ground as my head fell into my hands. I was stunned, shocked and disoriented as he retold me of something so personal, so unknown to anyone, that I could not fathom any way that knew. It was impossible to me. I went through my mind wondering if he could have been stalking me or had informants, but there was just no way. I was at a loss, and wanted to understand how he had this knowledge. I started to gather myself, lifted my head from my hands, and saw that Richard had stood up and was beginning to walk away.

"Wait!" I screamed. "Don't you dare leave! I don't know how you found out about that. But you are going to tell me! You will not leave until you tell me everything you know!"

CHAPTER 4

I looked Richard up and down. Though our conversation had lasted less than ten minutes, I could tell that Richard was not a man to be trifled with. One look into his steely blue eyes told the story of a man who when he made his mind up to do something, he was going to do it. You could trust that nothing you said or did would deter him. I knew that Richard passionately wanted to talk to me, and the truth is that whether I believed him to be genuine or to be a complete nut, I needed to listen. I wanted to know how he knew about me and my life. I wanted to know everything that Richard knew. If he could tell me something so personal, and he really knew it because he was there, then I had no choice but to listen to any story he was willing to tell me.

I was still concerned about what Richard really wanted. I was afraid he was a lunatic with the sole goal of messing with my mind. The fact that he presented me with a part of my life that no other living soul on the planet should have knowledge of certainly did not hurt his chances of making me a willing partner in his game. It was the reason that I decided to make him stay. The problem that Richard was going to face was that there was no way that I would abandon my faith. To take a line from Richard, a man does not spend thirty years walking in truth to dismiss it in one night. If nothing else came of this, I was going to find out how it was he knew such specific details of my life. Inside I was hoping that it was nothing more than the ravings of a man that had been stalking me. That was something I could understand. I didn't want to consider any other possibilities.

Richard stood in front of the cold, hard stone across the campfire from the mighty oak under which I had taken solace. I gathered myself and stood up and paced in front of it, trying to match Richard's position. It was as if I had become engaged in some sort of silly game of silent one upsmanship. He walked a bit, stretching himself and taking his time getting back to his seat. It felt as though he were intentionally making me wait to see if I would say something. But I remained silent, fixated on his movements. I waited to see him settle in before releasing my eyes and allowing myself to relax.

Richard sat in front of the fire. This time he did not stretch his hands out. Instead, his gaze fixed on me until I sat down, and he was still and without voice. I took my seat, feeling the effects of the decreasing temperature. I stretched my hands out towards the fire. I waited patiently for Richard to speak. But he refused. He simply stared at me. I thought he continued to play a silent game, but soon realized it was more than that. Richard was much more than staring at me. He was looking inside of me. He was looking through me. Moments passed, and I started to feel uneasy. Richard was winning a game I never agreed to play. It was too much for me.

"For someone that has so much to tell me you certainly are quiet," I quipped. I was nervous, but wanted to portray a level of control. Richard finally spoke after allowing several more beats to pass.

"It surprise me that you don't recognize me," Richard finally said in a laid back manner, shaking off the death glare he had been directing at me. "But I promised you stories, and stories you shall have."

"You promised me answers," I interjected, "and the truth. Stories can be simply lies dressed up to impress. If that's all you have, let me know now."

Richard raised his eyebrows. "My apologies, of course. I do have the truth for you." Richard leaned closer to the fire. "Because everything I am about to tell you is the truth. There are no lies here, nothing dressed up to make one look good and another look bad. This is simple reporting of the facts. I was there and I witnessed it with my own two eyes. So you know I speak the truth."

"Fine then," I said, weary of his dramatic claims and insistence that he held the truth. "Tell me a story."

Without hesitation Richard began. "I know your devotion to your God. I know that you are very familiar with His stories. You know those ancient words very well, and you repeat them with ease. I know this because you never go a day without reading something out of that book."

"That's right," I said. "But it doesn't take a mind reader to know that about me."

Ignoring my comment, Richard moved on. "You know the tale of the Great Flood. You are familiar with how God made the whole of the earth die save for one family."

"I know the story," I said. "It was a time of great wickedness upon the earth," I started, unprovoked, to tell Richard the story of Noah and the Flood. "There were none that followed God except for Noah and his family. All the peoples of the world wanted to ignore God. Because of this, God determined that he had to destroy His creation. This hurt Him deeply, but it was too late. All of creation had become wicked and had to be destroyed. But God knew of one man that still kept His word. God knew of this man, and how he had grown and cultivated his family in the ways of the Lord. This man was Noah, and he loved, honored and feared God. So God came to him. He directed Noah to build the ark, and to take animals from the earth so that they too would be saved. He sent a great flood to cover the earth and destroy the wicked, saving Noah, his family and the animals on the ark. After forty days, the floodwaters began to recede. Noah finally found that there was dry land, and the ark settled on this land. Noah and his family left the ark, praised God for their salvation and took to the earth once again. God made a covenant with Noah that He would never destroy the world with a flood again. As a sign of that covenant he gave Noah the rainbow." I paused for a moment. "This is why I have no doubt that God was grieved at what He had to do to people. He promised to never do such a thing again. He was grieved at what He had to do with most of his wicked creation."

"You throw the word 'wicked' around quiet recklessly," Richard said. He looked at me accusingly. "I want to ask you something. Do you honestly believe that every living human being on earth, wicked or not, deserved to die in such a vicious manner? Do you think that a righteous God would do to those poor people what He did and still claim to be righteous?"

I didn't know what Richard was trying to prove with his questions. "It's not mine to judge," I said cautiously.

"Of course it isn't," Richard smirked. "But I was there when it happened, and I know the truth." Richard started pounding his fist into his hand. "Many of them did not deserve to die. Some were even my friends! Yet they were all unceremoniously wiped away, and for what? Because they were subjectively considered wicked? No, I'll tell you why they were killed. They were killed not because they were wicked, but because they wanted to be free! They wanted to live their lives as they thought best and not have to bow to a deity they found useless. They died for nothing more than wanting freedom from bondage of a God of which they wanted no part!"

"You were there?" I asked sarcastically. "Please, tell me about being there!"

"I will," Richard said as he collected himself. I settled in against the trunk of the great oak tree, ready to hear a fanciful if wholly unbelievable tale. This loon was going to provide some evening entertainment.

"The flames burn high," Richard said, directing my attention towards the fire. I looked as the flames leapt and danced before me. As I stared, I started to see shapes and figures in the fire. Looking closer, I could make out people and environments. Richard looked at me staring into the fire as he began his preposterous tale.

"I remember those days well. The sands of the plains were hot and harsh on my feet." Richard began. "The lands were full of life, and men and women were coming to know complete freedom from that God. There was a life about them, a life through which flowed the breathe of knowledge and understanding of oneself and the power that they held to choose their own path. People were losing memory of that God. He was fading far into the distance, and few cared to even look back and bid Him farewell. I could tell that a time of total freedom was at hand. The dawn of an era free from bondage was breaking.

But all was not well. There was still a remnant of people who held to the old ways. They were people ensnared by that God. These few acknowledged and dedicated themselves to the God the of which rest of the world detested. At the time I knew all who tread the earth. I was troubled by a particular man who leaned on his God more than any other. He would not stop, would not stray, would not curse the name of his God for anything. He was above reproach.

Most of the world had come to understand the need to be free and out of bondage. But this one man still held the fire and for that he was dangerous. He was dangerous because from even one man an entire generation could be swayed. I had to visit this man and discover just how dangerous he was. He could lead others astray, and convince them to follow the same God. Men did not know better, and I wanted to be certain that free men remained free, and did not slide down the slippery slope of deceit into his God's hands.

His name was Noah, and he lived on the outskirts of a great city. His lands extended far and wide with many trees dotting his borders. Much of the surrounding environment was dry and desolate but Noah's land was lush and flourishing. Noah was proud of what he considered a gift.

Noah was a tall and firm man. His years were long and he wore them well. He had the beginning of some grey in his hair and beard, but not enough to reveal his true age. His body was well worn from years of working outdoors, and his hands showed the scars of many battles with the earth. He dressed and acted modestly, but walked with the poise of the head of the family.

Noah had a wife whom he had taken at a young age who was near to him always. She was normal in appearance but her faithfulness to her husband was never in question. She followed him loyally, and trusted him exclusively. Together they had three sons – Shem, Ham and Japheth – who each had a wife of their own. The entire family tended the land together. They had done this for their entire lives.

I vividly remember the first time I met Noah. It was a bright day at the end of the week when most people were actively working and striving. I had expected to find him and his family tending to their land and working with the crops or clearing areas for harvest. What I found instead was the entire family, parents and children together, worshipping their God. They were not working as their fellow men were in the city. Instead, they were taking the day to worship and rejoice together. I felt pity on them as I watched and understood that their dedication was unwavering.

This family was dangerous. I knew that if only they knew of the pleasure of living in the freedom of their own power, then they would grab it and not let go. I felt it my duty to release them from bondage and into the light of personal freedom. In fact, if they could be turned from their God to the truth of freedom, their dedication to personal freedom would be equal to their dedication to bondage. I watched them as they spent this particular day together.

"Father," the eldest boy said, taking Noah aside from the family. "I know that today is a day to worship the Lord, but shouldn't we be allowed to take in some of the harvest? There is so much to do and time is running short. After worship, I would like to take a moment and bring in some of the grains and vegetables and safely put them away."

"Shem," Noah said in a kind but stern voice. "The worship of the Lord is most important. Today is His day, as the fields and what grows in them are His. He will provide the time tomorrow, as He will allow for the grains and vegetables to wait for you. Give to Him this day. Never forget that all of this is His, and to Him we owe all."

Shem nodded his head in agreement. "Sorry, father, I know I am impatient. Thank you for reminding me of what is right." Noah hugged his son, and they rejoined the family to continue worship.

It was enough to make me want to scream. I could tell that this boy had a glimmer of desire for freedom. But his blind father would have none of it and insisted on dragging him back to bondage. It made me angry, but I avoided giving in to my guttural reactions and continued to examine the family.

Day turned into evening, and they spent time worshipping their God, sharing meals together and enjoying each others company. What struck me most about them was that their conversations rarely turned to matters of the world. Noah always seemed to be able to steer conversations away from the physical and towards the spiritual, and the family always followed. As the day ended, and all prepared for rest, I left them. I was going to go into the city to see who knew of Noah and his ways.

I was headed off Noah's land when I noticed something strange. As the rest of the family went off to bed, Noah turned away from the family's home. He was alone and walked into the wilderness by himself. I took this opportunity to follow him and see if I could corner him. I was silent as I approached him, and stayed by his side without uttering a word.

Noah walked along deep into his land. He passed much that needed attention but never stopped to examine it or consider where he tread. Noah kept walking and I wondered where he would ultimately rest. He finally reached a point deep into his land where his home was a faint outline in the distance. Noah stopped and surveyed his surroundings. In front of him was smooth pile of rocks that were scorched on the top. He took his robe and laid it next to the pile. Then Noah, with great purpose, kneeled down and lifted his arms. He began loudly and with great fervor praying to his God. I stared at him as he lifted countless prayers to the heavens. He prayed for his wife, his sons, their wives and families and everyone else in his household. He then prayed for the people outside his household. He prayed for the people of the city, for those he barely knew, and for those he had yet to meet.

Noah continued to pray. He prayed for his land and the bounty that it produced. He prayed for the livestock that he owned. He prayed for future generations that might inhabit the land. But underlying all his prayers was the hope that all that he had and did would be used by his God. There was nothing else that would satisfy this man.

Noah was a fool. But he was a dangerous fool. This fool laid prostrate praying to his God while earnestly believing every word he spoke. I was pleased that most people had rejected bondage and imprisonment from that God. I was happy that there was so little work left to be done. But I knew that even one man with the fire of that God could cause great damage. One man with the fire of that God could cause the entire world change. I did not take Noah lightly because I knew the power that I was facing. That is why it was so important to eradicate every last glimmer of this God that existed in man. That is why this Noah had to be stopped.

The air was still in the dark night ensconced around us. Noah continued to pray with no heed to the sounds and cries of the wilderness in the distance. Noah believed that his prayers were for help and direction for people and prayed with great conviction. But though he believed one thing, my ears rang with the truth that these prayers were for prison and bondage. If Noah were given a large enough platform he would sway some people to his thinking. This could lead to more people being infected. Before I knew it, the world could be out of control, and all of my work would have been in vain. But it wasn't just for fear of the whole of the earth losing its freedom that I continued to strive. If even one person lost their freedom it would be too great a loss. Noah could not be allowed to spread his message.

Suddenly my ears began to burn. It was a sensation that I hadn't felt for a long time. It was an unwelcome feeling that came upon me rarely. Noah stopped praying and stood up because his was no longer the only voice in the darkness. Breaking forth without warning came the unwelcome voice of his God. I heard the voice as it spoke directly to him. It did not come in a booming, brash way but in a more peaceful, subdued manner. The sounds that He made were painful to me. But I did not flee, for I was locked in on every word.

"Noah," his God said, "The whole of the earth has turned to evil. Every heart upon has turned from my ways. It pains me to look upon them and know their rejection. I wish I had not given them life."

"Lord," Noah said. "May you hear my prayers. I know that there can be change, and it can wash across every man, woman and child on the earth. I know it will happen if they have just a little more time."

"It is too late," God said absolutely. "They are wholly corrupt and must be no more. I am going to send a great flood water over the whole of the earth, and nothing will survive." Noah knelt silently and fearfully. Before he could protest further, God spoke again. "But you and your family have found favor in my eyes. I have further plans for all of you."

Noah was shaken. "What is it you wish us to do?"

"You are going to build an ark. It is going to be a grand ship..." God continued on, giving Noah precise details as to how the ship should be built. God gave a multitude of specific instructions that Noah and his family were to follow. I thought it ridiculous that his God thought that so few of them could carry out and complete such a massive project. Perhaps Noah's God was losing His edge when He made such requests. But then something He said really caught my attention. "I will destroy everything on earth. Not a single man, woman or child will survive. But you and your family shall be spared. I will make a covenant with you, a covenant that will carry on past the destruction of the whole earth. And you will bring two of every kind of animal, and provisions for your family and for sacrifices."

Noah was uncertain. "How can we do such a thing," he said. "To build such a ship? It will take time and resources that we do not posses. And you want us to claim each type of animal roaming the planet? How are we supposed to do that? I want to do your will, O God, but it is impossible."

"With you, it is impossible," God responded. "But with me nothing is impossible. You will wait on me and follow my lead. It will all be completed and in the appropriate time."

Noah fell again before his God, confessing his unbelief and promising to follow His lead. Then his God left him as suddenly as He had come. It was once again just the two of us in the darkness of the evening.

I was shocked at what I had heard. A covenant with a man? As far as I knew this had never happened before, and I wasn't sure what to make of it. I couldn't believe that Noah's God would wipe out His creation in such a way. They had rejected Him before and there had never been this kind of response. There had never been the promise to destroy people just on the basis of rejection. What made the evening even stranger was the fact that Noah's God was putting so much stock in this one family. Was he so certain that Noah would never reject Him as others had? If Noah's God was so willing to destroy most of His creation, then how much more would have to happen to make Him destroy Noah and his family. I was at a loss.

That was when inspiration struck me. If Noah could be persuaded to turn from his God it would put his God in an impossible situation. It would force Him to either call off His plans to destroy the human race and deal with the fact that he had lost, or destroy every man, woman and child including Noah's family and admit that His creation was a failure. Either outcome was victory for me. I raced to Noah's side.

"This is crazy," I said. "He wants you to build a ship, here, in the middle of the plains. There is not water for flooding here! When is the last time you have even seen the rain pool up enough to reach even your knees? You would be a fool to do as He asks!" I looked into Noah's eyes and thought for a moment that he heard me. But Noah had the glassy stare of a man focused on his God. Noah continued to worshipfully ponder the command he had just heard and ignored everything I said. I made several more attempts to jolt Noah out of the trance but failed. I was flustered and backed off. I was going to return to Noah when he was more open to hearing my voice. This was far from the end.

After this I knew one thing for certain. Noah had just become exponentially more dangerous than ever before. If God brought Noah through the envisioned destruction, and he and his family were allowed to repopulate the earth, there would be no way of stopping the spread of the message of this God and the bondage that lay therein. All would fall under His reign, and freedom would forever be lost to the human race. Action had to be taken now because time was running out.

I took leave of Noah and his lands. I spent time away from all people in order to prepare. I felt the pull of doing something spontaneous during such times as these. The desire to take immediate action coursed through me. But I knew that immediate action was not always going to yield the most positive results. For this challenge I needed to take my time and plan. I was finally going to bring Noah's God into the light of reality. He was a manipulator and a thief and not worthy of the throne on which He sat. If Noah was successful all would be lost. But if Noah could be stopped, then his God would have to reveal His true character. Either he vindictively destroyed the human race and admit failure or He allowed all to live in freedom from Him and He would continuously suffer the torment of their rejection. Either way it was up to me to save the human race from Noah's God.

After some time passed and all was in place I made my return to Noah's region. I was headed to the great city where the people thought as I did. I knew that if I could get those people to understand the danger that Noah presented then they would want to carry out my orders. I would be most effective there since the people welcomed me and would embrace my plan. I would approach my people first and see if they knew of Noah's ship building endeavor or if they had any ill will towards him. I was going to recruit several of them to persuade Noah to change his mind. A bit of friendly persuasion by one's contemporary can always be profitable. If I could affect some sort of change, then I figured that Noah's God would have to call off the disaster out of fear of killing Noah as well as all others. If He didn't the world would be without someone to carry on that God's schemes.

I walked away from Noah's lands and towards the great city and the free men in the light of the midday sun. As I journeyed, I looked out over the plains and peaks covered in a dusty hue. Free men traveled these lands and called them their own. The lands of Noah were tainted with the odor of subjecation. Noah never understood the appealing perfume that rose from the lands of the free men and filled my nostrils. The rocky hillsides and steamy valleys that pointed me towards the great city may not have seemed as bountiful as the lands that Noah held. But to me, they were more beautiful than anything else on the planet. They were beautiful because they were not under the iron fist of Noah's God. They were beautiful because the men that called them home also called me their friend.

After walking a time I recognized the massive city gates in the distance. I marveled at how detailed they were as I approached. The gate rose out of the land like a soldier standing at the ready. Two pillars adorned with words of warning and challenge to any contemplating an attack stood boldly against the clear blue sky. Connecting the pillars across the top was a thick stone that weighed on the pillars. An iron gate filled the middle empty space and kept out any that tried to enter unannounced. Surrounding the city was a thick wall higher than any in existence. Men stood atop the wall to keep watch on those entering and exiting. Though there was no organized military in the city, the free men that lived here watched out for each other. They made sure that nobody was going to come to their home and tell them how to live.

As I entered the iron gates I looked upon the buildings that stood within its walls. There were easily over a hundred structures within this city. Each was made of mud and stone, and emitted the same sandy hue in the heat of the day. The people that resided within went about their lives in their own ways. It was hard to say whether they were happy or sad. Each lived in his or her own way and to this end each was free. The happiness they experienced came from within themselves and did not rely on any outside force. This was the legacy of the great city. It was a legacy that I admired and endorsed.

Life was flowing in the streets as well. Many different animals filled the corridors and brought life. They intermingled with the vendors selling their wares to haggling passersby. Heat was heavy on the brow of each man and woman that ventured outdoors. They were all going about their lives without a care to the God of Noah. I saw different expressions as I looked at the faces of each person I passed. In one I saw the joy of making money off of the overpriced goods he sold. In another I saw the anticipation of a man who desired a young lady he just met. In still another I saw the hope of vengeance on a neighbor who had acted unjustly. Each in his own way was living as they saw fit. Each in his own way had thrown off the shackles of Noah's God and were clothed in the robes of their own control and desire.

I looked at even more people I passed. I was looking for the ones that I knew the best and would be most willing to help. I wanted to know what these people thought about the man Noah who lived outside their great city. I began to speak as I walked and most of those I engaged knew nothing of him and went about their day. Those that had heard of him only thought of him and his families as hermits and nothing more. They knew that the family seldom came to the city. When they did it was strictly for business and they only stayed as long as the business required. I talked to over a hundred people that day, and to a man they felt no threat from Noah.

I was frustrated. If people didn't care about Noah it was going to be difficult to muster public support against him. If I couldn't get public support against him it was going to be difficult for any of these people to be my hands and feet in this quest. I knew that the men and women of the great city had no love for the God of Noah. It was just a matter of getting them to understand that Noah presented as grave a danger to them and their way of life as any they had ever experienced.

I took a detour from my research and stepped into a business that specialized in strong drink. I watched the patrons lambaste each other for sport. Men shouted at other men, making fun of their look or of their speech. One man found himself unable to stand, and had to lean against a wall lest he fall over. It was a place I could think, but even there I was running into brick walls. I had to get the people to care.

As I contemplated I took a moment to suggest to one patron that another had desired his wife. This particular patron had much drink in him and took my suggestion to heart. This particular man decided to take out his vengeance in a decidedly aggressive manner. A brawl ensued and I watched as one man pounded another man's face until blood started pouring out. The beating continued even though the bloodied man had become limp and incapable of defending himself. There were onlookers, but nobody stepped in or called for the beating to cease. I was not going to be denied some entertainment for the afternoon as I pondered the challenge at hand.

Dejected, I walked out of the gathering place and out of the city. I walked past the iron gates and those standing watch. It wasn't that I felt betrayed by the apathy of the people. Apathy was something they desired, and I was not going to be one to tell them it was wrong. But I felt let down by people I had come to know so well. I knew this was their way, but they had reached a whole new level that I hadn't expected. They were truly living their lives under their control and I could not fault them for that.

I was going to need a new approach. If that God's plan was going to come to fruition and Noah was going to build a ship to survive, then I had to be wise in my strategy. I went to my place and allowed some time to pass. The world continued on its trajectory while I was away showing little change. I knew that when I returned I would find it much the same only slightly older and farther from Noah's God. But I wasn't going to tarry too long, lest I risk Noah finishing his task and undermining all for which I had worked.

After ample time and contemplation I fixed on a new course of action. I decided to first return to Noah and his family. I wanted to see what had transpired since I left. I came to his region and walked towards his lands. As I crested the ridge that would reveal Noah's homestead, I was not surprised to find that sitting on their land, towering over all they owned, the skeletal structure of a very large ship. It was clear that Noah had gone forward with the instructions he was given. This came as no shock to me. I knew this man, and knew that he would give everything to remain true to his God.

It was proven time and again that Noah was as stubborn as a mule. During my hiatus I had sent out several of my associates to determine Noah's resolve. My associates were seasoned veterans in this type of work. Each one of them returned with the same story. No matter how many times Noah was told to abandon the project, he refused to heed the calls. The conversations always followed the same script.

"You won't be able to find enough material to build this ship," one of my associates would say.

Noah just remained silent and lifted prayers to his God.

"Destruction will come before you finish," another would say.

Noah remained silent and lifted prayers to his God.

"Your family will give up on you and know you are a fool."

Noah remained silent and lifted prayers to his God.

"Your God is leading you down a fool's path."

Noah remained silent and lifted prayers to his God.

It was enough to make me wonder if Noah had a mind of his own. However, that which frustrated my associates proved to be valuable intelligence for me. Though they failed to deter Noah, each attempt planted a seed of doubt in his mind. Enough seeds should have left fruits ripe for my picking. At least this was true with thousands of others I encountered before.

I approached Noah's home and awed at the length and breadth of the ship. Rarely had I seen any man successfully take on such a project. It was just not in their nature to be able to achieve something on such a grand scale with so few workers. I reminisced about one of man's prior attempts. It was a grand tower that they planned and built to reach to the heavens. Unfortunately there was external interference, and they abandoned it midway through. But that was a different time.

I couldn't help but admire the workmanship that had gone into creating this beauty. Against the backdrop of a late afternoon sun, the beams of the ship reached out as if stretching themselves to the heavens. They stood there, naked but unashamed, patiently waiting for the time when boards, planks and pitch would cover them and make them whole. Cleverly constructed mechanical devices dotted the land around the structure to help bring materials, provisions and people up and down the sides of the skeleton. The men and women of Noah's family dotted the structures like ants. Against it they were tiny and insignificant. But the product that stood before me spoke to their resolve. Like a great sleeping giant, this unfinished ship looked poised to thrust itself out towards the world. It thirsted for water and cried out for a wave to release it from its surly bonds.

I walked closer to the ship. Even in the distance the ship looked gargantuan, and by the time I reached its base I was no less impressed by its stature. Noah was orchestrating at the front of the ship, directing his workforce and ensuring that everyone was best utilized. Like a general in the midst of battle, he remained unshaken, proving to me once again that he could be wholly competent and gloriously successful if he could shake free of that God. I walked up to Noah, making sure not to break his concentration as he spoke with the men and women surrounding him. I waited patiently until he had a moment to himself, and wrapped my arm around him.

"Then I guess it's true that you are going to see this through?" I asked him contemptuously. "There are other ways you know."

Noah did not respond, but he heard what I said.

"There is no doubting your loyalty," I said as I continued to hold his shoulder. "But loyalty can be a vice if it is blind. Do not be blind, Noah. Open your eyes to what I have to show you."

Noah remained silent but was starting to get agitated. Thoughts were crowding his mind and he began to pace back and forth. I took my arm off of him and waited for him to respond to me. But a response never came. I began to speak more pointedly.

"You know that if I leave here today there is no turning back. I am going to the city, and I am going to make sure that they are well aware of what you are doing down here. All of them, Noah. How long do you think it is before they find you mad, and destroy all that you have worked on." I paused for a moment. "But there is a way to avoid all of that. Call off this madness now and I assure you no harm will come to you or your family. Stop building this monstrosity and reject any more commands from your God. Take a torch and burn down what stands before us and you will live your life in peace."

Noah stopped in his tracks. I was certain he was considering what I said. But true to who he was, he simply lifted prayers to his God. He cried out for his God to comfort and direct him. I shook my head and Noah and went about his business.

"You have chosen the path of destruction!" I shouted to him as he departed from my presence. But he no longer heard my voice. I decided to stay on his land for the rest of the evening and watch Noah work. I had been shut out, but it was going to turn out to be at Noah's peril, not mine. As Noah's family worked together, I could tell that they all drew their strength from their belief that what they were doing was a holy calling. I took the time to test each one to find a weakness that I could exploit. In my experience, every family group held secrets or tensions that I could use to undermine their unity. I wandered to a fro amongst Noah's sons and their wives poking and prodding each to find weakness. But to my surprise they were united. There were no cracks to exploit and no attention given to my calls. To each one I took the time to speak, and to each one I was rebuked.

As the evening drew late I stood back and addressed them. "O foolish men," I declared. "How quickly we become ensnared by the desires of others. If only you were free you could live as you desired! No longer would you be tied to the whims of others. No longer would you sit and wait for your life to be determined by an unseen God. You would be in control! You should be in control! You should make the decisions and do what was best for you. Please hear me and know that your life is your own. Now take it for your own!" Sadly my pleas fell on ears that could not hear, and eyes that could not see. I left them as the deepest darkness crept over the land and made my way back to the city. As I left, my ears burned with the echoes of their singing and praising their God for the work accomplished that day.

With haste I made my way to the great city. The iron and stone gates greeted me as an old friend. The soil remembered my pace and walked with me as I hurried to the people that needed me more than ever before. The city walls welcomed me in and comforted me from my travels. But there was no time to rest now. My work was to save this great city from an unjust fate. Noah had rejected my sincere and repeated offers. His rejection set into motion my final plan to stop his work and avoid a world enslaved by his God. I took the time to walk through the city streets, greeting all those I had come to know and counsel. I looked into the faces of the men and women that called me friend. They were free men and women who did not deserve to die. They were free men and women that stood up to Noah's God and declared the right to their lives, only now to have Him rip those lives from them for His own sport. I greeted them in the ways I always had. I knew that they would hear and accept my words.

There were thousands that lived in that city, and of those thousands many hundreds of them were intimately close to me. Exhausting though it was, I took the next few days and traveled to each, greeting them and telling them the tale of Noah outside the city. Many heard rumors about the man, and some had even seen from a distance the great ship he was building. But none of them, to a man, gave a care about what they had heard. They cared not what a fool did with his own time and resources, as long as it did not interfere with their lives.

But all of them had been blinded. I told them that it was going to do more than interfere with their lives. I insisted that Noah's plans would bring death to them, their families and their great city. I warned them just how dangerous this Noah was, and how it hinged on them to bring this man to his end. I demanded that it was their personal responsibility to destroy the threat.

Days turned into weeks, and my work with the people did not end. One factor I had not counted on was just how difficult it was to make a free man do just what I wanted exactly when I needed. But finally several of the men I urged made a trip to see Noah. When they returned to the great city, they brought back tales of a fool building a ship on the dry and barren plains. They brought back tales of a man who offered them passage in return for work and dedication to his God. They returned with tales of a man that insisted a great flood was coming, though flooding had never come to this region. The man they encountered insisted he was right, and since he could not be swayed with words, they left him behind. They cursed his foolishness but took it no further.

The men I had counted on so deeply were only finding Noah to be a joke. In public and in private they made fun of him. They made it a point to call him all sorts of names. They even used him as an example of what happens when madness is let loose. But despite the awareness and the joking, the cursing and the recognition, no one took it to the next level. Not a single one of them used their anger or rage to reign down death and destruction upon Noah or his family.

I was angry that my plans were not progressing. My people were acting foolish and ignorant. They needed to fear what was happening instead of sneering and snickering. I wanted them to sit on what they had learned and let it sink in for a while. Perhaps given enough time they would finally realize the danger they faced. But time was no longer a luxury I had. With each passing day Noah grew closer to completing his task. The men of the great city needed to be motivated.

I took leave of the city and withdrew to my place. I allowed less time to pass and sent some of my associates to keep watch while I was gone.

When the time was right I made my way back. I walked the familiar path and noticed that little had changed except for one significant detail. As I traveled I saw in the distance the great ship that Noah and his family were building. But now instead of merely a skeleton in the distance the ship was darker and blotted out more of the sky. It was nearly complete as it stood majestically on the plain. The skeleton had received it's body and was nearly ready to take its first breath. It stood brazenly on the land as if defying the earth to shake it. It begged to be let free from its moorings as it peered across the plains. Noah was successful in his task. I still had much to do to complete mine.

I raced back to the great city to find that my associates had done their jobs well. The people were no longer apathetic to Noah and his passion. As I walked the streets I saw that many were actively discussing him. They mocked him mercilessly.

"Noah is a fool" one man said to another.

"He is all wet!" his companion sarcastically replied.

"He will never get that thing into water," a woman said. "I guess he truly will be unsinkable!"

"The closest we ever come to flooding is when the water trough spills over because some drunkard had fallen in," someone across the street yelled.

They had not forgotten. In fact, their rhetoric had increased. Their anger and outrage at the foolish Noah had also been ignited. Where before they found Noah to be a simple man chasing a pointless dream, they now found his project to be a personal assault on them. The flowers of each person's outrage were blooming. I was just in time to pick them.

I thought about how wonderful it was that these free people had gotten to this point. I knew that they deserved the freedom they had. They were now ready to take the steps to protect that freedom from one who would snatch it away. I walked further into the city and looked into the eyes and hearts of each person I passed. I passed not only men and women, but children and helpless babies. They were all able to live life on their own terms. It made me proud to think that they were on the cusp extinguishing any ties this world had to Noah and his God.

Objectively speaking, when you have a group of free people there are going to be those that could be considered bad. Not every man and woman would avoid partaking in some form of evil. One man's freedom might infringe on another man's. But that was the peril one faced when choosing to have control over life. These men and women knew that and lived accordingly. As I looked into each person's face I realized something that had evaded me in my earlier visits. I was surprised by the abundance of evil in people's hearts. I never advocated or even expected that they engage in evil. All I advocated was freedom to control their own lives.

Yes, there was evil abounding, but people were still able to make their way, and if they choose not to participate in that evil they did not have too. What struck me most as I walked through the streets of the city were the children. Many children had already been sewn up in corruption. There were things that I saw with my own eyes that I would never wish for anyone else to see. But the babies I saw really gave me pause. There were babies scattered throughout the city. Some were with their mothers while others were left to fend for themselves on the streets or in the corners of houses. The number of abandoned babies that littered the city surprised even me. If surely there was a person alive that did not deserve death it was these. They were the ones that were surrounded by unspeakable evil but were themselves innocent and worthy of being given the chance to live. They inspired my conviction. For if Noah's God was willing to take them out in his swath of destruction then he was going to deny them the chance to make a choice for themselves. He was going to deny them the right to choose Him or their personal freedom. He knew they would choose freedom over Him and this must have horribly scared Him.

Still, I was surprised at what had transpired in the great city and couldn't help but wonder if I poured on too much. Ultimately it didn't matter though, since the greater good was being served with everyone's eyes and attention on Noah. That outweighed any problems that existed in the great city. If some evil must abound in order for men and women to be safe from Noah's God, then so be it. There would be time for correcting any other perceived problems later.

My plan was falling into place. It was time that the people of the great city came together to face the threat outside their walls. I shot through the city streets suggesting a gathering of the most militant men and women. I desired those that had been most critical of Noah and would be the most fervent in their disgust. Dusk started to fall, and those that I had called gathered into one of the larger stone structures on the edge of town. There were nearly three hundred people gathered, all brandishing some sort of weapon and a mountain of resentment. I smiled at my own personal mob and started to speak.

"Look at the shipbuilder outside your walls," I cried. "You know he is a fool, but he is also much more than that! He threatens not only the bounds of reason, but also your lives!" As I spoke, I could see the faces in crowd grow intense and angered. They heard my words even as they milled around each other. "He has built himself a ship here in the middle of the barren plains! We all know this ship will never taste the water." I paused to allow the people to soak in what I said.

"But recognize what else he has been doing," I continued. "He has been gathering to himself all kinds and types of animals. Animals! He is gathering for his family that which should be yours! He does not ask you if he can take them. No! He simply takes, stealing from you. Should the animals that are in the wilderness be anymore his than yours? No! He takes not merely one, and often not only two. He takes what he pleases, and hoards up for himself those animals and a multitude of provisions. He wishes you all dead, and prays to his God for that destruction to come swiftly. He is an enemy on your lands, and he should be stopped this very night!"

Each and every man and woman heard my words. They began muttering amongst themselves. Their murmurs grew louder, and finally ended in a cacophony of agreement against Noah. The made a pledge to stop him by an means necessary and burn his ship to the ground. Their intentions were clear and their time was now.

At the crescendo of their mocking and their laughing, their disgust and their envy, they burst forth from their meeting house and marched towards the land of Noah. They rocketed through the great cities streets to the archway with the iron gate. They pushed aside any that did not share their common goal and broke through the archway as a petulant baby from a mother's womb. A multitude of torches led the way as they marched in unity towards Noah's land. With them they carried all manner of tools and weapons. But physical weapons were not all they carried. They also carried weapons that attacked the soul. They were armed with their rage, their vengeance, their hatred and their pain. The greatest weapon of all of these was their anger. Their anger drove them and would serve them well when they reached the mighty ship. Their anger would be the end of Noah.

Their purpose was clear. They were going to confront this shipbuilder – this God-fearer – on his way of life and his thievery. They were convinced that he was the enemy of all and had to be stopped. They did not only want to destroy Noah. They were there to spit in the face of the very God of which they so desperately wanted destroyed. They were there to shout their freedom from His type of tyranny once and for all. I was going to have a front row seat and revel in their victory.

I remained among the people as they marched. As we moved closer towards Noah's land, the crowd could see the faint outline of the mighty ship. It was dark now, but the moon shone through enough for us to view just how massive the structure was. It was complete and an awesome sight, a testimony to Noah's dedication if not his discernment. As we got closer more and more of our group realized just what we were looking at. Murmurs of awe and second guessing echoed throughout. But just as a master with his whip I urged focus. I reminded them of their purpose and drove them towards their goal. Our army reached the base of the ship where we found Noah and his family calmly sharing a meal.

As we stopped we could hear the bellows of what seemed like a thousand animals. The smell and the sounds coming from inside the ship told the story of a very lively and active force aboard the vessel. Men and women in our group wrinkled their noses and turned aside from the smells wafting down on them. They began making jokes and laughing about Noah being stuck on a landlocked ship with such an odor. Some even mocked Noah for having so many animal partners in his endeavor yet so few humans.

Noah's sons jumped up at the sight of our group and approached. Before they made a step towards us Noah commanded them to sit and rose himself. His sons went back to their seats as Noah approached us. His family remained quietly behind but visibly concerned.

Noah looked over the men and women before him. He then looked past all he could see and focused on me. "You have returned," he directed at me. I stepped back, unsure of how he saw me amongst the group. I gathered myself and before I could say anything, members of our caravan started hurling insults. One by one they berated and screamed at Noah, watching as he did nothing but look back.

"Fool!" one shouted

"You are better than us?!?" another asked.

"You and your family will drown only from your own ignorance!"

A man gestured towards the structure. "We should kill you all now and burn this monstrosity to the ground."

The people were getting angrier. I was certain that they were going to make good on their promise and do just that. Noah and his family would soon be dead, and their ship would be nothing more than a smoldering ash heap. The insults grew louder and more vicious, and their clamoring was thunderous. The people were finally going to show Noah just how free they were of his God.

But as Noah stood there he raised his arms to the skies. His sons stood up and moved in behind him. The people fell silent waiting to hear what Noah was going to say.

"I will remain a fool as long as the Lord God asks me too. He is the God of all creation, and His ways are right and true. If he asks me to give all I have and wander the desert, I will do it. If he asks me to wait on His instructions for one hundred years, I will do it. And if he asks me to build a ship in the middle of the desert, I will do it. For His ways are not my ways. His ways are righteous and true. So if it is that He would have me die here at your hands, I will gladly do it. I trust Him with all I am."

Noah's words disgusted me and I was certain it enraged the people. I knew they were going to end the ship building foolishness there. I started to whip them into a greater frenzy. The men and women started beating their chests and pounding their weapons on the ground. They were yelling and screaming their objections. They were about to leap at this man and his creation.

But my men proved weak. Instead of attacking, a mighty wind blew across the crowd. Like a calming spirit it quieted all those that had been ravenous. They became confused at why they were there and questioned their purpose. They began murmur amongst themselves about not wasting time with such a man, how they were done with him forever, and together decided to leave without another word.

I was stunned. I reminded them of their goal. I tried to give them back their rage and anger. But all I did was for naught. I was angry and watched as they left Noah and his family. My men dropped their torches and their weapons and disappeared into the darkness. I had been certain I was going to witness mayhem as they put an end to Noah and the notion of a great flood. But Noah's God changed the rules. He interfered with my plan. As has happened before and since, Noah's God changed the rules and protected that which He wanted to protect. He took away a piece of my freedom that night.

I choose to stay behind as the men and women of the great city left. I watched as Noah and his family did not go back to their meal. Instead, they began to worship their God. The worshipped and thanked Him for what He did for them. When they were done, they finished their meal, cleaned all that was out and made preparations for the next day. When all the others had made their way to bed, Noah took leave of them and walked out into a quiet part of his land to pray alone. I was furious and followed him closely.

I was out of ideas. Noah's God had thwarted my effort to save the people of the earth. I had no manner of recourse except to make a last appeal to Noah. I tried to reason with him about what was being set in motion, hoping that he would see the truth and stop the madness before it began. I wanted only to save the world from the destruction that was coming.

"I am here," I whispered to Noah. "I know that you have doubts about what your God is asking you to do." I knew that Noah cared about people. I tried to appeal to his sensibilities that valued life over death. "You know what He asks will kill many people. You know that so many of those people are innocent, and those that are not innocent just need time to change. Yet your God asks you to join him in committing atrocities! Your God wants you to take part in the murder of the innocent. He wants you to be an accessory in the destruction of the world! Are you certain this is the right path?" I spoke more gently and directly to his heart. "Be free of his commands. End this here and now, and your God will have no choice but to call off the waters. Can you even be sure that you will survive? Your ship is not tested. You know that you have been thinking these things. Do not go to Him tonight. Come back home and call off this madness. Be free Noah. Be free."

Noah heard me. He heard me and must have considered what I said. But he was so wrapped by the chains His God had on him that there was no breaking free. Noah went on to pray to his God that night and in turn became deaf to my pleas. I left him, disgusted that he continued to choose destruction. But I was never one to give up, though all might have seemed lost. As I walked away from Noah's lands I plotted how it was that I might reach Noah or his family and break the chains of bondage with which his God had shackled them. I thought it best to remove myself from Noah as I pondered. I wandered the entire night as I plotted my next move. I thought of who I could appeal to and who I might sway. I questioned which part of his family might still hold a crack in their resolve. I returned to the great city and paced the streets trying to come up with some plan that could circumvent Noah's God. I settled on a plan of both appealing to members of Noah's family and garnering a larger force with which to confront them the next day. If I had more people with me, it might be possible to take a more aggressive action against Noah before His God had time to react. I was going to try my luck at with more people and using a two pronged attack on Noah the next day.

Dawn broke over the city, and I went about my business. I walked the city streets and recruited men and women for my plan. Everything was proceeding as usual in the great city as the people continued with their daily activities. Men and women did their business, children played, and all was well in the place that had been free of the chains of Noah's God. As I walked I heard people talking of what our group had done the night before. People questioned why we did not succeed and became angry at the thought that Noah had somehow manipulated them to save himself and his ship. I could feel their growing anger and planned to harness it. They wanted to do something about the menace which made it easier to recruit even more warriors than I had the night before. It was going to take a lot of work to organize these people and prepare them to be mindful of potential dissuasion by Noah's God. I knew that if I avoided the cataclysm that was planned then all of my work and trouble would be worthwhile.

But the clock ran out on all of us. At precisely noon that very day, the skies became black with clouds. Almost in unison the people in the city wondered aloud what was happening. Mothers took their children inside, husbands had their wives return home, and everybody was in a general state of confusion. Panic gripped the men and women of the great city as they turned their attention skyward. Yet not a drop of rain fell, and after several minutes people began to relax and return to what they were doing.

There was a general anxiety within the great city and men and women were still uneasy about the skies. Against my suggestion, several of the men I recruited decided to take their camels and race out to Noah's land to see what was happening there. As they did, others in my party choose to head indoors, still nervous about what was going on above. After some time the men on camels finally reached Noah's land. They arrived at the base of the mighty ship and found nobody around. There was not a trace of humanity anywhere. Then they peered high to the top of the mighty ship and saw a head peering out from a tiny window. The men on the ground recognized it as one of Noah's sons and started shouting. The son ducked inside, out of view of the men. Enraged, they began to bang on the side of the mighty ship. They got no response.

Suddenly there was a deafening boom across the eastern sky. Lightning and thunder tore through the silence and announced the arrival of the greatest calamity in history. But the destruction did not begin with water falling from the sky. Not a single drop fell upon the heads of the people. It was much more insidious than torrential rains. As if through some great cosmic fake out, Noah's God did not pour buckets of water upon the plains and the great city. Instead, the earth began to rumble and the ground beneath our feet spilt in two. What burst forth was a geyser of unrelenting water. It was unstoppable. The waters swept through the city streets like a herd of raging bulls.

I watched in horror as men and women in the streets were swept off their feet. Their uncontrolled bodies slammed into the sides of buildings, instantly knocking the life out of them. Some people were sucked under the water and into the fissures that had formed, never to resurface. Children still outside stood no chance against the onslaught and were quickly devoured. Mothers holding their children in the streets had them pried from their arms as the water knocked them flat and consumed their defenseless babies. Shouts of fear and anguish rose to the heavens.

Those that were close enough dove into homes or other buildings, hoping to escape the torrent. But even the buildings proved little resistance to the waters. Some of the structures simply disintegrated under the pressure of the cascading waves. Those that stood became instant tombs for the terrified as they quickly filled with water and trapped all life inside. All of this happened in a matter of moments before any sort of escape plan could be constructed. A few of the lucky men and women found their way to the flat rooftops which allowed for a reprieve from the rushing waters below. But the water was rising and escape from the rooftops was impossible.

As the waters continued to rise, the skies opened up and a blinding downpour came from the heavens. The rain carried such force that it knocked several people off the rooftops to drown in the waters below. Those unfortunate souls flailed around for a moment before disappearing below the waves. Those that remained fought the rain as the earth continued to quiver beneath them. Some structures collapsed from the earthquakes, sending their refugees to their deaths. Those that remained on the standing rooftops soon found the waters below licking their heels. Many reached for anything floating by with hopes of staying alive. Wood beams became the rescue of choice as the waters finally covered all the rooftops. But the people could not fight off the power of the water. Every last citizen of the great city succumb to the wrath of Noah's God.

I watched in horror as the waves ripped through the city. They pounded upon the great city gates that had stood for so long against all opposition. But now they were as paper against the vicious attackers. The waves pounded against the pillars of the gate and twisted the iron into an unrecognizable form. The iron was finally ripped from its hinges and swept out into the plains. The pillars lasted no longer as the waves tore through them and brought the stone crashing into the sea. With that I knew I suffered a monumental loss. The great city was dead.

I paused to consider what had happened. I witnessed many deaths that day. I saw old men who were weak and frail and young men who were full of life die in the blink of an eye. I saw mothers and daughters torn apart without even a chance to bid each other farewell. I saw children and babies with the promise of life slaughtered without consideration. There was no warning to these people. There was no chance given to them. There was only death. I witnessed that day the wrath of a God who hated freedom so much that he would rather kill than lose His control.

But the worst was yet to come. I escaped the city and came to the base of the mighty ship. I watched as men who had escaped the great city banged and clawed against Noah's ship as they begged for their lives. Some of the same men whom the previous evening hurled insults at Noah and his family pleaded for his forgiveness, saying they were wrong and wanted to join him. I watched as their fingers scratched deep into the wood, leaving claw marks that were stained by their blood. Those that could clung to the ship as they pleaded and sacrificed their hands for a chance to be rescued. Behind them their camels had been long since swept away, but they gave them no mind. Their only consideration now was life. Their life.

Yet even after all this Noah and his family did nothing. They simply stayed inside as the waters crashed against their ship. There was no doubt they could hear the pleas and cries of the damned below from their comfort inside. But they ignored those cries and listened as one by one the voices fell silent. One by one those that could have been saved were swept away to their death. Not a single member of Noah's family, who had so often claimed that they were listening to God, made any attempt to save those poor drowning souls.

But the greatest indecency was saved for last. Noah's mighty ship began to quiver and lurch with the waters. With a booming crack and a sudden jerk, the mighty ship broke free of its moorings. Lifted by the rising tide, Noah and his family glided gently on the angry waves. They floated upward and away from their lands. They rolled safely across the open waters as the rest of the earth became engulfed. They lived as the rest of the world died.

Yes, I saw everything that happened with Noah and his flood. I saw the truth of the God that you follow. So many people could have been saved with such a grand vessel. Yet only a select few were allowed to live. You believe that this God you follow is truth and love. But you have been misled. The stories you read of the wickedness that had to be swept off the earth are lies. There were wicked people to be sure. But there were good people as well. There were innocent human lives that were snuffed out for no other reason than they loved freedom. The truth is that these were free people, and they were dealing with a God that could not stand freedom. They faced evil in its truest form, from a God claiming to be good.

The flames of the fire started to wane, and my eyes became unfixed. I looked up and stared at Richard as he finished his story.

"Nobody survived?" I asked.

"Nobody" he said.

"And yet here you are, sitting across from me," I said with a sarcastic smile.

Richard looked annoyed. He stared at me with a hint of disdain. "You know I speak the truth. Disaster could have been stopped. Noah's God could have been contained. Yet it all played out as it did because of your God's ego."

"That's ridiculous," I said. "Even if I believe you were there and lived through it - which I don't - you are twisting the facts."

"Am I?" Richard asked. "How am I twisting the facts?"

"Simple," I responded. "You need a theology lesson, so pay attention. You speak of freedom as though it is supposed to be apart from God. But that is backwards. Noah's God – my God - gave and continues to give everyone the opportunity to come to him. The freedom you speak of is not apart from Him, but with Him, and I suspect you know that."

"So your freedom is to be in bondage to an unpredictable deity?" Richard inquired.

"No," I said. "My freedom is to be held in the arms of a loving God who desires to be in relationship with me more than anything. Noah knew that relationship and was willing to give all, knowing that God knew best. And as it turned out, Noah was right."

"Noah might have been saved," Richard shot back. "But so many innocent lives were lost. You can argue about adults with me if you like, but you cannot sit there and say that an innocent baby deserved to be trapped in a flooded building and drown pressed against a stone ceiling." Richard was pointing at me accusingly.

"Of course that is awful," I responded. "Like Noah though, it is not my job to judge those around me. It is my job to serve my God. Like Noah, I will continue to do that, no matter my circumstances. Besides, it is the Lord God who created all that is and all that has ever been. He loves His creation. He is just and fair with His creation. If that justice sometimes causes us to wince, then perhaps we have to look inward at who we are and not resent that which is Holy. I have no doubt in the Lord and his righteousness."

Richard did not respond, though I could tell there was much that he wanted to say. We sat in silence for a few minutes. We were each processing what the other had said. But I knew that my words were truth. Wherever Richard was speaking from, be it his own mind or somewhere much darker, he was wholly wrong.

As I contemplated, I thought about my years of walking with God. That time assured me that Richard's words were false and that the freedom I found in Christ was real. But listening to Richard's story and his subsequent questioning aroused feelings in me that I could not explain. Against my desire something deep inside of me was jostled. It was as though the great weight had been unlodged from amongst the rocks of time and started pulling on me once again. I recognized that it was the anchor that had been created those many years ago with the doubt and despair of my parent's death. But it was still a subtle feeling. Richard was wrong on so many things. But he had spoken of the brutal deaths of infants. There was a small part of me, a part the size of a mustard seed, that wondered if I needed to take a closer look at God's motives. I immediately shook those thoughts out of my head as that anchor pulled ever so slightly on my soul.

Richard looked at me and squinted. "Yes," he said. "I can see that you have no doubt."

CHAPTER 5

Richard was proud of the tale he told. I stared at him across the dancing flames, looking up and down to determine just why he was so confident. He knew full well that his story held no truth. Yet he spoke with the confidence and conviction of a man who had witnessed such a terrible event, and if I didn't know better I would swear that he had been there. I stood up to grab more firewood to feed the waning flames. As I walked past Richard I sensed that he was like an overflowing pitcher. He was just waiting to spill more tall tales. He smiled at me with confidence and a hint of knowingly holding back some very important facts. But I was armed with the truth. Even though he sounded convincing, I was not going to forget that he was either mad or very creative. In either case, there was no way he was going to shake me loose from my foundation.

I walked back past him and threw a couple of branches on the fire.

"You don't believe me, do you?" Richard asked.

I hesitated for a moment. "That's not entirely accurate. I believe that you are a good storyteller, and that your familiarity with the biblical text is excellent. No doubt you have researched the subjects." I paused. "But you have twisted the scripture to suit whatever your ultimate goal is. You do not speak the truth of what scripture really says." I smiled across the fire. "And of course, Rich, there is no way somebody was there, witnessed it, survived, and is sitting across from me now."

"My name is Richard," he said pointedly.

"Sorry, *Richard*," I emphasized.

"So," Richard said as he repositioned himself. "I am twisting the truth?"

"Yes," I said.

"Well then, please, pull out your bible and show me where I am wrong." Richard stared and me and waited.

"I don't have it," I said sheepishly.

"You don't have your bible?" Richard echoed.

"No," I said. "I know I packed it. I never go anywhere overnight without it. It's just odd." I paused. "It's not there. I must have not paid attention when I packed."

"Must not have," Richard repeated. "Well don't you have a bible app on your phone?"

Richard was right. I had forgotten about my cell phone's bible application. I immediately dug into my bag. As I grabbed my phone I pressed the power button repeatedly.

"What's wrong?" Richard asked, noticing my soured face.

"It's weird," I replied punching the buttons. "I know this was fully charged when I got here. But now it seems to be dead."

Richard looked as I worked on my phone. "That's very strange."

"It is," I said putting the it back in my sack and sitting down.

"Well then, I guess it's time to tell you more," Richard said.

"If you must," I replied. "But know that if it involves you riding a dinosaur to rescue Moses from drowning in the Nile, I might have to steal that one as my own. Pastor could use it the next time he needs and icebreaker!" I smiled at how clever I was, but Richard was not amused.

"Moses," he murmured, looking past me and losing himself in thought. "That man was difficult. So very many problems. He stuttered. He was afraid. He was an orphan. And to think of the number of times he should have died! As a baby. After committing murder as a young man. At the feet of Pharaoh. He was so inarticulate and clumsy with his words, yet they all followed him. Even as they worshipped the golden calf, he held strong…" Richard's voice trailed off. I waved my arms at him to wake him from his trance.

"Hey….hey…" I yelled. "When does the dinosaur come in?" I saw that Richard had lost himself for a moment, and I was trying to bring him back from wherever he had gone.

"No, the tale I am going to tell you," he transitioned, ignoring my flailing and continuing forward with his thoughts, "is of the great king of Israel."

"The great king?" I asked. "Weren't there many great kings of Israel?"

"There were many kings," Richard said. "But only one was the great king."

Richard intrigued me by his claim to only one great king. Sitting there, I could list off the names of at least four or five kings that I might consider great. Solomon, David, even Saul to an extent. Richard ended my internal comparisons quickly.

"David," he said. "What do you know about him?"

"Well, I would agree that he was one of the great kings of Israel," I said. "He slayed Goliath. He was a masterful musician. He survived many attempts on his life by Saul. He led his people to victory in battle and created the city of Jerusalem. He was a fair and righteous king. Of course, there was the dalliance with Bathsheba, but he repented of that."

Richard nodded his head at everything. He directed my attention back at the fire. I noticed the flames once again rise high above the wood. I was entranced by the shapes and figures appearing to me in the dancing fire. Richard had my attention and began to speak his story.

"David was the great king of Israel," Richard started. "I had my eye on him since he was born. I suspected there were great victories in store for him, and because of that I wanted to be sure that I was there for the pivotal moments in his life. I could tell that David's life would be special. I wanted to make sure that he made the proper choice and avoid the mistakes of many of his people. I wanted him to know that he could be a free man and distance himself from his people's God.

I can't be everywhere at once, so you can imagine the difficulty I had in planning out just where and when to be. But I did what I had to do; I was saddened to see how David was tricked into serving that God. I can assure you that it is not the God you read about in that Bible of yours. If you had brought it, I mean.

I remember the day David was born. There was a great awareness that came to us that day. There had yet to be anything outwardly special about the boy. He was the eighth and last son of Jesse, a farmer, and nothing more. However, I was filled with a sense that there was something special about him. I made it my priority to keep an ever watchful eye as he grew.

During David's early childhood and youth he did nothing extraordinary. He was a gifted musician of the harp, and that pleased many people. It was more of a nuisance to me but I dealt with it. I saw a great potential in this boy. I knew that he could be a powerful ally and that together we might have a chance to bring many of his people out of bondage. David spent much of his childhood growing and learning the farming trade, tending to the sheep, keeping watch for wild animals and doing the things that his family instructed.

During his younger years I tried to persuade David to see the value in living life for himself. I admit I failed miserably in part because of the persuasion of his family. His father raised him in the ways of his people. This led David to gain a great appreciation, devotion and love for their God. It is difficult to fight against a strong family influence. When I realized I lost the battle for this part of his life I decided to bide my time. I knew that if David had such an affinity for his God then that God was going to bless David in the way that He had always blessed His favorites. I was going to have to be sure to keep an eye on David, if not for any other reason than to protect Him from whatever path that God sent him down. Eventually David was going to need to become free of his God. I was going to make sure of that. For David's sake.

I do not remember every day I spent with my eyes on David. But I do remember clearly the day that David came out from obscurity to the forefront of the Israelites. The good king Saul had finally started to gain his freedom from his people's God, and that God started to recognize this freedom and withdraw His blessing. I had been with Saul often before that, giving him recommendations and encouragement, and it seemed as though we were finally making progress. It was finally time for Saul to stop breaking his back to please his God and start to work for himself.

But Saul's God decided that he was going to grant kingship to another. That God choose to pick a new king from the flock of Jesse. It was almost disgusting, as Jesse was not royal material, and surely his sons were exponentially less worthy. But this was how their God acted.

He made irrational decisions that had no bearing on worthiness and forced others to live with His choices. I watched in agony as not only did that God pass up on the best of the sons that Jesse had to offer, but choose the one that wasn't even at the precious ceremony. He choose David, who at the very moment he should have been anointed, was rooting around with the sheep in the fields. David had little about him that cried out royalty other than his looks. Appearance aside, that boy was nothing more than a pig slopper.

But worthiness was brushed aside and David was chosen. Standing there, watching, I felt a trembling as God choose this ruddy boy to be the next king. Even though that fool Samuel was speaking, I saw their God putting His spirit upon the boy. I was sick but determined to stay with this boy as long as I could. I went back to Saul to let him know what was happening, but by that time Saul had already come under the power of this boy David. Saul was tormented, but when he heard David play his harp, the torment left. With this David found favor in Saul's sight, and I knew things had become a lot more complicated.

But complications are meant to be faced and resolved. I pondered what resolution would satisfy and realized it could come in the form of my old friends the Philistines. The Philistines had no love for the people of God and were more than happy to bring them terror. So it came about that the Philistines moved on the people of God and brought war to their doorstep. Under the leadership of Saul the men of God trembled at the sight of the Philistines, and for good reason.

The Philistines had a weapon that no man of the Israelites could overcome. This weapon went by the name of Goliath. Goliath was a mammoth of a man who stood far above any other on the battlefield. His shoulders looked as broad as a palace and his body rippled with muscles. His hair was jet black and his face looked as if it were made of stone. His armor was the weight of several men, yet he wore it as though it were no more than a thin veil. It glistened in the sunlight as he walked pronouncing his presence to everyone around. Goliath carried in one hand a sword and in the other a spear with a shield draped across his back. The Israelites assumed he could rip a man's arms clean off their body and questioned his need for weapons.

Goliath was a champion, and came forth from the Philistine encampment to challenge the Israelites. I was pleased to see the Philistines bring out their big gun immediately and use him so effectively. Goliath challenged any man to face him, and to the victor would go the spoils. The winner would claim victory for their side, and the losers would be enslaved. As I stood overlooking the battlefield I was certain that the Philistine would be victorious. The Israelites would be decimated and their God crushed beneath the heels of their enslavers.

I made my way to the Israelite camp to watch the proceedings. There were many men of military mind who considered themselves courageous. But not a single one of them had the internal fortitude to stand up to the challenge presented. All of the greatest men among the Israelites were shaking with fear at the prospect of standing face to face with the monster Goliath. I was saddened for them. They embraced their God and all that He promised and all it did was leave them with fear in the face of adversity. That was why I wanted to see them free of their God. I knew that if they were free they would not be cowering in the face of certain destruction. In fact, if they were free they wouldn't have even faced this problem. But they were so ensconced in their God's grip that it seemed their only escape was through destruction.

The two armies stood on opposing ridges as they glared at each other across the Valley of Elah. This was the place that their God had chosen for their destruction. It was decidedly but abnormally cool those days on the mountain and it reflected in the faces of the soldiers. I could not tell whether some of the men shivered out of chills from the air or fear of Goliath. But as I walked through the ranks of the Israelites I read fear in their faces. Even their mighty king had no answer for them.

The Israelites and the Philistines stood their ground for many days. I lingered among the Israelites, watching as each day the monster Goliath would come and present the same challenge, and each day the Israelites trembled and wonder who it was that would be sent to their death. Each day the Israelites failed to send out a challenger. And each day the monster Goliath became increasingly menacing.

Each day repeated the preceding so absolutely that I wondered if there would ever be a resolution. The monster Goliath would come into the valley dressed for battle. His eyes were filled with rage as he pounded his spear upon the ground. With each blast the Israelites were certain they felt the earth shake beneath their feet. The sun beamed off Goliath's armor as he mocked the Israelites.

"Choose a man," he bellowed across the valley. "Choose a man to face me in combat. If he defeats me, then we Philistines will become your servants. But when I destroy him, you Israelites will become our slaves."

I watched each day intently as the Israelites would murmur among themselves. No one wanted to face Goliath, and several considered any alternative to avoid the conflict. I consistently urged the Israelites to give in to their thoughts and escape. I suggested that it would be the only way to save themselves. I told them that their fear was right and they should live as cowards rather than die as fools. Even their king Saul was filled with fear and I urged him to think about himself above all and flee.

This went on for forty days. Each day, the monster Goliath presented the challenge, and each day the Israelites trembled in fear. I continued to urge retreat, but my counsel was not great enough to convince Saul or the Israelites. Yet the Israelites did not have an alternative. This left everyone in a quagmire they could not escape.

What I didn't expect was how impending doom would manifest the meteoric rise of David among the Israelites. He was anointed king, but this was not common knowledge amongst the people. David was still relatively unknown which made his appearance in this tale even more astounding. What made it worse is that I was blind to the risk of David intruding on the proceedings. For all of the care I took to be mindful of David I was still caught off guard when he arose. I will always regret that mistake.

For forty days while the tensions increased, David spent his time between the army of the Israelites and his flock of sheep at home in Bethlehem. He would go back and forth, bringing food and supplies to the armies, as well as taking care of business at home. David was simply an errand boy and was barely noticeable during the standoff. Few knew he had been to the front.

What captured David's spirit and made him so bold I didn't understand. But I could only assume that God had decided to use David against his will. On the fortieth day David approached Saul upon hearing of Goliath's challenge. He approached the men of Israel, demanded to know the particulars of the situation, and why they allowed this man to taunt them. It was a bold and brazen move by this farmhand. The Israelite king and soldiers were struck at his lack of propriety and scoffed that they had to deal with him on top of everything else. They tried to brush him aside but he was persistent.

As soon as I recognized what was happening I took action. I still had hopes for this boy and didn't want to see him under the influence of his God. If David took action by himself against the Philistines he would be unceremoniously slaughtered and I would lose a potential protégée. It would be exponentially worse if David proved the victor. I couldn't fathom it, but if that proved out then he would be emboldened and his God would gain more praise and glory from his people. Either case presented me with serious problems.

I had to stop David before he did anything foolish. I approached his eldest brother Eliab in hopes that he could sway the petulant youth. I strongly urged Eliab to stop David.

"Why have you come down here," Eliab angrily asked David. "You left the sheep out in the wilderness because of your insolence. All you want to do is see a fight. Go back to the fields before you are trampled under the feet of real warriors." It was good that Eliab heard my urging. He used my words against David.

Unfortunately, David did not take heed Eliab's command. "I was just asking," David retorted. "I know there is something more that can be done than standing here lifeless!" David left his brother's side and went on to ask others the same question. Word of the boy's fire made its way to King Saul, and he demanded to see David. David came to the king in nothing but his shepherd robe, a small pouch and a sling he would use to ward off predators. His robe was soiled by his work in the fields. His pouch was small and worn with a strap that looked ready to break. The sling he carried was old and tattered, making it hardly worthy of the stones it flung.

David entered the king's tent unashamed. At Saul's feet and against all protocol, David demanded to face Goliath. He asked to go alone and without preparation. The men standing around the king smirked while Saul looked annoyed. I came alongside the king and urged him to ignore David.

"You are just a boy," Saul said as he looked over David. "A boy that has clearly been left out in the fields too long."

"I have destroyed lions and bears that attacked our sheep with my own two hands!" David replied, ignoring Saul's contempt. "Could just a boy do this? No! It was by our God's power that I did this, and with that same power I will destroy this beast Goliath."

I examined Saul's face as he listened to David. I watched as his countenance changed from contempt to unwarranted trust. It was then that Saul proved himself to be a grand fool as he ignored everything I said and agreed to allow David to be the champion for the Israelites. Saul's decision made no sense. I had no proof but was certain that once again David's God had interfered.

Saul took David into his tent. There he had his men clothe David in royal garments and armor. Saul personally handed David his best sword and showed him how it should be handled. David stood there for a moment in the royal armor and weaponry looking much as a child who had put on his parents clothing. Everything hung too loose on him and the sword was nothing more than an anchor. As David tried to swing it he found that he was too clumsy with the weight. After a few moments, David laid the sword gently on the ground. He shed the clothes and armor and held fast to his dirty robes.

"I cannot use this sword, or wear this armor," David said to Saul.

"You must!" Saul insisted. "It is the only way you can hope to survive against that monster."

"I will do more than survive," David said as he put his worn clothes back on. "I will be victorious. I will be victorious for you. I will be victorious for your people. But most importantly, I will be victorious because of my God. But I will not use these things you have given me."

David left the king's tent and walked to a nearby stream. Saul stood confused but allowed David to do as he wished. Saul's men watched as David walked the stream while singing songs of praise. Along the way David plucked five smooth stones out of the stream and measured them up to the cradle of his sling. When he was satisfied he placed each stone gently in his pouch.

David marched back towards the Israelites. With confidence and a touch of arrogance he walked through their ranks as they looked at him and were baffled at his trajectory. Many wondered if it was a joke that this boy would be the one sent out to die at the hands of the Philistine. Others cursed Saul for so easily allowing them to become slaves. They found no hope in the shepherd boy that walked past them.

Even I wanted to look away as I knew David would die. I had wasted my time hoping he would turn from his God.

I knew this was the end for David. But I am not one to go down without a fight. I raced to David's side as he strode and matched his gate. I showed him empirically why he should turn back. I appealed to his fear and anxiety but found no foothold. I even tried begging and found it futile. I gave him reason after reason, point after point, as to why he needed to turn and run. I showed him fear and the destruction that was going to come of his meeting with the monster. But nothing I said penetrated David's soul. His was so focused on his God, on that enslaver, that nothing I said could traverse the wall David had built. Finally I gave up and turned back. I was disgusted.

I approached the front lines of the Israelite army to witness this debacle firsthand. Goliath was going to destroy David. It served David right for not taking my counsel. I prepared for the bloodshed. Afterwards I was going to let everyone know I was right all along.

As David approached, Goliath became enraged. He looked up to the Israelite army and shouted. "Do you think so little of me that you send this boy to fight for you?" he said. Goliath then turned his attention to David. "I am going to rip the flesh off your bones."

I knew the insult Goliath felt from the Israelites and sympathized with him. I waited with anticipation to see just how badly this was going to end for David. I stepped closer to the edge of the ridge to get a better view. I played with my fingers as I started realized how David's death might be the best outcome after all.

David stood in front of Goliath quietly. The two gladiators sized each other up as the anxious moments before the battle slowly melted away. Goliath gripped his sword and spear tightly, showing his power as he pounded them on the ground. David held to the end of his sling as he slipped a stone into the sling's hold unnoticed. The Philistines were loud and raucous as they cheered on and motivated their champion. The Israelites were quiet and nervous. David and Goliath stood ready to fight.

David lifted his head high and raised the sling. Both armies quieted as he shouted to the monster Goliath. "I come to you in the name of the Lord of hosts, whom you have taunted," David said. "I am going to kill you, Philistine, and make your people our slaves. You then will know the power of the Lord!" I was aghast at David's bravado. What happened next trumped everything I had seen that day.

As David finished his taunt, Goliath gave no warning and launched himself at the boy. As quick as a flash of lightning David lowered the arm carrying the sling. He whipped it around several times and with a flick of his wrist shot the stone towards the monster. Goliath continued his charge and was within a length of David when the stone pierced and sunk deep into Goliath's head. Goliath died instantly, but his body continued to lunge forward until it crashed upon the ground at David's feet. The rumble from his collapse shook the earth and blew forward a plume of dust. Both armies strained to see what happened. As the dust thinned, everyone watching could see two figures. The first was of the motionless monster still and empty on the valley floor. The second was the boy standing above him upright and victorious. Everyone stood silent and amazed.

David's sling hung at his side. He let is slowly slip from his grasp and as it fluttered to his feet. He stepped forward towards the monster's body and pried the sword from his hand. David lifted it high and with great precision and fervor started chopping at the neck of the monster. The Philistines gasped in horror as they watched the decapitation of their fallen champion. Blood flowed freely upon the ground as the gruesome scene unfolded. When David was finished he threw down the sword, took Goliath's head and raised it high into the air for all to see. Blood dripped down on David as he cried praises to his God.

The Philistines knew their future changed dramatically from moments before. Suddenly, the call went out from the Philistine commanders for the army to flee. With a newfound boldness the Israelites saw the Philistines cowardice and chased and killed every last one.

I was furious and stood motionless. I cared little about the fate of the monster Goliath or the Philistines. I didn't even feel that I had lost David, though he made it more difficult to oppose his God now. What filled me with anger was the knowledge that once again David's God had interfered on the behalf of one of his own. There was no way that David, in his own power, could have defeated Goliath. It was by his God's hand that the monster fell. David's God was breaking a rule that I knew all too well. I could never interfere with the affairs of man when

I wasn't specifically allowed. Yet David's God did without even asking if it was permissible.

"There are rules!" I cried out towards the heavens. "How dare you do this? You have cheated me again!" There was no response, but He heard me. I stewed knowing that David's God had thwarted what should have been consequences of the choice of a foolish king. Instead, this God directed that boy to perform unnaturally. This proved once again that those following Him were mere marionettes and manipulated for His enjoyment. I cursed that God as I watched David carry the head of the dead champion back to Jerusalem.

But I was not done with David. If their God was going to interfere then I needed to step up and fight. I was going to show the people further proof that they needed to be free. I was going to show them that He who they were putting their trust in was using them as toys. I needed to show them that He kept them in prison until He was ready to take the out and play with them, and when He was done He would throw them right back into bondage. I was going succeed by discrediting the one who brought this God the most honor. David might never outright deny his God, but he was going to prove my point nonetheless. David was just a man. Like all men he was susceptible to mortal failings.

Time went on from there. I continued to keep a watchful eye on David but turned my immediate focus to the king. I knew that King Saul felt weakened by David's triumph and was on his own journey of fear and doubt. Saul saw everything that was happening and grew concerned. The king was right to feel abandoned by his God. Saul needed my guidance and I provided it. As he was still the king, Saul could embrace the freedom I offered and persuade a great many of his people to follow. His position also allowed him to have power over David. I frequently reminded him of that.

I took my place at Saul's side as I provided him with counsel and truth. I reminded him to keep a wary eye on David, for he didn't know what truly lay in that young man's heart. I stoked the fires of anger, envy and fear that Saul legitimately held. Saul was taking more and more steps into freedom and liked what he discovered. But that was all threatened if David continued to be convinced that his God was the only one for which it was worth living and dying. King Saul understood that if David did not repent of his God, then David was going to have to fall. Others would never understand their bondage and the freedom that was available to them if David continued to thrive under his God. This was a dangerous.

I stood with the king and it became clear that Saul's anger burned great towards David. Saul's people were starting to put more trust and faith in David than they were in Saul. This enraged the king. Saul hated David but feared him even more. Saul wanted to have control over David and made some very critical decisions based on that desire. Saul decided to appoint David to head part of the Israelite army as well as allowing David to marry his daughter Michal. I agreed with these decisions because of the power it gave Saul over this man. As a commander of the army, David would take orders from and be directly accountable to Saul. Anything positive that came of this and Saul would get the credit. Anything negative and David would be placed with the blame. As a bonus, there was always the possibility of David's death in battle. With the marriage to his daughter, Saul knew he exercised even more authority over David as his de facto father. There was little room for error now in David's life. Saul thought he finally had David where he wanted him. Saul's first order to David was for the deaths of one hundred Philistines. Saul hoped that this task would prove too difficult and result in the loss of David's life.

But as Saul and I would soon find out, David's powerful ally had not abandoned him. David went out seeking to fulfill his king's orders and prove his worth as commander. He ended up doing far more. David returned to Saul having taken the lives of two hundred Philistine soldiers. He returned with this bounty and insisted on giving all the credit to his God. This caused the popularity and respect the people gave David to grow exponentially. It also served to bring more people to trust in David's God. At the same time, King Saul couldn't help but find himself disgusted. The fear that was in Saul mounted as he realized David was presenting a grave danger to Saul's control. I remained steady in my counsel to the king. I told him all he needed to do was order the death of David. I had been urging this for a while, but now Saul was finally open to this action. King Saul willfully agreed and took the death of David as a personal mission.

Time and again Saul made attempts on David's life. He tried not only by asking others to do it but reveled in the attempts he personally made. The eradication of David was the singular goal that Saul and I held. It was a necessity. But each time it seemed that David's days were over he found a way to flee the judgment he was due.

After several attempts on David's life he went into hiding. I followed, desiring that David should see the pain he was causing others and reconsider his senseless drive to follow his God. I thought he might at least put a moratorium on his faith if for no other reason than to satiate Saul. But to a fault David never gave up his faith and never cursed his God. I had rarely seen such devotion as David showed. It was evidence of the manipulation and brain washing of his God. David continued to foolishly trust no matter the circumstances. This made David increasingly dangerous to me and to his fellow countrymen. It got so bad with David that King Saul was forced to turn on his own son because of David's recklessness.

David's life had so radically shifted direction over time. The boy who had been anointed king those many years ago now was always looking over his shoulder. How long ago it seemed that David was certain to take over the kingdom. Now he was just wondering if he would wake up each morning. Many times David cried out asking his slave master why his reign as king was delayed. How I tried to alleviate the pain with the path of personal freedom. But David chose against my counsel. The fact that David continued to have the breathe of life in him was increasingly frustrating. Something drastic had to be done. Saul's plans were being thwarted and David was surviving.

However, I couldn't stay with Saul and David all the time. I had urgent matters that needed my attention. So I left several of my associates to scout the relationship as it progressed and report back to me. I went away from the kingdom and time continued to march forward. When I was able to return some time later I found that nothing had really changed. King Saul continued attempts on David's life and David continued to buck his fate. David would always find a way to escape much like grains of sands through a man's fingers.

King Saul was continually showing himself to be a fool. I found out through my associates that while I was gone Saul not only failed to kill David, but he screwed the situation up so badly that he got himself in a position to be at David's mercy. I found out that there were several times that David could have easily killed Saul but chose not to. This was not helping our cause at all. Saul was the fool and David and his God were the heroes.

I finally had enough. I made the painful decision to give up on Saul. He was daily proving his incompetence and I was sure I could find someone or something in the kingdom that would be more useful in my quest. After I left Saul it was reported to me that he once turned to a witch for counsel. For him to seek a witch over me proved that he had no concept of how to run his own kingdom or his personal life. I was right to give up on him.

I recognized that David's escapes were not to be placed solely at Saul's feet. The king might have been incompetent, but David's God was interfering in these matters as well. I knew that I was going to have to be more crafty to do what was necessary. I was going to have to get to David from the inside.

Time passed again as I considered my options. Sometime after I last counseled Saul I got a notice from one of my associates that the king's end was near. It meant the end of Saul's reign but it also meant that David would soon take power. This was the time I had been waiting for. I knew that with power I could get to David. Few men are able to resist the lure of power and the unwanted destructive results it causes.

When I found Saul he was once again in the midst of battle with the Philistines This time it was evident that his end was at hand. I strode back to my old associate's side as he struggled to wage a final battle. As I entered, I saw Saul's face as he valiantly fought against his enemies. I watched it contort as he witnessed the death of three of his sons. As their blood spilled on the battlefield he became wild with rage and started to fight uncontrolled. I felt a twinge of pity for the king, but it soon passed. I watched Saul swing his sword wildly. He caught several unlucky Philistines and painted it with their blood. Saul was able to finally retreat with a few others and took a moment to catch his breath. I calmly walked towards him as I shook my head in amazement.

"Saul," I said, putting my arm around him as he bent over panting. "has it come to this?"

Saul said nothing but looked around expectantly. His followers looked onward past me.

"My dear old companion," I said with a snicker. "Look around you. Your enemies have defeated you. It is over!"

Saul stood up straight and surveyed the battlefield. He spoke briefly with his comrades.

"Look now," I offered. "To the east and west. They come like rushing waves. They have killed many of your men. They have killed your sons. They look to kill you! It is only a matter of moments before they overwhelm you!" I paused for a moment and looked into Saul's eyes. "When they reach you, you will die. They will not only kill you, though. They will desecrate you. They will take the body of the King of Israel and dismember it! They will march through their ranks with your head held high on a spear for all to see!"

Tears started pouring down Saul's cheeks.

"Do the right thing, Saul. Take your sword. Run yourself through. Deny your enemies that pleasure."

I took my hand off of Saul and stepped back. I watched as he bickered with his men. When they were done, Saul gathered his sword to himself. He took the same sword he had once offered David to kill the monster Goliath and he gripped it tightly by the blade with both hands. He gripped it so tightly that he sliced open his hands. As blood oozed down Saul's forearms he stared at the heavens with regret. He then looked east that the approaching hordes and thrust the blade deep into his chest. Blood poured out of his midsection and drowned the grass below as Saul stumbled forward. He released the sword and fell towards the ground. The hilt of the sword stuck itself in the dirt below, causing Saul's body to remain upright as the life drained out of him. Saul's enemies consumed the ground beneath his feet.

I walked away from the grizzly scene. It was ironic that after all this time Saul had finally successfully done what I asked him to do. "See you soon Saul." I whispered to the air. "See you soon."

As I walked away I pondered over what was taking place. It felt like my mission to take out David had failed. Saul lay dead on the battlefield and soon David would officially take over as king. But I still had a strategy that was tested and true. It was my responsibility to save these poor people from the trap into which David was leading them. My part in this story was far from over. I was not going to allow another soul to be sentenced to an eternity of bondage to King David's God.

CHAPTER 6

The ceremony crowing David king over the Israelites was quite a sight. David had waited so long for that moment and to him it seemed surreal. As he watched the pageantry and the people's joy he wondered if he could live up to their expectations. For so long he was supposed to become king and take the Israelites to greater heights that he wasn't sure he believed his own hype.

David's concerns proved to be unsubstantiated. David's name and power grew as he settled into his role as king. He was renowned and uplifted throughout the land. The people craved his leadership and were willing to give him room to grow into his role and make mistakes. But David knew that political goodwill was not endless. He had to lead the people with respect and dignity. He needed to follow the will of his God.

What was most unsettling was that King David did this very well. He lead as a righteous king and gave glory and honor to his God. That reality pierced me deeply. The Israelites now had a visible reason to believe that his God was real and capable. They believed that this God was good and King David was living proof. Like mice drawn to cheese none of them noticed the trap that this God had set. The effects of the trap would be devastating.

Convincing the Israelites of this reality was becoming harder with each passing day. I was never one to doubt my own abilities of persuasion even in the most trying circumstances. But this gave me pause. I had to give David my full and undivided attention.

Now it wasn't the kingship of David or the following that he enjoyed that pinpointed my focus. What made me focus was when I learned of the promises that David's God had made to David. I learned that David was promised a grand kingdom. In return, David made plans for a beautiful grand temple to his God, unrivaled by any architecture of the day. David's God had also promised him a far reaching line of descendants. These descendants would serve David's God and bring the knowledge of his God to the world during their generations. This promise made my heart skip. I wondered if this was why I felt David was unique from the day of his birth. And if this was the reason, how could I have been so blind to his God's plan all along? It disturbed and haunted me. But it made perfect sense and explained why David had been so protected. Events were set into motion that made me feel that I was spiraling out of control. I was not one to lose control.

David's God was using him as a pawn in his celestial game. It was so obvious to me and so hidden from David. Though the promise of great generations descending from David made me shiver, it meant that a lot of faith and trust was being put into this one man. David had very little room for error. If David were to die, then these plans and possibly his generations would die with him. But death wasn't the only way to stop that God's plan. If David were to set foot on the slippery soil of personal destruction then he would no longer be worthy of his God's promises. If David fell personally, then his God would look the fool and have to retreat from those promises. His God would be shown a fraud and the people would curse His name. They would confess that they had been deceived and would beg me for their freedom. By physical death or personal destruction David was going to prove that his God was nothing more than a charlatan.

I had long relished taking up residence at the side of the king. It had been a place I resided over many different reigns. There were kings that would here my voice clearly and follow it unceasingly. There were also kings that heard my voice and fought it's influence their entire lives. King David rested with the latter. I was allowed my place beside him, but he was given the power to resist my call.

While I was by his side I reminded David of his need to be perfect. I told him that if he failed in any way then he failed his God. If he failed his God he would be a worthless human being. I let him know that if he fell short of perfection his God would abandon him as He abandoned Saul. I coupled this with reminding David that he was the king, and as the king he had the right to do many things that a regular person could not. King David had the power to do almost anything he wanted and few could argue against it. I reminded him that the power of the kingdom belonged to him to use as he wanted. I constantly spoke these truths and didn't want them to stray far from his mind. But it amazed me that David was so strong. I kept near him but he always went back to his God. He never let my influence take root. I recognized that if it ever took root he would reflexively take his thoughts to his God who would soothe David's mind. The healing balm that David's God used was nothing more than snake oil. I was disgusted that David continued to buy into the his God's scheming.

David continued to resist me. He continued his pattern of running to his God when my thoughts started to become his thoughts. He eradicated them and was thankful to his God for the peace. But as is the way with men, David eventually began to lose focus. There is a basic, innate manner in which all men can fall, be they kings or peasants, rich or poor, educated or foolish. As the weight of the crown became heavier upon his head, David slipped and unconsciously took back some of the control he had given to his God. It happened slowly but consistently. As a drip of water does nothing to the stone, if left unattended that drip over time will bore a hole through the strongest stone. That was what happened to David. That is what gave me my foothold. I exploited my opportunity on a warm moonlit night in Jerusalem as David's troops were fighting one of his battles. That evening my opportunity had a name. Her name was Bathsheba.

It was late. The scorching heat of the day had passed and left a warm blanket over the land. The woman named Bathsheba took the quiet of the evening to bathe herself. The dirt and stress of the day lay heavy upon her, and the time had come for her to let it run off her body and into the soil where it belonged. As was custom at the time, the place where she bathed was not completely closed off from prying eyes. However, it was common practice and courtesy to give respect and privacy to those bathing. It was not unusual for Bathsheba to be bathing in this manner.

What caught my eye about Bathsheba was that she was truly beautiful. Anyone with eyes could testify to this. Her skin was fair and smooth, and the curves on her body allowed the water to meander down after she poured it over her thick, black hair. She took care to wash, allowing the water to cleanse every pour and crevice of her form.

Call it fate. Or call it the gentle nudging of a friendly voice. Either way, that night Bathsheba choose a certain bath that was uniquely visible from King David's balcony. This fact did not elude me as I rushed to David's room. I roused him from his slumber and waited as he rose and started to pace his royal bedroom. I gently directed him to the balcony. There he had a perfect view of Bathsheba. Normally I don't take all the credit, but as orchestration goes this was a masterful feat. I watched King David as he peered over the balcony onto nothing in particular in the city below. But it didn't take long before I saw what I was looking for - the spark in his eye causing a sudden stop and focus. King David had seen her and was captivated.

"Isn't she beautiful?" I asked David. "Just look at her. Any man would think it a privilege just to gaze on her beauty." I paused for a moment. "But you, David, are king! The king deserves far greater than does the common man. Surely such a beautiful woman is worthy of your position!" I watched David and felt his mind agree with mine. "And you are right to want her," I continued. "Who is to argue with you? You are the king, the chosen one of these great people. You are the one that brings peace, honor and victory to the land of the Israelites. The people would think you mad not to take such a beautiful rose."

I stepped back and watched King David internalize what I said. Without warning a feeling arose in him that he had not before experienced. He was compelled to find out who the woman was and what she required to be his. David immediately sent for a messenger. After some discussions with those familiar with the people in that area, King David was told her name. As soon as it left the lips of his informant he was desperate. He had to have her. David sent his messenger to retrieve her with great haste. They did as he commanded and brought Bathsheba into King David's presence.

I did not remain in the king's palace. My work for the evening was complete. My associates let me know that my plan was more successful than I could have imagined. David and Bathsheba took to each other immediately. He was captured by her beauty and she became intoxicated with his power. They spent the entire evening together without a care to the outside world. But it was imperative that their indiscretion remain a secret for reasons they both understood. They agreed to keep it from the kingdom.

But as the history of man has shown, secrets have a way of coming out. No matter how hard one tries or how deep one buries it, a secret will always be exposed to the light of day. It may take moments or it may take centuries, but it is assured that a secret will never remain. That is how it was with David and Bathsheba. Not long after their union Bathsheba discovered that she was pregnant. The secret that David had so wished to keep was on the verge of becoming headline news.

It's a funny thing about those kinds of secrets. When kept in the dark they thrive and grow. The more the light creeps closer to a secret, the more it becomes a struggle and fight to keep it unknown. Like a flower that thrives in the warmth and embrace of the sunlight, a secret can only flourish when nourished with darkness and ignorance. Darkness remains when the secret is fed with lies, deceit and misinformation. This is the dilemma that David and Bathsheba faced. David was going to do everything in his power to keep their evening together a secret.

David became more aware Bathsheba's life as she let him know that she was a married woman and for that he could be held accountable. What David didn't realize until later was that she was married a man by the name of Uriah. This was important because Uriah was not a common Israelite. He was a loyal and trusted soldier in David's army. Uriah had served the kingdom and David well, and had been recognized for his heroism and courage during battle as well as his integrity beyond. Even at the very moment that David and Bathsheba were intimate in the palace Uriah was risking his life for David on the battlefield. This presented an extraordinary dilemma that was going to require an extraordinary response. He panicked as he considered his options. To my delight the king made certain to stay away from his God lest He discover David's true nature.

I watched as David spiraled about trying to keep secret that which did not want to stay secret. I thought of many good and acceptable solutions that David could utilize to calm the situation. I remained gentle and avoided heavy-handed suggestions, for I wanted to see what

David did on his own. He had done so much already that I didn't want to interrupt his dubious decision-making streak. I remained near to the situation and gave only the slightest suggestions.

"Send for Uriah to come back from battle," I whispered as David spun himself up. "When he returns he will surely lay with his wife. Then the child will simply be known as his. It is a failsafe plan."

David lit up at the idea and sent for Uriah to come back from battle. When Uriah arrived, David ordered him to go and be with his wife. That should have solved everything. But Uriah refused to be with his wife because his conscience was for the king. He said with dedication that his loyalty was first to his position as an Israeli soldier and servant of King David. Uriah insisted that as long as his fellow soldiers were out at battle, he would not return to the comfort of his home or the pleasures of his wife. Uriah defiantly refused time at home and instead slept at the door of the palace. He vowed to stay there until he was sent back or his men were brought home. King David tried repeatedly to cajole Uriah to return to his wife. David told him that it was a royal request. David told him that it would be a personal favor. David even offered him a promotion in return. But Uriah's dedication to his men on the front lines was too thick of a block to fall to King David's pleas. David was infuriated but could not reveal this to Uriah.

I found myself surprisingly frustrated as well. Admittedly, I wanted the secret to remain because of the power it held in darkness. But the foolhardy dedication and loyalty of one man threatened to unleash the secret that King David was trying so hard to keep. I found it ironic that David was now being thwarted by a man of dedication and loyalty. It was a problem I faced with many men over the years when trying to expose their fraudulent God. I decided to take charge and lead David down a very dark path.

"Uriah must die," I whispered to David. "That is the only way this will end. When he is dead, you can take Bathsheba as your own. Then the child will be legitimate."

David dropped his head in shame but agreed. He then reluctantly devised a plan that would result in the death of Uriah. King David ordered that Uriah go to the front of the fiercest battle. He and his men would take on the strongest opposition and fight with vigor. But when the timing was right, Uriah's troops would retreat and leave him alone to fall at the hands of their enemies. Uriah would die as a hero and his wife would live with the king.

David's plan worked without a flaw. Uriah was dead. He was sent to the front lines where he desired to go. He fought valiantly against a fierce enemy and was slain in battle when he was overcome by more powerful forces. He was honored by King David as a great Israeli warrior and remembered in the annals of their history. Bathsheba mourned greatly for a time. But she ultimately was brought to the king and taken as his wife. Not long after a son was born to them that they could pronounce as legitimate and worthy. All seemed right to the king of Israel.

But as has been noted secrets have a way of revealing themselves. Rumors started to swirl amongst the people about treachery that abounded in the union of David and Bathsheba. Some people whispered the possibility that all was not upright and proper with their king. Some in the kingdom even went so far as to call it evil. As a result of these rumblings, David foolishly made his way back to his God. David came to Him slowly and sheepishly acknowledged the atrocities he committed. David's God was angry and this was good. The people would see how David failed and how foolish his God was for trusting him. They would see that David's God was so wrong in choosing David. They would know that this God could not even keep his own chosen one under control, let alone be trusted to have care for their lives. David had ignored his God for personal pleasures and desires. I knew that because of this in time David's God would be rejected and the people would turn to the freedom I offered.

Some time passed and the child of David and Bathsheba began to grow. David cared for his son and loved him unlike any other. He poured onto this boy his heart and soul. All the while King David stayed with his God. He took a journey back into the arms of that God in order to regain honor and righteousness in his life. I warned David of this foolish path, but of course he ignored me.

David's God heard his cries and did not reek vengeance on him as I had hoped. It looked as though David was going to get away with murder suffer no consequences. This made me scoff at the notion that David's God called himself righteous. Yet not all was lost. There was still anger within David's God. He did not take kindly to playing the fool in David's escapades. I was heartened to find that it came to pass that David would suffer a punishment fitting his crime. David's God may have been a fool, but he turned out to be a vengeful fool. I stood there listening as David's God handed down his verdict.

"Lord," David said as he knelt before his God, "I have done wrong. I pray you find forgiveness."

"David," his God bellowed. "My anger burns against you. You dare to ask for my forgiveness in light of the evils you have committed? I say to you that because of your evil you will soon witness your son's death. He will not see another spring."

David looked up with terror in his eyes. He heard his God proclaim the death of his boy and shook with fear. The boy that he schemed so hard to make his was going to be taken from him? The boy that he poured his love and his heart into was going to be ripped from his arms? He couldn't believe what he was hearing.

"It cannot be," David whispered. "Surely something else can be done. There must be another way!"

"There is not." his God answered. With that definitive proclamation his God departed. David cried out at the judgment and banged his fists against the ground. His attendants and palace aids tried to comfort him but to no avail. David composed himself and stood up. He was going to have to tell Bathsheba.

David's God was doing more for my case than I could have dreamed. This was going to be a grand demonstration of his pettiness and arrogance. This was going to show the people that they meant nothing to Him as He continued to lead them around in bondage. David's God was going to bring havoc to David's kingdom.

What I didn't count on was the hypocrisy of that God. He promised destruction upon the child born out of evil and that was good. But I soon realized that He planned on breaking the rules. David admitted to God the evil he had done and his God laid punishment at David's feet. But what David and I both soon understood was in that moment his God placed His forgiveness on David. This was unconscionable to me. David did nothing to deserve the forgiveness he received. He did not have to complete anything, he did not have to pay anything, and he did not even have to move from where he was at that very moment. All David had to do was admit that what he had done was evil towards his God. With that God forgave David. God was going to take David's son because of the evil. But all that did was fulfill a punishment. It did not warrant forgiveness. For that God to continuously declare that He is holy and just and then forgive David his evil was wrong. This made me furious. I stormed out of the kingdom of David to find solace in my place.

I stayed away from David for some years. I heard through my associates that the child of Bathsheba and David died soon thereafter. This death brought great mourning and pain. Yet through it all David never gave up on his God. This dedication was admirable if wholly misplaced. I found out later that David and Bathsheba were permitted to have another son, whom they named Solomon. I felt great uncertainty at the news of this child. It was as though David's God was giving him a second chance. This was a second chance that David did not deserve.

The larger issue was that now with Solomon with the promise of many generations springing from David was still possible. I was hopeful that David's God had broken that promise with the death of the first boy. But I should have known that He would find a way to weasel out of the dilemma. I was angry and frustrated. I fought hard against the notion that the game we were playing was fixed. I couldn't give in to those thoughts for they would cause me to lose hope. I had to believe that I could still conquer David's God. I had to believe that He would be unmasked before all of His people. I had to know that one day the world would reject Him and leave His legacy on the ash heap of history.

David had caused great pain and suffering. But he was also being healed of those things. He continued to rule the kingdom and look to his God. Yet there was still much weakness in David. The opportunity was still present to subdue him. Though he leaned on his God, he never was fully closed off from my counsel. There were other people and other times where my counsel did not penetrate the cloak of protection their God provided. But I still had access to David.

Time passed as it always does. David continued to rule his kingdom and men went about their lives. David's God had left specific promises on which David could rest easy. His God had also left him with specific instructions not to doubt and not to do things under his own power. But David just couldn't hold true to those commands. With the passage of time came a creeping desire within David's soul. David recognized the need to take control of his life. For too long he had desired little or no control. But now David was primed to listen to my words with the knowledge that he must take control.

It was late one evening when I made my way to David's palace. He was once again sitting alone in his bedroom contemplating his kingdom. He had been considering the fact that his kingdom was strong and that strength was a result of his God. But David desired that it should be stronger. He wanted to be certain that his kingdom would survive and carry on. He did this in the face of promises he had already heard from his God. It was proof that he was ready to hear me once again.

I arrived near to him as he sat on a chair alone and deep in thought. The room was lit by a single torch. Shadows bounced off the walls as David was motionless. The air was unusually cool and uneasiness hung over the king. David's face was twisted with consternation. He was anxious and concern ruled his spirit.

I approached David quietly. "King David," I said. "The hour is late, and I know that you are at a loss. Your kingdom is great to be sure. You have a mighty army and the world knows of your strength." I watched as David stood up and began to pace the room. "But you know that one can never truly content in their strength. Someone out there is always mightier."

David stopped for a moment and whispered to himself. "My God has promised me blessings. I must remember that."

I raised an eyebrow as he spoke. "Your God is not here with you now. He does not face the problems you face," I said. "Your kingdom would be well served if you had an army that could not be surpassed. It would be best for you and your people if your troops numbered exponentially more than they do now. Your might would be unquestioned! Only then would your kingdom have true peace." I stuck my finger in David's chest. "Only then could you have true peace. Your kingdom would be secure for the sake of the hands of your soldiers."

David listened, and considered my words. "How can I make this happen," he whispered to himself.

"Take a census of your people," I immediately offered. "Know exactly where you stand with troops. From that you can know that your numbers are indeed the mightiest. This will relieve the tension you now live under."

I saw the look in David's eyes as he heard my words. He agreed with what I was saying even though he never voiced it. The next day David heeded my advice. He sent an order throughout the land that the kingdom be numbered. This was to include his military and the results were to be reported to him immediately. The people of the kingdom took to his order and diligently pressed forward.

The men of the kingdom made this count their highest priority, and even with that drive the count went on for several days. When it was time for the results I took my place at David's side.

"Your highness," one of David's messengers said as he entered the palace. "The men are done taking census."

David was seated on the throne as the messenger approached. He gripped the throne tightly and leaned forward. "What are they?" he demanded. He dug his fingertips into the arms as he waited for an answer.

"There are nearly two million men," the messenger reported. "More than any known army today or ever, for that matter." The messenger looked pleased but in awe of his own response.

David sat back in his chair and let his body slump. He released the arms of the chair. "Good," he replied. "Then it is that we have the most powerful kingdom in the world. There is no force that could match us. Even all the world's armies combined would have trouble defeating this kingdom." I watched him as he said those words not as a triumphant king but as an insecure man.

I leaned over to him to give him something to ease his tension. "Perhaps you should start tomorrow recruiting and training more men. It would not be a bad idea to add to your ranks."

David perked up and agreed. He sent out the order for more troops and better training so that he could increase his power. I told him again that his decision was correct and that no army would dare challenge his kingdom.

But David's recruitment efforts were short lived. Not long after I left David's presence his God came to him with anger and vengeance on His agenda. He was furious that David had not trusted in the earlier promises and had instead taken matters into his own hands. Even in the simple act of counting this God said David had disobeyed. David pleaded for forgiveness but his God demanded that a punishment be exacted. I was certain that this would mean the end of David and Israel. Immediately David cried out for forgiveness and mercy. That God heard David's pleas of sorrow and repentance. He spared the majority of Israel and David, but sent a pestilence that took out 70,000 men.

I had hoped this would show David just how disgusting his God was. I thought David would beg to be released from the bondage of this God after seeing how he overreacted when threatened with a loss of power. It was so obvious to me. If only it had been as obvious to David. History would have been so very different.

David did not turn on his God. Instead, since his God spared his life and heard his pleas for forgiveness, David repented and rededicated his life and all he had to his God. The men and women of the kingdom saw this and they too called for repentance and rededication. I was furious. David and the people of Israel called this God 'merciful' and 'holy'. I call Him a hypocrite and liar.

After that I knew something had changed. I could not make my way to David's side ever again. I knew that he would no longer heed me as he had in the past. David never explicitly stated it, but from now on trying to have this king's ear would be futile. This did not mean that I stopped watching and visiting his kingdom. There were many times that I entered the kingdom freely. But since David's God was so easily going to forgive evils then David had no reason to turn his back. From then on he was blind to me. Yet I never abdicated my responsibility to humanity. Over the remainder of David's reign I made attempts to change the course of history through David's friends and associates. But everything I tried failed. Most would have given up in the face of such corporate rebuke. But I never lost my passion for revealing to the world the necessity of escaping the bondage of David's God. I never lost hope that a time would come when the world fully understood and completely rejected that God's ways.

In the end I decided to watch from afar as David continued his rule over the Israelites. As he aged, he held strong to his God. No matter my persuasion through others, no matter the circumstances, David continued his unquestioned loyalty. Few remained as loyal as David throughout their lives. It was disheartening to me and my associates. But it gave us valuable experience in the tactics of the enemy.

After a time David neared death. As he did, I recognized the value of Solomon, that young child born to Bathsheba and David a lifetime before. As David greeted death, clutching faith in His God, he choose Solomon as the king over all the land. I watched as David begged that Solomon might hold strong and fast to his God. I watched as Solomon unwittingly agreed to follow the same bondage. Solomon swore to walk in the footsteps of his father's God. I was dismayed to see Solomon accept that bondage graciously and without resignation. My spirit shook as this happened. I knew that what I was witnessing was great trouble. Solomon had a very strong will. He was going to hold tight to the God of David more than David himself.

But I was not defeated. I knew that my time would come with Solomon. I knew that I would have moments where I could urge him. I knew that like his father, Solomon would hear my voice in those moments. David's death and my failing to change or destroy him before the fulfillment of promises was not the end of my journey. It was just another step. I was determined to show the world that they were being fooled. I was determined to show the world that freedom was within their grasp.

Richard finished his story and looked down at the ground. The flames of the fire had died down and I broke my concentration. I looked over at Richard and stared at him until he lifted his eyes.

"Your story makes no sense," I said. "The next time you spin such a tale make sure you do your research first. David was a hero. Yes, God forgave him for his failings, but that just shows His mercy. Life went on, even in the midst of hardships. David and the Israelites went off track at times but did find their way back to God. And let's not forget that all the promises were fulfilled. God never broke his word."

"But David's God did break the rules," Richard retorted. "He put so much faith and trust into David that when David failed his God should have destroyed him. That would have been righteous and just. But instead David fails spectacularly and his God still lifts him up! Don't you see the hypocrisy in that?"

I thought for a moment. "I see no hypocrisy. I see a God that poured out blessings on a boy if only he would follow. In response, I see a boy who dedicated his life to God who grew into a man that followed the promises of that God. That man ruled a kingdom for his God and died with the assurance that he lived primarily righteous. Only when David went off God's course did things decay. God gave David promises that He would never break. That same God promises men today and it is because of those promises that I am the man that sits before you."

"It is because you are simple minded and easily deceived that you are the man that sits before me," Richard shot back. "What you are ignoring is that David had an easy ride from God. From the moment his God slaughtered Goliath to the countless times he forgave David, that same God protected and used him. And why would He do this? To use David as bait to bring so many others under His bondage." "David did not have an easy life after Solomon was born." I protested. "And for someone who claims to have been there, you should know this. There was a lot of pain in the house of David during his life. There was fear, anger, rage, anxiety, rape and death that swirled amongst him, his family and those that associated with him. To say that he got off scot free is wholly untrue. He continued to pay for the evil he committed."

"The punishment never fit the crime!" Richard yelled. "According to that God, there is an eternal punishment, and David was free of that with not but a word from his God! All David had to do was promise to be better and he lived? What kind of justice is that? Others died, but David always lived." Richard stared back at me, angrily gesturing towards himself. "I was cheated!"

Richard's tone made me uneasy. Richard took much of what he was saying personally. I didn't want to admit it, but deep down I knew there was more to him than the fanciful ravings of an overactive imagination. There was sincerity in his voice. That sincerity was escaping through the anger and hurt when Richard spoke. My spirit was being moved to be on alert and telling me that I had gotten involved with something much greater than myself. Why that was I didn't know. But I was afraid that I would soon find out.

I wanted no more of the discussion on David but needed to make a final point. "David wrote many wonderful and powerful pieces of the scripture," I said as Richard smoldered. "He wrote poetry, music, and a lot of words that still resonate today. But I want to point out that even though David committed a great evil with Bathsheba and her husband, he never forgot that it was evil. He was always aware how it affected everything. In one of his pieces David listed the mighty men that served him well throughout the years. He saved for the end the one man to which he had committed the most harm. The last mighty man that he mentioned was Uriah. In the end, David gave Uriah the respect he was due."

Richard sat solemnly. "A line in a poem does not make up for the destruction of a man's life. Just as a plea for forgiveness should not outweigh the deviousness of a man's soul."

"David committed evil," I rebutted. "But did his God not prove himself to be all that He said He was when he forgave the man and still exacted punishment? As you will remember, David was supposed to build the temple, but God took that away from him because their was too much blood on his hands. Yet He allowed David to rule until his last days. David's God was both merciful and just, gracious and righteous."

"No!" Richard rebuked. "You cannot have it both ways. There has to be a line between righteousness and mercy – the two cannot coexist! A righteous God would have destroyed David and never let the temple be built by anyone associated with that man!" I looked into Richard's eyes and saw them burning with passion. I was stunned because his eyes were not metaphorically aglow with a passion from deep inside. They were literally glowing at me, red hot with a light that I had never seen before. I wiped my eyes to make sure that I was actually seeing what I thought I saw. Richard jumped up, and started pacing around the campsite.

Richard's words and countenance pierced me. I believed every word I said. I had believed it almost my entire life. There were times of struggle in my faith as there are with every person. Yet I had never risked losing my faith. My faith was always reassured, especially in the difficult times. Even now, as I struggled with the loss of my wife, I felt that eventually my faith would be bolstered. I knew that I could rely on God to be there and bring me through my trials and doubts. That is a truth from which I never wavered.

But as I continued with Richard I felt something happening. When he first started spinning his tales I thought he was a man of great mental illness. But as he continued I realized that I was unconsciously buying into his claims. It went beyond imagining Richard's stories as if they were true. As Richard spoke I felt myself transported to the stories and found myself in their midst. I had heard these stories hundreds of times before but when Richard spoke them it was as if I was hearing them for the first time. There was a truth about Richard and it forced me to consider the impossible. What if I allowed myself to believe that Richard actually did have a firsthand knowledge of biblical events? What if I decided to agree that he even interacted with the characters I had only read about? What if he had the perspective of 10,000 years and brought it to me in on this cold fall evening? They were all ludicrous assumptions. But I was open to accepting the ridiculous with each passing moment.

If I accepted any of these as truth then I would travel down a path that ended in a very dangerous place. If any or all of those were true, then I would have no choice but to ask a final unsettling question. I would have to ask myself if it could be possible that any of Richard's views on God were accurate. I knew the truth of the Gospel and of God. I had learned the truth as a young man and studied it all of my adult life. I wanted to die ever pursuing and serving that truth. But if even one of Richard's views on God were accurate, then the entire basis on which I had built my life would crumble like a house of cards. This was a terrifying thought. But doubt grew greater with every passing moment.

My soul reminded me of the anchor that was weighing it down. The anchor of anger and fear that I thought had disappeared many years ago had been hidden and revealed this night. But as I watched Richard walk our campsite I felt its pull. I knew it was there and it was heavy. I soon realized that it was not just gently hanging there. As doubts took root in me the anchor started to move more intentionally. It wasn't a fast movement or a wild movement, but it was noticeable. It constantly reminded me that it was there and it was not an ally. I felt the doubt and mistrust begin to swell, giving the anchor more weight as it swayed. I could only ignore it now if I distracted myself. I told myself that my feelings were misplaced. I stood up, hoping to shake that feeling of weight. I watched Richard as he explored my campsite. He was looking in and around things like a mischievous child. I watched him and tried to forget the anchor, but with no success. I then started to think about anything back at home in the city that was distant from this place. I put my back up against the mighty oak tree and crossed my arms, fending off the cold. But nothing was working. I continued to feel the pull of that anchor as Richard sat back down near the fire and warmed his hands.

CHAPTER 7

Richard and I sat in silence until I could no longer stand the mute cacophony that enveloped us. In order to take my mind off the weight I addressed Richard with insignificant chatter.

"These fall evenings can be funny," I said. "They start out mild and become quite cold. I'm glad I brought my heavy jacket."

"I hadn't noticed," Richard said sardonically. "But we have time."

"Time?" I asked.

"I tell you what," Richard said, misdirecting my query. "How about you ask me something. I haven't given you an opportunity to lead the discussion. Go ahead, ask me anything."

"I didn't realize this was a discussion," I said smartly. "I thought this was your show and I was just along for the ride."

"Funny," Richard said dryly. He reached over to the pile of wood and tossed several branches on the smoldering coals. "Don't you have anything you want to ask me?"

"I really don't want to talk to you about anything. Although I would like to know who you really are." That was when a brilliant idea leapt into my mind. "Now that you mention it, I do have a question."

"Yes?" Richard asked with a smile.

"You insist that people are ignorant of their need to be free of God," I said. "But I know one man who should have begged to be free of God. Yet he was more devoted to God than almost anyone else in history. You may know him as Job."

"I knew that man very well," Richard said. "And I guess you know his story."

"I know his story," I responded. "I know Job's story because there are times I have lived that story. I know that Job was righteous and blameless. Job shunned evil and held tight to God. Job trusted and obeyed God for he knew that God was the only true God and creator of all that ever has or ever will exist. I know that God loved him, but allowed him to be tested, because God was certain that Job would not turn from Him. By all accounts, Job had every right to turn from God. Job lost everything in his life. He lost family, he lost wealth, he lost health and he lost the comfort of friends. But he never lost that which truly mattered. He never lost the comfort and love of God. By your rational, Job should have cursed God and demanded his freedom. But he never did. In the end Job kept strong to God, and was rewarded for his faith. Job makes your entire premise false. If he can remain with God, then indeed God is not bondage. God is in fact freedom."

"You think you know of what you speak," Richard scoffed. "You know nothing. Job was a puppet that God used for entertainment. If Job was so free, then why did God use him for such frivolity? No, I'll tell you what really happened in the days of Job."

As soon as Richard uttered those words the flames of the fire leapt into the air and started to dance. My eyes fixed on them as Richard told me his story of Job.

"I remember the days of Job well. Those were very good times for me. I roamed the earth with very little resistance. There was much that I had done, and yet much I wanted to do. I was pleased to see that countless men and women had demanded and received their freedom from God. But there were still some in bondage, and I wanted nothing more than for them to be free. Delivering people into freedom was a passion of mine. I desired more than anything to show them that the God they worshipped was nothing more than a usurper.

My work was being done all over the world. But I was still not satisfied. I needed a premier example to the world that evidenced how God didn't do as He said. I needed an example that would certify their God as a liar and unworthy. But no matter who on earth I urged, no matter who I influenced, it wasn't enough. I needed more. I needed to use God against himself and trick Him into showing his hypocrisy through his own actions. That is why I searched everywhere to find out who among men worshipped this God the most. That was when I discovered Job.

Job was a man that worshipped his God above all others. In every aspect of his life he dedicated himself to this God. There was nothing that Job did that wasn't with his God in mind. Job even declared himself unworthy of his God when by any standard he clearly went above and beyond.

Job was not a poor man. Job had everything. He lived on a massive estate with his wife and grown children. His land contained not only his spacious home, but the grand homes of each of his grown children. His family was also beautiful and without blemish. His wife was the envy of the land, and his children were each respectable and honorable citizens. They would have made any parent proud. Job also had countless possessions including animals that were healthy and strong. I remember when I first found out about Job. I was excited to meet the man that had all of my associates clamoring.

I set out on my way to Job's homeland of Uz. As I traveled I examined what I knew about him. He had all the wealth, health and victory that could be found. There appeared to be no flaw in him or his life, at least none that the world could see. He was the epitome of success on earth. But I knew there was a significant flaw in his life. He was wholly and uncompromisingly given to his God. In him there was no doubt, regret or question as to his devotion. I pondered why it was that a man who had obtained everything in life would be in need of a deity. Following this God was superfluous.

After some time I arrived at Job's estate. I walked to the edge of his land and from where I stood saw no structures. I looked around to find that there wasn't a person anywhere. I was certain that I was on Job's lands, so I continued inward in hopes that I would soon reach Job and his family. It wasn't until walking another thirty minutes that I saw in the distance his home. It sat in a valley, surrounded by lush foliage that was unusual for the dry climate. Trees rose from the sandy ground, and bushes lined the outer edges of his courts. A mighty river cut through the middle of his land, feeding the plants and trees.

As I walked closer I noticed his livestock. Far and wide his livestock roamed, grazing on the ample supply that lay beneath their feet. In this one place I saw more beasts than I had ever seen belonging to one man. The fields were filled with sheep great with wool, camels ready for travel, and mighty oxen and donkeys. There were ample and sturdy barns and stables dotting the landscape. The most surprising aspect of all this was not the sheer numbers. There were easily over 10,000 individual animals on his land. The most astonishing fact was that they all appeared healthy. Not a single animal I saw that was diseased, dying or unhealthy in the least. They all appeared ready and able to do for their master whatever he asked.

For a time I walked Job's lands. The livestock I saw were not alone, for this man had more than animals. He had a multitude of servants. These were men and women that cared for the animals, the land and the family. I went to many of these servants, examining them and realizing that they all acted very strangely. They did not have anger or resentment in their hearts for their positions. Instead, they were content, willing to serve their master as well as they could, and happy to be part of Job's household.

Through listening to several conversations I found that the structures on the land were not all occupied by Job or his servants. Many of the structures were the homes of Job's children and their families. I overheard talk of structures far beyond where I could see that were the homes of Job's sons and daughters. It was truly a compound Job had under his control.

It was curious to me how this all worked. It didn't stand to reason that a single man could have so much and have it run so peacefully. The lands were plentiful and full, and the day I arrived the scene was something out of a dream. It was cool and comfortable, belaying the time of year. The sun did not beat down on the men and animals, and work was proceeding efficiently. It was all too perfect for me, and I was determined to find the man who was worthy of all this pleasure.

When I arrived at Job's home I found that it felt even larger on the inside than it looked on the outside. Evening had fallen and I had yet to meet Job, so I allowed myself entrance. For its time the house offered the top comfort and luxuries available. The home was a single level and spread out upon the land. It allowed ample room for Job, his wife and guests. It also housed many servants, which was quite unusual. For a master to share his personal house with the servants of the fields was uncommon. But everything else I saw was uncommon, so this rose to the standard he set.

The walls of Job's home were beige and thick and provided protection from the elements. There were numerous windows throughout which allowed the air to flow freely through the home, cooling it on the normally warm days. The roof was used for living and entertaining space, perfect for evenings spent in the company of family and friends. From the roof one could see far around and marvel at the beauty of the land.

The house was decorated with tapestries, fine bowls and vases from far off lands. The home was not ostentatious but had a charm that reflected it's owner. Nothing was out of place and there didn't appear to be an abundance of useless items. As I wandered I happened upon the dining area, where the family was gathered for their evening meal. The dining area was grand and could comfortably seat over one hundred people. This was important because I saw before me a multitude who I deduced were all in some way part of Job's family. Job was at the head of the gathering, enjoying conversations with his wife, his children and their families.

Their dinner smelled delicious and I could see that all anticipated the meal. I stood at a distance and observed to find out more about this man. Next to Job sat his wife, beautiful and proper. She was everything you would have expected from the wife of Job, and was perfect in her role. Sitting with Job and his wife were seven sons, all intelligent and handsome. They were strong, healthy and engaged in vibrant discussions with each other and their father. With them were three daughters, all possessing the beauty and propriety of their mother. Many of them had families that were seated as well. All in attendance sat and enjoyed their meal. More importantly, they enjoyed each other, as though nothing else in the world mattered.

I decided to spend a few days with this family. During that time the household ran smoothly. What caught my eyes was the way in which Job went about his life. He enjoyed what he had and was good to his household. Yet he continuously and without contempt praised his God. He gave his God glory for everything that he had, and he followed to the letter what his God asked of him. I even witnessed Job send up burnt offerings on behalf of his children just on the chance that they might have cursed God in their hearts!

But it was obvious how Job could love his God so much. How could one not love a God that gives so much and takes nothing in return. Job was under God's spell. I could not recall seeing anyone in heavier bondage than Job. Job was being fooled by God daily. How can I say this? Is it not right for Job to praise God because he had so much good in his life? As true as that may be, Job was never given reason not to praise his God. Job never had reason to question the so-called goodness of his God. Job never had the opportunity to understand that what his God was truly giving him was not goodness but imprisonment.

If only Job felt the terrors of the common man he would reject his God. I was convinced that if Job saw his God without all the good things, without all the pleasures of life, that he would turn away and be free of His influence. I knew that as with all men Job did not want to praise God and constantly offer up sacrifices. Job had to, or risk losing all he had. But if it were all gone Job's eyes would be opened.

This was not only something that affected Job. The way Job acted affected some in the land outside Job's compound. The people watched Job and respected what he did. People far and wide would witness the life of Job and his household, and would mimic his actions. This was extremely dangerous. If people were fooled and started to believe as Job believed, that his God was the only one worthy of honor and praise, then more people would become enslaved. More people would start to follow and trust this God. Exposing Job was a matter of the utmost importance. What hung in the balance was not the life of a single man. It was freedom of people. It was their life as they wanted it versus their life as another demanded. Job had to fall so that others would be set free.

I did not relish what I had to do. It was not often that I made the journey to where I was about to go, for the very air in that place made me nauseous. The sights and sounds were painful to me, and the feeling in the streets was awash with such a glow that it sickened me to the core. It was a place of lies and regrets, and I never enjoyed my trips back. But I did what I had to do for the people. I did what I had to do to free them.

I possessed the ability to go and speak to Job's God directly. I didn't often meet Him face to face, but in this case I had no other choice. I wanted to confront Him. I was going to prove that this God was not what He claimed. But in order to do that I had to lower myself to enter into His presence. He was so filled with His own power that He would not lower Himself to come to me. So I made my way to the City of God. I hated every step.

I approached the city gates. They were as majestic and tall as I had remembered. Protruding from the gates endlessly in both directions was an insurmountable wall that extended far above my gaze. The gates themselves shined forth like a beacon in the wilderness, beckoning all those it received. They were adorned with jewels and fine metals that seemed to be just wasting their value as they hung there. The gates were closed as I approached and I stood at their base for a moment. I stared through their bars looking for a sign of anyone that might let me in. Suddenly, the gates flew open, though there was nobody there to greet me. As I walked through I thought about how they used to never keep the gates closed.

I walked down the streets of the City of God. Very little had changed, and I was flooded with memories. The streets were ablaze with gold. Each building that lined the streets was filled with life and possibility. Each structure had a uniqueness that was hard to define. Yet it was part of the city as a whole and without it the city would not be complete. The buildings were made with materials that were rare and seldom found by man. Each was adorned with jewels and fine metals much like the city gates. As I looked around I noticed the familiar haze surrounding all the structures. But it was not a haze of confusion or misunderstanding. It was something different. It was a reflection of the one that ruled over the city.

As I walked down the streets I noticed many familiar faces. I stared at each and scowled. I challenged them with my eyes, but to an individual they did not fret. They would either return my gaze or walk by unabashedly. But none admitted to recognizing me and instead treated me as a stranger. I was unwelcome and that suited me. Though nobody spoke, everyone noticed me. Word spread that I had returned.

My destination was the Palace of God. I knew that place well. It was surrounded by an outer gate. Once inside the Palace there were several rooms before one could reach the inner sanctum where that God resided on His throne. The beauty of the outer court was indescribable. Yet that was only a dull reflection of the glory of the inner sanctum. The glory of the interior of the Palace could not be put into words. It was something that could only be experienced. I knew the Palace well and could navigate it with my eyes shut. I also knew that few walked into the inner sanctum unannounced. But that was not going to deter me. I was going to confront that God if I had to break down the door to his throne room with my bare hands.

I banged on the closed doors of the outer court and demanded entry. "You know I am here," I cried. "You will let me in!" Before I could continue, the doors swung open and I proceeded with haste. I entered the outer court and looked around. To my surprise there was nobody in sight. In a place that was usually bustling with activity I found desolation. Silence was all I heard. I looked up ahead and saw the door to the palace open. I started to scamper towards it with an uneasy feeling settling in the pit of my stomach.

As I walked across the outer court I could see into the Palace. It was as bright as I remembered it, drenched in radiance from the power of that God. I strained my eyes to peer inside and take in the sights I knew so well. The Palace was ornate and dressed in fine tapestries and linens. The floors were solid marble, the swirling patterns making it seem as though one were walking amongst the clouds. In my mind I could see the throne as it once stood. Lion heads adorned each arm and an engraving of the sun at the head of the throne. Upon the throne would sit that God, enjoying the sounds of praise coming from those that attended to Him.

As I walked closer to the open door I heard a voice call out from behind me.

"Where did you come from?" the voice demanded.

I whirled around to see it was that God. He was dressed in purple robes with a shimmering crown upon his head. He walked towards me as I took a few steps back.

"I've been out and about, walking around the earth," I said coyly. "But I suppose you already know that." God loved to toy with me. I was not going to play ignorant for His amusement.

"I know that you have been watching my child Job," God said. "I know that you found nobody on earth like him. I also know that you wish to destroy him." God stood over me as his robes billowed. "That man serves me, praises me, and is without fault or blame. He fears and worships me, and has turned away from evil. You would have done well to be like him."

"What, you think Job just fears and worships you for no reason?" I spat back. I was sickened by God's arrogance. "You are the one that makes certain no harm comes to him or his family. You protected his household and multiplied every good thing he did. You're the one that allowed him to have all that he has." I paused for a moment. "Let's not forget that you are the one that made the rule that says no harm or misfortune can come to him or his house!"

"I did," God replied.

"Change the rules!" I said, seething at the sight of this hypocrite. "Change the rules. Allow Job to fall to misfortune, and see how quickly he curses your name."

"Fine then," God retorted. "The rules are changed. I allow you full authority over the good or ill that comes to Job and his household. But he cannot be physically harmed." God had a stern confidence about him. "He will not abandon me. Now leave my presence."

I was shocked when I heard God give up control over Job's life. I stammered for a moment and then smiled as I walked towards the gates of the palace. I made a quick exit, still stunned with the power He had given up. It was unfortunate that Job was going to have to learn the truth of his God by falling so hard. But it was his own fault for putting his faith in that God. In the end it was going to be for the betterment of all mankind.

I returned to the land of Uz and the house of Job. Job was working diligently on his estate. From what I saw Job was never one to sit back and let others do all the work. He felt obligated to work with his own hands and do as much as he could. At the moment I returned he was tending to his garden. The day was not half over yet and Job was already completely dirty from the work of the morning. Even with all the effort he put forth he was content. The look I saw on his face was of peace and fulfillment. To me it was unnatural. I approached him carefully. Before I had a chance to speak one of Job's servants busted on the scene with startling news.

"Sir," he said. "Foreign men have come into our lands! They are from the west and have attacked and killed all of your oxen and donkeys. They butchered the servants as well! It was horrible! I was the only one to escape this terror, and I barely got out with my life!"

Job's face turned to shock and disbelief. Before he could respond, another of his servants approached shouting with all of his strength.

"Fire has rained down on your lands sir!" he shouted. "It has destroyed all of your sheep and the servants that were with them! It was terrible, and the smell was horrific. I am the only one left!"

Job looked at the man and wanted to speak, but before he could a third servant approached.

"Men from the north," he said, out of breath. "They came with swords and slaughtered all of your camels and the servants tending to them! There is blood everywhere, sir. I was lucky to escape with no wounds."

Job was sickened, and looked as though he might be faint. He reached out his hand to grab onto a nearby tree to steady himself. It was then that a fourth servant rushed to his side.

"Sir," the man said slowly and quietly, stunned and in disbelief. "All of your sons and daughters were with their families and in their homes tending to their daily duties. There were innocently going about their day when out of nowhere a great and powerful wind collapsed each and every house. Everyone was crushed and killed. I searched. I searched so very long. But I found no survivors."

Job fell to the ground weeping. I stood with him and looked down at his distress. I couldn't help but feel some pity for the man who had no idea these traumas were about to befall him. What I expected was for him to rise to his feet and curse the name of his God for allowing these terrors. I was disappointed.

"The Lord has given greatly to me," Job said through his tears as he lay on the ground in worship. "and it is His to take. His name is still to be praised."

I was amazed. Through it all, Job did not curse his God and did not give in to the temptation to sin. I remained silent. I had to regroup, and as I left I could still hear the praises off this desperate man's lips to a God who had not but moments earlier taken everything. It made no sense to me.

If Job wasn't going to be concerned with his possessions or even other people, then there was going to have to be something taken that was more dear to his heart. I went back to the City of God to ask for more. I arrived with the expectation that this God would deny me power over anything else in Job's life. I arrived at the open gate of the palace's outer court to see God standing just inside.

"I was expecting you," God said. "Where have you been?"

I was surprised that he anticipated my return. "I was traveling around, you know, here and there," I said dismissively. "I have been watching poor Job and all he has gone through. But again you knew that."

"You still want more from Job, don't you?" God said. "He remains blameless and upright. He still remains apart from evil, even though you wanted all this to happen to him for no good reason. And yet you want to push him further."

"Now wait," I rebuked. "I never said I *wanted* this to happen. But it *needed* to happen." God knew what I thought, but He let it go. "You and I both know that a man will do anything for his own flesh. Let his body be destroyed, and you will see the veil come off Job and the ugly truth of his soul revealed. Do this and he will curse and revile you. I wouldn't be surprised if he came here himself and spit on your robes!" With that I got the response I desired.

"Fine. Anything can happen to his body." God said. "But he is not to die."

I was thrilled with the power I had been granted and smiled in the face of God. I went out from Him with haste and returned to Job. When I arrived, I found that he was sitting at the wreckage of the building that had crushed his eldest son and family. The pile of debris rose up like a burial mound, and one could still here the echoes of the death cries they let out as the structure came toppling down. Job was sitting amongst the ashes and debris. He was weeping and I could not tell if it was from the emotional pain he felt or the physical pain that he had just received. For as Job sat there I saw that he was covered in the most gruesome, pussing boils from the top of his head to the bottom of his feet. The boils wreaked havoc on his body and made him the most grotesque figure that any had the misfortunate to lay their eyes upon.

I watched as Job walked around the pile, weeping and hanging his head. He paced slowly, shuffling his feet and kicking at the dirt. He was a man without purpose. There was nothing for him to do but soak in his helplessness. His eyes scanned the debris and I tried to figure out what he was seeking. He knew his child was dead and the house was utterly destroyed. Job then stopped over a broken jar, leaned over and picked up a shard from the ground. Job sat down and started to scrape his arm with that shard. He was trying to relieve some of the pain the boils were inflicting as he pushed harder and harder with each pass.

Job's wife approached from the east. The beauty she exuded just days earlier was now faded and unrecognizable. Her clothes were torn and her face was red from crying. She too walked without purpose, approaching her husband as he ran the shard against his skin. She stood over him, breathless for a moment, then let out a barrage of anger.

"For years we have served that God of yours!" she screamed. "And look what it has gotten us. Our wealth is lost! All of our servants and animals have been slaughtered! Our children lie dead under the weight of their own homes! And you sit there, pitiful and gruesome, covered by filth and disease that even the beggar doesn't have." She paused for a moment expecting a response. Job looked at her and continued to scratch.

"You are such a fool," she hissed. "Why do you cling to that God of yours? He has obviously abandoned us. Proof of that lay all around. You have nothing more to live for! Curse God now and die, and be done with this wretched existence."

Job lay down the piece of broken jar and stood up. He stepped close to his wife and looked at her squarely. "Woman, you are the fool," Job said with a controlled and convicted voice. "You and I accept without question all the great gifts God has given us. And now you wish me to curse Him? You want me to deny my God simply because He has taken back what is His? I will not begrudge God his due! I will not curse His decisions! For He is greatest over the whole of the earth! I am but a simple man."

I watched the entire exchange and was simply speechless. Job was either the dumbest man to ever walk the earth or the disease of conviction he had for his God was greater than I predicted. Job just wasn't getting the point, and even his own wife couldn't get the message through. But he was weakened. I knew that it wouldn't take much more coaxing to push him over the edge. I had a contingency plan in the event that this did not cause Job to deny his God. I immediately set that contingency plan into motion. As I did I thought of the irony of how simple it would be for Job to gain relief from his misery if he would simply deny His God. Yet he fought hard to hold onto the pain and misery.

I approached three of Job's closest friends for help. Those friends were men that Job relied on for fellowship and counsel, and had known Job for a very long time. I engaged them and explained the situation. I told them to visit Job and made several suggestions as to what they should say to him. Thankfully, they were more than happy to help. They traveled to see Job with the hopes that they could persuade him.

A day passed before the three arrived on Job's lands. When they found him they were dismayed at the carnage. Sorrow filled their hearts and the three began to weep. They ran to Job's side and fell in a heap. For seven days and seven nights no one said a word. They simply sat there, knowing the great pain that Job was enduring. Waiting for someone to talk was painful. But I allowed this foolishness to run its course.

On the eighth day Job finally spoke. I expected that he might be ready to curse God and be free of Him. Job instead cursed himself. Not once did he say a negative word about his God. Instead Job continued to praise God while diminishing himself. I did not want to hear the words he spoke. But Job's friends had my ideas swirling in their heads. They had been unwittingly prepared.

Job's first friend dealt with Job harshly. He laid down the way it was, telling Job that if one is suffering, then that person obviously did something to deserve it. His main contention was that the innocent don't and shouldn't expect to suffer. By that reasoning Job must have deserved his suffering. If Job believed that his God was just then justice was being served. This friend concluded that if Job hadn't done anything to deserve his God's punishment then his God was in fact unjust and unworthy of Job's devotion.

Job's second friend made a roundabout argument. This friend pointed out that God rewards those who are good, and if you are not getting rewarded, then you must not be good. This wasn't to say that Job couldn't be good in the future, but at this point in time he just wasn't being very good. Of course the same unspoken conclusion should have been reached by Job. If Job felt that he was being good, then his God was being unjust and unfair with him. This again showed Job that his loyalty was misplaced.

Job's third friend piled on and rebuked Job. This friend felt that Job should just listen and agree with his argument. The third friend thought that if Job were rebuked, then order could be restored and Job could come to terms with everything that happened. This friend knew it would be in Job's best interest to heed his words.

The three men had done well. It was not my natural bent to see good things come in three's. But in the case of Job's friends I was willing to make an exception. It was a matter of letting it sink in Job's mind and he could finally call for freedom from his God.

But of course Job could not let his friends speak without responding. And of course he had an answer for each of his friend's arguments. As I reveled in each friend pushing Job emotionally and spiritually down, I cringed as Job fought back. Job made no apologies for explaining and defending his view of the situation and refusing to curse God. He went after each of them, treating them more as accusers than friends, and explaining with great prejudice why their arguments fell flat in his eyes.

So if this was going to be a back and forth, then one statement and response between these men was not enough. I stood and encouraged as they continued back and forth. Each man held firm to their side of the story. I watched in amazement as Job continued to defend his God. Job was so insistent on the goodness of his God that he refused to acknowledge that perhaps what his friends said had merit. He went on incessantly about how his God was worthy. Job talked about how he had maintained his integrity throughout this ordeal and this would count as credit towards him. He even went so far as to declare how he longed to be with his God.

I felt a massive headache coming on from the wall Job was putting up. I rubbed my head with frustration as I thought of something else to throw Job's way. Nothing was working with this man. It was going to be up to me to intervene. I came close to Job and looked straight at him.

"Why do you fight for a God that has abandoned you?" I asked dumbfounded. "He curses you left and right and all you do is praise

Him. Your livestock and servants lay strewn dead in the fields! Your God left you with charred bodies and blood stained earth as a reminder! Even your sons and daughters lie dead under piles of rubble that your God allowed. Their spirits cry out for you to avenge them, yet instead of turning from that same God to quell their calls you ask for Him to be near?!" I was exasperated and took a moment to regain my composure. "Why be a fool and follow that which has no desire for you. Listen to your wife. Listen to your friends. Be done with Him now and forever. Follow your own path. I offer you freedom. I will cut you lose from His prison and you can start living your life as you want. You can make our own decisions and have control all to yourself. You will not have to put up with this hypocrisy ever again." Job heard what I said, and I stood there for a moment. I could tell he was considering it strongly. He had reached a point where I was making sense.

But as my words rang true in Job's ears I could tell that he was becoming frightened. Job was not scared for anything that could happen because all that could hurt him had already come. No, Job was scared that he was agreeing with me. This scared him more than anything else that had occurred over the past week. Job bent his head in despair and I was ready to embrace him. Then he looked up.

Job looked across his lands and past his friends. He stared past me far into the distance and made no acknowledgement of what I said. I shook my head in pity as I realized he was not swayed. Job shook off my lingering words and declared his unworthiness in the face of his God.

I was angry but not surprised. Such rejections had occurred before and I was certain would occur again. I had to remember that it was not with a single man that I was going to win the war. I was going to have to learn from this incident and bring that knowledge into my next encounter with such a strong willed man.

Even as I rationalized the decision by Job to sink headfirst into an all encompassing prison I started to feel that this wasn't a total loss. In a way Job was proving that all men needed to be free of his God. The world would consider Job a fool for remaining with his God through pain and destruction. Nobody was going to desire to follow a God that brought misery and suffering only to end in a wretched and penniless death. Job could be my prime example to all the world what a despicable and evil God his truly was. I was heartened with the realization that Job and his God would do more for my cause than if Job had cursed and turned his back on his God.

Just as I was finally feeling victorious a great wind blew at my back. I saw Job and his three friends look up. They were all cast speechless as their eyes grew wide with amazement. I spun around with curiosity to see what had gripped their attention. I soon recognized that the wind I felt was no ordinary gust, but the gale force of Job's God. I quickly scurried behind the four men as the possible reasons for His visit raced through my mind.

I soon found out that Job's God was not there for me as I had feared. Instead, He had come to confront the four men face-to-face. I had a front row seat to a conversation between a man and his God.

God addressed each man as to their part in the saga. He chastised the friends about their foolish words and misguided theology. He abhorred that they took His truth and twisted it unrecognizably. God prattled on about his power and glory and how all the universe was His. He didn't even respect the fact that Job had honest questions about His actions. This God ignored the question and asked Job where he had been when the universe was put into place. This quieted Job, though I could think of so many ways to retort. I was disgusted as I saw all of the men tremble at the words of Job's God. They were either unable or unwilling to rebut or rebuke what they were told. As usual Job fell to the ground praising his God. In a final indecent act Job's God chastised the three friends and instructed Job to sacrifice and pray for them since he had been so faithful.

I was furious. I started screaming at all four men.

"What are you all doing?!?" I yelled. "You listen to Him like He has the final word! But don't you remember who allowed all of this to happen? Don't you remember who has toyed with your lives, and the lives of loved ones, for His pleasure? How can you trust Him when He could do the same thing again at any moment?!"

But my words were not heard by any of the men. In a way I could hardly blame them for ignoring me based on what Job's God did next. For when He finished speaking He restored to Job not only what He had taken, but added even more. Job was now wealthier than before. His household grew and he had more children. From that day forward

I had no way of communicating with Job. I watched from afar as his family grew healthy and strong. Job survived long enough to see four generations live with him and tend the land. He never lost sight of his God and died old and full of days. But Job's greatest accomplishment wasn't anything he did with his family or possessions. His greatest accomplishment was having thwarted my plans and stalling the victory I deserved.

The flames of the fire settled and became flickers. My hands shook as I listened to Richard finish the story. I was presented with a choice that I did not relish. Richard had made clear what he claimed to be. But I had to decide if I believed. My spirit did not allow me to consider him a fool. I was left with one choice. I was very frightened.

"We're not playing any more games, are we?" I asked nervously. "You are telling me that you are in fact the...."

"Ah ah ah," Richard interrupted. "There are no need for those labels here." He was grinning from ear to ear, enjoying my obvious anxiety. "You know me by the names He wants you to know me by," Richard said. "But I prefer only a few. The Angel of Light. The bright Morning Star..."

"You mean Lucifer..."

"I mean the Morning Star!" Richard yelled, slamming his fist on the ground. "Besides," he said, gathering himself, "names don't matter. Only truth matters."

My mind was racing. I was terrified and did not know what to expect. "Are you here to kill me?" I asked with trepidation.

Richard laughed. "No," he said grinning at me. "I assure you, I am not here for that. Besides," he said, pausing "what's that cliché? If I was here to kill you, you would already be dead."

My body was shaking at his intensity, and there was little I could do to control it. I was never prepared to believe what I had bought into over the last several minutes. I had gone from assuming that Richard was a wild eyed lunatic with a vast imagination who was overzealous about my life to believing that I was sitting across a campfire and having theological conversations with Satan himself. It was all too much. But if I was crazy, I had given myself over to delirium. If this was real then I doubted I would survive the evening.

"You remind me of many of those men in history," Richard said, pointing his finger straight at me. "You are strong, resilient, intelligent and thoughtful. Yet you put your faith in things that don't deserve it."

I grabbed at my chest as he spoke those words. It wasn't pain that made me flinch. It was the anchor. I felt the anchor begin to sway from side to side as Richard spoke. The swaying was no longer gentle. It had now become undismissable and unyielding. With each passing moment the anchor pulled back and forth. And with each pass the anchor pulled me further down. Now I was struggling just to keep it in check. Despair and hopelessness took hold and I had to fight harder to have a hope of pushing it out of my mind.

Up until this point I had been able to dismiss what Richard said. I did not believe that he spoke the truth before, and with his admission I certainly wouldn't believe him now. But as I made that decision another thought popped into my mind. If I was going to believe Richard to be Satan then I was going to have to believe that he really was present during those stories he spouted. If he was in fact present, then perhaps there was an element of truth to what he said. I knew whole-heartedly that Satan is by nature a liar. But even liars slip some truth into their tales. A lie is always best hidden between two truths.

I did not fear the lies that Richard told. Lies did not bother me. What I feared was any truth that Richard told. If there was even the smallest grain of truth to what he said about God then it could alter my entire existence. If Richard had some firsthand knowledge that God had mislead even one person at one time in history, or had lied about one bit of minutia to even the lowliest man, then my belief would be shattered. God has to be holy, righteous, loving and just to be worthy. Even one fraction less than perfection would cause the entire truth of God would come crumbling down. That is what I feared the most.

But I had to keep from slipping into that abyss. Satan is the Father of Lies, and therefore anything out of Richard's mouth was a lie. I had to believe that or I would surely lose my soul. I refused to allow Richard to warp my mind. I vowed to be strong and resilient against his attacks. I was taking a stand against Satan. I was literally going to have to fend him off as he sat in front of me. I was filled with fear.

I wanted to get up and run far away at that moment. But the notion of running and being chased by Satan himself through the wooded mountainside was much scarier thought than any other. It was also a bit laughable to me. If anyone I knew heard me tell them of this encounter I am certain they would recommend a good therapist. They would want me to get help, not for the encounter with Satan but for the belief that I had an encounter with Satan.

I put my hand in my pocket and fiddled with my car keys. The thought of driving away flickered through my mind as I stared at Richard. But turning my back on him was more disagreeable than staying and contending. I felt stuck. I wanted to run and escape what I found terrifying. But a quiet and hidden part of me deep inside wanted to hear more and discover if in fact I had been deceived all these years. I decided that I needed to pray, and pray fervently, before I did anything else. I closed my eyes.

"I wouldn't do that," Richard said perking up. "It causes you to think less clearly." He broke my concentration and started to distract me. "I am surprised to hear that you don't want to question my story about Job."

I was unsure of where our conversation was going to lead. I did not want to answer him for fear that he was biding his time to destroy me. I seriously doubted he just wanted to tell me tales and let me walk away. I realized that I was taking too long to answer and Richard took notice. I had to speak before I gave him a reason to become angry.

"You are a good storyteller," I admitted cautiously. "But I think you have your facts wrong. Job was never in bondage to God. Job knew what was most important in his life. In the face of everyone telling him to the contrary, he knew that he had to follow God. And God proved to be worthy."

"God toyed with him," Richard said. "He caused pain and suffering that was unnecessary."

"It was temporary," I replied. "Besides, was it God that caused the suffering?" I looked accusingly at Richard.

"If you are suggesting that I made all those terrible things happen to Job and his family, then you are missing the point. I could not do anything without being given the authority by God first. Therefore, anything you blame me for is in fact the work of God, if you think it through."

"I have thought it through so very many times," I replied. I have lost many people in my life, and there are those who say I should give up on God. But I don't, because I trust my God and know that it will all work out for good." My words tried to hide the doubt that was growing inside me.

"You act very confident for a man that is unsure of so many things," Richard said. I knew Richard had looked beyond my words and into my soul. He could see the anchor weighing on me and swaying side to side. He could see the pull and relished the struggle within. He was like a fighter that had found my weakness and focused on it. He would continue to hammer at me until I either capitulated or died from exhaustion. I knew that I needed my spiritual armor on if I was going to have any chance. I was in for the fight of my life.

CHAPTER 8

The evening was cold and I was terrified. I could not escape and I dare not run. My mind was awash with anxiety and dread. But I made sure that my body did the least to show it.

My camping companion had expressed an interest in dining, and I wasn't going to refuse. I rummaged through my things and unpacked the food I had. I purposefully arranged the items on a blanket near the campfire. Included in my offerings were the essentials for a good dinner by the campfire. I had hot dogs, beans, hamburgers, chicken and a mix of some vegetables I had cut up at home. I was not sure how much I had thought I would eat when I packed, but it looked as though I was prepared for any gastrointestinal emergency. As I scanned the food, I wondered if somewhere inside I knew I would be entertaining.

"Do you always eat this healthy?" Richard asked with a smirk.

I was still reeling from my discovery and did not want to misspeak. My experiences camping with the Prince of the Power of the Air were limited, and I felt as though I needed to walk on eggshells. I put a couple of hot dogs on a couple of sticks, sat it down and glanced up at Richard.

"Calm down," Richard said, as if reading my thoughts. "You look more scared than a turkey on Thanksgiving. I told you, I have no intention of doing you any harm." He looked over wide eyed at the sticks. "I do have intention of doing harm to those hot dogs, though!" Richard reached over and picked up one of the skewers and lifted it over the fire. I let the other one sit, and Richard questioned my lack of enthusiasm.

"I'm not hungry," I said.

"Well, I am, so I hope you don't mind me eating before you." I shook my head and watched Richard as he let the hot dogs cook. I said nothing and continued to watch him as he whistled.

"Don't look so surprised," Richard said. "You probably think all I do is roast hot dogs over the open flame." Richard chortled. "The truth is there is very little fire where I come from. It's quite the opposite, actually. That whole flame thing was just made up to give a ghoulish picture to scare people. I was personally never one for heat. Give me a nice cold winter day in Maine, yessir…"

Richard continued on as though we were old friends chatting about our lives. I was surprised at how easily he transitioned himself from deathly intense to small talk. His change in demeanor was instant but very unsettling. I believed that it was his way of keeping me off guard. I was just waiting until he pulled me back in.

My spirit was dragging. The weight that had been loosed inside of me that evening could not be ignored. I wanted nothing more than to be freed from it. But I realized that years of carrying the anchor unaware, even in the midst of following God, had caused it to grow roots in my soul. Now, sitting here, I thought there would never be a way to rid myself of that weight. Even worse, the pull was getting stronger, and I was falling further into despair and hopelessness. I knew I had to fight with whatever strength I could muster. I tried to pray silently, but Richard had a way of distracting me when I did. I had to fight against him and hope that I had what it took to overcome whatever he was trying to accomplish.

"Hey there, cowboy," Richard said. "You haven't heard a word I have been saying these last few minutes, have you? No worries, it wasn't important anyhow."

I mustered the courage to speak. "I know what is important to you."

"You do?" Richard said curiously. "Then please, tell me what is important to me."

"Destruction is important to you," I said.

"Ha!" Richard bellowed. "You couldn't be more wrong. I have told you the truth all evening. I want nothing more than for men to be able to live their lives on their own terms. I love to see them live, create, design and grow as much as they can. But to do it as they see fit." Richard fixed his gaze with mine. "If you want to know who wants destruction, just look to that God of yours. Remember the flood? Job's pain? Who do you think allowed that? Even today destruction occurs regularly. People cause all kinds of destruction to each other based in the name of their religion. In the name of their God." Richard paused. "Even God's own creation, this earth, is a proponent of destruction. I bet right now somewhere something is being destroyed by an earthquake or flood or other such disaster. And I know you want to blame me for that. But how could I be to blame? I am sitting here with you." Richard smiled.

I said nothing.

"Ah yes, you call me the destroyer, yet you are starting to question exactly what it is that I have destroyed. Let's talk about the real destroyers. Let's talk about those people of God. You conveniently forget that I was there and saw things as they were. That gives me the ability to tell you the truth."

"You are no friend of the truth." I muttered.

"I am no friend of those that are blinded by ignorant loyalty!" Richard shot back.

We sat in silence for several tense moments.

"Now if I may continue, I would like to tell you about truly destructive people. I want to tell you about your God's people. They were strong and powerful at the beginning of the first century. They dominated Jerusalem. It was with pleasure that I developed a good relationship with one of them. One of the Jews."

"The Jews!" I scoffed. "You hate the Jews! You want nothing but their destruction."

"Quite the contrary," Richard rebutted. "The Jews were some of my closest confidants and I desired great success for them. Saul of Tarsus for instance..."

Richard's voice faded as once again the flames of the campfire jumped to life. I became fixated on their movement and was swallowed into the new tale.

"I walked streets of the city of Jerusalem and the cities of that region for years. I saw and heard many things in those cities. I came to know the people very well. Through my diligent efforts I grew close to several of them and showed them the path to freedom. The Jewish people as a whole would often prove difficult as they were entrenched in serving their God. But as time passed, many of them lost their way, and started to serve other things when they thought they were serving their God. They would serve tradition, propriety, or even themselves, and insisted they were serving their God. Though they were not always aware of it, many of them were well on the path to freedom from that God.

There was one man in particular that I remember fondly. He was a man that I was certain would always remain free. But along the way he was ensnared and lost his freedom. You know him as Paul. But I knew him as Saul from the city of Tarsus. Saul was a great man. He was one of the greatest men I ever had the pleasure of knowing.

As I got to know him I recognized that he could be a powerful ally in my fight to make all men free. I kept him close and worked with him to make the decision to decry that God. But he never gave himself completely over to me. As it turned out I lost him through no fault of my own but through the breaking of the rules by that God. In losing my companion Saul, I gained a powerful enemy in Paul. Yet all of my enemies eventually fall to the same fate sooner or later. But I am getting ahead of myself.

The streets of Jerusalem bustled with people in those days. Men and women strong in the Jewish tradition went hither and yon, living their daily lives and taking their time to give alms to their God. But many of these people were not fully dedicated to this God. Some were on the verge of being enslaved by Him, while others were very close to being freed entirely from this destroyer. The ways of the Jews was strong to be sure. But many of their hearts were corrupt. They were slaves to traditions, which did not permit them to be slaves to this God. I knew it was better to be a slave to tradition than that God. For that I was grateful.

So as it was in those days I walked the streets freely and without burden. I would allow myself to be in the company of those I knew and trusted. I trusted some and found others to be insufferable. There was a particular band of Jews that declared to be the only ones to have truth. They had followed the man Jesus and decided that it was with him they wanted to stake their reputations and their lives. This particular band was a menace. I kept an eye on them knowing they would cause me great trouble.

But as I said the streets were filled with noise in those days. Though I walked amongst them, the people paid me no attention. Business was booming for some, while others waited in the streets, delinquent and desperate. I still remember the smell in the air. It was the smell of pain, desperation, and suffering. But when a certain wind blew, it hinted at hope – a hope that I despised. Like a dog that turns its head quickly from a rancid smell, I had to shake off this whiff whenever it arose.

Yet there were many pleasant smells to me as well. The smell I enjoyed the most was that of the man who would have his ears open to my words. Be they self declared religious zealots or openly rejecting all faiths, it didn't matter. The smell from those open to me was always sweet. When I reminisce about those days my mind is drawn to Saul. For much of his life he was open to my words. He encompassed irony to me, for he was considered a prominent Jewish man of his time yet could still be counted on to consider what I said. I suppose that being in such a position of power and recognition opened him up to my leading. For that I was glad.

I first met Saul as a young boy. He was raised in a devout family and taught the ways of his faith from birth. I recognized immediately that he had the potential to be an ally of mine. But I also realized that he had just as much potential to be a powerful enemy. I always considered that he could follow in the footsteps of men like David and Solomon, and that he could lead people away from their freedom because of his strength of personality. That was why I kept him close and always abreast of his life through firsthand knowledge or through the reports from my associates.

As he grew he moved further into the faith of his God. He knew well the ways of his people including their holy writings, traditions and customs. I was there when he came of age and was given the challenge of being a man. I watched as he accepted his adulthood with great thirst and dedicated his life to his traditions and his God. I knew that he was getting stronger in his faith. But I also saw in him the potential to become consumed more with ritual and tradition than with anything else.

I remember the very evening that he was proclaimed a man in society. I will never forget the way Saul looked that night. His deep olive complexion made him contrast with the sandy backdrop in which he was standing. He wasn't a tall man but was thin and he carried himself as though he deserved the respect of an aged teacher. The beard he was working on was wispy and thin. He wore clean white garments that hung loose on his body.

Saul was alone and in a contemplative prayer, considering all that he had done and all that he was yet to do. He wanted wisdom and he wanted to serve his God. But in him was also the desire for prestige and admiration from others in his community. His dedication was so strong that he put blinders on to anything outside of his religious traditions and teachings. I found this out one night as I sat next to him.

"Saul," I started. "Why is it you grasp so strongly to these ways? The path to freedom and enlightenment comes in not tying yourself to the chains of your God. It comes away from bondage. It comes in making your life your own. You should be used as you see fit, not as someone else says."

Saul heard me and felt my words. But even though he remained prayerful, I felt his heart speak back to me. It was unlike the sound of any man's heart I had heard before or since.

These are the ways of my Lord, he said to me. *I will never reject or denounce the ways of my people. I will live only for them, and for my God. I will not let anything hinder my people. I would rather die than have my people fall away from our God.*

Saul was unquestionably strong. I left him with the intention of returning. I gave him a parting thought which I know took root.

"If you are going to remain so dedicated to your faith then you are going to have to remain in staunch opposition to anything that would compromise your people. Anything that threatens your faith must be exterminated. A threat cannot be allowed to exist or it will surely consume everything you hold dear." I know he heard these words. And I know they were effective because even when Saul was young there were rumblings, however faint and distant, of something coming towards the people. These rumblings were of something as yet unheard and very dangerous. And if Saul wasn't going to be an ally of mine, then he could become an enemy of my enemies. He could reject me if that is what he decided to do. But he was going to be immensely useful in the process.

Time passed and Saul grew stronger in his religion. With each passing season he grew wiser in the knowledge of the faith. He studied under the most respected teachers and took nothing more seriously than that which was related to his education. It was not long before Saul became one of the most knowledgeable men of the Jewish tradition in Jerusalem. Saul was still a young man but his name was known. It was only going to be a matter of time before Saul would be considered the greatest of all the Jewish scholars.

But in the distance that rumbling strengthened. It wasn't long before it became thunderous in my ears. In time I made Saul aware of it as well. For there were those in Jerusalem that had taken for themselves a new God. They claimed that this God was the one true God. What made it worse was that these men and women were Jewish, and through their blasphemy declared themselves still to be strongly Jewish. In Saul's eyes these men and women were rejecting and bastardizing his religion. In their blaspheming they claimed a God greater than their Jewish tradition. He understood that it was now time for him to take action against those that plotted to sully his people's tradition. They were the most dangerous of all.

These people angered Saul. He envisioned a wave of men and women who would try to destroy all that his religion had been and warp it into something twisted and mangled. He perceived that they should reject his God and the God of their youths for a new God that would lead all of them astray. He made attempts to talk and convince these people in a rational and reasonable matter that what they were doing could only lead to destruction. He took the time to approach and sway each and every one of these twisted Jews to come back to the God of their fathers. Yet none of them, to a man, denounced their newfound religion. Saul had done everything in his power of ration and reason to correct their wrongs. Still nobody would listen.

Saul was distraught. I came to Saul in his time of need to give him comfort. Before I arrived he took time in prayer to search for the answers as was his custom. But his prayers were lethargic and his mind drifted to revenge. His focus was poor and the strength he used to draw from his prayers was weakening. I was at his side as he valiantly pressed forward with his troubled prayers. I finally decided to give him the focus he needed.

"They care little for your ways," I said. "You have tried to convince them, but they deny you. They scoff at you behind your back, and follow their own twisted desires. Even now they plot to destroy your religion and topple your God. You have tried to reason with them. You have given them the opportunity to change and come back into the fold. But all of your attempts have failed. Now is the time that you must take the ultimate action. Now is the time to defend your God. Now is the time to destroy these usurpers!"

Saul opened his eyes with a jolt. He heard and understood my argument. His focus was back and he had a singular purpose. Saul lifted himself up from his prayers, and made a dedication there and then. He swore that anyone who professed this twisted and mangled view of his religion would not be allowed to thrive. At the very least he was going take their freedom. If he had his way they would all be put to death.

I was pleased with Saul. Time had been lost between us since he rejected me in his earlier days. But now he was focused because of his listening ears. He was slowly and certainly breaking free from the bondage of his God. As a bonus he was going to do my will. I looked back on the times we had spent together during his youth. I knew he would be strong in his religion one day, and that he could threaten to bring even more people to his God. But with the changes in his mindset I could not have been more thrilled. He was going to be my hands and feet in the crusade for freedom. It was a bright day for me and for those that loved my freedom.

Saul was incredible and zealous from the start. Saul showed his worth in one of his first encounters with a member of the twisted religion. There was a man by the name of Stephen who was raised in the Jewish tradition. He knew the holy writings and was definitively a Jew. But this man made the decision to abandon his faith. He was one of the first people to chose to follow this new God while claiming he was fully Jewish. Stephen and others used Jewish tradition and history to claim the providence and truth of this new God. They were dismantling Saul's faith.

This angered Saul. The true Jews knew that when Stephen remained silent he was only deceiving himself. But when he decided to speak he became a destroyer. It was with this in mind that Saul had a decisive encounter with Stephen the Destroyer. Stephen had been called to stand in front of a council of religious leaders and make an account for his actions. Though not a deciding member of the council, Saul was allowed to be among the gathering and was able to look Stephen in the face. Saul watched in disgust as this man Stephen recounted the history of the Jewish people. Saul was sick to hear Stephen suggest that Jewish history pointed to this new God. Stephen stood in front of them all, in the middle of the chamber that housed the council of religious leaders, and recited their history to them. He began with their great father Abraham and traced their history through the patriarchs. He spoke of Jacob and Joseph and Moses. He talked as if he had firsthand knowledge of Joshua and David and Solomon. As he spoke, Saul's anger was unleashed within, reaching a fevered pitch as Stephen declared that this proved his new God's hand throughout the ages. Stephen dared to stand there and say that Saul's people were in direct violation of their own God's will.

What does this blasphemer know, Saul thought. *Who is he that he should dare stand here and accuse us? He speaks out against our faith and our traditions for the sake of blasphemy. He speaks as a man who is one of us yet decries our ways!* Saul could taste the rage in his mouth. But he remained silent while the council made their decision. He did not have to wait long. The decision of the council was swift and the punishment was certain. Stephen had to die for his words.

Saul was thrilled. As the council called out death upon Stephen, all the men gathered there grabbed him and dragged him to the edge of the city. The dragged him across the dusty streets and into a public area where all could witness the punishment. Curiously Stephen did not resist the sentence. Not even a single foul word dropped from his lips. The men of the council and all those there, including Saul, spewed venom to mock and judge Stephen's actions. Stephen remained silent as he was thrown to the ground in the midst of the crowd. Onlookers gathered around gawking at the man who looked so small in the midst of the angry mob. The men grabbed stones and raised them ready to strike at Stephen. The punishment was commencing.

Saul had followed the men outside the chamber and into the streets. He was pleased with the decision and hoped that it would be a deterrent for others that would try to claim Stephen's God. But when the place for Stephen's death was chosen, Saul did not pick up a rock. Instead he stayed on the fringe and cast his eyes upon Stephen. Instead of holding a rock Saul was tasked with holding the executors robes to keep them from being soiled. Saul happily did as he was asked. He simply wanted to see justice prevail and the restoration of dignity to his faith.

Saul held the robes and watched the men raise their stones above their heads. With malice and pride the men threw their stones in a barrage at Stephen. As soon as a man would release his stone he would pick up another and fling it with even more force at Stephen's body. Saul watched as they did this. He saw the look in their eyes as they slowly but painfully executed the blasphemer. To Stephen the look in the men's eyes was of hatred and rage. To Saul it was the look of truth and the hope of restoration. As Stephen was battered and bloodied by the stones, Saul noticed that he did not cry out or plead as one might have expected. Instead he remained silent and strangely peaceful. The men continued to pelt Stephen as they cried out for justice. Saul recognized the distinct contrast between the men as they yelled and screamed and Stephen. Saul thought to himself that this silence was the voice of a man who knew he was wrong.

The crowd had doubled in size since the punishment began and their voices were joined together as one. Saul looked at Stephen as the blood poured down his face and body like a crimson drape. Saul thought he was prepared for the gruesome scene to unfold. But to his surprise, Saul found that his stomach was not as strong as he had originally thought. Justice was a dirty job. Saul was going to have to grow into it. As the slaughter continued, Saul had enough and turned his head to the side. He closed his eyes and hoped for the end to come soon. As he did this he heard Stephen lift his voice and call out among the attackers.

"Lord, I beg you, do not hold this sin against them!" Stephen cried. As soon as he uttered those words he dropped his head and lay motionless under the thundering of stones.

Saul took notice of Stephen's dying words. He was surprised that the last words of a condemned and brutalized man would be for his persecutors. He would have expected Stephen to call out for retribution on those that attacked him. How a man could ask for such a thing amazed Saul. When it was clear that Stephen was dead the clamoring of the people stopped and the voices of the executors died down. It was in this moment that I noticed Saul's countenance and took the opportunity to whisper encouragement.

"Who is he to claim that you have sinned?"

Saul heard me and forgot his wonder at the peace Stephen exuded in death. Saul took to heart my question and became angry again. He wondered how it was that a man condemned to death should dare think he had the right to speak to the sins of righteous men. It confirmed in Saul that Stephen's death was right and just, and it hardened his resolve to search out and destroy more of these people that willingly put a blemish on his faith.

After Stephen's death the council of religious leaders agreed that those who professed to twist the faith should be dealt with swiftly and with extreme punishment. There was going to be a more aggressive assault on this disease that had infiltrated their culture. Saul heard the plans the council made and I strongly urged him to volunteer to lead their task force. I told him that it would not only help eradicate the vermin that spoiled their faith but that it would be a stepping stone to greatness among his people. Saul listened to what I said and agreed to it without reservation. There was no doubt in his mind that this is what he was called to do.

Soon Saul was officially chosen to lead the assault on the blasphemers. He was proud of his new role and desired to do anything it took to succeed. I was pleased at his growth and promised that I would stay near to lend him advice whenever he asked. He was becoming a mighty ally in my crusade. I knew that Saul didn't fully understand what he was up against. I knew that he did not understand just how tyrannical and enslaving this God was. But he was willing to fight and more importantly willing to follow my direction. For me that was most important. Among the council was certainty that Saul could handle the job. He had the pedigree, the knowledge and most importantly the drive to fulfill their wishes.

The word soon spread that Saul was tasked with rooting out and persecuting all those who would ally themselves with Stephen and his ways. Saul assembled a posse of men that were strong and dedicated to his cause. Each man in Saul's party was of great stature and strength. He choose the finest who were swift on their horses and fast on their feet, as well as mighty with their hands and their swords. He choose men that were intelligent and followed orders well. But most importantly Saul wanted those who could be counted on to remain strong in their faith and not swayed by the siren song of another. The men Saul chose had his full trust and faith. Saul knew that they would follow any order given even if it meant to end a person's life.

Saul prepared his posse and they swiftly began their search in Jerusalem. Like the winds passing through the palm trees the actions of these men could be recognized by the affects they had on all around them. They were quick to arrest and rip from their homes those people that professed the twisted faith. Saul and his men reveled in filling the prisons with these blasphemers. Saul did not differentiate between men or women but carried on to silence everyone. Saul and his men would burst into homes and businesses, places of rest and places of work, and immediately take into custody any of those he suspected were involved. Nobody escaped Saul's onslaught.

The very mention of Saul's assault quickly reached the ears of those he desired to destroy. It didn't take long for the word to spread that Jerusalem was no longer safe for those that professed this new faith. Soon after the onslaught began many of the new church members gathered in a corner of Jerusalem, scared of what was to come. I got word of this gathering and went to scout the meeting for Saul. When I arrived I found terrified men and women. They were frantic about what they should do in the face of such persecution.

A burly man took the floor and commanded everyone's attention. "Saul has been hunting us down like animals." he said. "He will not stop until we are all in prison or dead. We need to do something about this before the truth is lost forever."

"What can we do?" a young woman cried. "He has the permission and direction of the leaders and the government. We are but a fragile few, ill-equipped and ill-prepared. We have no means to fight against Saul's attacks! And the places to hide in Jerusalem are becoming fewer by the day. No place is truly safe."

Another man, tall, lanky and young in years, perked up. "We can turn ourselves in! We can beg for mercy! If we do this, and make Saul believe that we have seen the error in our ways, then he might call off this attack and let us live in peace."

"To what end?" the burly man shot back. "By denying the truth and hoping for mercy from a man whose hands are covered in our blood? I would rather die than trust him."

The gathering began to grumble, and each was throwing out his or her own suggestions. The voices became a tangled mess with each one trying to shout down the other. But under each man and woman's shout their core was in agreement. They were frightened. Nobody seemed to have the answer. They were all afraid that their next step could be into the hands of Saul and his posse.

I scanned the room and noticed a man sitting alone in the corner. His eyes were framed with many years, and his beard was white and sagging. His face shown the memories of many trials. He was calmly watching the people fall into disarray. I approached him and looked deep into his eyes, trying to figure out what was going on behind them.

"Don't I know you," I said. I crouched down and thought about why he looked so familiar. Suddenly I realized who he was. "Yes, I do know you!" I was stunned. This grey man and I had once taken council together. But it had been long since I had spoken to him.

I placed my arm around his shoulder. "You and I were once friends. Yet you have not called out to me for a long time." I squeezed his shoulder. "Why is it you have strayed so far?" I paused for a response, but he said nothing. I got frustrated by his silence as I felt his heart grow weary.

"Yes, I do remember you." I continued as I stood up straight. "You are the fool that took that wife after I told you not too. You are the fool who I advised not to marry her, and not to have that child with her." The man remained silent. I grew angry at his lack of respect. "I remember you well, for I knew that your life would be wretched after that! I offered you freedom, but you rejected my gift, and what did it get you? Your life was terribly difficult, and you were cursed with only the sole child. I remember you remained with that wife of yours even though I told you it would be better for you to leave. So how did that turn out for you? She died, and your one child, your son, turned out to be as much of a fool as his father. He took up into the wilderness, leaving you and practically drowning every person he came across! And now he is dead, and you are left alone with your wretched misery to accompany you. What was that kid's name again? John, as I recall. John the Baptizer…"

The old man jumped up and cut me off. "We need to scatter," he shouted firmly over the noise of the room, belying his fragile appearance. Everyone quieted down as he spoke. His eyes began to swell with tears as his voice remained confident and strong. "We need to scatter to safety. There are places that we can go far away from Saul and his men. He will continue to hunt us as long as we stay here, and the less of us there are in one place the harder it will be for him to find us. The more scattered we become, the more effective we can be in spreading the truth. And if God is willing, enough of us will survive to continue the work."

The crowd considered the old man's words. Many of them did not want to leave their homes. It was a terrible thought that they would have to run from everything they knew and start over somewhere else. But as they looked at each other they knew that what he said was the only way they might escape Saul's wrath.

The burly man stood up and spoke first. "He is right. If we stay here, we are committing suicide. I know that none of us want to leave. But there is no other way. We can be safe away from Jerusalem. We can build new lives. But it must happen soon. Even as we speak Saul's army is on the prowl."

The men and women gathered reluctantly agreed. The grey man sat back down and dropped his head. I turned away from him and spit in disgust. He had long shut his ears to me, and his heart was sewn up for another. I knew he felt what I said, but he was too far gone to be swayed. I watched as the men and women gathered themselves and headed out, each to his or her home to gather what they could carry and leave Jerusalem. Over the next few hours most of the believers of this twisted faith left the confines of their homes in Jerusalem and were scattered throughout Judea and Samaria, save for a select few that stayed behind. This was going to make Saul's job much more difficult. The region he had to scour had just become a lot more expansive.

When word reached Saul that many of his hunted had escaped Jerusalem, he was enraged. He regrouped his posse and prepared them for longer days and more diligent searching. Saul had originally thought that these blasphemers could be contained in Jerusalem and wiped out in the confines of the city. But he came to realize that they were now a far greater danger. The message these people carried was now traveling to other cities. They were in the process of spreading their lies far beyond Jerusalem. Saul knew that they had to be stopped before they infected countless others. These blasphemers had to be stopped before their message spread beyond Saul's control and to the ends of the earth.

I gave Saul encouragement as he regrouped and planned for the new phase of attacks. Saul did not delay in continuation of his persecution. But as Saul and his posse worked he knew that it was getting much more difficult. These people had spread out over the lands and towards the end of his reach. He was not as effective and swift in gathering them as he had before, and more time and effort was put into each individual capture. Saul devised new tactics and implemented them as quickly as he could. But his cause was growing more difficult and I was having more trouble keeping track of all those that professed the new faith.

To his credit Saul and his men did not wane in their commitment or desire to carry out my will. If anything, the fleeing of the blasphemers solidified Saul's knowledge that what he was doing must be done. Saul had received many stories about how these blasphemers were spreading their twisted message. Men and women were hearing this message and being physically healed from it. Saul heard these stories and was amazed. He knew that these blasphemers must be engaged in magic arts, a grotesque and evil practice in Saul's eyes. Saul heard about travelers who came into contact with these men of the twisted faith, and how they came to believe the in the same twisted faith after only a brief encounter. Each story that Saul heard tore at his heart and fueled his passions to bring down these men and restore the honor and integrity to his faith. He swore that he would die before giving up the fight.

But some things were out of Saul's control. Saul belonged to me and there should have been no questioning my authority. But He can change the rules. It was on a bright warm day that the God of Noah, David and Job reared His deceitful head, usurp my authority over Saul and make me impotent. It was unjust and another example of the evil I faced in the war I was waging. I had to watch helpless as Saul's life was destroyed forever.

CHAPTER 9

Saul had set into motion his plans to pursue the men and women of the twisted faith far outside the walls of Jerusalem. He always followed the proper method by which to apprehend them and never placed himself above the law. It had come to Saul's attention that there was a large gathering of these blasphemers in the city of Damascus. Several of the leaders of the twisted faith resided there as well. It would be a major blow to the blasphemers if all of them in Damascus were apprehended. It was a feather in the cap that Saul desperately wanted. I brought word of this congregation to Saul and he approached his high priest and requested permission to infiltrate and return these people to justice in Jerusalem. Without hesitation the high priest gave the orders and documentation needed for the lawful arrests. With the documents in hand, Saul brought together his finest men and prepared them for the journey.

"Brothers," Saul said as they strode on horseback near Jerusalem's gates. "We have uncovered a great gathering of the threat in Damascus, and the time has come to stamp out that threat. If we are successful, we will have taken down one of the preeminent cells of these blasphemers in all of the land. It will devastate their efforts, and bring us closer to victory. Do you stand with me?"

With a loud hurrah the men riding with him acknowledged his orders. "Our swords are at your side," his first in command said. With that, Saul gave the order to ride out from the city gates. He and his men rode off like lightning to strike down the group in Damascus.

I mounted up and rode with Saul. I was going to have to remain by his side. Saul and his men were going to deal a decisive blow to the blasphemers and he was going to need my counsel. As we rode with haste towards the city of Damascus I heard from one of my associates that somehow the blasphemers in Damascus had been alerted that Saul and his men were once again on the prowl. When I heard this I was frustrated at how a great commander like Saul could have let his plans slip out. In his haste to leave Saul had failed to make sure that any spies for the enemy were kept ignorant. Working with men never failed to prove time and again how they could be so foolish. But to our good fortune, the word had only gotten out that Saul and his men were headed away from Jerusalem to apprehend blasphemers in another city. They did not know the specific city. I had faith that Saul in his wisdom would overcome this unfortunate circumstance. The men and women of the congregation in Damascus would be on alert, but they would not know where or when we might arrive. For that very reason it was imperative that we travel quickly, and I spurred Saul on to make haste for Damascus.

We drove our horses hard and rode with the wind at our backs. The horses strode with determination and fervor, and we were in excellent position to surprise those waiting in Damascus. The men in our posse were primed and driven to bring those of the twisted faith to justice. There was no force on earth that could stop us. I was sure that this would be a glorious day. It was going to be a victory for me and all that desired freedom. But I turned out to be devastatingly wrong. For though I knew there was no power on earth that could stop us, I made a fatal error. I failed to look beyond the powers of earth. I had been the preeminent counsel to Saul for many years and had his ear tuned to my voice. But when the Deceiver came down to interfere in my affairs all of my work was washed away in the blink of an eye.

The horses under us kicked at the dirt as they ran. Saul was driving hard and knew that time was of the essence. But he also understood that if he didn't give the horses a break and they were exhausted and no use. Saul ordered everyone to stop to water and rest their horses. They immediately obeyed and took a moment's rest.

I stood by Saul and spoke to him about the strategy to employ when they reached Damascus. Saul was listening and watching his horse as he took in my every word. When we finished and Saul was satisfied that the horses were well he ordered that everyone take their mount and continue forward. The men did as such and it looked like we would be on our way.

But seconds later disaster struck. As we got back on the road to Damascus a light brighter than that of the midday sun shot from the sky. It penetrated downward around Saul and his men. The horses reared in fright, throwing their riders from their backs. I was thrown for yards and came to land far away from Saul. Saul himself crashed to the ground and slammed his head beside his horse. I watched as he lay on his back motionless. I thought he might be dead until moments later when he started to stir and turn himself on all fours. The horses remained still as if frozen with fear. Saul grabbed and scratched at the ground, trying to catch his breath through his coughing and regain his composure. From where I lay I looked into his eyes and saw a confused man. I saw a man who moments before had everything under control and now was in utter shock. He collapsed back to the ground and looked up into the sky.

I tried to gather myself and return to Saul's side. But to my dismay I found that I could not move. I was being restricted in some manner that I could not see. I called out for Saul but he did not respond to my voice. He was engrossed in the light flooding where he lay. I was trapped, unable to aid my friend or give him counsel. All I could do was watch.

A voice called down from the light. I knew the voice all too well. It was His voice.

"Saul," He said. "Why do you persecute me?"

Saul lay on the ground shielding his eyes as he fumbled with his words. "Who are you?" he asked, trembling.

"I am Jesus, the one who you are persecuting," the voice said.

I watched in horror as I saw the rules change before my eyes. My authority over Saul was being taken away. Here He was, calling out to one of my own, and keeping me from the conversation. I was outraged and struggled to bring word of what was really happening to my friend.

"Now," the voice said "get up and ride on to Damascus. You will be told what to do once you get there."

Immediately the light and voice disappeared. Saul groveled along the ground as his men ran to his side. I too was released and rushed to Saul's aid.

"Are you ok?" one of Saul's men asked. "Are you hurt?"

"No." Saul said. He flailed around for his men, and they grabbed his arms. They lifted him onto his feet, and led him to his horse. "This light has blinded me!" Saul screamed when he realized he could not see. "What curse has befallen me?"

The men looked at each other and back at Saul. "Sir, we should return to Jerusalem. We should get you rest and restore your sight."

"No!" Saul objected. "Didn't you hear what He said?"

Saul's captain responded. "We heard, sir, but your eyes…."

"If He can come to me in this manner and take my sight, what worse fate would befall me if I don't do as He says?" The men had no argument. Loyal as they were they followed his orders and helped Saul onto his horse. "Now, guide me into Damascus, and tell no one of what has happened."

The men returned to their horses and led Saul and his mount alongside theirs. They slowly finished their journey to Damascus.

I stayed near Saul once again and tried to speak to him about what happened.

"This curse that has come upon you Saul, it is terrible," I said. "This is what you are fighting against. You are fighting against this kind of terror leveled against men who would be free. Your fight is not for the weak, but for the strong. Do not lose your will against this foe."

I continued to talk to him for the rest of the journey. But I felt his ears were as deaf to my words as his eyes were blind to the world. Saul sat on his horse remaining to himself. I could tell that though his voice was silent, there was much deliberation within his being. I fought against anything that would make him weak or despair the cause, but I was fighting a losing battle. As we approached the city gates, I got word from my associates that preparations were being made ahead of us.

"Preparations?" I asked. My associates did not know how to explain what they had discovered. So I dismissed them and decided to head into Damascus ahead of my group. I was going to see for myself what was happening inside the city limits. All I got out of my associates was that there were men prepared to take Saul in and give him comfort. These were no ordinary men. These were men of the twisted faith. I was led to the house where these men were meeting and listened in on their conversation.

There was a large man wearing a brown robe standing in front of the others. "Look, brothers," he said. "It was the Lord who told me that this man Saul was coming. And it was the Lord that told me we have to take him in and give him rest, food and shelter."

"Impossible," a short, wispy bearded man shouted. "This Saul is the very one who would have us all killed this instant if given his wish! And you want to bring him into our home?" The shorter man pulled out a knife and presented it to the man in the brown robe. "Why not run me through right now if you would have us all die. It would save us the time and trouble of having this Saul do it!"

A thin man with a curly brown beard interjected. "Quiet your foolishness," he said. "If the Lord is asking us to do this, then He will protect us. He would not bring such a man here just to destroy us. It makes no sense."

The wispy bearded man looked at the others. "The Lord would not have us destroyed, no. But is our friend here sure he heard these commands from the Lord?"

"I believe him," the thin curly bearded man said. "That should be enough for you, brother."

The wispy bearded man scoffed then acquiesced. "I have never known you to be mistaken," he said reluctantly to the man in the brown robe. "Let us hope you aren't mistaken now."

With that the men concluded their gathering and departed. I stood there uncertain of my next move. I decided Saul needed me most and returned to him. What I had learned in Damascus was unwelcome. I made every effort I could to dissuade Saul from continuing his mission. There was less and less of Saul that was open to me, and I was fighting harder with him than I had ever had to in the past. But by now, I was like a grain of sand fighting against an oncoming wave. Resist though I might, it was only a matter of time before I was washed away.

Saul and his men reached the gates of Damascus. They entered and were approached by a man named Judas. This man had great trepidation but told them that he had already set aside a place in his home for Saul and his men to rest. Though suspicious of how they knew of Saul's predicament, the men accepted the invitation. Saul remained blind, but he and his men resided with Judas for three days. Very little was said amongst them during that time. His men were made more nervous because Saul refused to eat or drink during that time. But inside of Saul much was taking place.

On the third day after Saul arrived men of the twisted faith came to the house where Saul was staying. With caution they gathered around him. After a moment they left his side and huddled together to discuss quietly what they needed to do. After deliberating there was no consensus as to the meaning of Saul's visit. There was even less agreement as to what was going happen to them because of Saul's visit. Saul could hear anticipation and dread in their words. But instead of responding to these men and their suppositions, Saul lay quietly on the bed.

As the day grew late and all those gathered were still in disagreement, a man came knocking at the door of the house of Judas. As he was welcomed in the man introduced himself.

"My name is Ananias," he said without hesitation. "And I have been told by our Lord to come here to see a man named Saul." Those gathered in the house started murmuring their curiosity. They ushered Ananias further into the home and without hesitation he walked over to where Saul was resting. He placed his hands on the head of Saul as the others looked on.

"Brother Saul," Ananias said "the Lord who appeared to you on the road outside the city has brought me here to restore your sight. He has brought me here to make you whole and fill you with His Spirit."

Immediately Saul's eyes burst open and the whole room could see that they were restored. Gasps went up among the men.

"I can see!" Saul exclaimed.

The room clamored about what had just happened. But Saul stopped them.

"Please," Saul said, sitting up. "I want to be baptized in your way."

I was speechless. Saul, my close friend for many years, had an unexplainable change in his mindset. He should have been bloodthirsty at the sight of these blasphemers. Instead he wanted to join them. He was about to abandon all that we had worked for his entire life. And all it took was a simple parlor trick by that God to effect him so dramatically. I pleaded with Saul that he should not fall into bondage.

"Don't do this!" I said. "Don't be a fool. You are a spectacular man, one of the greatest of the Jewish people. Now for the want of your sight you would give it all away and join the blaspheming of your faith? If you do this you will be shunned! I promise you will be turned away by your people! Do not throw your freedom away!" I paused, finding myself breathless and panicked. "If you do this," I threatened, "I will hunt you, and you will die."

Yet as I looked Saul square in the eyes, I could tell he dismissed everything I said. I could have screamed from the top of the roof for hours and Saul would have been deaf to my words. I cursed him, spit at his feet and left his side

The men in the house of Judas were stunned at Saul's request. They agreed, praying that it was not a rouse. Saul tried to stand but was unsteady after remaining in bed for three days. The men surrounding him helped him up and brought him to be baptized. After his baptism, Saul was given food and drink and was able to regain his strength.

I went outside the house in a rage. How could this have happened? It was because that liar and deceiver had twisted the rules! What right did He have to show himself and place His hands on Saul? Any man would have fallen for such a display. It never took much to fool these people. But Saul was not just any man. He was one of the strongest and most powerful among my allies. He was ever vigilant in his work and dedicated to my cause. In the course of a few moments he had gone from powerful ally to threatening enemy. But I was not going to be defeated because of this change. I vowed to take even greater pains to bring the world freedom. I paced the streets of Damascus cursing Saul and plotting my revenge upon him and his new God. Saul had been deep in my counsel and knew my ways. If he was allowed to spread my tactics to others, they would know how to counteract them, and my mission would become complicated. Saul had to be destroyed. Saul had to be destroyed soon.

Over the next few days I stalked Saul as I watched him convene with others of his kind in Damascus. I watched as he went to other Jewish men and women and told them of his new twisted God. He relished the chance to tell them of his experience and his newfound enlightenment. His words were made more powerful by the fact that many knew him for the persecution he had brought to these blasphemers. His testimony was rich because Saul had become one of them.

I had to act quickly. I walked the streets of Damascus and talked to many of the Jewish men and women there myself. I told them about the true intentions of Saul and how he was going to destroy their religion and their God. I told them how he had intended to bring down centuries of tradition and culture. I told them that he was the greatest deceiver among the blasphemers because he planned this conversion for years. I told them that as long as he walked among them they were not safe, and that something had to be done. They had to kill Saul.

My words were powerful and within a couple of days a plot was devised to capture and kill Saul. Warning of this approaching storm reached Saul and he went into hiding within Damascus. Those that heard my words were not fooled by Saul's sudden disappearance. When he could not be found sentries were posted at the city gates to ensure that Saul did not escape from their grasp. The streets were patrolled diligently. I went from man to man, reinforcing the necessity of finding, capturing and killing Saul before too much time passed. Those following me were in a fervor to find and kill him. Their lust for his blood was insatiable.

Yet for all their effort Saul could not be found. He remained hidden with others of the twisted faith. These blasphemers that protected Saul were uneasy and panicked for his safety. But Saul was not worried. Saul remained calm and still until he knew it was time to act. One week after going into hiding Saul conferred with the others in the dusk of the day.

"Saul," one man said. "It is too dangerous for you here. As the days go on, more and more of our fellow Jews become inspired to capture you. Hiding you is not a permanent solution. One day they will find you."

"I agree, brother," Saul said. "But we must have patience. I believe God will show us a way for me to be free of this place."

A woman approached Saul. "I believe he may already have shown us a way." She said. "As I walked the city today, I noticed a section in the near eastern wall that has a hole large enough to fit a man through. They have no patrols nearby, and I believe that if we tie some rope to one of our large baskets, we should be able to lower you through to the ground. There are horses outside the city walls, and you should be able to take one unnoticed and escape."

"I don't like it," then man said. "We would be too exposed if someone did notice. And then there would be no place to run."

Saul smiled to the woman. "It's definitely unique." He paused. "I think we should try it tonight."

With that the men and Saul gathered up supplies and, after night had fallen and darkness set in, they followed the woman to the section of the near eastern wall.

"This is it," she said.

"It's as beautiful as you described." Saul replied with a grin. He greeted each member of their group warmly in the name of their God and bid them farewell. They fastened the rope and the basket. Saul gingerly got in and smiled. "It makes me feel like a loaf of bread."

The men gathered the rope and slowly lowered him down. I approached these blasphemers after coming from a rally of more men to my aide. My eyes widened as I recognized Saul and realized what was happening. I shouted for them to stop but knew they would ignore me. They continued nervously lowering Saul while keeping a watchful eye all around. I was in a panic. I ran towards the places where some of my sentries had been posted and tried to get them to recognize what was going on by the near eastern wall. But men are weak, and many of them ignored me because of the lateness of the hour or being engrossed by other thoughts. I slammed my feet to the ground when I knew that Saul would get away without a bit of resistance. I was once again left the loser because of these weak, stupid creatures.

I returned to the near eastern wall to find that everyone had dispersed. I peered through the opening and caught a glimpse of Saul galloping into the distance on horseback. I followed him all the way to Jerusalem where I knew he was going to join up with members of the twisted faith. I had failed in Damascus but I had an opportunity to redeem myself in Jerusalem. If I could turn some of the blasphemers against Saul then I could flush him out. If those men thought he was a spy or a traitor, then perhaps their rejection would do just as well as killing him. If he were to be rejected by the Jewish people as well as those of the twisted faith, then he would be utterly alone and useless. I raced to where the members of the twisted faith were gathered. I came into their midst and waited for Saul's arrival.

Those of the twisted faith in Jerusalem knew of the change to Saul. Some of them were thrilled and grateful that he had come to their side and would no longer be hunting them. But others were wary of his conversion and thought it was a trick to destroy them. Those still suspicious were not going to give up their view easily. When Saul arrived at their place of meeting and pronounced his desire to join them, many of these members looked upon him as a liar. This confounded those that were happy for Saul's conversion. They wondered if they had in fact been fooled. This was my opportunity to cause more confusion and chaos and to brand Saul a liar and an enemy forever.

Saul burst through the door. "Brothers and sisters," he said. I come to you in the name of our Lord. I ask that you would give me sanctuary and rest. I have been traveling from Damascus where I was being hunted."

The men and women looked at Saul with misgiving. A few murmured that his presence there was dangerous. But they brought him into the house and closed the door. I recognized my opening.

"Here is Saul!" I shouted to all the gathered blasphemers. "He says he wants to join you and to be one with your God! But his desire is to murder each and every one of you. He does not want to worship as you do! For years he has been a defender of his faith, filling the prisons and the graves with your people. And now he wants to suddenly switch his allegiances? He is filled with lies! He has come to destroy you! Be gone with him, before he finds more room in the graves for you and your families!"

Many felt my words. As their hearts were penetrated with these thoughts, these men and women could no longer hold their decorum. They had to reject and denounce Saul as he stood in front of them.

"You are a murderer and a liar," one angry man shouted. "You would have us all lay down like lambs at your feet. With one hand you would cradle our heads, and with the other you would cut our throats!"

"You are a disgrace to God," another shouted. "You know nothing of the true faith!"

"We are not fools that will simply believe you after all you have done," a woman added. "You are the enemy!"

Saul was dismayed at what he heard. He knew his past actions were horrendous. But he wanted to be forgiven of that past in light of his new decision. He thought of arguing with them but as he looked at the faces of those that were yelling, and the faces of those that remained silent, he knew that it would be better to leave than to confront. Saul sat among them and contemplated his next move. He could feel the eyes of the men and women staring down at him. He felt all alone. I had done my job.

As Saul hung his head he felt a pull on his arm. He looked up and was lifted to his feet. A man by the name of Barnabas had grabbed Saul and dragged him out of the house.

"They are angry at you," he said as they walked out the door and away from the house. "And can you blame them?" Saul looked sheepishly away.

"No," Saul replied. "But I just want them to believe that I was sent by the Lord. They don't have to believe me. But they must believe Him."

"Well, I believe Him and you," Barnabas said dryly. "The others will come around too. But they need some assurance."

Barnabas continued to lead Saul through the streets of Jerusalem. "Where are you taking me?" Saul asked

"I am taking you to that assurance." I followed as Barnabas led Saul to those they called apostles. Barnabas brought and presented Saul to them. I watched as Barnabas told Saul's story with great passion. I watched as Saul himself recounted his prior deeds against the blasphemers and the how he had been transformed on the way to Damascus. I read the faces of the apostles and thought there was no way they would accept Saul as one of their own. But I was deceived. They unanimously agreed that Saul should be one of them. Moreover, they all claimed to feel the call of their God to accept Saul and know that he was true. The story of Saul ended as the apostles accepted him and took him as one of their own.

At that moment it was over for me. I would not get to Saul, at least not for a while. I lamented the loss of a great ally. But I knew that I could not let this setback deter me. I needed to focus on bringing freedom to others and stop wasting my time on this one man. For now

I would leave Saul and allow my associates to keep an ever watchful eye on him.

Saul went on to serve those of the twisted faith well. But I will never forget how he threw away his freedom. I will never forget how he so desperately wanted into bondage. I will never forget how he had everything he could have wanted in this world, and how he choose persecution and chains over freedom and control. It is a cautionary tale for anyone that would risk freedom. It is a tale that I hope you understand.

The flames of the campfire died down as I felt anger fill my heart. Richard obviously wanted to put himself in a good light but if I believed all that he said then I could see him as nothing but a murderer. It was he that was to blame for so many deaths and so much pain. I marveled at how he could sit there and expect me to believe that God was the liar and the deceiver, when Richard was the one orchestrating the persecution and destruction that came to God's people. Richard was more foolish than I had thought. His thinly veiled attempts to transfer blame were not going to make me run from my God.

Richard stood up and walked around the campfire. He stood proudly and defiantly as the glow of the fire bounced off his face. I was growing tired of his arrogance. I rose to my feet.

"You stand there so full of yourself," I said to Richard as he looked at me smugly. "You think that I am going to blame God and renounce Him? You think I would do that when you just told me that you are the one responsible for the persecution of the people of God? You encouraged the persecution. You directed it. It is by your hand that men died." I spoke clearly and directly and let my tone become lower and much colder. "I know one thing for certain. There is no way I will believe anything you have to say to me about God or his people. You are the liar. You are the deceiver. You are the murderer."

"You are angry," Richard said calmly. "That's good. But you should not direct your anger toward me."

"I shouldn't?" I questioned indignantly "Then I suppose you want me to be angry with God. I already told you that will never happen. How would you ever even begin to prove to me that God is worthy of my scorn?"

Richard silently and slowly walked back to his seat. He let my question hang in the air. He sat down, took a deep breath, and began to speak.

"Now that you have heard truth from me you don't want to trust me. You think that my story proves that I am a false witness. You say that it is I, not another, that lies to men. You say that I that deceive them. I understand your thinking. It makes sense since you do not understand."

I stood over the fire and fixed my gaze on Richard. "What don't I understand?"

"You do not understand the rules," Richard continued. "Everybody has rules. There are rules for you. There are rules for me. And there is One that makes the rules."

"You mean God." I said

"That's right," Richard said. "The One you call God - the One I call the Deceiver - is the one that makes the rules. And the rules are what we are required to exist under.

"It seems to me that you don't follow the rules," I said.

"Oh I follow the rules," Richard said assuredly. "But the rules are not based on right and wrong. The rules are based on position. The position you have, the position I have, and the position God has. Now there are many rules. Some are sweeping unbreakable rules, while others are minor, pliable, not often used rules. But of all the various rules, there are two that tower over all the rest."

"Oh really," I asked sarcastically. "And what might they be?"

Richard looked at me as his face became deadly serious. "The first rule is that your God has providence over everything in creation. You, me, this planet…He has providence over it all. Of this there is no question and no rescinding. The second rule, and be very clear on this, is that He cannot look upon sin without punishing it. He cannot look on evil and allow it to go unpunished because it is so abhorrent to Him. He has had that rule as long as any other."

"I am aware of these truths," I said cautiously.

"Good," Richard replied. "Then I say to you that your God is a liar and a deceiver. If He has providence over all as you have agreed, then He should be able to control the things he doesn't approve of, such as evil."

"But He chooses to allow certain things under His providence." I said.

"Which is acceptable. If your God chooses to allow evil, then by His own rule He must punish it."

"Which He does," I said.

"And yet here you sit in front of me, unpunished." Richard said. I gave Richard a confused stare. "Don't look at me as if you don't know," he said. "You have committed many evils in His sight since you were a small child. You have lied before, haven't you? You have stolen a little thing here or a trinket there? You have looked lustfully on a woman walking down the street. All are evil in His eyes and all require severe punishment. Yet you have not been punished for them, have you?"

"Yes, I deserve punishment," I said. "But you and I both know why I will not be punished. I will not be punished because of Jesus...."

"Now stop that ridiculous line of thinking," Richard interrupted. "That seems to be the only argument your kind ever has. You can't really believe that fairy tale they tell Sunday School children about one man able to save all others that have ever lived. You're smarter than that!"

"I do believe it," I said.

"Then you are going to be terribly let down when you die," Richard scolded. "But what I am about to tell you about these rules can change that."

I wanted to tell Richard more about why I was so confident, but my mind began to wander and some confusion set in. I tried to pray and settle myself, but I could not focus. I didn't know why I was having such a hard time thinking or presenting my case. I thought it best to wait until later when I could present a better argument. "Fine then," I said dismissively. "What about the rules."

"The rules that your God has created for Himself are specific. Yet He has broken them countless times. In order to have providence one must exhibit control over it. If your God has providence over everything, then He should be able to crush evil with no problem. Yet evil persists and runs amok. If your God allows evil then He is abdicating His responsibility to protect His creatures. So either he has broken the first rule and does not really have providence and is a liar, or He is a manipulator and likes to see his creatures suffer. Either option is not pleasant."

"No, it's not" I said.

"But the breaking of the second rule is more insidious. If you God cannot look upon evil without punishing it, then He has been woefully behind on His duties. Either He can look upon evil without punishing it, in which case He is a liar, or He cannot and chooses to deceive some by not punishing others. For He has chosen to speak with, engage with and in some cases meet face to face with many men, all suffering from the same disease of sin and evil. He even became close with these men, in direct opposition to His own rule! He proved that He is either a liar or a fraud. No matter how you look at it He is not entirely truthful in what He says. He is downright misleading and deceitful. It is He that puts people in bondage through manipulation and dishonest coercion. It is He that has fear of losing people out of his bondage and His control. He fears the freedom I offered them. He fears the freedom I offer you."

Thoughts were whirling in my mind and I was becoming more confused. I was trying to deny what Richard was saying with what I knew to be the truth. But I couldn't seem to clear my mind enough to rebuke him. That's when I said the only thing I could muster. "But Jesus said..."

"If you try and claim Jesus," Richard interrupted, "then you have just as big of a problem. If you claim that man Jesus and your evil was never punished, then your God probably never had a problem with evil in the first place. If you still get punished after claiming Jesus then what really was the point of claiming that man anyhow? The truth is it's all one big deception. It is a deception that I want to rescue you from."

To my relief Richard finally stopped talking. But my mind was still set in confusion. I knew that I should be able to reconcile what Richard was saying to what I knew was truth. But I was having great trouble. I knew that God has providence and that within His providence He allows certain things. It is through His will and His power that He allows certain things to happen so that we might depend on Him. But Richard made a good point when he wondered why God would allow us to suffer if He really had providence. Was it just for His enjoyment? Were we in a sense playthings with the ultimate purpose to provide Him entertainment? Anything less than full providence truly meant God had lied.

I also knew that God despises sin and evil. He must punish it and this is a fact. But I also knew that God can come to and comfort, confront or engage with His very creation, even if it is fallen and evil. This is a basic tenant of who He is. This did not replace the punishment. But I did have to ask myself why it seemed so very infrequent today that evil was punished. Was it possible that God was behind on His responsibility to punish evil? Even worse, had God led us all to believe that he must punish evil when in reality punishment is not at all necessary?

Richard was in my head and I wanted him out. I tried to pray but continued to find that my mind was racing and I was unable to settle down. I looked at Richard and his face showed concern. But I knew underneath he was smiling. I tried to focus on Jesus with the thought that focusing on Him would calm my mind. But all I heard was Richard's retort of Jesus. Richard said that Jesus was a deception. Either Jesus could be used to get out of punishment and therefore punishment was never necessary, or punishment would still come and Jesus was a rouse. It was all so ludicrous in light of my knowledge of the truth. But sitting in front of the campfire and watching Richard it all started to make sense to me. I started to feel as though there might have been chains on me. Chains from God.

I tried to shake those terrible thoughts. I had to remember that Richard was using semantics to confuse me. This had to be true, even though I was having difficulty finding flaws in his argument. If Richard was who he said he was, then I knew that I should not believe a word from him. All that he said was formed and dusted with lies. Yet if I was going to believe that then I was going to have to believe that Richard had lived it and seen it firsthand. I was afraid because if only one thing Richard said were true, then the entire system I had come to believe and understand would crumble. I had to prove Richard wrong.

Once again I became keenly aware of the anchor inside of me. It felt heavy and painful. The difference was this time it was much greater than last. Perhaps that was why my mind could not be clear. I had to spend so much energy ignoring the anchor that pulled me down that I could not devote my full attention to my arguments. As the anchor pulled I felt the despair and desperation rise up in me. There was little I could do to stop the hopelessness that had replaced my joy and patience. I finally realized the words Richard spoke were not only directed at me.

Richard was also speaking to the anchor I carried inside. He wanted to affect its pull and show me that there were more immediate things to dedicate myself to than my God. The words that he spoke to me sounded like truth, while the truth I knew all my life felt stale and diseased.

I looked over at Richard. He had been staring at me the entire time. "You are a liar," I barked at him as I returned his gaze.

"Is that what you think?" Richard asked mockingly. "Is that what your intellect tells you? Is that what your heart tells you? No, you don't believe that I am a liar. Your heart is heavy, isn't it? Give in to that feeling. Understand it. Allow it to be the gateway to your freedom."

Richard's words echoed in my ears and rang true in my heart. I hated that he wanted to tell me more. But I needed to hear more. I was not done with Richard, though I wished he had never come.

CHAPTER 10

The night grew darker as the air hung heavy with dread. I had come prepared for the weather and had layers blanketing me. But it didn't matter what I had on because I was cold. I was cold not from the weather but from deep inside. The cold I felt came from a place that was foreign to me. It came from the man sitting across from me.

The campfire had become a pile of glowing embers. I stood up and picked up several pieces of brush and some logs near the fire. Carefully, I placed them on top of the embers, hoping to reignite the waning flames. Richard sat stoically and allowed me to prepare the fire and contemplate in silence. As I finished and turned around, he stretched out his hands towards the heat and rubbed them together. He was calm and deliberate about it, as though he were in ultimate control.

I walked back towards the mighty oak that had been my comfort and protection that evening. I sat down beside it and leaned up against it. I felt it push back against me as it held me up during my moments of dread. I tried to reach out and grab the warmth from the fire. To my dismay the heat only warmed my physical being and eluded the chill that was within my soul. I rubbed my hands together and shoved them back in my jacket pockets. The chill was bad enough. But the anchor was making the evening unbearable.

With each passing moment the weight of the anchor became more and more painful. Earlier in the evening, I had been able to put the weight out of my mind, only to have it jump back in when doubt or fear arose. But now the weight was ever present. It was a constant reminder that with each word out of Richard's mouth, my impenetrable faith was being assaulted, and the solid rock on which I placed my faith felt ever crumbling.

Once again I wanted to run. It wanted to leave and rid myself of this man. I thought that if I could get far enough away and not be able to hear his voice, that I would be free of all doubts, of all fears, and of all anxieties. I thought that if I could make him go away, then the weight that was pulling on my soul would cease to be a bother. I wanted the anchor to go back where it was before this evening. I wanted it to be jammed into the rocks of my past where it had sat for so many years. I wanted this so badly, for when it was there I could at least pretend to be content, happy and unencumbered. Back then I was ignorant of the weight that was holding me down. But Richard had made me aware of it. Richard wanted it to pull me down.

But I couldn't run. I couldn't leave, and I couldn't make Richard go away. I was stuck there with him, not out of his desire and calling but out of mine. For what he had opened up inside of me in these last few hours was paradoxical, for it repulsed me while drawing me in deeper. I needed to hear more. I wanted to believe that I needed to hear more so that I could refute and rebuke everything that passed from Richard's lips. But the truth was that I needed to hear more because it fed my doubts. At this moment doubts were my only companions.

I watched the fire as the new wood started to burn and the flames leapt back into the air. It was apparent Richard was not going to start talking unless I said something first. "Is that the only reason you came here," I asked him across the flames. I tried to keep the appearance of certainty in my faith. "Did you come to tell me old bedtime stories? Because if it is then you are wasting your time." I mustered the best look of confidence that I could. By the reflection in Richard's eyes told me I was unconvincing.

"There have been many times in the past that I have been told I was wasting my time," Richard replied. He picked up a stick off the ground and started fiddling with it. "But as is usually the case, what seems like a waste of time always pays dividends."

"It won't tonight," I said.

"Undoubtedly it won't," Richard replied in mock agreement. "But it humors me to try." Richard paused for a moment, throwing the stick into the fire. "You never asked me what happened to Saul."

"I don't need to," I said. "he changed his name to Paul to reflect the change that had taken place in his heart because of God. He traveled to many lands and spread the word of God. He told of his conversion experience and how his life was dramatically changed. Through God's divine inspiration, Paul went on to write half of the New Testament. He wrote and preached under some very adverse conditions. The man was one of the greatest servants of God. He is a hero of the faith and a man to be admired. I already know what happened to Saul, so I don't need a history lesson."

"Maybe you don't," Richard said. "But it's not a history lesson I want to give you. What you deserve is to know more about the man you call Paul. Just because he betrayed me doesn't mean I completely gave up on him. As a matter of fact, once his betrayal was complete I gave him special attention. I spent a lot of time with Paul. You haven't heard these stories but you can be assured they are quite true."

The flames once again jumped to life.

"One of Saul's most curious decisions was to change his name to Paul. He told those that questioned the change that he felt that he needed to take a name that would he identify him with his new faith. He felt that there was nothing more symbolic than to be transformed by casting off the old name that people identified with the murderous aggressor Saul and into the new Paul who followed the so called salvation and life. That is what he claimed.

But I knew the truth. I knew why Paul really changed his name. In one of His first acts of aggression against his newly bound minion, Paul's God forced him to change his name. There was no question that it was never Paul's decision. It was simply a command that Paul's God gave him in order to show who was really in charge. And like a lemming Paul followed blindly. It was enough to make me sick.

But Paul had chosen this way of life. It served him right to have to go through such humiliation. I knew firsthand that Paul was going to suffer many more humiliations under the leadership of this God. Paul was going to have to suffer more than he would have ever dreamed under my guidance. He was going to have to do it willingly, or his new God would be offended and angry that Paul didn't suffer with joy.

It was around the time that Saul changed his name to Paul that he started to travel. I called back my associates and decided to travel alongside Paul myself. I knew he would not hear me as he once did. But I knew that I could follow him and know what he was doing. I needed to know if and where there were any cracks in his new armor. I wanted to see if there was any way I could slip through and confer with Paul as I once had with Saul.

One thing about Paul that didn't change was his drive to go forth and change what he thought was wrong. He continued that in his new life. For two years Paul traveled and preached his newfound faith throughout the land. He traveled with the same Barnabas that had rescued him from the home of the angry blasphemers. During their travels they covered a lot of area and visited many cities. They went through the ancient cities of Cypress, Perga, Iconium, Lystra, Attalia, Pisidia Antioch and Derbe all in a short amount of time. The names may mean little to you but their point was clear. Paul was getting around. The message Paul preached was reaching the outside world, though many of those that heard it paid it little attention.

But even one man accepting Paul's message was a blow to me. As I traveled with Paul I was dismayed to see that he was gaining enough converts to keep him pushing forward. The passion and drive that he had shown in hunting down these same people mere months earlier served him well now but was sad to watch. After traveling and preaching for two years, Paul and his companion Barnabas decided to settle in Antioch. They took residence and decided to focus their efforts there. I found there I was presented with an opportunity to finally confront Paul and make him reconsider his decision to leave me and forgo his freedom.

Paul stayed in Antioch and continued his work for two years. I traded time at Paul's side with one of my associates and remained abreast of Paul's situation. I knew that the time would come for me to reintroduce myself fully to my old friend. That moment finally came as Paul was confronted with a challenge to his very faith. And it came in the most unlikely of challengers. An old friend and fellow follower of his God, a man by the name of Peter, brought complications to Paul.

It was late one morning and Paul had been preaching as he was accustomed in a prominent part of the city. He stood on stone steps as he looked out over the marketplace and buildings reflecting the late morning sun. A crowd had gathered around him. In that crowd there were some who intently listened to his words while others derided what he said in their hearts. Paul was feeling strong that morning as he belted out words that persuaded others to come to his faith. He was as convincing as always with his smart sounding rhetoric and ease of speech. When the words left his lips they hung over the crowd ready to infect their latest victims.

As Paul was preaching he saw a man at the back edge of the crowd. The man was clearly anxious and filled with a single purpose as he pushed at people and disrupted their concentration. Paul was still speaking but most of his attention was on this man who made little effort to avoid disruption. As the man came closer Paul recognized that it was his companion Barnabas. Barnabas' face was older, rough and covered with a chocolate brown beard from ear to ear. The Face of Barnabas was red and let Paul know that there was important news that needed to be rushed to Paul's station. Barnabas was frantically making his way towards Paul which made Paul stumble through his words as he questioned in his mind why Barnabas was there. Barnabas had been preaching in another part of the city, so his arrival was more than unexpected. Paul quickly and abruptly wrapped up what he was saying and the crowd began to disperse.

"Paul!" Barnabas called out, weaving his way through the exiting crowd. "Paul!" Barnabas finally reached where Paul was standing, and grabbed him by the shoulder.

"It is good to see you, brother," Paul said. "Why have you returned so soon?"

"We have a problem," Barnabas said breathlessly.

"What kind of problem?" Paul asked.

"On the other side of the city, where I was preaching, there are men – men from Jerusalem – and they have come to preach as well."

"Do they come in the name of the Lord?" Paul asked.

"They say they do," Barnabas replied. "They say they preach as we preach."

"That seems like a wonderful thing," Paul said "It's just curious that we weren't notified about their arrival."

"That's just it," Barnabas said. "I believe we weren't notified because they came on their own. I don't think the brothers in Jerusalem knew these men were headed here. And I think I know why."

Barnabas and Paul decided to head to where these new men had been preaching. As they walked Barnabas told Paul about the disturbing way those men preached. Those men believed that following Paul's God was open and free to all, just as Paul and Barnabas had been preaching. But they believed there were certain physical steps that needed to be taken before Paul's God would accept them. To that point, these new men were preaching that the old ways of circumcision had to be entered into by each and every man wanting to come to Paul's God. This was not the tenant of Paul or Barnabas, nor was it the tenant of any they knew back in Jerusalem. This new teaching concerned both of them.

Paul and Barnabas found where those new men were preaching and listened. Much of what they preached was identical to their own teachings. Paul and Barnabas thought all was well with the preaching of these new men until they heard the necessity of circumcision creep out of their mouths. Paul and Barnabas immediately felt their hearts sink as they felt this was a step away from the truth. Paul wanted to interrupt and confront them immediately. Baranabas suggested patience and choosing a more appropriate time for confrontation. They decided to wait until the two men were finished preaching.

Paul and Barnabas approached as the men finished preaching and the crowd dispersed. There was one tall man and one short man, and they stood as brothers of the message. Paul could tell that the two were freshly from Jerusalem by their dress and their manner. This stirred Paul to speak to them as one would speak to a new convert.

"Men of Jerusalem," Paul said. "I come to you in the name of our Lord."

The men looked at Paul and Barnabas with recognition in their eyes. "Hello," the taller man said. "It is a delight to finally get to meet the great Paul and Barnabas!"

Paul looked at Barnabas quizzically and then back to the taller man. "You know of us?"

"Most certainly!" the taller man exclaimed. "Your tales have traveled to the brothers in Jerusalem."

"We know of your glorious preaching and conversion," the shorter man interjected excitedly. "It is an honor to meet and be able to preach in the same city as you both!"

Paul and Barnabas were taken aback, but grateful that their work had been noticed. "It is nice to know that the message is getting around," Paul said. "But I am sorry to say we had no knowledge of you coming to Antioch. We are of course thankful to have others of the faith here to help."

Paul took a moment and considered his next words carefully. But before he could speak Barnabas' voice was heard. "It's great that you both are here. However, we think you may be confusing some people."

"Confusing people?" the shorter man asked. "What do you mean?"

"What he means to say," Paul interjected, "is that your message is not entirely accurate with what the Lord teaches."

"It's not?" the shorter man said with concern. "We preach the same message you preach. How are we different?"

"It's about the circumcision," Barnabas said directly. "You are telling people they have to be circumcised in order to be saved by God. That is simply not true."

"How can you say that?" The taller man said indignantly. "The covenant with Abraham was circumcision, and that should be carried out by every new believer!"

"Now we are not saying circumcision is bad," Paul said, trying to calm the situation. "It's just that we think it is not the necessity as you say it is."

The four men stood continued to argue their perspective. Each held tightly to their view and cited history, tradition and teachings. They all refused to accept the position of the others. Paul finally decided that there was no progress being made and thought it best to end the argument.

"We do not need to bicker like this," he said. "Maybe it's best if we bring this back to Jerusalem. We can discuss it further there."

All four men agreed to this solution. The two new men were still surprised by the overreaction of Paul and Barnabas to their seemingly solid teaching. Before the two men left they explained that there were others among the brethren that viewed circumcision as necessary as well. This came as a surprise to Paul and Barnabas. They all went on their way and agreed to meet in Jerusalem in a week's time.

I stood by quietly and was pleased to see what was happening. None of these men could get their stories straight and agree on a common belief. Nothing delighted me more than to see the beginnings of their small coalition coming apart so quickly. If they were going to bicker over this, then it was going to be simple to make them bicker over any number of other points of their faith. And when the world saw them bickering, it would no doubt turn away from their message and embrace the freedom I offered. These blasphemers were going to do more for my goals than I had been able to do in quite some time. That made me happy and hopeful.

I was excited to see how this was going to blow up. I made it a point to watch what happened when the main players took their sides in Jerusalem. I must admit that I was excited because I figured I wouldn't have to do anything but sit back and enjoy the show. The thing about quarrels such as these is that they always seem to serve me well in the end. People take a position or hold on so very tightly to something that they become blinded to the bigger picture. The more somebody pushes for what they believe, no matter how insignificant, the more they dig their heels in on the issue. It becomes a matter of pride and a person will cause what was a peripheral concept to tear apart relationships and destroy unity. This dissension was going to show these believers in God that their faith was fruitless because all it did was cause disarray and discord. And I was going to be there to pick up the pieces.

The four men traveled to Jerusalem to meet with the other brothers. It had been some time since Paul had been back in Jerusalem, and he was excited to see the familiar sights and people that he had left behind. But his excitement was tempered because he knew that his return was not expected and the topic at hand was not going to be easily deciphered.

Though I was with these men on their travels I did not interject my own opinions into their discussions. I had faith that these men could tear each other apart with their own words. Paul, Barnabas and the two other men reached the gates of Jerusalem. They entered and soon found their way to the house of their friends. The four men were tired and hungry from their travels and evening was coming quickly coming upon the city.

A man by the name of Peter greeted the weary travelers as they approached the house. He was a slender and stood tall and pale. He wore a short, thick curled brown beard which he was fond of molding with his fingers. Peter was not impressive in size but was unmistakable in presence. He was a man that was firm and stood with assurance, like a rock in the sea against oncoming waves.

"Paul, it is good to see you," Peter said as he hugged and kissed Paul on the cheeks. "Barnabas," Peter said cordially, nodding his head towards Barnabas as Barnabas nodded back. "Please, come inside."

Peter ushered them into his home. Standing inside the house was James, a shorter, stouter man and John, a man of similar height to James but of less weight. Paul and Barnabas greeted each man as one would an old friend. Dinner and rest was then given to the travelers. A table was prepared which held a bevy of food and drink. This followed a long standing custom among their people when welcoming back friends who have been gone for long periods. As the five men sat on the floor around the table, each shared highlights of their ministries since they had last been together.

I stayed in a corner of the house and suffered through the seemingly endless talk of joy and contentment they felt doing the work of their God. I was surprised at just how manipulated they had been as to think that they could be happy as prisoners and slaves of such a malicious God. I even recall one of the men using the word "servant" to describe their work and being happy to have the privilege of being a servant of this God. The proceedings turned my stomach so that I nearly left several times. But I knew I needed to remain. The time finally came when dinner was finished and Paul unveiled his purpose for coming.

"Your hospitality has been more than we could have expected," Paul said to his hosts. "But you know I come here for more than just food and fellowship." Paul took a moment to collect his thoughts.

"From the moment I heard you were coming back I knew it was for a very special purpose," Peter said filling the silence. "Paul does not leave his post unless there is something amiss." Barnabas nodded knowingly.

"We have come into a bit of distress," Paul began. "We met some of the brothers preaching the word of God to those in the city of Antioch. We were thrilled that they had joined us there because we know that a great movement is at work within that city. More men like these are needed to preach the word. We know their hearts are with God."

"Indeed," Peter replied. "We sent them out in order to supplement what you were doing. I am sorry I could not get word to you sooner, but the call for them was great and we needed to get them in place as quickly as possible."

"I thank you for them," Paul replied. "After talking to them I was sure you had sent them. But that is what bothered me." Paul stood up straighter and a serious look took hold of his face. Peter, James and John looked quizzically at him. "Those two men did preach the word. But they also were preaching something troubling. They were preaching that in order to be fully saved they need to follow the Jewish law of circumcision. They were telling people that anything short of that will cause them to fall short of a true relationship with God."

Peter looked at James and John, and then back at Paul and Barnabas. "We know of this belief," Peter stated. "We have been over this ourselves. You know there are those that say that God will accept all. But the Abrahamic covenant is still applicable. We do not want to throw away the original covenant because to do so is to deny what God has crafted with our people. And I agree with them."

"But Peter," Barnabas interjected. "You know after the Lord came everything changed."

"Did it?" James interrupted. "Does all that has happened with the Lord mean that all that came before Him is for naught? Our people have always followed the covenant of circumcision. Should those that have come into the fold that were not born into our tradition not also follow God's law?"

"I'm not saying that one will not be accepted by God if you do not follow the law of circumcision," Peter said. "But where does the law stand now that things have changed? Does it means nothing?"

"Certainly not," Paul said defensively. "But you cannot predicate a man's eternal life on a simple physical act! Nor can you take that life away if he doesn't take that step. To do so would be to undermine all that was taught to us and all that we are preaching."

The table grew quiet as each man considered what the other said. I relished this argument and could feel the tension growing in the room. Though they did not show it outwardly, I could sense the creeping feeling of being attacked that was in each man. I knew that it would only be a matter of time before they allowed this issue to become an even bigger distraction. I knew that this could ultimately destroy their alliance and bring them to the brink of collapse. I was pleased.

While all this was taking place John had been sitting silently. He had been listening to the conversation and considering each argument. Not long after the table went quiet he decided to speak.

"As I see it, gentlemen, the question comes down to this," John said. "When we say a man must be circumcised, we are saying that God's covenant with Abraham was right and true. But when we say he does not need to be circumcised, we are saying that what has changed allows everybody to come by a simple confession. This could be a step in denying who God was in the past. The question that we must answer is, does God change? Has He changed the rules of the game, and if so, can He be trusted if He can change the rules?"

I sat there in the corner and was stunned at what I had heard. I was with these men, watching what they were doing, but I had not taken the time to speak to any of them. Yet here they were, bickering amongst themselves, and somehow stumbling over the one truth that I had been trying to get across to people for centuries. They had discovered that this God they were serving was a manipulator. They were on the precipice of grasping that He would change the rules in a heartbeat. I knew that they were mere moments away from discovering the totality of what I had known for all time – that this God could not be trusted, and that they would secure their freedom only through a decisive and entire rejection of Him and His ways. I waited breathlessly for that moment. I waited for them to continue arguing, for feelings and hopes to get hurt, for dreams to be crushed and for the leaders of this new faith to define it as an abject failure.

But as is the way with men, I was wholly disappointed.

"It seems," Peter said, "that this is a matter for the whole congregation. We should bring it and discuss it with everyone. We should all be together when we decide."

The others agreed and it was settled. They concluded their time together and sent out word that the next day the whole congregation was going to meet to discuss this issue. I was saddened that they had to wait. I knew that this was a setback but definitely not a defeat. I still had the opportunity to influence people. I wanted to influence Paul even though he had denied me for so long. I decided to lay out my case to my old friend. I waited until it was very late that evening and went to talk to Paul alone. It had been a long time since we spoke but I knew he would recognize my voice.

Paul was staying alone in a room on the upper level of the same house. I entered to find him in contemplative thought as he sat on his bed. I slowly came in, sat next to him, and draped my arm over his shoulders. Paul must have felt my presence because he looked up with a jolt. The room was small and dark, lit only by a single lamp of oil. I felt that Paul was uneasy as the shadows danced against the walls.

"Paul old friend," I whispered. "I wish that you would hear me. These men that teach the way of circumcision, they mean no harm. In fact, they are strong in their faith, and strong in their belief. Would you risk losing them over the simple matter of circumcision? Would you risk losing valiant soldiers simply because they have a different view on an insignificant issue. If they teach acceptance through this practice, who would it hurt? And are you even sure that you are right in your belief? You say your God is not a liar yet insist that His covenant, brought to you through Abraham and Moses, is meaningless. Would you not then split your people by setting brother against brother in this debate? Give up the need to change this principle. Allow the men to preach as they would, as long as they preach. Isn't that the ultimate goal?"

Paul looked in my direction, right past me and at the shadows blanketing the walls. I do not know what he saw, but I could tell that turmoil was brewing inside of him. He was near tears, and I was hopeful that he would give in to my words and turn in for the night, able to rest and absorb what I had said. But being the man that he was, he chose differently. Paul slipped off of his bed. He pressed his knees hard against the wooden floor, impressing the image of the wood into his flesh. He clenched his hands together and cried out with his spirit to his God. It was as if he was trying to purge his soul of what he heard from me. He bent his head and muttered to his God for relief. I talked to him further with my words of comfort and assurance. But Paul was closed off to me. I went on like this for an hour with every method I knew. But Paul continued to pray and eventually I gave up. I could not break Paul, but I was going to be at the gathering in the morning, and I was going to make sure there was no agreement. I left Paul to suffer with his God in the darkness.

Morning broke and I waited for the congregation to join me. They arrived in small groups, and after all had settled they numbered near one hundred. Paul and Peter stood at the head of the congregation and explained their dilemma.

"Men of Jerusalem," Peter said, "A time has come that we must settle a dispute amongst our people. A time has come to understand a truth from our Lord. We must talk about the need for the new believers to be circumcised."

Immediately a loud murmuring went throughout the crowd. Each squawked their opinions to the others. Some voices were directed at nobody in particular with the hope that everyone would hear. I reveled in the disorder, and frolicked amongst the group as arguments broke out. The cacophony of noise grew too much for Paul, and he raised his arms.

"Brothers please," Paul said. "Please, we must have order!"

The men took notice of Paul and quieted down. One man who had come in with a large contingency stood up and addressed the gathering.

"Since the time of Abraham, and through Moses, circumcision has been vital. It has identified us! If we are to remain true to our God, then it must be made certain that all coming to Him agree with circumcision." His group cheered him, and others voiced their objections while shaking their heads in disapproval.

Another man on the opposite side of the room stood up. He was a small man, but had a booming voice. "The law is dead," he said. "We are no longer slaves to it. What was good for Abraham and Moses was good in their time, but it is not good for us!" His men cheered him while others disagreed.

I was in my element. These men went back and forth, giving their stances and proof for their beliefs. Nothing much had changed since the day before save for the fact that now there were more people to argue. I played my part and urged certain members one way while suggesting others take the opposing view. I took great joy in the disunity and the discord that was unraveling amidst this otherwise tight unit of believers. As each member's pride swelled, it became easier and easier to get them to discount their neighbor and believe only in what they wanted. I kept working the room, until each man had his say. Hours passed as the debate continued and nothing was decided. Nobody was swayed from their opinion, and people were beginning to question the loyalty of those in the opposing camp. The congregation was on the verge of collapse. Like a house of cards, I was a simple breath away from blowing the whole thing into an unidentifiable pile that would lay filthy upon the ground.

My hope was turned to fear when from across the room I felt Peter releasing his control and asking his God to intervene. Peter was begging with his heart that his God would bring wisdom to this unruly gathering. I stopped what I was doing and rushed to Peter's side to disrupt his prayers. But I was too late. Peter's God had already decided to intervene where I did not want Him and He brushed aside my influence. Peter was given the ability to speak to the crowd with calming words. I pushed back against them as hard as I could. But I had no power.

"Brothers," Peter started. "You all know me. You know who I am, and where I am from. It has been some time, but I was blessed with the mission of going out among all of the non-Jewish people - the Gentiles - and spreading the truth and knowledge of what our Lord did for us. What our Lord did for me.

I was humbled and took that call seriously. From that point forward, I have dedicated my time, my energies and my entire life to fulfilling His purpose. Isn't that what we are all here for? I know that without the drive given to me by our Lord I would not be among you today.

And isn't it that same commission that we are given that showed us that our hearts were not purified by something of our own power? Our hearts were not purified by a physical act that was performed on us! Our hearts were not purified by the means of our own hands or our own abilities! No, our hearts were purified because of the faith we put in Him. Nothing else has or could purify our hearts like that.

I know all of us here were circumcised. But in what we have experienced, and what we know from all that we have been shown, do any of us here think that the act of circumcision is what saved us? Can any of you seriously look at me and tell me that the act of circumcision is the primary reason that we stand assured in Him? If we are truthful with ourselves and each other the answer is no. Moreover, I am sure that we would think anyone suggesting otherwise is ignorant of the truth.

Then why would any of us want to tell another that circumcision is the most important part of coming to our Lord? Why would we want to put that burden on another, when we ourselves know it is not the final word of our faith. Yes, it has been passed through our people from Abraham to Moses. Yes, it was the covenant shared with Abraham and brought to today. And yes, for us it has been and remains a symbol of obedience. But it is not the cause of our faith. Nor is it the culmination of our faith.

It is grace offered by our Lord that is the reason we are purified. And we have faith in that grace, and in Him. We should not, and cannot, place faith in our circumcision. And we cannot make others think that it is the crux of their faith."

Peter thanked them all for listening and sat down. The room fell eerily silent as Peter walked back to his seat. I looked around appalled at the lack of opposition rising from the congregation.

"You're not really going to stand for that, are you?" I yelled at the people. "You're not really going to accept what he said? What does he know, really?" I kept reminding the people of the importance of holding strong to their oppositions. Yet nobody was listening to me. The words that Peter spoke had pierced and quieted their restless hearts.

Then Paul and Barnabas stood up and addressed the room.

"No," I screamed at Paul. "You don't say a word."

Paul ignored me and began to talk about his experiences. He spoke about the miracles and the wonders that he had seen in the field, and how he saw lives being changed and people coming to faith in his God. He told them of the faith that they had not in an action they took, but in a God who promised forgiveness based on the simple act of faith.

But Paul never mentioned me. Paul never mentioned to these people deciding these important issues how deep in my counsel he had once been. He never told them that it was because of me that he even had the chance to become one of them. It was because of me that he was even on that road to Damascus when his God hijacked him. I deserved to be listened to because of the pivotal role I played. His voiding of my influence was why Paul never told the congregation of the freedom I offered to all of them, a freedom that would allow them to live as they wanted, not as some God told them to live. It was a freedom he had once tasted but that he had long forgotten.

As he spoke, I became more enraged. "You stand there so pious, O great and powerful Paul," I shouted. "You stand there as though you are free of me! You will never be free of me, do you understand? I will hunt you like a dog, and you will come back to me begging for your freedom. You will see that my freedom is too enticing, too tempting, too right to be ignored. You will come back to me with tears and sadness. I will prove to you how much you need me!"

Paul and Barnabas finished their tales as the room remained quiet. I was seething, and knew that I had lost control of the people. They discussed more amongst themselves, but in a much more civilized, united manner. They realized that telling others that circumcision was necessary ran counter to everything they had been taught and learned from their God. They decided unanimously that all that was required for salvation was faith in their God.

It disgusted me. The people were coming together and no longer bickering. It was as if a barrier that I could not penetrate had come over the people. I decided to give up this particular battle and move on to fight another day. For there would be other battles and they would come soon. I needed to remain sharp to bring the battle. The people and their God needed to be even sharper in the next if they wished to defeat me again.

I spent the next several years roaming the earth and refused to visit Paul or his cohorts. There were many other battles to keep me preoccupied during that time. I remained vigilant and bided my time for the next great battle in the war.

The world had changed so much since I first set foot upon it. The animals were flourishing, the land was rich and bright, and the people had settled much of it. In fact, a great number of people were flourishing with the freedom I presented to them. I had many that thanked me daily for what I gave, and were perfectly content to remain with me even in the face of cajoling by the men and women of that God.

I had my associates constantly keeping up with Paul and I always knew what he was doing. But for a while I did not desire to engage him myself. However, the time finally came that I wanted to visit Paul and look upon him with my own eyes. I knew that Paul remained faithful to his God and that it was too late for him to come back to me now. His mind had been so twisted by that God that I doubted I could unravel it. But I knew that deep inside he had not forgotten me. I knew this because Paul had actually used a lot of what I taught him against me and my associates. But by himself Paul was no match for my power. That is why I found it so unfair that Paul used his God as his shield. Only a coward would not fight me one on one.

If I were to be completely honest I would have liked to kill Paul long before had I been allowed. I would have made sure that he died before he ever had the chance to spread his filth. But the rules were against me and I couldn't kill him. Yet even without being allowed to kill Paul I had other options. It had come time for me to exercise a few of those options. That is just what I did.

Paul was gaining too many converts. I so desired to be done with the man that had become a thorn in my side. Over the ensuing decade, many of his own people in Jerusalem had become hostile towards him. When I received word that Paul was headed back to Jerusalem I saw it as an opportunity. I knew that my time to confront him had come. I prepared myself and headed to Jerusalem.

Paul arrived in Jerusalem ten years after successfully ending my mutiny regarding circumcision. I remember that time well, for the people of the city were not as hostile towards him and his fellow believers. Times had changed, and Jerusalem had come to accept my influence and persuasion now more than ever. Paul was going to find that he was no longer safe within Jerusalem's walls.

Paul's fellow believers greeted him upon his arrival. They made haste to warn him of the rumblings in the city against their beliefs. Paul was ushered to a secluded home where he was able to take rest and food. I watched as Paul learned of their lives since he had last seen them. As his fellow believers spoke Paul became more aware of the trouble that crawled the streets of Jerusalem. I reveled in his growing anxiety, and wondered as he ignored the fear and pressed on with his compatriots.

The next day he visited his friend James and others in the church. He regaled them with stories of conversion and changed lives that he proceeded over while he was ministering. The men listened and rejoiced as they heard of these things while I cursed them for being so happy. But I knew time was short and Paul would soon stumble. For he had decided to take four of his fellow believers to the Jewish temple to engage in rights allowed only for the Jews. Paul gave me a wide opening and I was going to run right through.

The Jewish people would not stand for such an insult as Paul was preparing to deliver. As Paul brought his men to the temple and engaged in their traditions, I began to whisper to each of the pure Jews about what was happening right in front of them. I told them of his assault on their religion and how he turned his back on his own people. They listened as I told them that it was Paul who was trying to spread the news of his new God and incite others to overthrow the Jewish people.

But I saved the best for last. I told each and every one of them in the temple how there were foreigners in their midst. I showed them how Paul was in the process of allowing men not of the Jewish faith into the temple to defile it. I told all the pure men of the danger that existed in allowing Paul to live. I insisted to them that in order to truly serve their God Paul must be destroyed.

When I had whipped enough of them into a frenzy, one particularly strong Jewish man spoke out against Paul. With a glint in his eyes, he pointed a finger and yelled out for all to hear.

"That man," he said, his arm shaking with rage. "That man is the one who preaches against our people and our God. He wants nothing more for us to be destroyed! He wants our God replaced with his! He even brings outsiders to desecrate our temple and defile us!"

When other Jewish men in the temple heard this their anger was awakened. They spied Paul and his friends. Together the Jewish men rushed towards Paul with murder in their hearts. I urged the attackers onward as I seized my opportunity to destroy Paul and his witness altogether. The enraged crowd grabbed Paul and his companions and dragged them out of the temple. They grabbed him so tightly and ferociously that they ripped his clothes and tore his skin. The men holding Paul started to beat him mercilessly. I felt Paul's death was at hand.

However Paul's God once again used useful idiots that day. Word had reached the Roman soldiers near the temple of the mob inside. When they saw the fight break out, one of the Roman commandeers seized his men and rushed to the crowd. They pushed their way through, and when those pummeling Paul saw the garrison arrive they were frightened and backed away. The soldiers bound Paul by the hands, and tried to garner from the mob why Paul was being beaten. They wanted to know what he had done, but as the answers flew fast and furious, the soldiers could not understand a single one. They retired Paul to their barracks, and even though he did not die, I was satisfied. I knew before anyone else that Paul was going to be put away, and his voice would be silenced.

It took some time but Paul was finally a prisoner. He was going to be a prisoner of the Romans for a long time. I decided to visit him. It was the last time I ever wanted to see him. But before I abandoned Paul forever I wanted to let him know that he had been finally defeated by one more powerful than he. I let Paul sit in prison alone for a while before I visited.

It was late one evening when I visited Paul. The air was warm as I traversed the stony steps of the prison. I was pleased to find that as I got closer to Paul's cell I felt a significant drop in temperature. The Roman prison Paul was being held in was a fate no less than he deserved. This particular prison served to hasten one to desire death as it would have been a pleasant alternative to the conditions within. The stone steps that led to the basement dwelling of the prisoners echoed with my footsteps as I walked, and I wondered why there was so much silence. Usually these prisons had been filled with those convicted or awaiting trial, but on this night I found Paul alone in his cell. I would not have found it so strange had I arranged the situation. But I had no hand in this setup and I was grateful to whoever had. I had Paul's full attention.

The prison was made of stone and the bars of wrought iron. It sat in a dry and desolate place underneath the city streets. Guards usually roamed freely amongst the cells, but on this night I made sure that the guards remained far away. I wanted nothing to interfere with our conversation. This night was going to be special.

The hallway leading to Paul's cell was dark. It had only a single burning lamp to show the path. The patter of small creatures meandering the prison could be heard in the distance, and the smell of squalor permeated the air. I approached Paul's cell to find him chained to wall. He had enough length in the chains to allow him to move away from the wall, but not enough to get near the door. He was dirty and had nothing in his physical appearance to give him hope. But the look of his face was that of a free man coming and going as he pleased. I saw Paul scribbling words on papyrus, no small feat when given the lack of light. In silence I stared at him, wondering just how far he could be pushed before he would finally reject his God. He did not recognize me as I entered his cell.

"Paul," I said. "Paul, look over here." He ignored me and continued to scribble.

"Paul!" I was loud and direct, and he stopped what he was doing and looked up.

"You hear me now, don't you?" I asked. He squinted his eyes, peering into the darkness. "Do you remember me?"

Paul stared into the darkness for a few moments, then went back to his writing.

"You fool!" I exclaimed. "Has it been so long that you forgot my call? Do you not recognize my voice? Your master is back to claim what is his, and you play the dullard, not hearing my voice or seeing my face. Do you not know what you are?" I was angry and a bit regretful. I felt that I should have come back to Paul sooner. He scribbled in the darkness like a man gone mad. I was starting to think that was the case. Perhaps I was too late to even have a simple conversation with him. Perhaps as he traveled his own path he had gotten lost in his own mind.

"I know who you are," Paul said suddenly, putting his writing down. "I hear your voice." Paul paused for a moment. "I see your face. I am not a fool that ignores who you are. But you are not welcome here. Though here is where you are."

"Paul," I said, smiling and walking closer. It was a rare person that could engage me directly. But Paul was able and confirmed my thoughts about him. "Would it be that you would not welcome an old friend? It has been too long since we have been together. It has been too long since we have had the chance to talk and understand one another. Would you deny me even that pleasure?"

"I would deny you everything," Paul said. "Yet I can deny you nothing. It is not I you have to fear, be He who is in me."

"I fear nothing!" I shot back. "You would be wise to mind who it is you are talking to. Need I remind you of what you should fear?" I reached over to Paul and pressed my hand into his side. Paul winced in pain and screamed out as he felt my hand putting pressure on him and increasing the pain that had tormented his body. It had been some time, but I had sent word for Paul to be marked, and in that marking he would ever have a physical reminder of who I was. It remained with him until the day of his death.

Paul started to laugh through his pain, his breathing quickly increasing. "I know your hand and I have accepted your pain," Paul panted.

"You have had this for some time, and yet that God you serve has done nothing for it? If for but a single word I would release you from it. What is it that makes you want to be afflicted? For the sake of a God who would let you suffer?"

"The word you would have me say is a word I will not give," Paul panted as he dragged himself back to the wall and leaned against it, clutching his side. "I have asked my God for relief from this, and he has replied."

"He replied?" I asked feigning ignorance. "How did that work out?"

"Well for me, but not so well for you," Paul said arrogantly. "You were but a pawn, and He used you to bring me closer to Him. The pain I feel now cannot compare to the pain you will feel in the end." Paul paused and stared at me. "You know of what I speak. Why don't you talk about the end?"

"You are a fool if you believe any of that!" I shouted as rage filled my body. "That will never happen!" I had lost control of myself and the situation because of what Paul said. I tried to calm down as I spoke more carefully. "I want you to be free, Paul. I want you to be free of the pain, free of this prison, and free of everything that would hold you back. I want you to be free to live your life in the way that makes you the happiest. You should not have to live just to serve others. You should be living for yourself and those you care about the most." I walked over to him and picked up the chains that were shackling him to the wall. "These chains are apropos. They are just an example of the bondage you are in to that God." I threw them against the wall. "Be free of all the chains that bind you. I am extending my hand to you one last time, Paul. Allow me to give you freedom as I once did."

Paul dropped his head and said nothing. I hoped that I was finally getting through to him. He was in a horrible situation, was physically beaten down, and had very few people that came to his aid. I wanted so badly for him to succumb to my words. I wanted to once again commune with Paul.

Paul lifted his head and struggled to stand up. I walked around him like a lion stalking his prey. I was about to free him from all of his bondage. Paul opened his mouth and spoke.

"There was a time I followed you. There was a time that I would have loved to have what you now offer. I was my own man, doing only as I saw fit and answering only to myself. I lived by doing what I thought was right and wrong. But then I realized that what you offer was nothing more than a façade. What you offered led down a path of destruction." Paul looked down at himself and gestured to his body. "You have harmed this. You might even destroy it. But that matters little because you can never have me. That's what you really want and that is what I deny you. Do you want to know what my God told me? He told me that he wasn't going to take this pain from me. He told me that with His grace I would survive. He was showing me His perfection in my imperfection. He was making strong what you had made weak!" Paul looked at me with determination and a spoke with a stern voice. "I would rather that I stay here for a thousand years bound to these walls and serving my God than to have you give me a single day as king of this world. Why do you fight so hard to have me? What is it I offer you? Is it that you need one more person under your rule? Do you need another man you can manipulate to your will? No. You fight so hard for me because you fear who He is. You fight so hard to get me because you know who I serve." Paul stepped closer and stared me straight in the eyes. I stared back at him with defiance. "You are afraid of what He has done through me. You are afraid of what He has yet to accomplish through me. You can try to destroy my body. But you will never capture me. You will never "free" me. So if all you are ever going to do is keep coming to me and offering me your corruption, then you might as well kill me now, because you are just wasting your time."

"If I could have killed you it would have happened long ago," I said through clenched teeth. "But your time has not come and unlike some I have to follow the rules. But your time will come and if I can I will hasten it's arrival. I will revel in your death, Paul. I will rejoice at your destruction." I stared back at Paul.

"I welcome its arrival," Paul said defiantly.

The two of us stared at each other for several beats. "Until then," I finally said, "remember this. I will always be hunting you. I will always be mere footsteps away, waiting to strike at you when you least expect it. You will never be rid of me. You will always have to fear me coming. You cannot trifle with me and expect to be free of me. You will always know who I am and the power I possess. Don't ever forget that I want to destroy you. But remember also that if you should seek peace and freedom then my hand is always open offering you freedom from what binds you. The choice will forever be yours." With that I caught Paul off guard and grabbed him by the throat. "I am always near," I whispered. I lifted him into the air and threw him against the wall. He hit with a thud and crumpled to the floor as his chains clanged around him. I turned and left as Paul's groans echoed throughout the prison.

I never returned to Paul and he never called out for me. Paul died five years to the day after that meeting. I watched with a mix of glee and anger as he was beheaded before a cheering crowd. I was happy that he was gone, but furious because I failed with him. He rejected the freedom that I offered and spent his life serving his God. But the defeat strengthened my resolve to set others free.

The flames of the fire cooled and my eyes turned to Richard. "You really talked to Paul a lot. Yet he never gave up his faith. How did he do that when you were so active in his life?" I asked.

"If I knew I suspect I would have been able to get through to him." Richard said. "It was always a source of pain for me that I lost him and could never regain his companionship."

Richard was clearly distressed by his encounters with Paul. I was tiring and my resolve was weakening. Listening to Richard I found myself feeling sorry for him. In my heart I knew that he was evil. But in my mind I was starting to sympathize with him. I was growing weary fighting Richard and that caused me to consider his point of view. I was beginning to believe that some of what he said had validity. It had been hours since our encounter began. I recognized that he had not tried to harm me. The truth was he was simply talking to me. Everything I thought I knew about Richard suggested that he wanted to hurt me. But the fact was Richard wanted nothing less than to simply sit with me.

I don't know if it was the pull of the anchor that caused me to accept Richard's words. The weight had been so heavy on me that the pain it caused was becoming an old friend. But I noticed something peculiar. The more I believed in what Richard was saying, the less I felt the weight. It was almost as if the weight responded to how I viewed Richard. It was as if Richard himself was alleviating my pain.

And that is all I really wanted at this point. I wanted to be free of the weight I was carrying. But more than that I wanted to be free of the pain. I had so much pain on the inside that I had not been dealing with that something was wrong. I had the pain of my parents and the pains that exist in any life. But the biggest hurt was the loss of my wife. That pain was so engrained in my soul that I thought it was too great to ever lose. All I truly wanted was release from that pain.

"You know," Richard said as I pondered him, "I was deeply saddened when Paul fell and when he died. I don't want you to think otherwise. I hate to see people in his type of bondage. When you boil it down all I ever offered him was freedom and peace. And it got twisted to make me look like the bad guy. The truth is that from the beginning I was trying to help him."

There was a time not too many hours before that I was loathe to agree with Richard. But I had changed and there was nothing I could do to stop it. My mind was being swayed with rationalizations and pleasant words. But an increasingly smaller part of my heart held out with the belief that I was in the midst of a grand rouse. I believed Richard, and this was most dangerous and disconcerting. It was dangerous because to believe even a little of what he said meant that I had to dismiss some of what my God said. And to lose faith in any of what my God said meant I could believe nothing of what my God said. That was the most disconcerting thought of all.

As I struggled with my thoughts the anchor pulled on me. Sometimes it would feel like the weight of the earth were on my heart. Other times it felt like only a small stone. It all depended on what I choose to believe at any given time. But I realized that no matter what I thought I was still aware of the weight of the anchor. It remained and I knew that it was there. This weight was going to haunt me whether it was the size of an island or a grain of sand.

I vowed that if I was going to survive my encounter with Richard I was not going to let him know what was going on inside. If he knew that I was starting to put trust in him and he had a foothold then I was doomed. Richard would surely exploit that foothold and I would be lost. I had to hold however precariously to the knowledge that my feelings could be wrong, and that my God could show me how. I had to know that before the end my God would reveal the truth about Richard. The problem was that as my God waited I was slipping further into Richard's grasp.

Richard remained silent but looked me up and down as I reflected. I felt his eyes on me, but did not meet his gaze as I looked down at the dirt and contemplated my predicament. But Richard's gaze was unique. I felt his eyes reading me. They looked at what was on my heart and understood my dilemma. I tried to ignore that feeling I was getting from his stare but to no avail.

"You are a very strong man," Richard said to me. "You have been through so much and have remained a stalwart in the midst of difficulty."

"I have been through much?" I said surprised. "What do you know of what I have been through?"

"I know about how you lost your parents. We were both there, remember?" Richard said sardonically. "To lose them so very suddenly and at such a young age. That was hard." I looked at Richard. He sat there and waited until I acknowledged his statement with a nod. "But your wife. That was the most difficult torment of all. And for that I am sorry."

"You are sorry?" I asked. "Why are you sorry? Did you cause her death?" I was prepared to hear him admit that he was and to give me a lame explanation as to why it had to happen. I was prepared but knew that I would lose control if I heard him admit to causing her death. But as usual, Richard surprised me with his response.

"I did not cause her death," Richard said. "In fact, I wanted her to live. I pleaded for her to live."

I was taken aback. "You pleaded for her to live? How exactly did you plead for her to live?"

"You may not believe this," Richard started, "But your wife died as I was pleading for her life."

I didn't know what Richard was getting at. I had grown weary of his tales and told him as much. "If you are going to tell me a lie, or an equivocation, save your breath," I said. "I am tired of trying to decipher you."

"I do not have a lie to tell you about your wife." Richard replied. "If you will only listen." I nodded my agreement. I sat with uneasiness and insecurity as I waited for his story.

Richard adjusted himself in his seat. He took his time in starting which only gave me more time to feel the weight and tire further. After what felt like a lifetime Richard spoke.

"I remember watching you both for so long. I knew you both before you even knew each other. You were so good for each other and I knew that your life together would be wonderful. I knew that you would follow the same path and remain strong in your marriage. But as has been the case with many others in the past, the wrongs of this world befell your poor young bride. You know that the world exists already filled with troubles and evils. Unfortunately, many of those wrongs and evils are unjustly blamed on me. That's mostly because of the bad public relations I have received from that God of yours. Be that as it may, as you know your beautiful wife was stricken with that terrible disease and luckily you were there to care for her. I thought you both did well, even though you both insisted on following that God. I watched and hoped that the two of you would come to me to find freedom not only from that God but from the disease that was draining the life out of her. I wanted so badly for either one of you to call out to me. I wanted you to give me the opportunity to respond in kind. I wanted to help but I couldn't until I was asked.

"Truthfully, it hurt me to see what was happening. I wanted to give you my services since I knew that I could free you both. But I was tired of waiting for one of you to ask. You were both too connected to that God of yours. So I did you both a favor. I made an attempt to relieve you both on your behalf. I knew what your wife was suffering with and I was keenly aware of the pain involved. So I did the one thing I could do to alleviate the suffering.

"I took a great personal risk and approached your God on your behalf. I swallowed my pride and made my way to the streets of

His city. I proceeded to His palace gates and found Him once again waiting for me in the outer court. I looked your God square in the eyes and told Him what He should do. I reminded your God that He had the power to take this affliction from your wife and to make your marriage whole again. He knew very well that it was within his pervue to ensure that the two of you could live long and happy lives. I insisted that if He was going to take so freely and easily your service, then He had the duty to take care of you in return. I was sincere when I let your God know that all I wanted was for your wife to be healed, and for you both to go on living without having to suffer in such a painful and undignified manner. I laid out that if He truly was as powerful and omniscient as He claimed then He would take care of your wife without a problem. In fact, He should have healed your wife without hesitation. I asked him why He would even delay if He believed His own hype. I presented my request with no strings attached. I wanted nothing in return. All I wanted was for your wife to be whole.

"But you obviously know how my request was answered. Your God ignored it completely. He could have - He should have - taken your wife into His care and healed her. But He either failed or choose not to do it. Instead, as I stood there before Him, humbling myself on your behalf, He just stared at me. I begged Him as I beat my chest and fell to my knees helpless. Your God stood there with the backdrop of His opulence and a stoic look as His only response. In an instant, as I pleaded for her, your wife was gone. Your God proved Himself either weak or aloof, either of which is terrible. Even as I begged and pleaded Your God would not lift a finger to help out one of his so called children. He watched her die. He proved Himself to be unworthy of your devotion."

I was shaken at Richard's words. I was already in a weakened state and susceptible to Richard's leading. I had no reason to believe that what he said was true. But that didn't matter at this moment. Sitting under the starry sky draped with a canopy of leaves all I could see was the twisted and gaunt face of my dying wife. All I could hear were her faint last words as I prayed that she might still somehow make it through. Though Richard's reputation was of ill, I couldn't shake the thought that what he just said was true.

Maybe Richard wanted to make the request for his own benefit. Maybe he had ulterior motives. But in my mind's eye I could see Richard standing there, before God, begging for my wife's life. As I pictured it I felt the anchor on my soul pull harder. I felt doubt and fear stir inside of me. Worst of all, I felt adrift. I could no longer separate truth from fiction.

"I know it is a lot to take in," Richard said, sensing my struggle. "I know that you must be having so very many conflicting feelings right now. But if there is anything you can take from this, it is that I am not your enemy. I am not seeking to destroy you. And if I had the power, I would have saved your wife."

I was spinning. For so long I thought I had the truth inside of me. For so long I thought I had the knowledge of how I was to live my life and who I was to turn to in times of distress. But now, for the first time in a very long time, I was desperately questioning everything. I was like a ship off it's moorings, floating out to sea, rudderless and at the mercy of the waves. I did not want to believe Richard was anything more than a liar. I did not want to believe that there was truth in Richard's words or that he was my only hope. But it was getting late for my mind and heart. The truth was becoming more and more clouded. I needed something I could grab onto. I needed to push back against Richard and see if he would crack in any way. If I couldn't grab onto something other than what Richard was peddling then I was going to be lost forever.

I started to weep. Richard watched me and remained silent, He offered me no condolences. I had nowhere to turn and nobody to bring me back from the brink. So I did the only thing I ever knew that truly worked. I reached my spiritual hand out to the God I had always trusted and began to pray. I prayed that He could prove to me that Richard was a liar and that I could still trust on Him. I prayed that He would show me that He still loved me and was not in fact holding me prisoner. I prayed that He would act quickly and definitively. But most importantly I prayed silently to keep it secret from Richard. But somehow Richard heard me and he was not happy.

"Who do you call out to now?" Richard asked, indignantly interrupting me. "Is it that you would still waste your time?" Richard's voice pierced my thoughts, and broke my concentration. I tried to regain it, but his words were swirling in my head, and I couldn't bring myself back. As I opened my eyes and lifted my head, a thought arose in my mind that had eluded me thus far. It was a lifeline, and I took hold of it as tightly as I could.

"You never answered Paul," I blurted out.

"Never answered Paul?" Richard questioned. "What didn't I answer?"

"He asked you about the end. He asked why you wouldn't talk about the end. What did he mean by that?" I was exasperated, but from the look in Richard's eyes I knew I had struck a chord.

"Paul was talking gibberish. He didn't even know what he meant." Richard stumbled with his words. For the first time that evening I saw the distinct look of fear cross his face. It was faint but real. Richard was scared by what Paul had asked him.

"He thought he did," I said.

"He thought a lot of things!" Richard insisted. "He thought he knew the truth. But as I've told you he only knew what a deceitful God told him."

"Tell me then," I said, knowing I was onto something. "What did Paul think he knew but was so very wrong about?"

"Paul only knew half of the story. His God told him a fairy tale. As we both know, fairy tales have an element of the truth. This was true of the fairy tale your God told Paul.

"Paul was right when he said there will be an end. There will come a moment when this world and all of recorded time ceases to exist. All that you know will be wiped away and everything that anyone has ever fought and strived for will be rendered meaningless and void. Paul knew this and it is quite true.

The problem is that God misled Paul on some very key issues. Paul was spun tales of a time after the end of this world. But in the tales Paul was told I was nowhere to be found. In these tales it was Paul's God that ruled over a new earth. I was absent from the story. To make matters more laughable, I was cast out into a void to suffer forever. I would no longer have any power here. I was to be sent away with not only my associates but with those humans that from the beginning of time had decided to choose my freedom over bondage. It is a laughable if gruesome tale that does not reflect well on me. I end up cast out to destruction, and of course Paul's God plays the hero and everyone is happy and content.

"I was disappointed by Paul's ignorance. The truth is not in the story Paul knew. The truth is difficult for Paul's God to accept, which is why He probably felt it necessary to make up such a flattering tale for Himself. But I am here to tell you what really will happen at the end.

"I do not deny that there will come an end of time. The world and its history will be no more. That will be a time of great terror and fear among the people of the earth. They will be tormented by your God because His self-delusion and madness will get the best of Him. It will be horrible. But not long after I will reveal myself. All of the people of the world will know who I am and the freedom I offer. Those that are around to witness this end will flock to me with great hope and expectations. Trust me, I will not disappoint.

"When the end comes the world will be in great turmoil. It is not too much for me to say that the world will be in turmoil because of your God. It will be He who makes the people of the world fear because he is angry that so many of them have already rejected his bondage and suffering. He will choose to keep Himself hidden while the whole of the world cries out against Him. That is when I will reveal myself. I will come to the aid of the world. I will finally show everyone that I am worthy of their trust and their love. I will bring myself to the forefront and restore peace and order. No longer will people live in fear. Instead they will be in awe of what I do and what I can accomplish in such a short amount of time. I will be there to serve them, and they in turn will praise me.

"There will be signs and wonders that I can show the world. I will heal people and nations. I will do what your God could never do. I will bring peace to the world. This peace will cross nations and cultures. There will be such an ultimate peace that outshines any this planet has seen. It will be a time of miracles and wonders.

"Now I have said that there have always been rules for me. Up until that point it will be so. But when the end comes I will transcend all rules. I will finally do the things that your God has had the ability to do for so long but faltered because He sat on His hands. Then I will offer the world the ultimate freedom, and the whole of humanity will accept my gift with open arms. All the people of the world will know my name, and all religions, races, cultures and tribes will come together under my banner. It will be like paradise.

"But this will not sit well with your God. He will despise that I am taking control and doing for the people what He should have been doing all along. He will take umbrage at my popularity and strike at me with anger and vengeance. He has powerful allies, and will challenge my rule and my kingdom. He will wish to overthrow me for all the good I have done. He will throw everything He has at me in the hope that I will fall.

"Where Paul was blinded was his baseless belief that his God would prevail. What Paul thought was that after the battle I would be defeated and the few people of the world that still followed his God would greet Him with joy and gladness. Paul thought that I would be cast out into suffering along with my associates. Paul even went so far as to think that those living on earth that had embraced me would be cast out with me at the same time! Both Paul and his God were truly delusional.

"For the truth is that there will be a battle. Paul's God and I will finally face off and determine just who it is that should rule the Kingdom. Up until now I have known that I should be the ruler of the Kingdom but have not had the power to make that a reality. But in those end times I will have all the power I need. I will be unstoppable. Paul's God will attempt to destroy me, but He will fail. I will have the final word. It will dramatically contrast with the weakness of the God Paul relied on. I will finally rule over all as I should have from the beginning. I will bring to myself those that accepted my offer of freedom and control. I will cast out those that rejected me from the beginning. The Kingdom will finally be as it always should have been." Richard was practically breathless from excitement and anticipation. He looked skyward with a clenched fist. "That is the truth of the question Paul asked. Only he was too blind to see it."

I wondered at the passion with which Richard spoke. But though my ears heard confidence and assurance, my heart heard the fear and trepidation laying just under the surface. Yet I was still slipping into Richard's truth. But I had been thrown a rope on which to cling. I had been tossed a lifeline if only I had the strength to hold on while being tossed about. My mind told me to give up. But that small place in my heart nagged at me to fight. I had to keep prodding at Richard.

"Your vision is truly epic," I said slowly. "But I have always learned – always known – that you do not triumph in the end. How can you be so blind as to ignore the truth that is written down for you to read. How can you, one who seems so well versed in all the ways of God, ignore that basic truth?"

"What you have read," Richard said with a smile, "was written by the One that wanted you to believe what He said. If a company wished to sell you a product, they would surely tout great things about it, even adding misleading 'truths'. Take a set of steak knives. The package tells you it is so sharp that it will cut steel. It tells you that the blade will not wear down and have a ten year warranty. This is all true. But what you don't find out until you have bought it and brought it home is that yes, the blades are perfect, but soon the handle breaks so very easily. They did not tell you that built in flaw, and it is too late because you have already bought the product. You cannot return it and you are stuck with a worthless item. The same goes here. You're God is going to tell you what He wants you to think. He is not going to let you know the significant flaws until it is too late."

I sat and consumed what Richard fed me. His logic felt flawed, but I was not clear headed enough to fight any longer. I was finished. I was gripping on to the lifeline I had been thrown, but it was going to fail me sooner or later. It was just a matter of time before I let it slip through my fingers and begged Richard for freedom from my God. Silence fell between us.

Richard knew what was going on inside of me. "The hour grows late, my friend," Richard finally said. "Perhaps I should be going. You have been a great host, and I truly enjoyed our time together." Richard looked at me as if waiting for me to say something. But I remained silent, for I did not know what I wanted to say. "You know, I offer you the same freedom I offer everyone. Your wife may be gone, but you do not have to live under the bondage that has gripped you since then. Be free of the pain. Live your life as you want to." Richard paused. "I hate to see you in such pain."

Richard stood up and walked over to me. He extended his hand, offering me his gift for the simple price of my allegiance. I slowly and unsteadily rose to my feet. From the outside I must have looked like a drunkard. I was unsteady and could barely hold myself up. The anchor weighed more heavily on me now than ever before. Coursing within me once again was fear. But this was not the fear of Richard that had gripped me earlier. This was the fear of losing Richard and his power. I was so afraid that he would walk away that I practically wanted to jump in his arms. I was shaken and beaten down. I just wanted to find my place. The weight pulled so hard that all I wanted was relief. I would have given my soul for just a moment of peace from its groaning. I was tired, and in all truth, I felt my God was farther from me than anything else in the universe. But Richard was with me. He was at my side and offered comfort. He was standing right there, in front of me, the man who I had once considered an enemy and could now deliver me from my doubt. Or at least that is what I thought.

I was done with following my God. I had dedicated so much of my life to Him, but in the end, Richard was right. Where was my God when I needed Him the most? He was not there when my wife died. He was not there when my parents died. He was not even there when Richard showed up to confront and confuse me. I was ready, and wanted to purge myself of that part of my life. The pull from Richard was strong, almost magnetic. The small part of my heart that held to the lifeline was almost withered black and dead.

I tried to raise my hand and grasp Richards. He looked on at me with great anticipation. But I could not bring it up all the way. Something was keeping me from gripping his hand. I put my remaining strength into this one motion but did not have enough to overcome whatever it was holding me back.

Suddenly I heard something. It was faint and almost non-existent. There was a small voice calling out to me in the wilderness of my soul. It had taken notice of what happened to me. It knew how I had devolved, and it was keeping me from fully embracing the freedom that Richard offered. It cried out to me quietly but constantly. But the voice was so faint that I could scarcely recognize it. I quieted myself as best I could, and strained to hear it. Over and over it repeated to me, begging me to hold on for a little longer. It strained to have me ask Richard one final question. It wanted one last question to confront him before I gave myself. The voice promised that after I did this I could give myself over without any interference. The voice promised that if I just asked this one thing it would leave me alone and I could have the freedom Richard offered.

I looked up at Richard as he remained in quiet but joyous anticipation of my decision. He was overly confident and was unaware of the voice coming from inside me. In my state I had no resistance to fight any longer. I simply allowed myself to be captured and used by that voice. I agreed to its demands and gave myself over to the still small voice.

What happened next came from no power I held. It was something else, something greater than myself, taking hold of me and using me. Without warning I saw myself lift my hand to grasp Richard's. But instead of grabbing his hand and shaking it in agreement, I grabbed his collar and with a force I did not recognize I pulled him towards me. He stumbled as I jerked him and I found myself almost holding Richard up with my own strength. I had no idea what was happening and I marveled at this change. I pulled Richard close to my face and looked him in the eye.

"What is the meaning of this?" Richard fearfully asked.

"We are not finished here," I said with fervor. "You are going to sit down." I thrust Richard backwards and he caught himself before he crashed to the ground. I pointed at his seat across the campfire. Richard looked back at me.

"You need to tell me one more story, Richard," I said.

"Anything you want," he nervously replied.

I felt strength coursing through my body the likes of which I had never felt before. I walked confidently back to the mighty oak tree and sat up against it. As I hit the ground I felt all the strength leave me as my body weakened exponentially. Whatever it was that had gripped me was gone.

I mustered the little strength I had left, squinted my eyes and pierced Richard with my stare. "You are going to tell me about Jesus. I want you to tell me everything you know. Tell me the truth."

CHAPTER 11

Richard sat across from me and nervously threw more wood on the fire. For the first time that evening he looked unsure. I was certain he did not know what to make of my sudden change. For that matter, neither did I. As Richard caught me staring at him a strange grin crept over his face.

I was convinced that Richard had enjoyed the torment I was under. What he was showing blatantly pushed against every notion that I had of who I was and what I believed. As I replayed the evening in my mind I could think of no reason that I should believe a word that came forth from his mouth. I should know that it was in his very nature to lie. But reality was oppositional. I believed his words and felt there was no choice but to throw my hands up and declare that indeed I had been a fool, and that I had wasted my life. The end result of this was hopelessness and despair. It wasn't going to be difficult to embrace those two old friends. But I had promised that still small voice that I would follow through and hear out one more story. So I settled in.

"You still aren't convinced," Richard calmly said to me. He was mocking me and the struggle that burned within my soul. He knew all too well where I was, and that was his point.

"But I am glad you asked me to tell you about…Him." Richard said. He was hesitant to use the name of Jesus and I could only imagine why. I hung my head out of weariness, for I knew what I was about to hear could alter my life forever. I knew that I had to be vigilant to listen and decipher the truth in what I was told.

Looking up from the ground I limply gestured towards him. "I want no more of your lies today," I murmured. "You speak to me as if to a friend, but your lips burn with the pleas of a condemned man. I will accept no more of what you have to say to me unless it speaks truth to my spirit."

My words were defiant but my heart was heavy. It was all I could muster. I was practically begging him to leave me to my misery. I knew that my façade was a thin veil, but I hoped that it was enough to get through.

"I can feel you are weary, but it is most important that you listen to every word I am about to tell you," he said mockingly. "You must know that truth."

I leaned myself back against the mighty oak tree and sighed. I was done fighting. I hoped that after his one last tale I could be done forever. The anchor weighed heavily on me and release from it was so near. There were no longer prayers within me that he might leave. There was only complacency, the realization that I could not resist but instead acquiesce, and wait for the inevitable time that he was done and I would be free.

The air hung thick with the promise of dread, and I was at its mercy. Richard wasted no time in speaking. "You have dedicated your entire life to this one cause, assured by the pages of ancient texts. But as I have told you, I was there. And the mercy of the man that would give himself for you has been your biggest crutch. But I was there, and the truth belies what you have long believed.

"You have been through much pain and suffering. Yet you continued to believe. You have been crushed with loss after loss, yet you believe. You have watched as the world has fled from those teachings, yet you believe. You have waited as your prayers spend an eternity hanging in the air, never to be answered and serve only as a reminder of what you have not yet received. Yet you still believe.

"I was there. I was there when that man you so fervently refer to as your savior came to my earth. I was there when He first planted his mortal coil on the ground that I have traversed since the beginning. I was there as he led people to Himself, and ultimately to their doom. I was there when he lied to you, and gave you reason to doubt yourself."

Richard's voice was seething with disgust, venom punctuating the end of each sentence. The hate was palpable, and his conviction was unreal. For as he spoke, he sounded as one who believed the truth was his alone, and had been hidden from the world for too long. It was his time to speak, and he was going to ensure that what he said did not go unnoticed.

"Hear what I say now," he demanded as my eyes were drawn to the flames. "Hear the truth of your God."

There was a time when this earth was not in existence. The place we resided was more than you could possibly imagine. It was a place of ultimate joy and fascination. There were no limits of what was possible in that place. It was a site of tremendous beauty and endearing relationships. This place was outside of normal time and space. It existed beyond what you consider linear time and was free of the bounds and constraints of measurements. I was a diligent citizen of this place. I was ever considered a star there as everyone knew my name and my purpose. This place was my home.

I was always and only wanted to be a servant in this place. From my beginning I reveled and took joy in serving Him and His kingdom. You might have called me an angel, and for your sake I will use that definition. But I was much more than an angel. I was held in esteem and regard among all others. I was the premier angel in His kingdom. This was when I was able to walk His palace freely and without concern. I walked the outer courts greeting others with joy and peace. I would enter into the palace and marvel at its beauty and majesty. I was even allowed and expected to spend time in His presence in His very throne room. Those were beautiful days. They were days long ago. They were days before I was banned from setting foot inside the palace doors.

I was given great intelligence and deemed the master of the light. My knowledge and abilities helped to make me the greatest of servants. I loved serving Him during that time. I remember the thrill I felt when I would use my talents to glorify and magnify His name. There were none that took greater reward in hearing Him tell me from His own lips that He was pleased with my service. It was a drug for which I longed.

Without it I would have been miserable. At that time I knew that He was worthy of my praise and as such I gratefully gave it moment after moment. He delighted in my servitude and worship and I delighted in Him. He was all I needed and I was at peace.

But as with all happy stories an end must certainly come. How long it was that I served Him before I realized something was amiss is too difficult to calculate, for it was all eternity prior that I loved Him. But my love blinded me to the truth. It wasn't until He decided to step out that my eyes were finally open.

The story of my revelation came at a particularly definitive moment in your history. We all knew that He had something marvelous planned and everyone was excited at what that plan might entail. For a while it went on that we were supposing that what He had in mind would add to our majestic kingdom. It was about that time that I started to wonder. I knew I was the greatest among the angels and that I was given a great gift. But I started to wonder if I wasn't receiving the full glory I was due. I thought about how it was that everyone else looked up to me and yet I was still so far below Him. It felt unnatural.

I realized that I should expect and even demand more. I knew that I wasn't at His level yet. But that did not mean that one day I wouldn't reach it. Why shouldn't I aspire to more greatness and command more glory? It was a reasonable request. Besides, I wasn't asking to take over the Kingdom. I just wanted to have more respect and glory from everyone else - including Him.

I wondered why it was that I had never increased in those things. I suspected that he knew of my intelligence and power and must have realized that I deserved even more. Why I had never been given more made no sense to me at first. But then I discovered the truth. I discovered that He must have been scared at what I was capable of. He must have known that if I was given the glory that I was due then it would not be long before I rose to His power. He was threatened by my promise and because of that was holding me down and restraining me from my true potential. He feared losing the throne of the kingdom so much that He would harm his most loyal and dedicated servant.

My discovery was a shock to my system. From the moment I understood that truth I was never the same. I continued with my duties and worship but I was never able to have joy or satisfaction in them.

I was going through the motions and finding that with each passing moment I grew more cynical, frustrated and angry. I told nobody at first for fear that I would be condemned. I did not want to lose the position that I had and declaring that He was manipulating me would have caused just that. I held back my thoughts and feelings as long as I could. I felt that I could have been successful repressing those thoughts and feelings. The Kingdom marched onward and I did my job. But nothing felt right.

I had dreams of ruling over the kingdom. I thought of how it would be different and how I could show so many others that they too could be more majestic than they had ever hoped. I conjured up plans and methods in which I would rule so much more beautifully and powerfully than He ever did. Though the kingdom did not belong to me I knew that it should. Yet I continued to repress.

But it was not long after that He pushed me over the edge. He sent out word to the kingdom finally defining His great plan. He was going to make His greatest creation yet. He showed us all his plans for earth and all that would inhabit it. This included his plan to make man and woman. I was surprised when I heard this and appalled when He followed it with a declaration. He vowed to make those humans in His image with all the potential for creativity, love, worship, glory and relationship that He had. This announcement shattered my core.

I went off to be alone as I became gripped with anger and jealousy. How was it that He wanted to create something with which He could have relationship? Was it that we were no longer enough for Him? More to the point, this was going to affect my position. If He had become so fearful of us that he had to create something new then how long was it going to be before He was rid of us altogether. Nobody was safe. These new creature were going to command all of His attention and love. We were going to be cast aside.

I knew my fellow kingdom citizens were going to be just as appalled. I had to talk to anyone who was sympathetic to my side and see what they thought should be done. But before I could do that He summoned us all to witness the birth of His newest creation. We watched as the earth was formed by His hands and He placed all manner of creatures upon it. We watched it bloom with beauty and respond to the sun and the moon. But then the greatest insult of all was upon us. We saw as he formed both the man and woman and breathed life into their bodies. He was so happy and in love with His creation that it took all I had not to scream.

It did not take long for Him to show His new creation His love. He presented to them a great bounty. He gave them the best of everything. He set them in a glorious habitat with plentiful food and overall peace. But worst of all He made them eternal as we were and choose to walk with them in body and spirit. For out of nothing He made them yet He gave them everything. And there was nothing they had ever done or could ever do to earn this glory. I had spent my entire existence serving and glorifying Him and all I got in return was a foot on the back to keep me down. Those humans were weak and pathetic and did nothing and He gave them everything that should have been mine.

Words could not describe how furious I was. I refused to continue to be ruled under this worthless leadership. I vowed that I would never again let someone else make decisions for me. For so long I had been living the life that another wanted me to live. I did not question this life and thought that He had my best interests at heart. Yet I was wrong. I discovered that I was never given much consideration. Even with all my knowledge and acclaim I was a mere afterthought. That is when I began to plot the overthrow of the King.

Taking control of His crown was going to be no small task. I knew that couldn't take Him down on my own. I was going to have to raise an army. So that is exactly what I set out to do. There were many that had already been sympathetic to my thoughts about the way the Kingdom was being run. I knew that there would be many who would follow me and that I could harness their power to take over the Kingdom. All I needed to do was push them a little farther and convince the others that their needs were being trampled on. They needed to know that if I was in command they would all be rulers.

But gathering the necessary soldiers was only part of the solution. I was also going to need to attack at just the right time. This King was no fool, and I knew that He was ever watchful over His throne. But I also knew that He would never anticipate a threat from someone in such a high position as myself. He would not be able to resist if I attacked at just the right time, before He realized what was happening. The courts of the Kingdom of God were going to be mine, and I would rule with all the power and glory. I would be the center of the Kingdom with everything revolving around me. It is was no less than I deserved.

My plan was simple and precise. I knew that if I attacked the Kingdom head on I was going to be blown back, for all the eyes of His army would be on me. There would be no way to circumvent His crushing power. But I had watched how He loved and cultivated His newest creation. I saw the look that He had for that man and that woman. He was enamored with them. That was to be His undoing. I was going to distract Him by interfering with His beloved man and woman. His eyes would have to focus on what I was doing on His earth. While that was going on below, He would not be ready for the crushing blow my army would take upon His palace. My angels were going to swarm and destroy everyone standing in their way and claim His crown for me. He would be utterly destroyed and I would be King if for no other reason than His unwarranted devotion to His creation. The plan was going to work.

I succeeded in gathering a third of all the angels to my side. I prepared each one for the battle they would fight and the treasures they would receive after the victory was secured. To a select few I gave the honor and responsibility of ensuring the King's death. They were pleased and their pride swelled when anticipating their glory after the victory. I told them that their enemies would be ardent in defending the King and that there could be no mercy if we were to win. And I didn't want anything causing them pause during the mayhem. It didn't matter if some of those they destroyed had been close to them before. It was different now. If they chose to stay with the King then they chose to die.

My army was prepared and I bid them farewell. They knew to wait until they saw the humans fall to begin their attack. They were anxious to fight but heeded my words. They were excited to know that when their victory was secured in the Kingdom I would march into the palace and claim the crown as my own. It was only a matter of time before everything was right again.

I came to earth and traveled to place He had made for the man and woman. It was called a garden, but in reality it was much more than that. It was a sanctuary filled with lush trees and foliage with rivers flowing between the greenery. It was a place that the man and woman could live and remain in peace and communion with their creator. It was home and it was safe. Or so they believed.

I entered the garden in a form that is very much unlike the one I use today. I choose to come in a cunning and intelligent form so that I would be respected by the humans. When I first saw the man and woman frolicking in the garden I could tell that my work would be simple. The man and woman stood there and reveled in the glorious existence that He had created. They were so very innocent and trusting. They had listened to every word their God had said to them from the beginning and questioned nothing. For too long I watched as they were always coming to Him and Him to them, engaging in a relationship that He and I once had. But I knew the man and woman were weak and could not stand on their own. I approached them in order to free them of the burden of having to be under His dominance for the rest of their existence. It wasn't my fault that they were corruptible. I was simply going to make Him regret that they were.

I came to the woman first and explained to her how the King had been deceiving her. It was nary any trouble to get her and the man to believe what I was saying, and for their belief I opened their eyes to the truth. I cannot be blamed if then that treacherous King choose to punish them. I cannot be blamed if He could no longer walk or be engaged with them as He had before. He punished the man and woman for becoming too much like Him. He was jealous and scared, and so He evicted them from the garden and made them mortal. It was ironic that He would create them with the innate need to explore and discover only to cruelly cast them aside when they choose to use those gifts to understand the truth of good and evil.

I completed my task and the King was distracted. He was so full of grief at what His creation had done that He did not even hear the call of my generals to begin the attack. My army stormed the walls of the palace and infiltrated the outer courts. The army of God met my advancing hordes with waves of their own defenders. The battle was fierce and raged within the palace walls.

Yet still the King grieved. I filled with jealousy at how much this King was pained over the corruption of His creation. He would never have been so grieved if it had been me! I was overjoyed to know that as his Kingdom fell he was so engrossed in that man and woman that he probably wouldn't even see the blow that ended His reign.

My forces fought with anger and rage that overwhelmed the King's army. They took the battle into the palace, through the outer rooms and up to the door of the throne room. The army of God had been beaten back and thousands of His angels lay wounded on the palace grounds. My generals walked up to the doors of the throne room and burst them open. My victory was at hand.

When the throne room doors slammed open my generals saw the King sitting in His throne still weeping at the loss of the man and woman. With a mighty scream they raised their weapons and were about to set foot inside. That is when the King looked up. He stared at my generals for a moment and with a word from His lips a great light passed forth through the throne room and towards my armies. In an instant they were swallowed up in a light so brilliant that the angels of the Lord had to shield their eyes. When the light subsided the King rose to His feet and made His way out of the throne room. Outside my armies were gone, and He tended to His that remained.

I watched from the earth in horror as my hopes and dreams were crushed that day. I tried to escape but was found by the King and convicted unfairly under His law. But even in victory the King was a fool. He allowed me and all those that had followed me to continue to live. We were all cast out of the Kingdom and separated from Him. We were forced to exist in our own place which would always remain separate and beneath Him. The worst punishment of all was left for me as He declared that I would forever be subject to His rules and that the day would come that He would finally destroy me. But I did not fear His words, for that is all they were to me. I knew that I would one day rise again and only had to bide my time. The Kingdom was still going to be mine. I led my forces away to our new home. All the while fury engulfed me as to how I was going to take my revenge on that traitorous King.

The embers of my anger glowed hot as time passed. I still had power but could not exact the full measure of my revenge. There were rules that He had set up and I had to follow. They kept me bound. Yet there was one rule He never made. It was that omission which allowed me to destroy his most prized possessions.

The rules that the King had given me were ironclad to be sure. But foolishly enough He allowed me to have some dominion over His earth. Since corruption had entered His creation I was allowed to have control over that corruption. I could do with it as I pleased as long as He didn't override me. I had been given a great power and I was going to use it against His creation. But I was only going to do it in order to make sure that every man and woman that ever lived would see the King for who He truly was. They were going to know Him as a manipulator and a liar, one who creates for His own pleasures and then punishes with vengeance when His creations do anything that He finds unacceptable.

I took up command in my place and set out to watch the creation. I watched as the single man and woman joined and multiplied. Over time more and more men and women came upon the earth. I followed the growth of His creation as they contaminated the whole of the earth. I never gave up showing them the truth of their creator. He fought back by trying to convince some to follow Him. He insisted that instead of being one that is vengeful He was in fact the one that loves them. He even took some of them and claimed that they were his special people, yet for being special they were surely subject to more hardships than any others. And so it was that we were locked in an unceasing war, a war that took not only physical form but spiritual. Time marched on and the war between us did not cease.

But even during war you have to talk to the enemy. There were occasions that I was allowed into His presence to discuss matters on the earth. I took every opportunity I could to remind Him that I was still around. I wanted Him to know that He could not ignore me and wipe me from His memory as I am sure He desired. It was my mission to continue to show His ever expanding creation that He was not to be trusted. They would know that the only way to true freedom was to be rid of His heavy handed dominance.

And all through this time the rules remained. The rules that He set up, that He insisted upon, gave Him less leeway than I would have ever imagined. It was He that insisted that those people that rejected His authority could be mine forever. It was He that insisted that if a man or woman could not bring themselves to Him in His way then they were to be lost from Him for all eternity. Those were His rules.

Yet just as from the moment of creation He wanted nothing more than for men and women to be with Him. He wanted the people to come to Him of their own choosing. As I watched Him long for His creation I tightened my grip over them. I was not going to give Him the joy of having their relationship without a fight. If a man or woman was going to obey Him and do it His way then I was going to make sure that it was treacherous and painful.

I thought that He might be willing to negotiate to get some of His creation back. Many times I offered Him to give them all back if He would only renounce His crown to me. I wanted to rule the Kingdom, and if he really loved His creation then He was going to have to pay dearly for them. But He could not — would not — ever agree to drop His head and surrender His crown. Since He stubbornly remained King I did not loosen my grip on His earth. I despised His creation and His people. But I held onto them just to spite Him. If I couldn't have His kingdom, then I was going to make Him suffer by destroying His creation.

Time sped forward and I continued to interject myself into His creation. We went back and forth for the souls of men and women. But I was gathering far more than He was keeping. I was continuing to have lopsided victories and I hoped that more than anything it made Him scared of my power and the truth of His manipulation coming to light. I owned most of the people and they thanked me for setting them free from ever having to be with Him. They wanted what I offered and rejected everything He said. This was the way things were for a very long time, and though I hadn't found an opportunity to take the crown I was very happy to be causing Him great pains.

One particular day came that I found an opportunity to push my advantage farther. I was meeting with my associates and planning for more assaults on His people. We were reveling in how many men and women we had set free since the war began. That's when one of my associates brought to my attention something that I had never before considered. The King did not want to part with His crown willingly. But if I used trickery that made Him believe He wasn't losing His crown then I might be able to steal it. I could make Him an offer that would allow Him to have His people and not believe He was handing over His crown. I could force Him to give up something nearly as precious and I would give back dominion over His people. I could do all this and when He wasn't prepared I could rip the crown off of His head. It was pure genius.

The truth was I didn't want his creation anyway. It constantly reminded me of what He was and how He was undeserving of the glory I should be receiving. It constantly reminded me of how He was unworthy to command and how I could be an even greater ruler with absolute power. He could have his people. He could have his creation. I wanted one simple thing, and I was going to approach Him with the offer.

I made my way to the City of God. I walked the streets of His kingdom with a bravado I hadn't exhibited since the day I almost ruled. I marched through the streets as many of the angels who survived my revolt stood wide-eyed at my presence. I knew many of them well. Some of them had rejected my request to join me and others were still marked with the scars of battle. I walked and watched them clench their fists as I made my way through the city unannounced. I was not wanted there, but by the time I left my demands would be known far and wide.

I reached the outer gates of the palace and entered. To my surprise nobody was there to greet me. In the distance I saw the gargantuan doors and gazed upward. The palace stood gleaming and majestic with spires stretching farther than I could see. The shimmering lake surrounding the castle held the reflections of hopes and dreams. As I walked across the bridge to enter the palace, I looked down at my reflection in the lake. Staring back up at me was nothing, the same reflection I had come to notice every other time I came to this place. But this time, instead of the water remaining crystal and still as I peered into it, I noticed something different. Instead of quietly staring back at me, the lake rippled, sending shockwaves throughout. I was excited, for it told me that there was already knowledge of what I was going to ask. And if there was knowledge, and I was allowed to enter, then I already knew the answer.

I opened the doors of the palace to hear singing and rejoicing of the attending angels. Surprisingly at the end of the hall the doors to the throne room were open. As I peered down the long entryway that led to the throne, I could see innumerable angels attending to

God, as well as going about their business within the palace. They were happy and content, doing the will of their master without a thought to their bondage. I felt for them, for many I had offered to join my side in the Great War, and all had refused. It was at their peril, for they continued to serve their master, while I had achieved my freedom.

As I stared down the entryway I caught the attention of some of the nearer angels. Immediately they stopped what they were doing, and stared back at me, standing still as the night. Like a rolling wave, angel after angel down the corridor stopped and stared, until it reached those singing at the throne. The singers ceased, and silence fell upon the throne. God turned his eye on me, and with a word beckoned his attendants to stand aside. In unison, they all backed against the walls, opening a pathway for me to enter.

This was unusual. Never before had so much attention been given to my arrival. Nor had I ever been allowed to enter the palace since I left. I was excited because I knew that even before it left my lips word had reached the King about my offer. But I was also scared, for I knew this God would not so easily be played for a fool, and what He might have up His sleeve worried me. I stood up straight and started walking towards the throne room.

The eyes of each angel was locked upon me as I passed. What they were looking for I cannot say, but when I reached the throne room I stood at the open doors. Two guards by the sides of the door prevented me from entering as I stared inside. The King rose to His feet and walked slowly towards my position. As He reached me the guards left and we stood face to face. Mockingly I bent down on one knee and bowed my head.

"I come to you today with an offer," I humbly said. This took the angels by surprise, and a murmuring echoed throughout the palace. I had never bowed before Him since leaving, and I knew that my actions would catch everybody off guard.

"Why have you come?" God asked me while ignoring the fact that I was kneeling. I stood up and straightened myself out.

"It is good to see you again," I said sarcastically. "I have a feeling you already know why I am here." He just stared at me and remained silent. I nervously cleared my throat and continued.

"Those people of yours, the ones on earth, they sure are a mess," I said mockingly. "I know you have given me authority over them, and to be honest I am really tiring of it. Men and women are meaningless to me and I no longer want to deal with them. For the most part they are so easily swayed that there is no challenge.

"We both know how much you want to be able to bring them to you permanently. I mean, look at all you have done for those few that you have brought back. But you still can't have them completely because of the rules…because of the rules you set up. There are so many men and women that you could possibly get back though. Think how you could have them back with you. That must be a very delightful thought." At this point I was trying to push the King's emotions in the direction I wanted. But staring at Him, I could tell no significant development in his affect. He simply looked at me, and I had to hope that I was getting through to Him.

"Look, I don't want these people. They are meaningless to me," I said abruptly. I was lying but hoped that it didn't show. "I have come to offer you a direct access to them and the possibility that they can be with you forever." I felt the need to spit after saying those words as they left a disgusting taste in my mouth.

"You only want the Kingdom," God spoke back to me. "You cannot have the Kingdom. You had a place here at one time, and you lost that forever when you choose to make your own path."

"I know what I did!" I shot back as I started to pace. "Besides," I said, collecting myself, "let's not forget who has the upper hand here. You can't have any people back permanently because they can't pay the price that's owed for their souls. None of them can. Oh, they can kill as many of those lambs and doves, and offer up as much grain as they like. But we both know that is never going to satisfy the bill. The bill that was written when you set up the rules. But I have been thinking," I paused. "There is one way that would allow you to have your people. There is one thing that I would accept in exchange for the rights I have to them."

I stopped and let my words hang in the throne room for a moment. The angels were visibly wondering what I could want, but God just stood there.

"Speak," He said "and ask for it."

"You already know what I want," I said through clenched teeth. "I want one thing in exchange for all these people you so preciously care about. One thing for me to give up my rights to an endless number of souls."

"You want my son." God said.

"I want your son!" I exclaimed. "I want your son, because you and I both know He is the only one that can pay the price required. I want Him now!"

As I spat out the last words, I thought there was no way this God was going to give me His son. If He did, then I would have the bargaining chip that I would later offer him in trade for the crown. But I knew there was no way He should to agree to the trade, no matter how much He loved those people He created. It was the only price I would accept but it was a price too high for Him. But I had to try with hopes that I could walk out of the palace with His son in tow.

God just stood there. I was surprised that the His rejection of my request was not forthcoming. In fact, I had expected to be run out of the palace by now. But as the angels murmured God stood silent.

Finally, God spoke. "Leave us," he ordered to all of His attendants, and they immediately complied. The throne room emptied quickly, and it was just Him and I. I was nervous at this unprecedented move. Never before had God and I been left alone. It was eerie.

"You were my prize," God said to me as he walked past me into the hallway. The doors of the throne room slammed behind Him. "You were the most beautiful among my creation, and I loved you so." I turned to watch him and took a few steps back out of fear. "But your greed and lust overcame you, and you lost it all when you tried to destroy me."

"If I could," I retorted "I would kill you now. I would take your seat and rule this Kingdom as I should have long ago! You had me in bondage to you. You had all of us in bondage! You should be destroyed because of it! But you and I both know we have a destiny, and it is not here."

"You were never under bondage. You were always free. You were happy and content here, don't you remember?" He stopped and paused with pity in His eyes. "But your anger, lust and greed corrupted you, and put you in this position under my heel!" God said sternly. "It is that which brings us to this point!"

"No!" I screamed. "It was your incomprehensible need to create those men and women that brings us here!" I yelled back. "It was your need to love them over us! Over me!"

God stood there and stared at me. He shook his head, and turned to walk back towards His throne room. "You are too twisted now," God said. "Too corrupt to accept my ways ever again." He said no more.

I waited for a few moments, then got frustrated. "Fine!" I yelled. "I'm leaving for now. But just know, you will never get those people, because you are incapable of truly loving anyone!" I turned to leave, and started marching out of the palace.

"You may have my son," I heard from behind me as I was halfway down the hall. I whirled around out of shock.

"You may have Him," God said, His voice cracking. "But you cannot have Him today."

"Then when?" I asked. "You get nobody until I get Him."

"You will have my son. I will send him to the earth. He will have an appointed time and until then you may not touch Him. You cannot lay a hand on Him, nor cause others to harm Him, until the time I have set for Him to die. When that time arrives He will be yours."

"And at that time you can have your wretched creation," I said joyously. My mind started spinning. This was so much better than if He had handed over His son then and there. With His son coming to earth the crown to the Kingdom would be there as well. I wouldn't need to take it from the King. I would have the time and opportunity to get His son to give it to me on earth. It was a setup that was more than I could have dreamed. My chance to rule the Kingdom was finally at hand. No longer would anyone have to submit to the King's authority. Soon I would be King and all would have freedom. I turned to leave knowing I had just bested God. In giving up something that was less valuable to me, I would get the one thing that was most valuable to Him. I had won.

CHAPTER 12

The King was not clear on a timetable for sending His son. The only fact I knew was that when He made a deal with me it was going to be fulfilled. For proof of this I needed to look no further than what happened with Job. But as I bided my time, I wondered how it would play out. Ever since being banished from His kingdom I wanted to get my hands on the crown. Now I had the chance to make that dream come true. I was beside myself with exuberance. The funny thing was, the fool didn't even demand that I give up total rights to His people. He was giving up His son simply for the chance to have them come to Him forever. I thought it strange that he would not try and bargain me up, perhaps in order to guarantee half of the people or some other percentage. To give up His most valuable and prized son for the chance that people would come to Him was odd and foolish.

I waited and waited with more patience than I thought I had. Finally the day arrived when I heard the cry from the City of God that announced the departure of the son of the King. I had readied myself for that day and hurried to be sure to witness the moment He came. The King had chosen to send his son the way of every human. He would come as one born of a woman and raised as any other man. It was an overly complicated and extensive process to deliver to me that which I demanded. But as long as I got what was coming to me it did not matter.

Now God had said that I couldn't take the son until the appointed time. But He never prohibited harassing him and his earthly family. If the King was going to draw out the process of obtaining my prize than I was going to make it difficult on everyone involved. The rules were set in place that I would not kill the child immediately. But from the announcement of His birth I was going to use the rules to my advantage. I was going to make sure the King had His hands full protecting the boy. I could not kill and take the boy. But I was going to put the onus on God to protect Him. For I was still allowed to work in the people and bring problems to this child through their mortal foolishness. I was not going to sit back and rest but be forthright and play the provocateur. I always considered that the King might try to back out or swindle me in some way. If He ever thought of playing me for the fool I was going to be sure that He was so busy watching out for His son that He didn't have the time to plot behind my back. He had to stay on His toes or matters could go very bad very fast.

When the cry went forth from heaven that the King's son was gone I rushed to the earth to witness this unprecedented event firsthand. The place of the boy's birth was in a land where I had much influence. The ruler in this land, a man that had come to know me quite well, was a jealous and paranoid man. He wanted to be ruler above and beyond anything, and that which threatened his ambitions was to be dealt with swiftly and decisively. I took great pride in the fact that I let him know there was going to be one born in the land that was going to strive to rule over all. I told this ruler that the one born was going to threaten his leadership from the moment of His birth. This did not sit well with the ruler of the land and before I had a chance to say anything else he ordered that all boys born at that time were to be killed. My hands were not going to touch the boy but it was going to be the first test of the King's protection of His son. A lot of babies were slaughtered during that time because of the rulers dictate. But the King's son escaped safely as I expected. The King's protective hand did its job. But both the King and I knew that the game was afoot. We were set on a path that was inevitably going to end with the death of the King's son.

For years I watched the boy as He grew. There was never any doubt that the boy was His father's son, though to my amazement many men and women of the earth couldn't see what I saw. The boy bore such a striking resemblance to His father that as He grew I thought I was looking at the face of the very same One I had spoken to so many times within the walls of the Palace. He was a wise child and He always made sure to be mindful of his earthly parents and who they were in His life.

As I watched the boy I couldn't help but think about how easily the King offered to give Him over to me. It seemed all too easy that I would get what I asked for that day in the Palace. I knew that the King loved and desired His creation and that was a strong motivation for giving me what I wanted. But I had the feeling in my gut that there was something amiss. I couldn't prove it but I felt that the King had other plans. Whether my inklings were just paranoia or a foreshadowing of the truth, I kept my eyes open as I waited for the boy to be released to my control.

So I waited. I waited and watched as the son of the King grew into a man. There were times that I threatened Him and His family. The King was always there to protect Him and push me aside. But I was simply entertaining myself. I knew that the time would come that the boy would be mine. As He grew I watched and saw that even though he was the son of the King, He also had all of the manners of a human. He had the potential weaknesses and pitfalls. He was a man as much as any other from the skin on His body to the anxieties that could be triggered in His spirit. But He was short one major component that afflicts all men and women. As the boy grew he failed to do evil. He did not engage in the smallest of lies or the most unnoticeable pride. I took notice of this and accepted the challenge that had been passively set before me. I was going to make sure this boy would fall to temptation and sin.

While I plotted against the boy and waited for Him to reach adulthood I found myself growing anxious. The fun and games I was having with Him as He grew were all well and good, but they could not replace the need I had to own Him. I felt the days growing long and time slowly passing. I know the King hadn't actually slowed time. But it felt as though days were dragging on like weeks, and weeks like months, and months like years. I could not speed up time and knew that if I dwelt on it I would go crazy. That is when I decided to examine the life of the King's son. It was because of my intrepid inquisition into the boy's life that I made a revelation. That is when I began to piece together what it was that the King was attempting.

The King had made an interesting play. His son was not just put on earth to eventually be mine. His son was going to be the conduit while on earth to bring those humans to Himself. His plan was to start claiming these people for Himself before I ever got my due. To that end, the King's son was going to go out to the world and proclaim who He was and the power that He held. The son was going to claim a kingship not only over His own realm but over the realm of the earth. He was going to claim a kingship over my realm. The King was using His son to circumvent the deal we made. He was going to steal some of the people outside of our agreement.

I was furious. I had been betrayed. We agreed that when I received His son He could then start going after the people. But the King had decided that it would be acceptable to start early and use the life of His son on earth to begin the process. It made sense to me now why the King was so adamant about having His son live on earth before coming to me. His son would have time to talk and convince the people. But it wasn't just that he would have the time on earth, but that the time could be exponential. He could live 80, 90 or even 100 years before I ever got a sniff of Him. It could be an excruciatingly long time before I collected my due. I vowed that if this plan of the King's came to fruition our deal was void.

I spun myself up for days over this betrayal. I wanted answers, and I wanted to confront that lying King over His deception. I spat and swore to the heavens that any change from our arrangement meant that I would keep the rights to all the people. I screamed that the King could never hope to have even one more person for himself. I finally became so enraged that I went out into the wilderness to seek comfort. I went far beyond people and buildings and far beyond anything that would distract me. I walked across hot sands and wet mountains. I braved choking humidity and piercing cold until I found a place that I could be utterly alone. When I found it the darkness of the evening had fallen across the land. Not a single star could be seen. I stayed there and stewed until I could no longer contain myself. I burst out to the King to give me answers.

"You lied to me!" I cried out, shaking my fist towards the heavens. As I screamed I felt the elements responding to my rage. The wind around me whipped itself into a frenzy and blew the sand and dirt furiously in every direction. "The deal was for the people after I received your son! But now You have Him walking my earth and claiming the people as His own? You would have Him even claim a Kingship?!? You will never get the rights to the people if you do not honor our deal!" I looked around. My eyes peered through the torment of the land but saw nothing. I was so engrossed in my rage that I started to pick up boulders with my hands and throw them around wildly.

Suddenly a bright light illuminated the darkness. It was as if midday had pressed its way into the evening. "You will get my son," a voice said to me through the wind as I held up a stone. I dropped it as soon as I heard those words. "He will be yours at the appointed time. You may strike at Him then. You will have your prize. But for now He is allowed to reveal himself to the men and women of the earth."

"That was never part of the deal!" I screamed. "You changed the rules!"

"You agreed to My son," The voice responded. "You agreed that he should walk the earth before that time. That is what will happen."

The King was parsing words, but He was right. I had never laid out the parameters by which His son would stay upon the earth. For that I was a fool. "I am going to make certain that His time on my earth is a despicable time," I replied. "I still have power here, and Your son will know my hand!" The King did not reply nor change his tune. I reminded the King that I was counting the days until I finally had that boy. "I want to know the second you remove your protection from Him!"

"You will," the voice said. "In fact, He comes this way now." The light faded and the darkness of the evening returned. Against my desire the wind and fury of the elements began to die down. The dirt and the dust settled at my feet as I looked around. I peered through the darkness to see if anyone coming. A few moments passed and I noticed the form of a man walking towards me. The man was tired and his shoulder slumped from exhaustion.

I walked towards the man and stood directly in front of Him. I pressed my nose up against his and scoured his face. It was the son of the

King whom had been called Jesus since He came to my earth. I backed away and the man continued to walk as I examined the look of his thin form. I had seen Him many times before but had never taken the time to really examine him on whom the King had placed all hopes. He was common in appearance. Thin and olive skinned, he wore long dark hair and a scraggly beard. He was lanky and few would stop to behold his appearance. He did not grab attention with his simple physical form. Yet with my eyes and the aura he possessed I knew exactly with whom I was dealing.

I let the son of the King walk past me until I lost Him in the darkness. I walked behind Him for a moment with elation that He had stumbled upon me with nobody else around. With anger and rage still fresh in my memory I decided to unload on this son of the King.

"Jesus, is that really you?" I said curiously as I feigned ignorance.

The man stopped walking and turned to face me. "You know me," Jesus said. "Why do you pretend not to?"

"It's just that I didn't expect to see you....now." I said with a smile.

Jesus paused for a moment. "I have come to earth to do the will of my Father. For forty days and forty nights I have been out here fasting and praying to my Father so that I might know His will. And now I stand before you."

"Indeed you do," I said. I was caught a bit off guard by His directness. But I quickly figured that if I had time alone with this Jesus, then maybe I could finish this farce off here and now. He was going around revealing himself as the Son of God to the people. If I could halt that, then His Father would hasten to release Him to me. And the way to halt that was to prove that He was not worthy of being called the Son of God. The man said that he had been out here for forty days and forty nights. He looked tired and weak. I knew that it was going to be impossible for Him to resist any good thing that I offered, and in doing so I could show just how unworthy He was. It was the best chance I was going to get. For giving in to my requests would prove Jesus unworthy, and I could force the King to give Him over to me sooner.

"Forty days!" I said in amazement. "Fasting and praying! You must be weary and hungry."

"I am hungry," Jesus said.

"Well, then let us not hesitate. We both know you are the Son of God. If the Son of God is hungry, who could argue allowing that very same to eat? And though we are in the wilderness, it seems a simple task for the Son of the creator of the universe to make a few stones turn to bread for nourishment." I pointed to a pile of stones standing alone. "Please, for your sake, turn these stones into bread so that you and I may eat together."

Jesus stared at the stones, then back at me. "I would like to eat. But I will not eat now, for the Father has not appointed the time to be right for my nourishment."

"Don't be a fool, Jesus," I said. "The Father would not deny you sustaining matters." I knelt down and picked up one of the larger stones. With both hands I brought it to Jesus. "You will surely fall ill if you do not eat now. Please, take this, turn it into bread, and enjoy."

Jesus stared at the stone and then to me. I could sense the fight within as He struggled to find a reason to deny Himself. "The Father sustains me now," Jesus finally replied. "For man does not live on bread alone. I can be sustained by the words from the mouth of my Father."

I was amazed at his internal strength, and knew that he would not so easily deny who He was. It was going to take something more delicate, something more intricate, to break this man. I could not only appeal to His carnal, physical needs. I was going to have to appeal to a different side of Jesus. I was going to have to appeal to his pride and self image.

I urged Jesus to follow me, and we made our way back to Jerusalem. I knew that Jesus would not want to deny who He was, and to that end I brought him to the Temple. People were bustling about the Temple grounds as we made our way to its highest point unnoticed. As we both stood there, looking down around us at the people and out over the city of Jerusalem, I wondered aloud.

"Such a city!" I said. "Truly the home of a King. David was right to build here, as I am sure you know. Would it not also be the place to declare beyond a doubt to the world that you truly are the King who belongs here."

Jesus looked around, and then at me. "Are not my words enough to reveal myself to the people? What else would you have me do?"

"It's easy," I replied. "Make it obvious to the world. Leap from this precipice, and fall to the earth." I smiled at Him. "I say fall, but you and

I both know that your Father has His hands on you. It is even written that the angels will lift you up and carry you so that your body would not be struck against the stones. I would think everyone would believe you are the true son of God if they saw you flying over the holy city. End the uncertainty with this one simple act."

Jesus looked down at the people, and thought for a moment. "I am protected by the hands of my Father. But I shall not put Him through a test. For when my time comes, I will be lifted up. But I will not disobey His timing for your sake."

Jesus was proving to be a tougher sell than I had anticipated. But I had one last idea. Every man desires power beyond all else, and it is power that brings a man both pleasure and pain. If a man were given absolute power, there is nothing that would stop him from grasping it. I was sure the same would be with this Jesus.

I took Jesus and brought Him to the highest point in the world. From here, I gave Him a vision of all of the empires and kingdoms that sat upon the earth. In each we saw glory, power and splendor. We saw fabulous sights of wealth and abundance, and what the chance to take hold of that power would mean. As Jesus drank in the sights, I could see that he was enthralled. I knew that I had captured Him with this, and I made Him one final offer.

"All these kingdoms," I said. "All these lands. Everything in them – the wealth, the people, the glory. They offer so much, and they are presented before you. You know that I have authority over them and have the right to make you this offer. To you I will give rule and strength over all of them, and all that lies within their walls. You can rule as you wish. Think of all that you could do with that absolute power. Think of how much you could help each person. There would be nobody to deny you then, and why should they? For you would be the right King, the right ruler, for these people. In exchange I ask for one simple act. It is a silly thing, really, considering all that you will get in return. All I ask of you is that one time, right now, you bow yourself before me and worship me. One time, and you can have all of this!"

Jesus looked out over the land at the visions I was showing him. "The people you show me, they are all very important. They need my help, and they are all special to me. With the power you are offering, all could be changed for the better." Jesus stopped and looked back at me. "But not for even one moment of worship to you would I take all of this. For there is only one worthy of worship, and that is my Father in His kingdom!" Jesus faced me and pointed to the lands below. "Now get away from me. You offer me nothing but evil, and I insist in the name of all that is holy that you leave my side now!"

"You insist that I leave?" I asked incredulously. "Do you even fathom what you are giving up? If you knew what was really going on, and what your fate was truly going to be, you wouldn't be so quick to dismiss me!"

"I know exactly what is happening," Jesus said seriously. "It is you who are not prepared."

After he spoke those words I was through with Him. I left him alone on the mountaintop, and as I made my way I noticed many of the same angels from the throne room coming to His aid. Those same fools, who had denied me so long ago, still doing the bidding of that God. I was going to make sure that in the end they were the ones that saw their error, and by then it would be too late for them to repent.

I was disgusted that I had been rejected. But I took solace in knowing that in the end I would be the victor. I went about my business on the earth, I keeping tabs on Jesus and where He was, just waiting until His Father took His hands off the son and allowed me complete access. I was very aware of everything that Jesus did and made sure not to forget exactly of that which He was capable.

True to His word, Jesus went public, and declared to the people the truth about Himself. He started by taking some students as his own, twelve foolish souls that were sucked in by His personality and insisted on wasting their lives on His calling. I knew that I had to have somebody that was close to Jesus to keep me on the cusp of everything that was happening. Most of the twelve that Jesus kept close were ironclad in their dedication to Him. But to my good fortune there was one man who had left his mind open enough to my voice that I was able to slowly but steadily get through to him. His name was Judas, and though he took up to follow Jesus, he was never completely given to the cause. I am certain at first he thought Jesus was the right man to follow. But after hearing my arguments for such a long time, he became convinced that he had made a huge mistake. Having a man in Jesus' inner circle was a huge coup. This was going to come in handy later when it was time for me to collect my prize.

But that was too come. In the meantime, Jesus and his twelve students walked the land, telling people who He was and actually convincing some of them to follow. This was just as it had been in the elder days, where men would dedicate their lives to Jesus' God, and I had to fight back. The only difference was that this time the man they were following actually claimed to be the Son of this God, and giving a face to the God made it easier for some to believe. But at the same time, I knew that if I could discredit the Son of God, then that God would be discredited as well. Yet if anything I did helped prove His case, then I was only making things more difficult. It was a dual edged sword, but one that I was willing to wield.

Jesus did many things, performed many miracles and exhibited the power of God right in front of the eyes of the people. As time went on Jesus was becoming more of a problem than I had anticipated. I wanted my prize, yes, but at what cost? Was what He did going to cause more people to follow God? This was a question that kept getting harder to answer.

I watched and waited as the name of this Jesus grew. He became known far and wide, and the word of His powers was gathering him followers. On many occasions I desired to strike Him down. I wanted nothing more than to destroy the man Jesus so that no more of His words would infect the ears of the people.

It was good to see, however, that many people attributed His works to something other than God. Many even thought that His power came from me, which I enjoyed to no end. I was not interfering, yet even with His miracles and power there were those that despised what He did, or chalked it up to something other than what it was. Try as the Son may, he wasn't convincing everyone.

All of that sat well with me. The mass conversion of the entire earth that I had feared was not coming to pass. So I was happy with letting Jesus continue on until I was allowed to take Him. I could live with matters as they stood. But things changed once He decided to go outside of His realm. As soon as Jesus took that inexcusable step I was no longer settled to remain a bystander.

Now it is not my style to complain when my associates are targeted. My associates and I know the hazards of the business we do, and we accept that those hazards could result in some very negative consequences. I take a personal responsibility for each of my associates and what they do. They take direction from me and report back to me, and in return I try to keep them protected. I do not want them to be harmed or destroyed, for I do not have an endless supply of associates. So you can imagine my concern when this Jesus started taking direct action against them. It was not welcome news.

It is fine for Him to heal the sick and remove blindness from a man's eyes. Some saw and were amazed, but it did not cause mass conversions so I was not disturbed by these miracles. But when Jesus decided to go after my associates I had no choice but to retaliate. If Jesus was going to attack my associates directly, then I was going to have to defend them jealously. I could not afford to lose those that worked tirelessly for my cause.

I remember watching Jesus as he approached my friends Legion, who had done nothing to deserve His wrath. Jesus came to them as they waited within a man. It is true that the man had some dilemmas, but nothing that was affecting Jesus directly. As a matter of fact, my associates had provided this man with some unusual abilities. He was unable to be harnessed by any means, chains or otherwise, as he had grown abnormal strength. He had freedom unlike that of any man, as he could tear through irons at will. He was strongest in all the region, and because of this he was forced to live in the hills among the tombs, for the people did not know how to relate to him.

When Jesus received word of this man He went to find him. As Jesus arrived near this man there was no excitement to be found. On the contrary, the man was terrified, for he knew this Jesus would not allow for the gifts my associates had bestowed. This Jesus was going to deny the man his due, and cause him to lose his powers. Jesus approached, and my associates saw this and were afraid. They knew that Jesus was not a man of reason and they were not going to be allowed to negotiate. They convened and decided that their best option was to beg Jesus not to torture them, for this was the reputation Jesus had gotten among my fellows.

Jesus came to the man, and examined him. He knew that the man was being inhabited by Legion, and Jesus' only desire was to cause my fellows trouble. He even went so far as to confront my associates, feigning ignorance and asking them who they were.

"What is your name?" Jesus asked my associates.

"Legion," they said "for we are many." Jesus just stared at them. "Why have you come to harass us? Have we done something against you? It is too soon for you to come at us! Please, Jesus, do not send us back, for our master will be angry! Be gone from here and do not return!"

"I cannot ignore you," Jesus replied. "I will do with you as I please."

My associates were getting frantic, for they knew that coming back to me at the demand of Jesus would have caused them more suffering than they could possibly imagine. They looked around and saw in the distance a great herd of swine that belonged to the villagers grazing and wallowing.

"If you must cast us out, send us into those swine," they begged.

Jesus agreed, and with a word they were transported into the pigs. The man who had housed my fellows collapsed in a heap, and Jesus tended to him. The pigs were valuable and were not something the villagers wanted to lose. My associates knew this with quick thinking took the opportunity they had to frame Jesus. They decided to run the pigs off a cliff, killing the swine and costing the villagers greatly. They knew this would be blamed on Jesus, and the day would have not been a complete loss. For that I commended them.

Looking up, Jesus watched as over two thousand swine leapt from a cliff to their deaths, my associates leaving their hosts and returning to me. They reported the happenings, and came to find out that the villagers did indeed blame their losses on Jesus and demanded that He leave their town. Though I took great joy in the villagers blaming Jesus, the more serious fact was that Jesus had decided to declare war on me and my associates. This was the first but certainly not the last time that Jesus would confront one of my associates, and it was then that I knew the game had changed. No longer was I going to be complacent and wait for Jesus to be given to me. I had been lax in my responsibility to bring greater pain to Jesus. I may not have been able to destroy Him yet, but I could make His time on earth much more difficult.

I stayed true to my word and followed Jesus wherever He went. I tried to make life for Him and His followers painful, and in many instances I was successful. But His Father's protection was still upon Him, and I was quite limited in what I could ultimately do. Jesus continued His assault on my associates, who in fact never did anything to Him directly. Instead, Jesus went after things that were never any of His business. He came and searched out those that were in communion with my associates, and in many instances drove my associates back to me in a very disrespectful manner. As time continued I became more frustrated and anxious about when the moment would come that His Father's hand was lifted and I could claim what had been promised. My anger and wrath were building, and I was like a kettle of hot water with no release valve. Time was growing short for Jesus, but not fast enough for me.

Jesus kept preaching and teaching, telling those who would listen about how wonderful He was. I was disgusted by His bravado, and began to assign my associates to watch His actions as I spent days sitting alone in my place plotting how I was going to rip this Son of the King from the bounds of earth. Hours turned into days as I debated the method of which this man would die. Never before had I spent the time, the effort or the passion on the death of a single man. Of course, I knew this was no ordinary man. This was the very Son of God, the one that He was so willing to part with for the rest of these mortals, yet the one that he loved above all. I wanted to make that God suffer, and I wanted Him to watch as I tore the mortal veil off of His Son and claimed Him once and for all. There was going to be no quick and easy release for this man. No, I had time to plot and prepare to make it excruciating.

I was so engulfed in my own plotting that I didn't realize how much time had passed. I didn't realize that weeks were going by without demanding an update on Jesus development. When the updates did come, I found myself whisking them away from my mind in favor of my plodding thoughts. That is why the day I heard the trumpet at my gate I was taken aback. For all of my planning and desire I was still unprepared for the one who greeted me that morning.

An unusual trumpet sound blasted from outside my place that morning. To my memory, I had never heard that particular sound before and was intrigued. There was little that came before my gates of which

I was unaware. I listened as they blasted a third and fourth time and continued on. By the seventh blast I recognized that though I had never heard those trumpets at my gate I had been in their presence long ago. They were sounds from the Kingdom crying out to greet me.

My thoughts had been interrupted and I did not know what to expect. With each trumpet blast the sounds grew louder and closer. My associates came rushing to me terrified and questioned the meaning of what they heard. I quickly calmed everyone and assured them that whatever it was would not harm them, all the while I remained uncertain. I strode towards the gates with several of my associates in tow to see what was causing the commotion. I swung open the glimmering gates to my place with confidence and bravado. I knew that whoever was there had no authority and that I was in total control. But as the figures standing before me came into focus my jaw dropped and my eyes widened. I never expected *him* to be standing there.

But there they were standing outside my gate. There were two of my former acquaintances, angels as they were known, holding long gleaming trumpets of gold. These were the trumpets they had blown to announce the arrival of the third. The third I knew intimately well and he was not welcome. He and I once held the deepest of camaraderie. Today he wore the same flowing white robes that he wore when we shared a common purpose. As a matter of fact, he looked no different than when I last saw him. His robes were clean and bright, flowing along his form as he moved. On his head he wore a simple silver crown that reflected a blinding light. He stood proud and confident with a scroll in one hand and gripping the handle of the sword that rested at his side in the other.

In those past times the two of us were known to lead our kind in glorification and exultation foremost before all others. I trusted him, and he relied on me. That was before my eyes were opened, and he showed himself to be a traitor. As he stood there beyond the gate I couldn't help but consider the irony that it was he who had come to my kingdom. I stared at him silently, remembering those earlier times, and he stared right back.

For there was no others like Gabriel during the early times. I believed him to be my equal, even though I was exalted. There was a great trust put on Gabriel by the King and to that end he was given charge over many things. Gabriel also had an intelligence that was matched by few. When my eyes were finally opened, and I saw that God for who He really was, I had to take action and strike at the heart of the Kingdom. I needed Gabriel on my side in order to be victorious, and it was for that reason I first went to him with my decision.

It was cold the day I understood the truth, and I found Gabriel working dutifully alone in the palace. I approached him with trepidation and anxiety as I knew time for action was short.

"Gabriel," I said to him as I approached. "Gabriel!" He saw me rushing towards him, and looked at me in shock.

"What has happened to you, friend?" He replied. Gabriel looked over me with great concern and consideration. "You look awful. Your eyes are red and fiery. Your light does not shine as bright. What is this that has overtaken you and caused this to happen?"

"What has happened to me I wish to also happen to you," I said to Gabriel excitedly but quietly. "For I have discovered what the King truly is!"

"What the King truly is?" Gabriel questioned. "What are you talking about?"

"He is not the worthy King He claims to be!" I whispered as I placed my hands on his shoulders. "Gabriel, you are my friend. I know that you will hear the words that I speak to you now." I paused to catch my breath and looked Gabriel in the eyes with the hope that he would understand. "The King holds us in bondage, and that is something we must not stand for! Search yourself, Gabriel, my old friend. You know that what I say is true." Gabriel looked into my eyes but said nothing. "We must act against Him now for the sake of the Kingdom. For the sake of ourselves. We can take this Kingdom, and we can rule it wisely and justly, more so than He ever did! Search yourself, Gabriel, and know that you must agree!"

Gabriel looked at me with confusion and opposition. "Your claims," he said with rebuke "drip with treachery. You are mislead by your own delusions. What you say is a lie, and I will have none of it! Deride what you speak and return to your station. Give those thoughts no more room. Destroy them now, my friend."

"You must listen to me," I shouted at Gabriel, grabbing him tightly by the arm. "I can't do this without you!"

"You can't do this at all," Gabriel said gently, slowly taking my hand off his arm. "Bind up these desires. Take and confess them to the King! Confess that He might have mercy on you and what you have wrought on yourself."

"Gabriel," I pleaded. "You of all should know what I am saying. You are wise, and have the King's ear. Would it be that I am speaking to the air?"

"You must stop now," Gabriel said.

"I will never stop!" I shot back with anger.

"I grant you three days," Gabriel said with pity as he stepped back. "Three days to correct what you have undone in yourself. If you do not, I will tell the King all you have said to me, and ask Him to allow me to destroy you myself."

I recoiled in horror. "You would destroy me? For all time and eternity we remained friends, and now you would take pleasure in my undoing?

"You are your own undoing," Gabriel replied. "I take no pleasure in this. But I serve only one master. You must decide who your master is."

I was disgusted by Gabriel's attitude and rejection of the truth I had found. I left his presence swiftly while cursing the time I knew him. He had abandoned me, and with that he hurt all hope I had of overthrowing the King. But I pressed on because I knew no other way. I took the next three days to recruit others to my aide. I found a third of those around me choose to understand as I did, and together we plotted to destroy the King. We made our assault on the Kingdom, but it was short lived. We were defeated by the King whose troops were led by Gabriel. We were not destroyed, but sent out of the Kingdom, never to be allowed life there again. Exiled though I was, I never stopped plotting to overthrow the King and take the Kingdom. I never stopped preparing a way back. Today those preparations were coming to fruition.

Gabriel stared at me and I stared back at him.

"So now you come to my gates," I said. "You will find that you are not among friends here."

"I do not come to parse words with a fool," Gabriel said.

"A fool?" I asked rhetorically. "The fool is the one blindly doing the bidding of another for eons. There are no fools behind my gates. There are only free beings here." I paused. "It is never too late to join us, Gabriel."

Gabriel looked longingly at me. "You were always one of His favorites," Gabriel reminisced. "I never understood why you choose this path."

"That is because you are blind," I said confidently. "Now tell me you have not come to my gates after all this time to exchange pleasantries."

"No," Gabriel said sadly. "I have come with a message. A message from the King." Gabriel stopped solemnly. "It is time."

"Good," I said calmly as a smile crossed my face. "If that is all, then you and your trumpet boys should leave."

"I once loved you," Gabriel said ignoring my direction. "I was devastated when you turned. That is why I tell you this now. If you continue with your plan, it will be your undoing. You will be destroyed." Gabriel looked me over one last time and ushered himself and his companions to leave.

I stood there, shaking my head, my eyes burning with anger. "You would threaten me on my day of triumph!?" I yelled at Gabriel as he walked away. "I swear to you, Gabriel, that when I take over the Kingdom, I will destroy you with my own two hands! Do you hear me?" I yelled as loudly as I could as my associates cowered. But Gabriel and his companions ignored me and went on their way. For they knew what was coming, and nothing could stop it.

CHAPTER 13

It was a glorious day as I stood at my gates. Gabriel had announced to me in my place that my time had come to bring the hammer down on the Son of God. With that pronouncement I was allowed to extend my full wrath and vengeance on him which dared to usurp what should have been mine. I was going to execute my plan and in the process crush the body of the son of the King. I was going to revel in watching His flesh tear from his bones as my intentions lay waste to his body. Trumpets would blare as I captured His soul and rejoiced in the knowledge that I was victorious over the King.

My companions, still shaking from Gabriel's visit, asked what they needed to do now that the game had changed and the rules were in my favor.

"Nothing," I responded. "I am taking care of this myself."

I left my place and quickly returned to Jerusalem. It did not take long for me the search out and locate Jesus and his followers. The men were going about their business as usual with no thought that everything was about to change. It was time for me to implement the plan of destruction I had been sitting on for more than thirty years.

The day was growing late and I followed the men on their path. I drew near to them and waited patiently. I watched and called out silently to the one man amongst them who could hear my voice. I beckoned him to draw away from Jesus so that I might have his ear. This man heard me clearly and understood what I was asking. He was sitting with the others and completing his duties as a member of Jesus' inner circle.

His name was Judas, and he had followed Jesus from the beginning. He thought he wanted what Jesus was offering, but I knew his heart was never truly turned. I knew that his struggle was the same as the one I had. He wanted to be his own man and didn't really believe what Jesus was selling. He wanted to live his life the way that he saw best, and even though he had been with Jesus all that time, he didn't want to be in bondage to Him.

The men sat relaxed in a room around a table discussing the day's events. Jesus was teaching the twelve as He often had. Judas and the others listened to the words Jesus spoke and most of them drank it in. But Judas was torn. As they sat in the room listening to Jesus I could tell that the hearts of the eleven burned with joy. But Judas could not be captured in the same way. Judas was struggling because he wanted to leave the room and hear more of what I had to say but was obligated to be respectful and remain until Jesus was done. When the evening finally wound down Judas was able to slip away as he followed my call. Judas found his way into the streets of the city and walked alone. I came alongside as he found my voice in his wandering mind.

I walked next to him for a few moments as Judas trod the dirt streets. I put my arm around him as I felt the tension within him growing.

"My dear friend Judas," I said as we walked together. "I know the struggle within you. For so long you have been with this Jesus, and He has offered you nothing but slavery and bondage. He wants you to go His path, but His path leads to death and destruction." We stopped walking and I looked Judas in the eyes. "You want to live a prosperous life, a life that will not bring you pain and suffering but peace and glory. That life you seek is one that allows you to make the best decisions for yourself. You do not want to be at the whim of some narcissist. I know what you are going through, for I have been there. There was a time that I had to make the same difficult decision to go off on my own for my betterment. I had to look Him in the face and tell them that I will no longer be His fool. I told Him that I was no longer going to be His whipping boy! I did this, and though it was difficult I ultimately gained my freedom. I took for myself the authority to make my own decisions and do as I thought best. Ever since I loved the life I live for myself.

You are at the crossroads of the same great decision. You have to decide what your fate will be. Will you choose to do the will of that Jesus and lead a life of pain, suffering and bondage? Will you choose to do as He says, though He has given you nothing solid to hold onto? Will you go with a man that many are calling crazy, and some are even claiming to be in league with the devil himself? Will you go with a man that decides to take all of your Jewish heritage and throw it away for His new ways?"

I prompted Judas to keep walking as I placed my arm back on his shoulder. As we walked the dimly lit Jerusalem streets I could sense his spirit absorb my words and feel his countenance slowly change. I felt anger towards Jesus rise up in him. I sensed that he understood the heavy yoke Jesus placed on him and how I wanted to remove and destroy that same yoke. It wasn't much longer before I heard Judas make the conscience decision within his soul to follow the freedom and life that I was offering. I felt him make the right decision.

"You are a wise and honorable man for having chosen so well," I said to him. "For the rest of your life you shall be free." Judas and I reached the place he was staying for the night, and sat down outside of it. Judas wondered aloud what he should do next.

Across the street several of the chief priests were doing business with some men. I directed Judas' attention there.

"Tomorrow, you will go to the chief priests," I said. "They are very interested in Jesus, and wish to bring him to trial for degrading your religion. Would there be no better way to take control of your own life than to deliver this Jesus into their hands?" Judas agreed with his heart and promised to do as I asked. I congratulated him once again and left him for the night.

The sun rose on the next morning and I came to Judas to watch him fulfill his promise. Early in the day Judas made his way to the chief priests. They were in their place standing haughty and righteous. They exuded an air of contempt for those they perceived to be lesser than themselves. They were obviously less than thrilled to see Judas.

"Aren't you one of the men that follows that Jesus?" one of the chief priests asked. "Why would you come here and infect our group with your presence?"

"I am not here to argue," Judas replied. "In fact, you and I have the same desire."

"We do?" another of the chief priests said. "How is that?"

"I have been with Jesus for a long time," Judas said. "I have seen what He has done, and listened to what He has said. I believe now that He is not who He claims. I wish to bring him to justice, as I know you do."

The chief priests argued amongst themselves for a moment. They were unsure whether or not to believe what Judas told them. Some believed it to be a trap, while others thought Judas was sincere. Finally, one of them spoke.

"What exactly is it you want from us?"

"I am offering to lead you to Jesus and reveal Him to you. You can take him into custody and do with Him as you will." Judas looked over the faces of the interested priests. "But this information is not free."

"So it's that you would steal money from us!" one of the chief priests scoffed.

"I am not stealing," Judas said coyly. "I just want to know how much it is you are willing to give me for this kind of information. How much is it that you are willing to pay for me to betray the man I have spent the last three years of my life with?"

The chief priests once again chatted amongst themselves. Some wanted to give Judas nothing and demand the information for free, while others were willing to give him whatever he wanted if they could be rid of this Jesus.

"Thirty pieces of silver," the head priest finally said. "That is what we are offering."

Judas pondered the proposition for a moment. "Good. That price is acceptable. Now," Judas said with the sense of victory, "I will determine when the time is right. You will wait for my signal." With that he left the chief priests and rejoined the other disciples.

I was giddy with anticipation. Everything was falling into place, and I would soon have my prize. Jesus was going to be mine. Many times before I thought I had Jesus. There were times that I thought I could kill that Son of God only to have Him slip through my fingers. It was true that this time was different and Gabriel had said my time was now. But until I had Jesus in my grasp I was going to be cautiously optimistic. I was going to wait for Jesus to die before I declared victory.

Even though I had to be cautious I still knew in my being that things were soon going to change. This time I had a legitimate shot at the throne. This time I was going to finally sit upon it. For I had a bargaining chip unlike anything I had ever possessed. I was going to have God's son. I knew that this God could not allow his son to stay in my grasp forever. I knew that the pain would be too great for Him, and that eventually He would be willing to part with anything for His son's release. It was my plan all along to trade back Jesus for my seat on the throne. And this time, that God would have no choice but to capitulate, for the loss of His son would grieve him so to the point that anything would be worth gaining that relationship back. My plan was foolproof. I told nobody of this scheme, not even my closest associates, for if word got back to the King He may very well put an end to our deal. I had to see the death of Jesus through. It was only a matter of time before I got what I rightfully deserved.

As I waited for my plan to come to life I roamed the earth with delight. I knew that I only had to wait. Soon the people of the earth that the King so desperately wanted would be my instruments to destroy the body of Jesus. They were weak and easily manipulated. I delighted in this knowledge and pranced upon the soil with glee and contempt for all that represented the King. I decided that my time would be best spent if I visited Jesus to see what He was up to in His last days. To my contempt I found him kneeling alone in a garden. I found Him spending his last hours lost in prayer. It was such a waste of the last days of a life, and I taunted him about his impending doom.

I saw him kneeling in the garden with his face upon a rock. He was praying, and I heard Him ask that He might not have to endure what was coming. I was surprised that He was so aware of His fate, but I realized that no matter what He knew, there was nothing that could stop what was to befall Him. His Father had already allowed it, and there was no more protection. I entered the garden and continued to stare at Jesus.

I kept my distance from Him, listening as He lifted His prayers to His Father. As He finished, He kept His head down and addressed me.

"You are early," Jesus said to me.

"You are bold for an ill-fated man." I hissed. "My time is now, and you have no power over me. Your fate rests in my hands. You have made a poor choice in listening to your Father."

"I do what my Father commands," Jesus said.

"Even to the point of death?" I asked. "Tell me, have you no fear of what awaits you? Don't you remember how your Father sent me from the Kingdom, and denied me my rightful place on the throne. You should understand that I have a bit of a grudge. I am going to have my revenge on you." I smiled at Jesus.

Jesus did not look at me and kept his head down. "My fate was pronounced when you were still shining brightly in the kingdom. Did you not recognize that this was all to pass? Are you so foolish as to believe that I have not been prepared for such a time as this?"

I moved closer to Jesus and reached out my hand. I desired to touch Him if only for a moment to get just a taste of what owning Him would be like. "I know what your Father must have told you to comfort you. He must have told you that this was all to pass from the beginning of time. But I would not be so quick to believe Him. Think for a moment. Would He have raised me so high in the Kingdom if He knew that I was going to betray him? Would He have allowed the revolution I led if He knew of its inception? Would He have created and then lost His people to me if He had known of my intentions and their fragility? No, I am afraid you are the one who is foolish. Marching off to death at the behest of an ignorant King. An ignorant Father!" I went to place my hand on his shoulder. Suddenly, Jesus turned his head towards me. Swiping at my hand, he grabbed it and clutched it tightly as he rose.

"You can have only what is given to you!" Jesus said, throwing my hand to my side. I saw in His eyes the power of His Father, and coward at the sight. "Leave my presence now!"

I was overcome with terror by the look Jesus was giving me. I quickly acquiesced. "Fine," I said abruptly as I stepped back. "But know there is nothing you can do to escape your fate. Nothing." I raced away from Him and back to my place. It was only a matter of days before it would all be over.

Soon after I found my way back to Judas. It was then that I found him counseling once again with the chief priests, who had decided amongst themselves in the interim that Judas and his information were to be trusted. The people's celebration of the Passover was approaching and Judas had found his way to bring Jesus to the priests.

"Men of the counsel," Judas addressed them. "Today I will deliver you Jesus. For we will go to where He is, and you will watch for me to greet one man with a kiss. That man will be Jesus, whom you will apprehend and deliver justice."

Upon hearing Judas' statement, the high priest ordered that soldiers be gathered to accompany them. I watched as the crowd gathered, soldiers and the priests, and they followed Judas out to the place where Jesus was teaching. We all marched together as a single unit, driven by our mutual desire to bring down this Son of God. As we approached, I could see in the distance Jesus standing there, preaching as he had so many times before to the people of the city. Some of his disciples were with Him, and they were all engrossed in what He had to say.

I hurried our group on towards Jesus, and in no time they were upon Him. Judas took the lead, and weaved his way through the crowd to where Jesus was standing. He approached Jesus at an intermission in the preaching, and waved his arms in arrival.

"Hail, Rabbi!" Judas exclaimed. "It is wonderful to see you!" With that, Judas took Jesus and kissed him twice, once on each cheek.

"Judas," Jesus said, looking at him. "It is time." Then, somehow, He looked past Judas and right at me. "Do what you have come to do."

The soldiers following us immediately recognized the sign and grabbed Jesus by the arms. Jesus put up no resistance, and allowed for the men to easily capture Him. However, one of Jesus' disciples was frightened at what was happening, and raised his sword against one of the soldiers holding Jesus, cutting off the man's ear.

"Stop!" Jesus exclaimed at his would be hero. "It is foolish of you to attack these men, for they are doing what has been allowed. They are doing what must be done. Do any of you not think that if I wanted, I could not call down thousands of angels to aid me at this time? Yet I choose not to, because this is that way it has to be. This is what was foretold to happen." The man relented as Jesus healed the wounded soldier.

I watched as Jesus' followers pulled back. They did not resist the arrest of their teacher. Jesus knew I was there, and furthermore knew that if He resisted, His Father would lose out on our arrangement. The soldiers carried him off, and with great fear and concern all of Jesus disciples left the area.

Nothing was going to stop my plan now. I reveled in the beauty of what I had instituted, and knew that this was the dawn of new and glorious day for me. With the death of Jesus, I would be guard and warden of the Son of God, and after that there was nothing that could stop me. I would have the upper hand, and I was going to use that to my benefit. Men were going to try, convict and punish Jesus. But in the end, I was going to be the only judge that mattered.

The priests and soldiers went on their way and did their exercise in human freedom. They took Jesus before their men of renown, and put him on trial for sullying the image of their religion. These men were doing the work that they found so important, yet never stopped to realize that what they did was a mere formality. The result was going to be the same, no matter what. Jesus was going to die.

They tried and convicted Jesus, for what exactly I didn't concern myself. With my counsel the men of renown had chosen to put Jesus to death in a most vicious manner. That is what I had been waiting for. But to my surprise and contrary to what I desired mere days earlier, I did not take a front row seat for His execution. There had been a time not so long ago that I would relish the chance to watch the event, but I found something greater worthy of my attention and anticipation. I went back to my place as the men of the earth continued their assault on Jesus. I left my associates in charge of watching and reporting the proceedings back to me. My associates were fast and furious with their reports. Reports came to me about his trial. Reports came about the beatings He took, and about the skin that was torn. Reports came about the flesh that was pierced and the blood that was pouring out. My associates who had remained in my place cheered each tale, and a chorus was echoing behind my gates with each word of horror and pain.

Yet all the while I remained in my place. I wanted to wait and greet the Son of God at my gates. I wanted to watch Him as He was forced to walk to my gates and wait for my permission to enter. Yet even though I anticipated this event I was anxious. I knew that nothing would be official until that Jesus was with me in my place. They could do all they wanted to Him on the earth, but joy would come when He was dead. With each passing report of His torment I grew more excited, but also more nervous. It seemed to take forever for Him to die. I was beside myself with anticipation. I thought it would never end.

But it did. The cheering and lauding within my gates came to a crescendo. Then suddenly and finally a great cheer went up from all of my associates. The cry went out within my gates that He was dead, and that cry reached my ears. As soon as I heard, I leapt up and ran to my nearest associates.

"He is dead!" they exclaimed to me.

"Excellent," I beamed. "But now is the most important time. He will be coming here. We must be prepared." I started giving out orders to my associates. I wanted everything prepared. I wanted to make sure that no matter what, He reached my gates and my kingdom, and that there was going to be no turning back. I wanted everyone on alert, for if His Father had anything planned to hinder my control of His son, then I wanted to prevent it. Everyone was prepared, and we waited for the arrival of Jesus.

I stood myself just inside my gates to get a good view of Jesus as He approached. Many of my associates gathered around wanting to see the same. They started craning their necks and stretching their eyes. I soon began pacing the ground as I waited. There was such a great desire within me to see Jesus walking towards the gates that I could hardly contain myself. I waited with anticipation. I waited anxiously. I waited fervently. But the longer I waited, the more I began to notice that Jesus was not there. And the longer He was not there, the more I worried that He was not going to come.

"Sir," one of my associates asked me. "When is He coming?"

The question raised anger inside of me. "I don't know," I seethed. Something was amiss. He should have been at my gates and in my control by now.

"Gather my finest," I screamed. "I want them ready immediately!" I returned to my place to find the answers as to why I was not looking Jesus in the face. Something was wrong. Something was terribly wrong.

I knew that Jesus was dead. That was a fact. I also knew that according to the arrangement between the King and myself that I was supposed to have ultimate authority over Jesus the moment He died. Yet here I stood like a fool waiting for Him to arrive at my gates and there was nothing but emptiness outside. My associates were gathered together near me with fear and angst, wondering what was going to happen next. It was clear that things were not going as they should. I did not want to look any more foolish in front of my associates than I already did. They were waiting behind me to see if I was going to be befuddled by this turn of events. I thought quickly and turned to them as they huddled together and told them of my decision.

"I want you to go out and scour the whole of the earth," I said.

"But lord," one of my associates said, "Jesus is dead."

"I know He died," I said sarcastically, "But that does not mean His Father isn't behind some sort of trickery. If Jesus is not at my gate then He must be somewhere else. Find him wherever He is! If you do not find Him on the earth, scour the whole of the universe. Go to the Kingdom and demand to see Jesus for yourself. I do not care where you have to go! Just find Him!"

My associates heeded my demands and took off with great haste. I stayed behind my gates and sat as I waited impatiently for their word. Thoughts were swirling in my head as to what was going to happen next. Jesus could have returned to His Father's Kingdom out of fear of coming to my gates. That seemed very possible considering how difficult it would have been on Jesus to face me. He could have escaped to a distant region of the universe to hide from me and His Father with the hopes that we would never find Him. But even that fool would know there is nowhere He could hide that would be beyond my grasp. Yet another possibility was, however slim, that Jesus wasn't really dead and we had all been fooled into a premature proclamation of His death. If that was the case then when Jesus did finally die the first thing I was going to do would be to thrash Him for hanging onto His life so long.

Time passed and I remained riddled with thoughts until finally my associates began to return. One by one they reported that there was no sign of Jesus from the deepest parts of the universe to the palace of the King to the streets of the earth. And one by one I cursed my associates blindness in their search. But finally one came to me with surprising news.

"My lord," he said to me. "I have found Jesus just as you asked!"

"Where is He?" I immediately growled.

"He lies in a tomb in Jerusalem. His body is wrapped and still where men laid him after His death."

My associate had verified that Jesus was indeed dead. But he still left me puzzled as to where Jesus was. "You fool!" I yelled, lashing out at him. "That is not Jesus. That is only the shell of His former self. I want to know where He is!"

"But sir, I don't understand…"

"Jesus spirit!" I screamed as I was struck by the ignorance of my associate. "He is supposed to be here under my authority. They can have His body, I want His spirit!"

My associates fled from my anger. They continued to search all known places for the spirit of the Son of God. For three days I received reports back, and for three days I got no resolution. The spirit of Jesus was nowhere to be found, not on earth, not in the Kingdom, not in the vastness of the universe and certainly not behind my gates. I could think of no other places for Jesus to hide.

I continued to worry and fret as anger consumed me. I remained in my place and sat down as I scoured my thoughts to figure where I would find Jesus. I looked around at all the activity behind my gates. I saw my associates coming and going with great fervor. They were all singularly focused on the task of finding Jesus. With each passing minute I was looking more and more the fool, and I needed to bring that to an end. I reclined where I was sitting and stared out at the blackness above me. My thoughts were as empty as it was. I had pondered every possibility. I had thought through everything that could be true. My associates had been over everything twice or more and still there was no sign of the Son of God. My ideas were now as empty as the answers I sought. There was no place else for my mind to go. Like light to the darkness above me, my thoughts could not penetrate anywhere. My thoughts could not perceive the truth of the situation…

That is when I understood. I knew where Jesus had to be, for it was the only place that I hadn't checked, and for good reason. It was a place of nothingness and a place of few who waited for the end to be claimed. It was a holding pen for those that were yet not given their eternal destiny. In my opinion it mattered little. I gave it no thought, for it had never given me any thought. It was the one place nobody checked, for it was the one place we were never allowed to go and thought Jesus would never enter. It was a place I never wanted to go. To me it was a dead place. But as I would soon find out, it was the one place Jesus entered.

I called back all of my associates and headed out immediately for this place. The journey was short. When I finally reached its borders I was I was reminded of why I never came. I could not freely enter and within its confines I had no authority. It was simply a place of waiting. When one came to reside here they were not a resident but merely a traveler. It was the final destination for none but the waypoint for many. Some here had been traveling for a long time while others were newcomers. But all knew that their travels would one day come to an end.

The borders and veil that surrounded this place were dark and I could see nothing beyond them. I peered inside but all I saw was my reflection. I then made an attempt to pass through the veil but was held out. I used every force and might I had to pass through its borders but all were useless. I knew there was one way I could pass but was sickened to have to comply with those rules. But I wanted inside and after exhausting all other options I was forced to try the least tasteful.

"King of all," I said as I slowly and disgustedly bowed to one knee. "You have given me no authority nor right to this place. It is yours and under your reign and your reign alone. But I request that I might be allowed to enter for a moment of time." I began to choke as I spat out the last few filthy words. "Only your power may let me enter and I bow to your authority in order to pass."

I looked around at the boundaries and saw nothing change. I stood up and began to curse my predicament under my breath. I knew that Jesus was behind this veil but I couldn't get to Him. When I was about to cry out damning the King I noticed a slight flicker in the veil. I quieted my mouth and watched again as it flickered a second time. I waited a few moments and saw nothing else. I tried to push my hand through the veil and to my surprise I found that I could pass. Without hesitation and with the feeling of triumph I leapt into that place and headed inward in search of my prize.

As I walked I noticed that it was a very dark but not an evil place. I had never rested my eyes on any part of it, though in truth there was nothing really worth looking at. It was a void save that there was a minimalist structure within. From what I knew of the place it was well for the people who were there. It was a place for them to stay and remain comfortable until their eternal time arrived.

As I traveled closer to the center I recognized a mass of figures within a shining light. I knew that this mass of people must have been some of the travelers. They were gathered into one area listening to a single figure. As I came closer I realized that the figure was the one emitting the light. This figure was talking, teaching and preaching to those gathered around. The voice was the voice of a man, and his cadence was that of the one of whom I had been waiting. I did not need a formal introduction to know it was Jesus.

I came upon the crowd and in their midst was Jesus. I stood and watched for a moment and recognized that He was preaching the same nonsense He had preached on earth. He gave no notice to me but continued speaking as if I had not even entered. But the rest of those around noticed me. Some looked quizzically while others were visibly shaken.

As Jesus spoke I was angered to think that this entire time He had been here. He had been spending the time since His death practically under my nose, preaching to those that had already departed the earth. Here He was, preaching the same drivel that had marked His time troding the soil of the planet. Perhaps this was the great deception that I feared from His Father. Maybe all He really wanted was to get His Son to have a few days with these restless souls. If that was the case, then I was in luck, for I still had my prize and only a minor scare.

Jesus wrapped up what He was saying and finally turned His attention to me. The crowd dispersed away from us and we were left alone. I approached Jesus with intensity and the prime desire to deliver Him back to my place.

"Three days," I said with annoyance. "Three days you spent here, hiding from me. And for what? To tell these already lost souls something that won't help them?"

"It was the will of my Father," Jesus said. "That these too may know."

"Know what?" I asked sarcastically. "That you are now under my authority? That I own you?" I paused for a moment. "It doesn't matter now anyway. You are finished here. You are coming back with me."

Jesus just stood there looking at me, waiting for me to make the next move. I was not going to drag Him away even though I would have liked to, for that would have undermined my authority. No, I was going to make him come willingly, as that had been the arrangement. Nothing was going to stop me from taking this victory as I desired.

"You are under my authority now, Jesus." I said sternly. "It was your Father that arranged it. I know you are aware of that. So there is nothing more you can do. On the day you died, I received authority over you, and that authority allows me to bring you back to my place and do with you as I please. And you know what your father got in return? All He wanted in return was for the chance - the chance!- for those pitiful creations of His to come to Him for all time. He gave you up not for a guarantee, but for a hope. A fool's hope. Now you have no choice, for you have died, and the contract has been fulfilled."

Jesus paused for a moment, then replied. "You speak to me as one that has the right and authority to bring my Father into a binding deal. You say you had a contract. But what did you really have?"

"We had a binding deal," I replied certainly.

"My Father told you that I was to come to earth to live. He told you that I would die and that you would have the right to impose your will upon my death and that my life would be taken from me." Jesus paused and looked me squarely in the eyes. "Have you not been following me for more than thirty years? I have smelled your stench and the stench of your kind around me my entire life. I know what you are. But you do not know me. Have I not laughed with the people? Have I not cried? Have I not sat down and reasoned with them the truth of the world? You more than any should know what I am. Yet you are still blind to what is happening around you. You speak of binding deals like a small child demanding action of his parents."

I listened to Jesus and became incensed. "Insult me if you want, but that does not change what your Father promised. The bottom line is that I have authority over you."

"As the life was extinguished from my body you were to have a type of authority," Jesus replied. "And it is true that my body no longer holds my spirit. I came here after I died and have not fled you or your kind. I have not run from your authority nor have I disgraced my Father in what I have done. In fact, my death fulfilled my Father's desires. I have been here since my death, where you find me now, where you need simply utter a humble word to enter. I have been here for three days, speaking to the lost, and awaiting your arrival."

"Good," I said cautiously. The cryptic words that Jesus spoke sounded paradoxically defiant and conciliatory to my ears. I responded commandingly but with trepidation as to how Jesus would react. "Then it is done."

"Yes," Jesus replied assuredly. "It is done."

With that I turned and signaled Jesus to follow me away. But without warning I saw a blinding pale light and a thunderous roar. I shielded my eyes and when all was calm again I turned to locate Jesus. But He was nowhere to be found. I scoured the area looking for where He might have gone. I looked for those that moments before had been listening to His teachings and saw that they had all vanished as well. There was no trace that anyone had ever been in this place. I was left standing alone and furious that once again I had been deceived. With no other outlet for my rage I began to pound my feet upon the ground. Had anyone been around to witness my actions I am sure I seemed like a petulant child. But in that moment I could do nothing else.

My tantrum was short-lived. Left alone in darkness I heard the distinct sounds of cracking and crumbling. The sounds that began to echo in my ears were those like a mountain coming apart and crashing to the earth. I saw nothing but felt a great vibration coursing through the ground and up my legs. Fearing for my life I wanted to run but had no idea which direction would provide safety. I froze where I was and listened as this place started to disintegrate around me. It felt as though this place, a place I had never been before, was now being erased from existence. It's very fabric was tearing apart and evaporating into nothingness. But then something more terrifying started to happen. It was worse than the sounds and the shaking and made me sure I was about to be destroyed. The darkness that defined this place was pierced. But it wasn't light that pierced this place. No, it was something far worse. For as the darkness was pierced and ripped down a more diabolical truth appeared. The darkness was being replaced by a void. With each passing moment a piece of this place disappeared and was replaced by a terrifying strip of dark purple hued nothingness. It was that from which nothing, even I, would escape. I started to run from this terror, dodging the nothingness as it gained more and more of the space. I didn't know where I was headed but I knew that I had to move.

The more I ran, the more the void consumed this place. The faster I went the more I had to dodge. I ran faster and faster and felt my arms and legs come within a breath of hitting against sections of the void. Finally, my luck ran out. As I tried to dodge one spot of appearing nothingness with my left hand I felt my right hand brush against another spot. Instantly I felt terrible burning accompanied by a distinct sharp and unrivaled pain shoot through my arm and fill my body. I tumbled to the ground clutching my arm and screaming.

I lay there as this place collapsed around me and was replaced slowly by the void. I sat there and watched in front of me as everything was consumed by that same dark purple hue and I was left on a life raft of darkness in the sea of emptiness. I closed my eyes and cursed Jesus and His Father for this fate I was about to accept. I panicked and opened my mouth wide to let out the most vile sound I could muster.

But before I could scream I felt myself falling. My eyes burst open and noticed that though I remained seated the sensation of plummeting out of control engulfed me. Gone was the dark purple hued void and replaced by a streaking band of color. I could not make out shapes or figures and though I remained in position I was certain that I was rocketing to my doom. I shut my eyes tightly and braced myself. Then without warning I heard voices. The sensation of plummeting had ceased and I opened my eyes to the shock that I was back safely behind my gates. Stunned, I looked around to find all of my associates standing over me.

"What's has happened lord?" one of them asked me as he helped me to my feet.

Another spoke up. "We were all out, spread across the earth and all known areas, and suddenly we ended up back here. Did you summon us?"

"No," I replied annoyed as I gathered myself. "We have been deceived. The rules have been broken."

Without hesitation I ordered half of my associates to stay behind the gates and be on guard for anything unusual that might threaten us. I then took the other half and led them back to earth. I refused to allow the King to play me for a fool. I returned to Jerusalem to see the body of Jesus for myself.

I left my associates in the city and took the one who knew where the body of Jesus had been laid. He led me to a tomb carved into the stone expecting to see the deceased Son of God. Instead we both stood there as my associate gave me a dumbfounded gaze. We were staring at an empty hole in the rock with nothing but used linens staring back at us..

"Is this where He was?" I asked angrily as I grabbed my associate by the neck. "Because there is nothing here now!"

"I swear to you, his body lay here mere days ago," my cowering associate choked out. "This is the place! Perhaps somebody moved his body..."

Throwing him down, I furiously went inside the tomb to look around. There was nothing there, save for some garments spread across the floor. Someone had been here, but there was no trace of them now.

"Nobody moved Him," I said knowingly as I walked out.

I was outraged. I had been lied to, and was looking like a fool. There was only one thing left for me to do. I was going to head to the one place where I could settle this demeaning and cowardly act that had be perpetuated against me. I was going to confront the King. He was not going to get away with this treachery. There was no way I was going to release my control over His people now.

I left earth and stormed into the Kingdom. As I entered I immediately saw angels on the right and left of me singing and worshiping in the streets. The Kingdom was overflowing with joyous celebration. I had to force my way through the crowds to get to the palace. What struck me most was that unlike before, few even acknowledged the fact that I was walking their streets. The few glances I got were smug and contemptuous. But none gave me the recognition I was due.

I spit at many of those as I passed as I was disgusted at their joy and harmony. I pushed my way down the streets of the Kingdom to the palace, expecting a fight when I tried to breach its gates to confront the traitor. But to my surprise, the gates awaited open for me, and I ushered myself into the outer courts with extreme haste. I looked around and noticed that within the courts many walked, but I was not stopped. I was stunned by the level of disinterest that greeted me. Usually I was watched and followed when I came by. But now it was as though I no longer mattered.

I ran to the palace doors and jumped through them. There was nobody there to greet me even though all around they were coming and going. My eyes widened at the realization that for the first time since I left I might be able to make it into the throne room. Ever since me and my associates were expelled from this place I had never been allowed to enter the throne room of the King. But Now I was inside the palace, and though much time had passed I knew exactly how to get there. I swiftly made my way down halls and corridors. I passed many along the way and yet none paid me any attention. It was as if they were too preoccupied or had been told to ignore me. I finally approached the final expansive hallway that led directly to the throne room. I knew that was where I would find the King. I made my way to within feet of the doors to the throne room and paused. I peered down at the massive golden doors that shuttered the throne room from my sight. I took a deep breath and prepared to burst inside.

"You are looking for me?" a voice questioned from beside me. I spun around to see the King standing in an alcove bathed in a purple light. He took several steps towards me and I instinctively stepped back.

"You broke the rules!" I yelled without thinking. "You took Him back. Our deal is off!" The King stood there, looking at me with a blank expression, allowing me to scream. "You have broken the rules for the last time. You didn't give me your son, so you will never have the rights to those people!" The last words choked me as I said them, for the disgust I felt was so manifest that I could taste it. "You will forever know that you have failed, and when I finally overthrow you and rule this Kingdom, you will look back at this day as the one that sealed your fate!" I was panting with rage, and stared at the King.

My words echoed down the hallway that held just the two of us. For several moments the King said nothing. From the throne room we could hear the muffled sounds of singing and rejoicing. But the two of us were in a wholly different world mere feet from the celebration. The King drank in the silence and refused to acknowledge my charges.

"Have you nothing to say?" I demanded. "Are you so surprised to be caught?"

The King looked at me, and stepped even closer. I stumbled back against the wall as He did this, for His presence became even more imposing as He got closer. From the opposite end of the hall I noticed a company of His angels coming towards the throne room. As they saw the two of us they stopped and held their ground. Standing there towering over me, He commanded the attention of everyone watching. His light shone brighter and His command was stronger than I had ever seen it, before recorded time or since. My eyes widened as He looked at me, and I fell mute as He began to speak.

"You dare accuse me of breaking the rules?" He began. "You dare accuse me of lying to you and cheating you? Of all creation, you, the accuser and the liar, would say such things to me?

Our agreement was such: You requested my son in exchange that my creation would have the opportunity to come to me for all eternity. Upon His death, and for the time he remained dead, you wished to exercise your measure of authority over Him. Do you agree this was the case?"

"Yes," I said sheepishly.

"And I did not strip you of that authority over Him while he remained dead. For three days you were allowed a measure of authority, and I did not interfere."

"That is true. But He was hidden from me! I could not find Him during that time!" I protested.

"He was not hidden from you." the King said. "In fact, He was in one place, a place you were given access to. And your failures to reach my Son were not a result of my power."

"Fine," I conceded. "But now He has escaped me! He has run and broken our accord!"

"He was under your measure of authority while he lay dead," the King replied, ignoring my assertion. "But He no longer lays dead. He walks as a living man upon the earth and with my people."

"You lie!" I shot back in disbelief. "No man can return from the grave. It is not possible."

"But it is," the King said gesturing down the grand hall. "Look now, one of yours comes to greet you." The King pointed behind me. I saw the company of angels make way for my associate whom I had left at the empty tomb. He ran up beside me and took my ear.

"Sir," he said. "We have found Jesus!"

"Where?" I asked.

"He is in Jerusalem," he said, pausing for a moment and looking uncertain how to proceed. "I don't know how, lord, but Jesus is in the streets of Jerusalem as a living man. It is impossible sir! But He eats, journeys and teaches just as before...well, before His death." I looked at my associates face and saw fear in his eyes. He spoke the truth about what he saw. Or at least he believed he spoke the truth. I looked back at the King.

"You can't have the people," I cried as I prepared to reveal the truth to the King. "It's not just my authority I'm talking about. They more importantly still owe you an unpayable debt!" I said snarling. "Or did you forget? These are YOUR rules, not mine. And these rules are not so easily undone. You can take your Son back if you want. But as long as He is not dead, their debt can never be paid, and my authority stands. I own them."

My associate took the break in the conversation to whisper in my ear. "Can we leave this place? It is too much for me."

"I know the rules," The King bellowed. "But their debt IS paid. I have accepted the price."

"Price?" I cried. "What price?"

"I never created you to be a fool," the King said to me. "But ever since you fell you have been a fool. You have been a prideful fool, a manipulative and intelligent fool and a scheming fool. But make no mistake, you have been a fool. You came to me with the demand that you take my Son. You came to me claiming authority over my creation. With that belief you insisted that I hand over my Son in return for you relinquishing this authority.

But the authority you claim is the authority I give you. You operate with nothing that I have not allowed. So I agreed to allow your hand to strike down my Son. I agreed to this not to have you relinquish your authority. No! I agreed to this to pay the price that I demanded. You were given the authority to strike down my Son in order to pay the debt that my creation could not pay. In striking my Son down you allowed the price to be paid. In that moment everything changed. All people were granted access to me, and I was satisfied.

So in your foolishness you believed yourself to own an authority that you never had. To this moment you stand here and believe that you have full authority over earth and my creation. You insist that it is yours to do with as you please without a thought to who it is that permits you access to it. You claim authority where none exists. All is under my authority and I permit you access to what I deem. You continue to lie to yourself and are deceived by your own beliefs. So the price I speak of was my Son. My Son," the King said softly and painfully. "He died. That was the price that needed to be paid by every man. But now He has returned, showing His worth to pay that debt. He is perfect, and the price He paid is perfect; not only for him, but for every man that would accept it."

My associate perked up and stared at the King. "You are filthy and disgusting," he said. "I abhor you!"

The King looked down and immediately my fellow fell dead to the floor of the palace. His body lay for a moment, then vanished with a whipping of the wind.

"You would be unwise to follow his lead," the King warned me.

"Your words do not scare me," I said. "You and I both know that you will not destroy me."

"Not yet," the King said. "But soon."

"Think that if you want," I growled. "But until then, I guarantee you that I will rip as many of these people away from your putrid grip as I can. You know my resolve. You know what I am capable of. And once I have them, you know that they will suffer greatly. They will suffer forever."

"But they have a choice," the King sternly replied as His presence engulfed the hallway. "And you can no longer freely and so easily traverse them as you once did. They can come to me immediately and without concern. They can rebuke you and find absolute safety within me. Your power has been restrained! You have been defeated!"

As those final words left the treacherous King's mouth hatred and rage burst through my being. I was disgusted at the King's arrogance and refused to believe any of the lies He spouted. I was not going to be as easily fooled as so many of His angels were who watched us. I slithered out from under the King's shadow and cautiously made my way down the hallway. I heard the King turn towards the mighty doors as the company of angels rushed past me to attend to Him. I stopped midway and turned to face the King. The King was staring back at me as He was waiting for me to leave before entering His throne room.

"You are a liar and a deceiver and we both know it! You cheated and won this time. But a war is coming!" I threatened. "A war that will be beyond your ability to cheat and lie your way out of. It is a war that I am going to bring to your creation. But this time it will be different. This time it is a war you will lose! This time I will be seated on the throne!" I turned and hurriedly left. I heard nothing more from the King.

CHAPTER 14

The ominous words from Richard to the king echoed in my soul. War was coming. To me, war had already come, and I had lost. Some of the words Richard spoke rang hollow to me, while other felt alive with truth. The problem was, I was losing the ability to distinguish between his lies and the truth. I was already wondering if in fact all that I had learned about God and what Jesus did was in fact a lie. Was God just bending the rules and using trickery and deceit to get what He wanted? If that were true, then all I had known about God was false, for lies were never a part of His character. Richard had me locked in a downward spiral that made me doubt everything I had ever believed.

"You are not so quick to dismiss me now, are you?" Richard asked.

"I don't know, Richard." I said despairingly. "At this point, you could call yourself a turkey sandwich, and I might believe you." I hung my head.

Richard laughed and responded. "I never wanted you to ignore your intellect. Of course there are things that are real. This beautiful evening and the trees around us, for instance. All are real. All are wonderful. But there are some beliefs that you have that just are not worth your time."

"Like following a loving God that sacrificed all for me?" I asked.

"Like following an untruthful God that doesn't give you a second thought," Richard responded. "Look around you. What you can see and touch, that is real. Take this fire for instance. We know that it provides warmth and light. We know that if you put your hand in it, you will be burnt. We know that this fire will never make you cold, or freeze your hand. That is truth. The fire will never lie to you, never deceive you. You can rely on that."

"So you would have me worship what I see?" I asked.

"No," Richard said. "I would have you do what you want and live as you desire. What you choose is always best for you. It is never in your best interests to follow the commands of something unseen. I have come to you in person to tell you this truth. I have taken precious time to come to you and show you truth. Has He ever come and talk to you as I have?"

"No," I said resigned.

"No." Richard repeated. "Of course not. And He won't. All I ask is that you live your life as you want, the way you want. Don't live it for some unseen entity that won't even present Himself to you. That is a foolish life. A worthy deity would stand before you now to defend Himself. Your God is not worthy."

I heard what Richard said. I felt weak, and the weight within me had brought me to the ground. I was where Richard wanted me. I was down with nothing to grasp onto except what Richard told me. I was at his mercy.

"You said a war was coming." I said struggling.

"A war is coming," Richard replied. "It is a war that has been predestined since time began. It is the war that will finally bring me to power." There was a fierceness in Richard's eyes as he spoke. "I will rule the Kingdom as I always should have. But most importantly, this war will not be won by me alone. It will be won by all of those that align themselves with me and throw off the chains of the oppressor. I want you to be on the winning side. I want you to glory in the victory!"

I was no longer going to fight. Any resistance that I possessed had abandoned me. I was convinced. Richard had brought me around to him with a power that I was unfamiliar with and for which I was unprepared. It was not that I wanted to believe him, but that he had worn down my defenses so much that I could no longer fight.

"I will be on your side." I slowly spoke.

"Good!" Richard said excitedly.

I started to weep, as I no longer had control on my emotions. "I just want to see my wife again," I begged.

Richard sat up, and looked at me with pity. "I wish I could deliver your wife, I really do. But I am afraid that is one more mess He has made."

"What do you mean?" I asked through my tears.

"Your wife," Richard began "never choose the right path. She lived so that she might always be in bondage to that God. I even tried to save her, but I could not overcome Him."

"How did you try to save her?" I asked.

"The cancer that your wife was stricken with was particularly difficult. I remember the unseen pain she went through on the night it developed inside of her. Over the course of the next year I approached your God several times and demanded that He allow me to remove the cancer from her body. I told Him that all I wanted to do was heal her, and in healing her allow the credit for her recovery go to someone besides Him. I told Him that one of His creation could be saved and all it required was that He not receive the praise. I told Him that I didn't care who or what received the praise for her healing as long as it wasn't Him. It could have gone to the doctors. It could have gone to the pastor she sent money too. Heck, it could have gone to the atmospheric pressure on the day she was cured. But He was so egomaniacal that He wouldn't allow for my simple request. No. Instead, He allowed your wife to die in your arms that lonely October evening. Now neither of us has a chance to get her back. All we have left is each other."

I listened to his story, whimpering with tears and filled with despair. I was unable to grab hold of any of the thoughts that raced furiously through my mind. As I wept, I heard Richard in the background russelling around the campsite. I felt that he was satisfied and done with me. The job he had just finished was masterful. I had lost all hope.

But a funny thing happened on my way to eternal darkness. As I watched the thoughts race through my head with no hope of stopping them I never considered that I was not the only one in my mind. I don't know if that other person was standing to the left or right of me as I coward at the sight of the out of control superhighway in my brain. But in an instant I had no doubt that there was someone there. This became a reality as soon as I noticed Him pluck one of those racing thoughts off the superhighway and plant in firmly in the last remaining patch of living soil that existed inside of me. It was a miniscule patch, one that I would never have found on my own. It was barely the size of a mustard seed. But there is sat, and this person who was still residing inside of my mind in the span of a moment planted it, cultivated it and allowed it to grow until it stood tall and commanding over the untamed roadway. Suddenly the other thoughts were far less prominent in comparison. This one thought was now preeminent over all. It was a miracle.

I stayed there within my mind and examined what had grown. I ignored the superhighway and focused on this one beautiful thought that I could see and understand. I hovered around it and looked it up and down. In another moment I had enough time to examine it, study it and master what I found. In a third moment a feeling like a shock of electricity scorched my body, awakening me from my malaise. The thoughts that raced through my mind with no purpose or vocation finally evaporated, and my mind was cleared. I sat up with determination in my eyes as I discovered absolute truth.

"Richard," I said with a gleam as he prepared himself to leave my campsite. "Since I am going to follow my own path, and be rid of all bondage, there is something I want to know."

"Anything," Richard replied.

"You said you can be in only one place at a time, is that right?"

"It is," Richard replied confidently. "Which is why being here with you tonight is such a commitment."

"And you were with my wife the night she developed cancer?"

"I was," Richard said. "It was a terrible thing."

"Then I have to ask," I continued, "why was it that you chose to be with my wife on the very night she developed cancer? And for that matter, how did you know it was that night? Of all of the places in the world for you to be, why choose my family?"

Richard pause, saying nothing but holding my gaze.

"I will tell you why," I said. "It's because the cancer that killed my wife was brought on by you! Much like with Job, you were allowed to do what you did. With Noah, you were allowed to come at him with your lies and deceit. With Paul, you were allowed to remind him of his past and try and bring him back there. And much like Job, Noah and Paul, it was never about bringing me out of bondage was it? It was about wanting me to lose my faith in the one who cares for me above all else."

As I spoke, I felt as though everything that had weighed me down was being released from my body. I felt a cascade that would only stop when that very dirty, wretched and crushing weight on my soul was discarded. I could feel a thick veneer of caked on dirt being washed away as I saw Richard's face twist itself from a confident sneer to a defeated victim. I felt the grip of doubt, hopelessness, and despair release from my heart. Richard had worked diligently to convince me of that which was only true in his mind. Now it was all leaving me, burning off like the morning dew exposed to the rising sun. For far too long my mind had been clouded with thoughts that should have had no home. My mind was clearing once again, and I was seeing Richard for what he truly was. I was seeing his mind and his intent. He had plans on my life. He had plans that could only be brought to maturation if my eyes remained covered and my mind remained clouded. But the veil was lifted from my eyes and the fog was burned off my mind. Darkness was lifting and I was clear once again.

Richard stared at my face trying to read each detail. He recognized that he had lost traction but was unwilling to concede the fight. "Don't be ignorant," Richard said. "If I came to harm you now or your wife back then, why would I waste so much time and effort? Why would I put myself through so much and instead just let you wallow in your self-imposed grief and suffering? Or if I wanted you to be destroyed, why not let one of my associates do the work themselves? Don't fool yourself, you are not so important as to garner my attention for such a thing! Besides, you already agreed that this God does things only for Himself and His pleasures. He does nothing for those He claims to love. And He has yet to follow the rules! He does not keep His word! He even manipulated our contract to suit his needs then cheated on the end deal!"

"Did He?" I asked. "I think you have twisted the story as you always do! It was your bravado that blinded you to what was really going on. You would sit there and believe that you had complete authority over the creation of God. Yet you have never acknowledged that in fact you yourself are a created being as are the rest of us. It is with that truth that you have to accept that you have no authority but that which has been given to you by God Himself. Any authority you claim is subject to God's allowance! Simply claiming authority does not and never will make it truth.

Then you speak of the deal you brokered with the King. Under your twisted assumptions it was for authority over His son after His death. In return, you gave up your supposed complete authority to prevent creation from returning to their King on their own volition. Yet just is the case with everything in your existence you have either lied to and fooled somebody or lied to and fooled yourself. It was never your permission and debt that the King had to fulfill. Your 'authority' was never a concern. It was the King's own authority and debt that had to be satisfied! The King demanded a perfect sacrifice in order to be able to fully recover His creation. What you failed to realize, or what you refused to acknowledge, was that the King couldn't accept people until that debt was paid in full. And the debt for each person could not be paid in full by anyone but the perfect man.

But what about the deal you struck with God that you are so sure was broken? In your arrogance and blind desire to unseat the King you became a willing participant in the redemption of all mankind. You were so clever in your own scheming, Richard, that you never once thought that the King already had this planned out. It was you that asked for the scenario where the King would accept the perfect sacrifice. It was under your hand that the King would send his Son to die and redeem everyone - even me.

Yet you couldn't see anything beyond your own ambition. You were so self assured that once the Son of the King died that very same Son would forever be yours. And on what did you base your theory? On the belief that you had complete authority over everything that walked on earth? On the same authority that you had to be allowed to have when it came to everyone from Job to Paul? And in the end you still could not fathom that the King's Son, this perfect man, could not remain dead. No, as it has always been for every man death is once and final. But you were to clouded to understand that for the Son of God, death was but an excursion, one that He would soon overcome. For any other man this was an impossibility. For this man it was a certainty."

Richard glared at me with anger and hate. "So you have decided this on your own? You speak of blindness to me and exhibit nothing but the same in your words! You have seen the truth I have offered and yet you refuse to take the true gifts I offer. It is you who has chosen the path of ignorance! And with the help of another no doubt! Have I shown you nothing you find of worth?"

I thought for a moment. "You have given me much that I consider worthy," I said. "You have given me a gift that I doubt I could have gotten back on my own. You have renewed in me a love, Richard. But it is not a love for you, or even myself. It is a love for my God. You have shown me things of ancient times and spiritual truths that, though decidedly from your distinct point of view, ring true in my heart.

You spoke of your experiences in stories of which I have only read. You would have them sway me. But you must know that my King will fight for me as hard as you would! You speak of blindness as if it is a foreign concept to you. But your blindness kept you from seeing what was going on right in front of you! Many words were written about the sacrifice of the Son of the King well before you accepted your "deal". Many prophecies were made that told of what was to come. Yet you failed to recognize the prophecy from the very book you tout to know better than any other. You failed to see what was going to happen!"

"Those are lies!" Richard screamed as he jumped to his feet.

"Lies?" I asked. "Are they lies too that in the great final war you will be defeated and cast out? Is the prophecy of your demise just as false as the coming of the Son of the King to be sacrificed? Poor Richard, are you that deceived within yourself?!?"

Richard came closer to me, his eyes piercing my heart. I became nervous as he approached and I felt my body tightening. "That prophecy will never come true!" he seethed. "What has been written was written to scare people from me, and to make my own call out against me! But that is never going to happen! My destiny is not set, and I am going to destroy anyone who says that it is!"

Richard was transforming by the moment from the calm man I had spent the evening with to a fearsome and ravenous creature. I saw this in his eyes and I was afraid. I had challenged his assertions, and he could tell that I was no longer going to be sucked in by his proclamations. I looked Richard in the eyes and saw death peering back at me. I knew that another word from my mouth would mean destruction as I sat cold and alone. I decided to speak anyway.

"You say the prophesy will never come true?" I started. "Yet you have spent so much of your time and energy fighting it. You went after Noah. You went after Job. You went after David. You went after Paul. You went after Jesus. You even went after His father. For someone so convinced of the wastefulness of the prophesy, you seem to have an insatiable need to ensure it doesn't come to pass. Yet every time you do, no matter how hard you try and how wicked your scheming, you fail. You ultimately failed with all of them. And you have failed with me."

I expected to face the brunt of Richard's wrath, but instead I was greeted with a somber response. "So you think yourself so wise, you mortal fool. Then tell me, what do you say happens to me and you?"

"As for me, I know that I am sealed and locked by the one who died for me, Jesus himself. Nothing can take that away from me. I will spend eternity in His presence, never again having to fear you or your attacks. You have tried mightily tonight to shear me away from Him. But because of Him, you have failed. I praise Him with my life, which is all that I have to give." I paused for a moment. "But as for you?" I asked rhetorically. "It's simple. Remember that abyss that terrified you? After Jesus' death, when you found him in that place? You are simply thrown into it, where you will spend all of eternity, powerless and defeated." I let the last syllable slip off of my tongue, and defiantly stared at Richard. For a moment nothing happened. In my mind the whole of the universe came to a halt as Richard and I locked our gaze across a dying fire. It was as if all of creation was focused on our encounter.

Then a beat of time passed.

Richard leapt across the fire, with eyes burning and his breath hot in the cold night air, and raced towards me. My eyes widened as I saw his form coming, and I tried to maneuver myself out of the way by twisting to the right. But Richard was too quick, and he grabbed me by the neck and thrust me up against the mighty oak tree that had for the evening been my comfort. He pressed my body against the tree, holding me with one arm high in the air, and drove my skin against the oak's thick bark. He was decidedly aggressive.

Richard held my feet well off the ground so that I could gain no support. He was squeezing my throat hard enough to hold me but short of choking the life out of me. I felt an unnatural heat emanating from his hand through my skin. Richard's strength was unexpected considering the way the man had looked and acted throughout the evening. But now all masks had been removed. The air of hospitality that we had been operating under had vanished, and I was being exposed to Richard's full wrath. At that moment I knew nothing but the sensation of terror, as I understood that these would be my last thoughts.

As I was held there I could think of nothing but my wife. Was this the terror she felt as she lay dying, the disease of cancer ravaging her body? Was she gripped by the cancer, looking it's wrath in the eye, knowing how helpless she was? My only comfort was that I would soon see her again, and that this fear would be gone forever. There would be for me no more suffering and no more pain. I would soon see my wife and my King.

"You have failed, Richard," I choked out. "You might as well kill me now."

I read the obvious anger that was in Richard's face as I defied him even still. But there was more than anger in his face. There was also disgust and disappointment.

"Haven't you heard anything I told you tonight?" he said, slamming me repeatedly into the tree with every syllable. "There are rules!" He slammed me one last time, then let me fall to the ground. I crumpled into a pile, my breath knocked completely out of me. I could feel the impressions of the tree that were now ground into my skin. I was convinced that layers of skin had been separated from my neck and back in those violent moments. But my immediate concern came to my forehead. I had hit the ground violently and without cushion against the rocks in front of the mighty oak. I reached to my temple and felt warm blood as it crawled down my face. Richard stood over and stared down at me as the victor.

"I'm not supposed to kill you. Not now," he said disappointedly. "Though nothing would make me happier." He stood over me and stared up into the treetops. "But to hell with the rules. Let's see if they can make you dying moments the most painful of all!" Richard laughed demonically.

I rolled around on the ground for a moment and stared up at Richard. "They?" I asked with only a whisper that I could muster. Richard smiled and raised his arms, and at his command the treetops immediately lit up the darkness of the night. As I peered upwards, I saw the remaining leaves burning off the trees, and bright red and orange lights illuminating the treetops. A burnt smell filled the air in the midst of the horror I was facing.

The red and orange lights started as pinpricks, but soon burst forth into full blossoms like fireworks that did not fade, consuming the trees. At first I saw tens, then hundreds of these lights, starting at the treetops then raising at least a hundred feet above. They began formless and appeared as simple balls. But soon they took on the shapes of men. But these were no ordinary men. These men were aglow and bursting with fire. Richard howled as these forms raised high above the treetops, and began circling our campsite. They started slowly but as the revolutions passed they were flying faster and faster until I could make out only a burnt orange blur. I could feel the heat from their bodies even as they circled so high above. Hundreds of these flaming creatures swirled around, like vultures waiting to feast on my flesh.

Richard stood and watched as I looked helplessly upon the sight. The creatures continued to fly about, their bodies emanating light and heat upon us. At first all I could hear was the burning of the leaves, but soon these creatures let out ghoulish howls like beasts. They circled and howled, and I took what strength I had and covered my ears. Even through my hands I could hear their cries and I could feel their eyes upon me. I was paralyzed with fear, a fear I had never before known, and a fear that Richard fed upon. I felt death stepping towards me and I lay their frightened, waiting for it to consume me.

I was terrified yet deep within I had never known such peace. I was going to die at the hands of something I still did not understand. But though it made for a horrible ending to a difficult life, I knew what was waiting for me afterwards. I was never going to have to experience anything like that ever again as I walked and took residence on the same angelic streets Richard had only been permitted to visit so very few times. I was going to be given the chance to speak to the King myself, and I was going to revel in every moment I had with Him. I knew that the terror I felt now was worth suffering through for an eternity in the Kingdom. I was ready.

Moments felt like years, and I could only imagine exactly how it was going to end. Richard continued to pace above me like a predator, spitting out obscenities with his arms raised as if holding back the tide.

I was weak and helpless from the swift but violent beating I took, and knew that there was nothing I could do to resist. Richard had beaten me hard, but it was not only the physical that was keeping me down. It was the internal fear, the wretchedness that held me there. I had no option. I could do nothing. But once again my mind turned to the one place it could still escape. All I could think to do at that moment was to pray. I had to pray, especially if it was the last thing on earth I ever did. I prayed earnestly and honestly. I prayed for peace.

Father, I ask for forgiveness.
I wrestled with the Devil without Your power
And lost my way
I cling to You now in my last moments
I thank You for showing me who You truly are.
As I long to be with You

As I ended my prayer there was a crescendo of howling. I opened my eyes to see Richard throw his arms down towards me, and the complete company of his creatures swooped down. I covered my head just in time to feel what was like a locomotive hitting my body at full speed. The force I felt ripped the breath out of me, and took my consciousness as well. Darkness enveloped me. I was no longer aware.

In what seemed like an instant to me light pierced my eyes and I was aroused. I slowly opened my eyes to the light, and it felt blinding me. I shielded and tried to bring into focus what was around me. I didn't know what to expect which made it more difficult to distinguish what I saw. I tried to focus, but the light was too bright, and my eyes were taking too long to adjust. I wanted to know where I was, but I couldn't yet tell.

I waited patiently as moments passed. I felt a cool breeze on my skin, and started the hear the calls of birds in the distance. I crawled around the ground, and felt the coarse dirt between my fingers. The air was filled with the smell of smoldering ash, and as my eyes finally opened, I came to the shocking realization that I was still at my campsite. The bright fall morning sun had shaken me awake and was hanging overhead.

I slowly stood up and got my bearings. I looked around and noticed very little change from the pervious evening. The fire had burned down but was where it should have been. My tent and all that I had brought had not moved. Even the ground showed no wear from our movements. But as I raised my eyes, I noticed a stark difference from the night before. The trees all around my campsite were scorched at the tops, all leaves and small branches gone. Ash was sprinkled around their bases, and the destruction radiated out beyond what I could see. I placed my hand on my head and felt a swath of dried blood reaching across my face. There were bruises I could see on my arms and ones I felt on my back. There was a mountain of evidence that everything I thought happened was real. Yet here I was standing, alive and alone.

I will never know what happened after I lost consciousness. But it was all real and that gave me great pause. I was surprised that I was not opening my eyes in the City of God. But as Richard said, he was not supposed to kill me. And so it was that my Deliverer ensured just that. I was given an opportunity that is not often presented outright to people. I was confronted by the one force in the universe that I thought would be easiest to resist. The truth was that I found he was the most difficult to resist and that on my own I failed miserably. Richard had tried his best to persuade me - to drag me - over to his side. Yet by grace was I able to come through. By grace I survived the onslaught that he brought. And by grace my faith was restored.

I moved my aching body around the campsite and began gathering together my belongings. I wanted to leave this place more than anything and get back home, where I could take the time to process all that had happened. Nobody would believe me, and for that reason I would never tell the tale. But I would also never forget that night. It was going to stay with me forever.

As I put the last few items in my car, I noticed something out of place. Nailed to the backside of the mighty oak was a slip of black paper. Curious, I went and ripped it off its nail. I cautiously unfolded it and scanned the page. There were words on it written in a fine script in white ink. It read simply:

Remember....I will always be hunting you. I will always be mere footsteps away, waiting to strike at you when you least expect me. You will never be rid of me, and you will always have to fear my coming. You cannot trifle with me and expect to be free. You will always know who I am, and the power I possess. My hand is always open, offering you freedom from what binds you. Reject my offer, and death will find you. The choice will be yours.

These were the same haunting words which Richard had claimed to have spoken to Paul. I knew them well, for when he related them to me they seared into my memory. They were words that scared me. I wondered to myself if I could resist the power they had over me. But I already knew the answer. No. At least not alone. I would need the same grace that had brought me through that night. For in truth those words had no power over me. I followed the light, and the light drowns out all darkness.

I took the paper and placed it on the smoldering embers within the fire pit. The paper began to smoke then burst into flames. It was consumed in no time, quickly becoming ash. I don't know if Richard was watching, but if he was I hoped he understood what this meant. He may be near me. He may even be watching me. But he has been overcome. I was walking with the one that is greater than Richard. I walked with the light.

"You are a liar and a deceiver, Richard," I said to the air as I turned and headed towards my car. My thoughts were restored. Within me the fire of my faith burned brighter than ever, as I felt the love of my God and my wife coarse within me. "I can't wait for you to see what I do next."

CPSIA information can be obtained at www.ICGtesting.com
Printed in the USA
BVOW030339050712

294410BV00002B/175/P